# Royal House of Corinthia

*Royally wed... by Christmas!*

This Christmas Princess Arianna and
Crown Prince Armando of Corinthia are
facing the biggest challenges of their lives.

Pregnant Arianna flees to New York
to se~~~~~~ only to find
her ver~~~~~ Charming!

*Christmas Baby for the Princess*

Crown Pr~~~~~~royal bride—
so why can't he stop thinking about his
~~~~~~~~rti?

*Winter Wedding for the Prince*
Available December 2016

You won't want to miss this delightfully
emotional new duet from Barbara Wallace,
brimming with Christmas magic!

# CHRISTMAS BABY
# FOR THE PRINCESS

## BY
## BARBARA WALLACE

First Published in Great Britain 2016
By Mills & Boon, an imprint of HarperCollins*Publishers*
1 London Bridge Street, London, SE1 9GF

© 2016 Barbara Wallace

ISBN: 978-0-263-92031-4

23-1116

To Susan, Selena and Donna,
whose emails help get me from page 1 to page 220.

And to Peter, my personal Prince Charming.
Merry Christmas, sweetie.

# CHAPTER ONE

HER WALLET WAS MISSING.

Arianna was going to be sick. Stomach churning, she slumped against the brick wall and took a shaky breath. Then she checked her bag a third time.

Lipstick. Hand sanitizer. Passport. No wallet.

How? She distinctly remembered double-checking her bag after paying for breakfast, and her wallet had been there, nestled against the silk lining.

Times Square. There'd been that woman who accosted her and needed help reading the subway map, and another man who jostled her while she was trying to break free. One of them must have reached in while she wasn't paying attention...

Stupid, stupid, stupid. This was what happened when you tried to run away from your problems: you got more. Arianna closed her eyes to keep the tears from burning their way free. A few weeks, a month at most—that was all she'd needed.

For what had to be the one-hundredth time, she cursed her own foolishness. If she had listened to her instincts, she never would have had to run away in the first place. She wouldn't have to decide between a loveless marriage and a royal scandal.

Now, thanks to the pickpocket, she was going to have to make the choice sooner rather than later. Without money, she couldn't stay in America. She had no money for food, not to mention that the owner of that terrible hotel where she was staying expected her to pay her bill at the end of the week or, as he so sweetly said, he would toss her pretty rear end on the street.

Her *child* deserved better.

Amazing how one tiny pink line could change your life. When she first missed her period, she blamed stress. After all she and Manolo had just broken up. Besides, they had only been together—like *that*—two times. Two misguided attempts at deepening feelings that weren't there.

When the second month came and went, however, she couldn't blame stress anymore. The world stopped turning the moment she saw that extra pink line. She didn't know what do to, so she ran. Disappeared, so she could decide which of her no-win choices was the lesser of two evils.

Just then, a cold November wind blew down the street, the chill swirling around her shins before creeping up her skirt. Nature's way of reminding her how serious her predicament really was. Tucking her collar about her throat, Arianna lifted her chin with royal stoicism. No sense dragging her feet. With luck, a decision about what to do would come to her while she was on a plane back to Corinthia.

A few feet ahead, a deliveryman exited one of the businesses, maneuvering his cart over the threshold with a clank loud enough to be heard over Manhattan traffic. The place was called the Fox Club, according to the letters emblazed on the side of the maroon awning. Goodness only knew what kind of club the place was, but no matter. It was open and, hopefully, had a telephone she could borrow.

Except it wasn't a club. It was a time portal. How else to describe what lay on the other side of the door?

The room looked like it belonged in an old-fashioned American detective movie, like the ones they sometimes played on television late at night. High-backed booths covered in rich burgundy leather, wood so dark it was almost black. Iridescent glass chandeliers that bathed the room with a smoky white light. The hair on Arianna's arms started to rise. Sleek and sensual, the entire space pulsed with expectancy. A simmering promise of *something* for all who walked in.

To her left, a large bar lined the wall. More dark wood, only this time the dark was accented with brass rails and shelves filled with glassware. A stocky black man, dressed to fit the setting, stood by the register. His pomade-slicked head was bent over a clipboard, on which he was making notes. The man didn't look up when she approached.

Arianna cleared her throat. His attention still on the clipboard, the man reached under the bar and produced a sheet of paper that he thrust toward her. "Fill this out. I'll tell the owner you're here."

"Excuse me?"

"You're here about the job, right?"

He hooked a thumb at a sign that had been discreetly tucked in the corner of one of the windows. Through the glass, she could make out the backward outline that read Help Wanted.

"I…"

Arianna paused. It was a silly idea. Her, working in a restaurant. She'd never worked a day in her life. Not a proper job anyway.

On the other hand, if she could find a job, she would earn money, and money meant she could postpone going home.

She would have time to think.

Make the right choice.

Ignoring the voice telling her she was making yet another reckless decision, she set her bag on the bar and, before she could change her mind, announced, "Yes. Yes, I would like the job."

"I appreciate the enthusiasm," a voice replied. A low, smooth voice that definitely did not belong to the bartender.

Arianna looked up and caught her breath. If the club looked like something out of a movie, this man was the movie star. He approached her end of the bar with an elegance that was almost surreal in its smoothness, his double-breasted suit shifting and swaying in a cadence only a custom-made garment could achieve.

His cheekbones were sharp enough to cut glass while his eyes were the color of Mediterranean slate. Only a slightly crooked nose prevented his face from complete perfection. Interestingly, the flaw fit him perfectly. As did his surroundings.

"Max Brown," he said.

Arianna started to nod, the way she always did when someone presented themself, then remembered where she was and quickly stuck out her hand. "Arianna."

"Nice to meet you, Arianna." His grip was solid and sure. "Is there a last name?"

"Santoro." Arianna cringed as her real name popped out.

Fortunately, he showed no signs of recognition. "Pleasure to meet you, Arianna Santoro. You're interested in the waitressing job, are you?"

"Yes, I am."

"Glad to hear it. Have you filled out an application?"

"Not yet," the bartender said.

"I only just walked in," Arianna explained.

His smile was as charming as could be. "That's all right. Why don't we have a seat, and we can fill in the spaces as we go along." He motioned toward one of the booths lining the wall. "We don't need much. Just the usual stuff. Name, address, social security number. Oh, and your firstborn child, of course."

Arianna's stomach lurched.

"Relax, I was only kidding about the firstborn part," he said, touching her elbow. "Are you all right?"

"I'm f-fine." She supposed it was nerves making her feel queasy. What was she going to say when he asked for details about her identity? Squeezing the bar rail, she focused on breathing through her nose, hoping the lump would work its way back down. Having something in her stomach might help, too; it was past lunchtime after all. "Could I get some chamomile tea and dry toast?" she asked the bartender.

"You're ordering food on a job interview?" The man shook his head.

Max continued to keep his hand on her elbow.

"Might not be a bad idea, Darius," he said. "I wouldn't mind a fresh cup of coffee."

"You want me to go grind the beans for you, too?"

"And grow the chamomile."

The bartender muttered something about his job description, but obliged nonetheless. As soon as he disappeared behind a swinging door, Arianna felt the grip on her elbow tighten.

"Why don't we take a seat," Max said as he gently pulled her away from the bar rail, "and you can tell me about yourself. Starting with why you want to work for the Fox Club."

If only he knew… "Why does anyone want a job?" she asked as she felt herself being propelled to the booths on the other side of the room.

"Generally, because they need money. Is that why you're looking for work? Because you need money?"

"Of course. Why else?"

He looked her up and down. "No reason."

No sooner had she settled onto the leather bench then Darius returned with a serving tray. "The *toast* will be ready in a minute," he said, his face a scowl as he set a small ceramic teapot in front of her. "You need anything else?"

The question was directed to Max, who immediately smiled. Apparently, he found the bartender's abruptness amusing. "I'm good. You want to sit in on this?"

"No, hiring people is your thing. I'm perfectly happy with my supply order, thank you very much. Liquor bottles don't make special requests." Shooting a scowl in Arianna's direction, he turned and headed back to the bar.

"Don't mind him," Max said, shrugging off his jacket. The cloth of his white shirt strained against his biceps as he rolled up the sleeves. "He isn't nearly as put upon as he likes people to think."

"If you say so." She tried to glance over her shoulder, but the bench was too high to see over.

"Trust me, underneath that brusque exterior beats a very soft heart. Ah, this smells good." Coffee cup raised to his lips, he closed his eyes and inhaled. "We import the beans directly from South America. Our own custom blend."

"Really." She hoped she sounded enthusiastic. Usually, she liked coffee, but lately the aroma made her queasy.

"A bad cup can ruin the whole dining experience. Last thing we want are customers leaving with literally a bad taste in their mouth. Not if we want them to come back."

"No, I suppose you don't." She thought about the five-star meals she'd enjoyed over her lifetime. The coffee, like every aspect of the meal, was always impeccable. It never dawned on her to expect otherwise. "You've clearly paid a lot of attention to details."

"I should hope so. Details are what make or break a restaurant."

Then she suspected the Fox Club was "made" because Max Brown seemed to have thought of everything. Like their booth, for example. Not only did the high seat backs ensure privacy, but they'd been designed for two, essentially making them intimate little nooks.

The atmosphere seemed even closer with someone as exceedingly...solid as Max Brown. Suddenly warm, Arianna slipped off her coat. Underneath her turtleneck sweater, her skin tingled as heat spread across it.

Oblivious to her discomfort, her companion had put down his drink and was chivalrously pouring tea into her mug. "So, getting back to my original question, what makes you think you should work at the Fox Club? I mean, besides the fact you need a job."

"I, um..." She reached for a napkin and dabbed at the dampness forming on her upper lip. Where on earth was her toast? The strongest of odors was emanating from her cup, a combination of grass and another plant she couldn't place. Had chamomile tea always smelled this noxious? Her stomach lurched again.

Swallowing back the acid, she started over. "I don't... I mean, there isn't one specific reason. I..."

"You're new to the city, aren't you?"

"Yes," she breathed, grateful to have an excuse. "Very. I arrived a few..." She caught the word *days* before it could slip out. "Weeks ago. How did you know?"

"Because anyone who's lived in New York for any length of time knows the Fox Club. At least if they're in the restaurant business they do." He paused for another sip of coffee. "So, you're new to the city, and you need a job."

"Yes."

"Where are you staying?"

"The Dunphy Hotel." Actually, dirty and dated, the Dunphy barely qualified as habitable, let alone a hotel. It was also the last place anyone would think to look for a princess, which was why she had picked it.

"Interesting selection," Max remarked.

"I'm on a budget."

"I see." Something in his tone made her stomach roll again. This time, a layer of anxiety accompanied the nausea. It wasn't possible that he recognized her, was it? Her fingers absently combed the ends of her hair. She'd been monitoring the headlines since she arrived, and thus far, there had been no mention of her or her running away. Then again, Father would no doubt take great pains to keep her running away private. Even if news had made the press, she'd done her best to alter her appearance. Following advice she gleaned from American crime shows, she cut several inches off her hair and dyed the natural blond color a deep black. Since the Corinthian royal family didn't garner that much attention—the paparazzi preferring their British counterparts—she figured even the most ardent of royalty junkies would be hard-pressed to recognize her.

The gray eyes assessing her from across the table, however, made her wonder. The open scrutiny would make her nervous, whether she was hiding or not. He seemed to be examining every inch of her.

She forced herself to meet his gaze, while pressing a hand to her abdomen. The churning was getting worse. She could feel the acid creeping up her esophagus again.

"Experience…?"

He was talking to her. "Experience in what?" she asked, pressing her lips into a tight smile.

"Waiting tables. Now that the holiday season is getting underway, we're going to be busier than usual. A lot of groups book tables this time of year so we need someone who is used to juggling multiple large parties. Have you done large parties before?"

Swallowing back the queasiness, Arianna nodded. "Several." It wasn't a complete lie. She'd been standing in as her father's hostess since her mother died a decade ago and had assisted in planning more than her fair share of state dinners. Surely, memorizing dinner orders and bringing them to the table couldn't be more difficult than memorizing dignitaries' dossiers and defusing potential international incidents.

"Great. Where?"

"Where?"

"Where did you wait tables?"

"Oh, right. Italy," she replied, falling back on the cover story she'd rehearsed in case someone asked about her accent. Out of all of Corinthia's continental neighbors, the Mediterranean country was the closest in terms of language and culture.

"Any particular location or did you serve the entire country?" While his coffee cup masked much of his mouth, she could still see the hint of a smile.

Naturally he expected more specific details. To buy a few seconds to think, she took a drink, only to gag as soon as the liquid passed her lips. The stuff tasted as botanical as it smelled. Worse, actually. She shoved the cup to the middle of the table.

"Miss Santoro?" Max asked.

"I—"

No good. Her tea, her breakfast and everything else in her stomach jumped to the back of her throat. Clamping a hand to her mouth, she sprinted from the table.

\* \* \*

"Second door on your left," Max called out as she rushed away. Not that it mattered all that much with the restaurant empty. So long as she made it to one of the restrooms, they'd be fine.

"What the…?" Darius had just come around the bar carrying a plate of toast. "Usually it takes two or three dates before the woman runs away from you. What happened?"

"Very funny," Max replied. From behind him he heard the soft thud of a restroom door closing. She had made it somewhere at least. "Do me a favor and get a glass of ice water. She's probably going to need a cold drink when she comes out." Poor woman was as green as her tea.

Definitely not your typical job interview. Or applicant, for that matter. Not too many out-of-work waitresses that he knew walked around wearing cashmere. He might not know women's fashion labels by name, but he recognized expensive when he saw it. Besides, she moved like money. That posture screamed "private school."

A cashmere coat, and she was staying at a rat hole like the Dunphy? New to the country or not, the two did not go together. Women as beautiful as her stayed in five-star suites and not alone. They didn't apply for temporary waitress positions.

"You notice the haircut?" Darius asked, returning with the water.

Yeah, Max had noticed. Right after he noticed the coat. A total home job, and not a very good one at that. "She's trying to hide from someone."

"If she's thinking that hair will help her blend in, she's crazy."

It wasn't just her haircut that attracted attention. It was the whole package. "If she wore it up, it'd look okay." Even if it didn't, most people would be too distracted by the rest of her to notice.

"Don't tell me you're considering her."

"Something tells me she's in a tough spot."

"Great. Another one of your lost puppies." If his friend rolled his eyes any further, they would see the inside of his head. "Didn't you learn anything from what happened with Shirley? You can't save the whole world, you know."

"I never said I wanted to save the whole world." The few desperate souls who crossed his path, is all. And just because some, like his former piano player, chose not to be saved, was no reason to stop. It was definitely not a reason in this case.

He lowered his voice in case Arianna happened to come back. "She's staying at the Dunphy."

Darius whistled.

"Exactly." If that wasn't enough of a red flag, there was desperation in her eyes. An anxious shadow that said things weren't as she pretended. Max knew that shadow well. He had seen it in his mother's eyes all her life. Okay, so maybe Arianna wasn't running away from an abusive bastard like his father. But she was running away from something. And there was no way in hell he was turning a desperate woman out in the street. His mother's eyes haunted him enough; he didn't have to add a second pair.

"Besides," he said, shaking off the ghosts, "you've got to admit, she would look amazing in the uniform."

"Maybe, but can she wait tables? All you did this morning was jaw my ear off about how hard it is to find decent help. Do you really want to take the risk? Christmastime is crazy."

"I thought it was the time for goodwill toward men."

"Very funny." A soft cough cut off whatever else Darius was going to say. Arianna had returned to the table. Despite shaking and being white as a sheet, she still managed to look gorgeous and self-possessed. Max felt the stirring of attraction deep in his belly.

"Everything all right?" he asked.

Her nod was as wobbly as her legs. "Fine. That is, I was feeling light-headed, but I'm much better now."

She was a horrible liar. *Better* would mean color in her cheeks.

"Thank you," she said, noticing the water.

"No problem. Figured you wouldn't be looking for the tea." His coffee had long since grown cold, but he drank it anyway. Wasn't the first time—wouldn't be the last. "So," he said, from over the rim, "you were telling me about where you used to work."

Her eyes immediately dropped to her glass. "Right. Where I worked. The thing is…"

"It was a long time ago?" he suggested.

"Exactly." She grabbed the excuse like a lifeline, gratitude in her voice. "I'm not sure they would re-member me."

Max sat back and took a good look at her, trying to think like the businessman he was. Ten to one, the only experience she had waitressing involved leaving a tip. Darius was right: he had no business offer-ing her a job.

But then he saw how hard she was struggling to keep her composure and his conscience beat down his common sense.

"That's all right," he said, "I'll take your word for it. Do you think you will feel well enough to start tomorrow night?"

Her eyes widened. "I have the job?"

In a flash, Max understood how every private eye in every mystery movie fell prey to the femme fatale. The way her face lit up was absolutely criminal. He smoothed his tie and did his best to hide his reaction. "You did say you wanted it, didn't you?"

"I did. I mean, I do." She leaned forward, the subtle scent of high-end perfume accompanying her. "Thank you so much," she said, clasping his hands. "You have no idea how much this means to me."

Definitely criminal. Reluctantly, he disentangled himself from her grasp and stood up. "Darius will go over everything you need to know, including where to get your uniform. Welcome to the Fox Club family, Miss Santoro."

Out of the corner of his eye, he could see Darius shaking his head. Honestly, sometimes his friend was too much the glass-half-empty kind of guy. They were helping a gorgeous woman out of a tight spot, is all. What was the worst that could happen?

# CHAPTER TWO

SHE WAS THE worst waitress he'd ever seen. Quite possibly, the worst waitress on the planet.

"I tried to tell you," Darius said, sliding Max a cup of coffee. "But you and your white-knight complex wouldn't listen."

Biting back the retort he wanted to give, Max forced his features to remain expressionless. "She's a bit rusty, I'll give you that."

"Rusty? The past two nights she's dropped three trays. Not to mention all the orders she's messed up. Lorenzo and his staff are annoyed—they're threatening to refuse any order she puts in."

"Yeah, well, Lorenzo better think twice about that, considering I'm about to drop a small fortune upgrading the kitchen."

"It's not just Lorenzo. Darlene and the other waitresses are annoyed, too. Apparently she keeps disappearing into the employees' lounge during her shift."

So Max had noticed. In fact, he'd been paying quite a lot of attention to his newest employee the past two days. Enough to realize it wasn't only his desire to help that had made him hire her. She looked breathtaking in the waitress costume. He'd personally ordered the dress after seeing a photograph of Grace Kelly wearing something similar, the idea being that his waitresses would be smoldering but classy. On Arianna, the concept took on a whole new meaning. Every man in the room had to be cursing how the neckline didn't dip low enough to reveal anything more than bare shoulders and a hint of cleavage. Max certainly was.

She'd fixed her hair, too. Pulled it into some fancy twist that showed off a long, graceful neck. Max had dated his share of women—beautiful women—but none as enticing as his new waitress. As a rule, he didn't get involved with the help—made for an awkward work environment when he moved on—but with Arianna, he was seriously tempted.

"Darlene asked her if she was sick, and she insisted she wasn't," Darius said. "You don't suppose she's using, do you?"

"Nah." Enough addicts and alcoholics had crossed his path over the years for him to know the signs. "Nervous stomach, more likely." He'd caught her stealing crackers from the salad bar. "All the same, tell the other waitresses to let me know if they see anything odd."

"That mean you're going to let her keep waiting tables?"

"How else is she going to get up-to-speed? Another day or two and she'll be fine."

There was a loud crash.

"Another day or two, huh?" Darius said. "You sure?"

Across the room, their newest employee had just

spilled a salad on… Oh, Lord—was that the deputy mayor?

Max ran a hand over his face. "Send a couple bottles of Amatucci reserve to the table, and tell him the entire night is on the house." He watched as the mayor's right-hand man slapped away Arianna's hand before plucking a piece of arugula from the lapel of his gray flannel suit. Hopefully the drink and a few profuse apologies would be enough to soothe the man's ego.

"And your new puppy? What about her?"

"Move her to somewhere where she won't cause damage for the rest of the night," he said.

"You mean you're not going to let her go?"

He'd certainly fired employees for less. Only he couldn't shake the memory of her anxious expression, or that she was in a roach hotel to beat all roach hotels. Attraction to her aside, there remained the fact she was a woman clearly looking for an escape. What kind of man would he be if he cut her loose?

"Tomorrow we'll try her at the hostess station." Now that he thought about it, he should have assigned her that position to begin with. Who wouldn't want to follow her to their table?

"You're the boss," Darius said, with a look that said he disagreed. "I just hope you know what you're doing."

So did he, thought Max. So did he.

"Arianna, may I speak to you for a moment?"

The fussy, nasal voice of the maître d' had the uncanny ability to cut through the restaurant din like an upper-crust trumpet. By itself the tone was enough to make Arianna's insides cringe. When coupled with the distinct sound of disapproval, it made her feel sick to her stomach. Or *sicker*, as the case may be. What had she done this time?

Javier stood at his seating station, impatiently tapping his pen against the wood. His rigid posture reminded her of the music instructor her father had hired when she was twelve. A dictatorial virtuoso who she'd been certain had moonlighted as a prison guard. Come to think of it, she wouldn't be surprised if Javier moonlighted at the same place.

Smoothing the front of her waitress dress, which was doubling as a hostess outfit for the evening, she excused herself from the diners with whom she'd been talking and headed toward him. He immediately tilted his gel-slicked head toward a corner away from the crowd. "I thought I asked you to seat the last party in section four," he said, once they were out of earshot.

"I did." At least she thought she had.

"No, you seated them in section three."

Section three, section four...what difference did it make? Four people needed a table, so she gave them a table with four chairs.

Apparently, from the maître d's dramatic sigh, it mattered a great deal. "Did I not tell you that restaurant seating is like a mathematical equation? You make a mistake on one side of the dining room, then the entire scheme is thrown off-balance. Now I'm going to have to redo the entire seating chart. Again."

Arianna lifted her chin. Perhaps, she wanted to say, if she'd been allowed more than five minutes to study the floor plan before the restaurant opened... Traditionally, memorizing information on quick order wasn't a problem, but lately it seemed her brain was constantly foggy and sluggish. It did not help that the majority of her energy these days seemed to center on trying not to run to the ladies' room.

Apparently, Javier wasn't done lecturing her. "And did you tell a couple they couldn't sit in one of the back booths?"

"They were walk-ins. You told me the booths were reserved."

"I also told you customer service is our number-one priority. As the first face they see when they come into the Fox Club, you are in a sense Mr. Brown's ambassador, and as such, you never tell a customer you cannot accommodate their request."

"But I thought I wasn't supposed to disrupt the seating chart."

Javier glared at her. "From now on, come and get me if there's a special request. I don't want you making decisions on your own." He reached for the reservation book while muttering under his breath. Arianna caught the words *empty-headed* and *useless*.

They were enough to make her see red. Raising herself to her fullest height, she stared down her nose at the maître d'. "Listen here, you…"

"Excuse me." A tall, elderly woman approached them, preventing Arianna from finishing. The newcomer wore a pale green gown that, while dated, Arianna immediately recognized from the stitching as a designer original. She was carrying a leather tote bag and a large brown canister.

"Javier," she said, in an upper-crust voice to rival the maître d's. Another time, Arianna would find it amusing that she, the actual royal, had the least affected voice. "It's five past seven. Mr. Riderman and I distinctly requested a seven o'clock reservation. I mentioned it to this young woman, but she told me I had to wait."

"The rest of her party hasn't arrived yet," Arianna told Javier, figuring that he would appreciate the defense, since he set the rule.

He didn't, though. He snapped to even greater attention. "My apologies, Mrs. Riderman. She is a new employee. Had I seen you walk in I would have attended to you personally. May I send you and Mr. Riderman a cocktail with our compliments?"

The elderly woman's hand fluttered at the offer, her gigantic cocktail ring spinning on her thin finger as she did. "Mr. Riderman isn't drinking this evening. I, however, will have an extra dry martini."

"Very good." Arianna had to force herself not to roll her eyes at the bow Javier offered the woman. The palace guards weren't that effusive. "Now if you follow me, your regular table is ready."

There was another exception to his rules? If he was going to allow exceptions, then there should be a list for employees.

Javier glared at her when he returned. "You are very lucky, Mrs. Riderman is a forgiving person," he said.

Oh, no, she refused to let some uptight little man lecture her on this. "You specifically instructed that no party was to be seated unless everyone was present."

"The entire party *was* present."

"No, Mr. Riderman…" She stopped, suddenly re-

membering the bronze vase. "You mean she is eating
with her dead husband's…?"

"Will you keep your voice down?" he said, almost
hissing. "Mrs. Riderman is one of our oldest and best
customers. She's also an influential voice in the New
York arts society."

*Who eats with her husband's ashes?* "Does Mr.
Brown know about this?"

"Of course he knows."

"Oh." And he wasn't disturbed? "I'm sorry. I'll
make sure that doesn't happen again." The next time
a party arrived carrying a jar of remains, she'd make
sure to seat them promptly.

"It most certainly will not," Javier replied. "You've
done quite enough damage for the evening."

Arianna stiffened as he touched her elbow. She still
wasn't used to being touched so casually. In Corinthia, only her family and closest confidants took such
liberties.

And Manolo, she added ruefully. He had taken a
lot of liberties. But then, she'd been foolish enough
to think the words coming out of his mouth were
sincere.

"Are you sending me home?"

Javier shook his head. "Only Max can do that."
Arianna was certain she heard a silent "unfortunately" prefacing the sentence. "For now, I just want
you out of the way."

"Doing what?" As if she couldn't guess.

Folding tableware. Tucked away at the corner of the
bar, with a stack of linen napkins and a silverware

tray in front of her, she was quickly becoming an expert at the task.

Take a napkin off the pile, fold the cloth carefully into a triangle and stack a knife and two forks by the fold. Then tuck the corners to keep the silverware in place before rolling them into a cylinder. Within five minutes she'd built a small pyramid. At this rate, the restaurant would have table settings to last until New Year's.

She should have called home by now. If she was back home, she'd be curled up in her big comfortable bed right now waiting for a servant to bring her a cup of lavender mint tea.

Instead, her feet hurt, her back hurt and her stomach wouldn't stop lurching from the constant food smells passing by her nose. All she wanted to do was close her eyes and sleep for the next twenty-four hours straight.

Worse, after three days, she was no closer to deciding what she should do.

As if on cue, a wave of nausea hit her, forcing her to press a fist to her lips. If she didn't know better, she'd say the child inside her was voicing its opinion. Too bad she did not know what side the bambino was on. Then again, how could an embryo know what to do when she herself didn't?

If only she had not seen Manolo's true colors. Then perhaps the idea of spending a lifetime with him would not seem so...daunting. Her father, of course, was thoroughly impressed by the man and had been thrilled when she and the industrialist began dating. A wedding and grandchild would send him over the moon.

But wasn't wanting to please Father what had gotten her into this dilemma? Knowing how happy the relationship made her father, she'd ignored the questions whispering in her ear. If Manolo's kisses failed to make her head spin, or if there were times when she thought he loved being with the king more than with her, it was her imagination. After all, no relationship was perfect one hundred percent of the time. Perhaps if they were intimate her doubts would disappear...

Finding another woman's underwear in his apartment had shown her how wrong that idea was. Unfortunately, the shutters were pulled from her eyes a little too late.

"You're doing that wrong," a voice said from behind her.

Max. A quiver struck low in her stomach. The bambino seemed to have an opinion about him as well. Since that first day, her stomach insisted on wobbling every time she and the owner crossed paths.

He reached over her shoulder to take the setting from her hand. "The ends have to be tucked tightly or else the silverware will slide out. See?"

Arianna could feel his breath on the back of her bare neck. In Corinthia, it was considered disrespectful to stand so close to a member of the royal family. A deferential distance had to be maintained at all times. Max's arms were nearly wrapped around her. She could feel the edge of his jacket brushing her spine as he leaned forward, the feathery touch causing goose bumps.

"Now you try."

She tried to repeat the steps she'd done dozens of times throughout the night, but her fingers had grown clumsy. Instead of stacking the silverware, she fumbled and knocked them over. "It would be easier if you weren't breathing down my neck," she told him.

"Sorry." The space behind her cooled as he took a spot at the bar next to her chair. Better, but not by much. Arianna could still feel his slate-colored eyes watching her every move. Taking a deep breath, she rolled the napkin into the tightest cylinder humanly possible.

"Good," Max said. "Although next time, you might want to include a spoon."

Her shoulders sagged. Out of the corner of her eye, she saw Darius slide a drink across the bar. Max wrapped his hand around it without looking, and settled back against the bar rail to survey the restaurant. Unable to help herself, Arianna stole a look.

The man had the most effortless grace about him. You could see it in the way the glass dangled from his long fingertips and in the way he moved. Yet for all his smoothness, he wasn't overly soft. Just like how the scar on the bridge of his nose kept his face from movie-star perfection, there was strength beneath the elegance. A toughness that said he wasn't a man to be trifled with. In a way he reminded her of the ancestral portraits lining the halls of Corinthia Castle, with their impenetrable gazes that followed her every step.

They always left her feeling very exposed, those paintings. Max's stare did as well.

"I hear you're having trouble catching on to hostessing," he said, his gaze thankfully still on the dining room.

*Trouble catching on* had to be an American euphemism for making a lot of mistakes. "It was not all my fault," she said, defensiveness kicking in. "No one told me the woman was deluded."

"I beg your pardon?"

"The woman in the green dress. How was I to know she wanted a seat for her husband's remains?"

"Ah, Mrs. Riderman." Understanding crested over his features. "You're right, Javier should have warned you. She and her 'husband' come in every Friday."

"Every week?" With her dead husband? "Does that not violate some kind of health code?"

"Probably," he said with a shrug, "but seeing how she owns most of the buildings on this street, we're willing to risk the infraction."

"Oh." Whatever vindication she felt faded away. "I did not realize she was so important."

"All our customers are important," Max corrected. "Without them, we wouldn't exist." He took a sip of his drink. "Did he tell you that every time you move a party or seat them at the wrong table, that he needs to redo the seating chart?"

More times than she could count. "Yes," she said.

"Did he also tell you that having to start over causes even longer delays?"

"No, that he did not mention."

Arianna fiddled with the napkin roll she'd just completed, twirling the black cloth back and forth between her fingers. Whereas being upbraided by the likes of Javier set her teeth on edge, Max's criticisms made her feel foolish and inept. She couldn't imagine him ever making as many mistakes as she had these past few days.

"I had some trouble memorizing the seating chart," she said meekly. "My brain, it…"

She shook her head. Max didn't need to hear how her brain had become fuzzy and sluggish, or how it took all her energy to keep her ever-present morning sickness at bay.

"I'm sorry," she said instead. "I'll pay closer attention in the future."

"Afraid it's too late for that. Javier's refusing to let you back up front."

"He is?" That was not fair. She did not make that many mistakes. "What am I supposed to do then?" Surely they had enough tableware.

Max didn't reply, beyond staring into his drink. "I don't know," he said after a moment. "You can't hostess for Javier anymore. And I can't put you back out there as a waitress. Not after what happened with Deputy Mayor Esperanza. The man you dumped a salad on last night," he added when she gave him a blank look.

That man was the deputy mayor? While Corinthia didn't have the position, she knew enough about the title to assume that in a city the size of New York, the title was an important one. "No wonder he asked if I knew who he was."

She must have said something amusing because the hint of a smile played on Max's mouth. "Yes, well, Deputy Mayor Esperanza is a legend in his own mind, that is for sure."

"Was he very angry?" If the way the man turned a deep shade of crimson was any indication, he had been. She'd done her best to apologize, but the horrid little man simply slapped her words aside and told her to leave him alone.

"Nothing a couple bottles of super Tuscan didn't cure," Max replied.

"Good." She would have felt terrible if her mistake caused real damage to Max's restaurant. "I'm glad."

"Me, too. Although between you and me, the guy could use an arugula shower now and then. To keep him humble."

Setting his drink on the counter, he shifted his posture, leaning his weight on the elbow closest to the bar so he once again faced her. The smile he'd been fighting had found its way to his eyes, the shine bringing out flecks of blue in them Arianna hadn't noticed before. Her lips curled upward in response and for a moment, they silently shared the idea.

"So," Max said, reaching for his drink again. "You've never waited tables before, have you?"

"Of course I ha— How did you know?"

He arched his brow. "Did you seriously think I wouldn't notice your lack of experience?"

"No." Certainly not with the way he was watching her. Still… Her cheeks growing hot, she looked down at her feet. "I had hoped I would catch on quickly."

"How's that plan working out?"

"Not so well."

"You think?"

She'd prefer anger to sarcasm. "If you knew, why did you hire me?"

"Because I'm a sucker for a sob story, that's why," he replied.

Sob story? "I did not tell—"

"You didn't have to," he said, frowning into the last of his drink. "I guess I'd hoped you'd catch on quickly, too."

But she hadn't, and she felt like a fool for even trying. "I didn't realize it would be so difficult." All those people speaking so rapidly, barking orders at her. "Everything moves so much faster than I expected."

"Problem is, this is our busiest season. I need a waitress who can be up-to-speed immediately. I don't have the time to train someone."

"I understand," Arianna replied, though that didn't take away the sting. Before, she'd been merely foolish. Now she was foolish and useless, too.

Seemed like all she'd done the past few weeks was let people down. Her lower lip started to quiver. How on earth was she going to be able to do what was right for a baby? She hadn't so far.

"I'll go get my coat."

Sliding off the stool to her feet, she barely got a step before Max's hand caught her arm. "Hold on," he said. "You don't have to go so fast."

What was the point in staying? So she could fold more napkins?

"We're on the last round of seating. Why don't you grab a good hot meal, and wait until closing. I'll take you home, and we can talk about what you're going to do. Okay?"

How could she say no when his eyes were filled with such concern? Seeing their warmth helped to soften her disappointment. If she had one good memory about her brief stay in New York, Max Brown looking at her right now, with soft, sexy, sympathetic eyes, would be it.

Plus, she would be foolish to turn down a five-star meal. Her stomach, with its usual unpredictability, leaped for joy when he made the offer. "All right," she said. "I'll wait."

"Good." He looked pleased. Maybe it was wishful thinking, but she swore he had looked as disappointed about her imminent departure as she felt. "I'll send Darlene over with a menu.

"And hey, chin up…" His fingers caught her jaw, tilting her face toward his. "Everything will work out. You'll see."

"Sure," she whispered after he left. "We'll see."

Leaving Arianna at the bar, Max retreated to the sanctuary of his office. He had the sudden need to bury himself in paperwork and clear away thoughts of pale skin and black sateen dresses.

What was he going to do? His office chair squeaked as he collapsed into it. There was no way he could keep Arianna on staff; the woman was a disaster. Javier spent ten minutes ranting about her inabilities and swearing on his mother's life that he would not work with "that woman" again. Over-the-top? Sure, but the man was also one of the finest maître d's in the city. Max couldn't risk ticking him off. Especially since he'd had a similar "discussion" with his chef the night before.

So what did he do? He choked. He'd walked out there to fire her, but right when he was about to say the words, they died on his tongue. Killed by a pair of soulful blue eyes.

His mother's eyes had been brown. Brown and surrounded by mottled purple smudges she would try to cover with makeup. It never worked. Max always knew. No matter how much she applied, makeup couldn't cover split lips.

Not for the first time, he wondered if Arianna was running away from the same nightmare as his mother. His gut said no. Well, his gut and the fact that her alabaster skin would bruise too easily for her to hide it.

Or maybe he was rationalizing to soothe his conscience.

His conscience was still nagging him a few hours later when Darius knocked on his office door. "Just wanted to let you know the last party is getting ready to leave," he said.

"Thanks. I'll be out to close out the till in a bit."

"Okay." Except instead of leaving, his friend wavered in the doorway. "Is it true?" he asked. "Did you really let your new puppy go?"

"Stop calling her that," Max said, bristling. Arianna wasn't some stray off the streets. "And who told you I let her go?"

"The pup—lady—herself. When Darlene brought over a steak, she told me it was her last meal at the Fox Club."

"Oh." Apparently, he'd made his point after all. Now his conscience really stung. "I suppose it is."

"It's for the best, you know."

"I know." Didn't mean he had to be happy about it, though.

Stepping all the way inside the office, the bartender pushed aside the brass lamp and took its place on the edge of Max's desk. "Look, man, no one appreciates what you were trying to do more than me, but things don't always work out, you know? If you still want to help her, write the chick a check. Unless..."

His voice drifting off, Darius's attention shifted to the desk's surface and an invisible spot that he suddenly needed to scratch at with his fingernail.

Max narrowed his eyes. "Unless what?"

"Unless, it ain't just about helping a girl out. You said yourself she was hot."

"I didn't say she was hot, I said she'd look good in the uniform...and I was right." Over on the side of the desk, Darius let out a snort. One that said Max was splitting hairs, and they both knew it.

Truth? Yeah, he was attracted to the woman. She was different from other women who had crossed his path, and not because her appearance screamed money—although that did make her stand out. It was her personality that truly set her apart. She had the oddest combination of haughtiness and innocence about her. One moment she was icy and entitled, the next she looked vulnerable and scared. Most women, he could read from the get-go. They were either women from his old life, looking to rise up from their lousy circumstances, or they were women from his current world looking to hook a successful businessman. In either case, their faces were open books.

Not Arianna's, though. As much as he could read her, there was a layer he couldn't get to. It intrigued him.

Excited him, too. The way she wore that uniform, like it was a real Dior. He'd have to be a dead man not to appreciate that fact, and even death wasn't a guarantee that he wouldn't, seeing as how every swish of her skirt and sway of her hips sent awareness shooting below his belt.

A smile played on his lips. "Oh, brother," Darius said. "Just admit you want her already, will you?"

Max refused to respond. Spinning in his chair, he turned and looked out his office window. The view wasn't much, an alley and the emergency exit for the building on the next lot, but he'd certainly had worse. Behind him, the dining room was quiet except for the sounds of chairs being put on the tables. In between scrapes and rattles, he heard the soft notes of a piano over the din. Some song he'd never heard before. Reminded him of a Christmas carol, but not quite.

"When did you switch on the radio?" he asked. Normally, he wasn't big on plain piano music, but this was nice.

"I didn't," Darius replied. "That's the piano on stage."

"Are you sure?"

"Positive. Unless the speaker over your door is blown."

Max frowned. "Shirley?" Last he heard, his former piano player was behind bars. "You think she got out?"

"Doubt it. Besides, she was never that good."

Rising, Max made his way to the office door, with Darius not far behind. Together the two of them stepped into the main dining room. "Well, what do you know...?" Max said, giving a low whistle.

Arianna sat the piano, head bent over the keyboard, playing with the agility of a trained expert.

# CHAPTER THREE

ONCE SHE FINISHED her dinner, Arianna didn't know what to do with herself. Most of the patrons were gone, and the staff was busy getting ready to close. From the looks they gave her, it was clear they did not want her assistance.

She couldn't sit there and do nothing. Her nerves wouldn't let her. In a little while Max would emerge from his office to walk her home, ending her career at the Fox Club. She would be back to where she started three days ago: looking for a way to postpone her return home. Only this time, she doubted there would be another handsome white knight waiting to ride to the rescue.

Looking around, her attention stopped at the piano on the stage. She'd noticed it her first day here, but had yet to take a close look. Her spirits picked up a little. Surely no one would mind if she looked now. Reclaiming her heels, having kicked them off while eating, she slipped them on and headed over.

For as long as she could remember, the piano had been a close friend. When she was a little girl, she would sit on the bench next to her mother and accompany her by plunking out random notes. Later, the discipline of practice helped her survive the pain of losing her mama. And again when she mourned her sister-in-law's death.

Of course her instructors would say those were the only times she appreciated discipline since she spent most of her childhood ditching formal practice in favor of playing lighter, more enjoyable pieces.

She hadn't played much when she was dating Manolo; he'd been more interested in being seen than in listening to her play. The club's baby grand might not have as sophisticated a soundboard as the palace piano, but it was in excellent condition, and more importantly, she thought as she smiled and pressed middle C, it was in tune. Taking a seat on its bench felt a little bit like greeting a long lost friend.

Stretching her fingers, she played a scale, followed by an arpeggio. Because she was rusty, her fingers fumbled, and for a moment, it was like when she tried rolling tableware. Quickly, though, she loosened up, and the notes began to flow with ease. Confidence restored, she started playing one of the handful of songs she knew from memory: "In the Bleak Midwinter." The quiet, melancholy song seemed fitting, given her circumstances.

When she finished, she realized everyone in the club was watching her. Including Max, who stood near the front of the stage.

"Bravo," he said, clapping. "That was amazing."

Arianna blushed as satisfaction swept her from head to toe. Her entire life, people had showered her with compliments regarding her playing, and she'd basked in them all, but none of the accolades had affected her as much as seeing the admiration on Max's

face was. Knowing she had his approval left a thrill
that started at the base of her spine and spread out-
ward, to the ends of her fingers.

He hopped onto the stage to join her. "You've been
keeping secrets. Why didn't you tell me you could
play the piano?"

"I didn't realize it was important," she replied.
After all, she'd applied for a job as a waitress. If she
had known it was important, she would have touted
her skills first thing.

"Play something else," one of the waiters called
out.

"Sounds like you've won at least one fan. How
about it? You got any other songs tucked in that pretty
head of yours?"

"A few." Running through her mental library she
decided upon a Corinthian folk song, a simple melody
that had been a childhood favorite. She did her best
to ignore the fact that Max was watching her. Hard to
do with him propped against the curve of the piano,
his long fingers curled around the rim.

"Pretty," he said, after she'd been playing a moment. He was smiling, bringing the blue to his eyes
again. "How long have you been playing?"

"Since I was old enough to sit at the bench without falling over," she replied, adding a glissando for
flourish.

"That old."

"My mother played. When I was little, I would
watch her. Playing was a natural progression."

He leaned forward, a curious look on his face. "I
don't suppose you sing, too?"

"Perhaps." If only he knew. Both she and her

brother had to study voice. One could hardly lead the people in the Corinthian anthem off-key. "Why do you ask?"

"No reason. I was curious, is all. I have to close out the till. Would you mind playing a little longer? I think people are enjoying the concert."

Arianna looked out at the waitstaff, some of whom were nodding their heads in time with the music as they worked. Even Javier looked to be tapping his foot. "But of course," she said. It would be nice to leave them on a positive note after so many mishaps.

She played every song she could remember, an eclectic combination that ranged from Beethoven to Bocelli. Finally, there was but one song left that she could play from memory: "*Tu Scendi dale Stelle*," a popular Italian carol her grandmother used to sing. She hadn't meant to sing, but the words came out automatically.

In a flash, her head filled with memories of home. Of making candied fruit for Babbo Natale and pastries for Christmas Eve and how the whole country seemed to smell of evergreen and wine. So many traditions and she loved them all. She was Corinthian to the core.

Her heart jumped to her throat, choking off the words. She couldn't go on. "I'm sorry," she whispered as she stepped off the stage.

Max came out of his office as she was rushing toward the coatroom. "Is everything all right?"

She couldn't answer; the lump was still stuck in her throat. Brushing past him, she kept going until she was safely shut in with the coats and hangers. There she squeezed her eyes tight.

This was ridiculous. Getting emotional over a Christmas song. So what if the words reminded her of home? It wasn't as if she wouldn't be returning to Corinthia again.

Although if she chose not to marry Manolo, she would lose the country's respect, and that was as bad as never going home at all.

Footsteps sounded behind her. "Arianna? What's wrong?"

"Nothing is wrong," she told him, sniffing. "I felt a little homesick for a moment, that's all."

"Homesick, huh? Maybe this will help."

Out of nowhere, a handkerchief appeared before her. It was such an old-fashioned, chivalrous gesture that she couldn't help smiling as she dabbed at her eyes. The square smelled faintly of aftershave. Woody and masculine. Without thinking about what she was doing, she pressed the cloth to her nose and inhaled the scent. "Are you always this prepared?"

"If you're asking whether or not I'm a Boy Scout, absolutely not. I've just learned to keep a handkerchief on hand in case I run in to emotional women."

"Do you run in to them often?"

"More often than you'd think, unfortunately"

And what would they be crying for? she wondered. Because he had broken their hearts? It certainly wouldn't surprise her if those slate-colored eyes left a whole trail of women in their wake. Manolo had his assortment of conquests, did he not? And he wasn't nearly as handsome. Or, as gallant.

That gallantry was on full display as he took her coat from the hanger and held it for her to put on. "Where is home exactly?" he asked. "I mean, where in Italy? You are Italian, right? Tell me that much is true."

Arianna paused to enjoy the way his hands settled on her shoulders, the touch providing a comfort she hadn't realized she needed. It would be easy enough to say yes and end the speculation. For some reason, though, she couldn't bring herself to lie to him again. "Close."

"Close?"

"I'm from a small island country off the coast. I doubt you've ever heard of it."

"Probably not," he replied, brushing her shoulders again. "I always sucked at world geography. If a place isn't on one of the six continents, forget it."

"Seven," she said, smiling over her shoulder. She liked how he knew not to ask any more questions.

The grin she got in response made her forget all about homesickness. "Antarctica doesn't deserve full billing, if you ask me. Come on. Let me get my coat, and I'll take you home."

"You know, you really don't have to…" She followed him back into the dining room and into the darkly paneled room that passed as his office. "I will be fine on my own."

"Are you still staying at the Dunphy?" She nodded. "Then, yes, I do need to escort you. Besides, you and I need to talk about your future."

Which future was that, she was tempted to ask. Because she still hadn't figured out an answer. "I did not think I had a future here," she said instead.

"Did I say that?"

"You said you didn't have time to train me."

"As a waitress, I don't," he said, reaching behind

the door for his overcoat. "But you clearly don't need training to play piano."

Arianna's pulse quickened. "Are you suggesting I play the piano? Here?"

"No, at Carnegie Hall. Of course I mean here. It's the perfect solution, really. Every good movie nightclub has a chanteuse."

"A what?"

"A sultry lounge singer. My former one, she was unable to fulfill her contract. I planned to hire someone new after the holidays. Now, I don't have to. You're perfect for the job."

No, she wasn't perfect. Playing piano meant being in the spotlight. Far different from waiting tables or passing out menus, jobs where she had limited interaction with people and if someone recognized her, she could easily claim coincidence.

"I can't," she said, shaking her head. "I'm sorry, but I just can't." She looked away rather than meet his eye.

Several beats of quiet followed, where the only sound in the room was that of him shrugging into his coat. Arianna prayed his silence was because he'd decided to accept her answer without asking for a reason.

"I had a feeling that would be your answer," he said after a moment.

"You did?"

"Like I told you before, I'm not an idiot. Anyone with half a brain can tell you don't want to be recognized."

She should have realized her crude efforts at disguise wouldn't make it past a man as sharp as Max. "How did you figure it out?"

"Honey, I knew the minute you walked through the door. The cashmere coat and do-it-yourself haircut were dead giveaways.

"Don't worry," he added, as her hand flew to her neck. "It looks better pulled up. Makes the haircut look less obvious."

"Here I thought I was being clever."

"You didn't do that bad a job."

"I could not have done a very good one either if I didn't fool you."

"Only because I've seen more than most people."

Like what? What made him different than everyone else?

Because he was different, in so many ways.

Once more, his hands found their way to her shoulders. Despondent as she was, warmth still managed to travel down her arms. Like metal to a magnet, she felt herself leaning against him.

"Look," he said, "I don't know what your story is, but if you're in some kind of trouble…"

Arianna sucked in her breath. Max's breath warming her temple made it difficult to think too clearly, but one message managed to make it through the fog, and that was that he didn't recognize her. He only recognized a woman in hiding.

She relaxed farther into him. "Thank you."

"I'm serious, Arianna. If I can help… If someone is trying to hurt you…"

"No." She whipped around so they were eye to eye. "That is not the case at all!"

"Really?" He looked skeptical.

"Yes, I promise. I never meant to make you think I was in danger." No wonder he had been so patient with her. "You're right, I don't want to be found, but I'm not in trouble. Not *that* kind of trouble," she said with emphasis. "I just needed a few weeks by myself, to sort out a few things."

"And you needed to change your appearance to do this?"

"It's complicated."

"Most things are." There was a pause as he contemplated what to say. "You know, if you need someone to talk to—"

"Thank you, but this is something I need to handle on my own."

"Okay." Finally, he appeared to let the topic drop. For now at least. "How about we get going then?"

Ever since Max had walked out of his office that first day, Arianna had wondered if, when removed from the vintage surroundings, he would still look like a movie star. He did. The atmosphere followed him. Standing on the sidewalk, she shivered appreciatively as tendrils of frosty air curled from his lips like cigarette smoke. With barely a raise of his hand, he signaled a passing taxicab.

"I know it's not that far a walk, but I'd rather ride if you don't mind."

He wouldn't get an argument from her. Not tonight. The temperature had to be twenty degrees colder than the night before.

A gust of hot air greeted her legs as Arianna slid across the seat. The heat felt so good, she immediately kicked off her heels and wriggled her toes in front of the floor vent. She'd thought she was prepared for late November in New York, but apparently not. Max's coat, chilled from their short time in the cold, brushed her legs, each feathery touch leaving a trail of goose bumps.

"I'm going to go out on a limb and guess it doesn't get cold on your island," he remarked.

"Not this cold, no."

"Well, hopefully whatever it is you need to sort out won't take too long, and you'll be back to warm weather."

"I was under the impression we weren't going to talk about it anymore."

"Did we say that?" he asked, his grin lighting the darkness. Whether or not he could see her expression, Arianna frowned anyway. "Fine," he said. His coat brushed her leg again as he settled back into the seat. "We'll drop the subject. After I say one more thing…"

Before she could argue, he held up a hand. "You would have made a far better chanteuse than Shirley ever was."

Maybe sitting in the darkness was a good thing since it kept him from seeing how pink she blushed over the compliment. "Thank you." Then, because her conscience twinged over saying no, she added, "I'm sorry you needed to find a replacement."

"So am I," he said, his sigh heavy with regret. "But as Darius loves to tell me, you can't save the world."

"What happened to her? If it is all right for me to ask."

"She got arrested trying to sell drugs in Washington Square Park."

"That's awful." When Max said the woman couldn't fulfill her contract, she assumed there'd been some type of dispute or perhaps an illness. But drugs? Was that what he meant by being unable to save the world?

"I really thought she had her demons beat, too," he replied, "but her boyfriend must have dragged her back in."

"Perhaps now that she has been arrested, she will get some help."

"Maybe. At least she'll be away from her crack-head boyfriend. Then again," he said with a sigh, "who knows? Maybe she'll get out and go right back to him."

She could hear in his voice how heavily the failure weighed on him. Arianna wished she could ease his frustration. "At least you tried to help her," she offered. "There's that."

"Would have been better if I'd succeeded." He shifted in his seat again, and while his voice sounded far away, every move brought his body closer. "For the life of me," he continued, "I'll never understand why women insist on staying with losers when they know it'll kill them."

"People do foolish things when they're in love." Or think they are.

"Suppose so," he replied, his voice oddly flat. "All the more reason to avoid ever falling in love in the first place. All it does is cause trouble."

As good an argument as any. Perhaps, then, marriage to Manolo wouldn't be as awful as she thought. Since she didn't love him, his infidelity and duplicitousness wouldn't break her heart.

"Sounds like a lonely way to go through life," she said out loud.

"You say lonely, I say smart."

"You make it sound like love affairs never end happily."

"Have you seen one that ended well?"

"My parents were happy. And my brother and his wife. Very much so." Father's face would light up like the sun whenever Mama walked into a room.

"You said *were*."

"My mother and sister-in-law have both passed away."

"So they didn't end well."

No, they had not. Both men still mourned their losses deeply. Both of them spent their days cloaked in sadness. In fact, the only time she could remember Father showing any type of true joy was when she began dating Manolo.

Her insides suddenly felt hollow. Settling back into the shadows, Arianna trained her attention on the world passing outside her window. Times Square, normally bright and colorful, was extra festive thanks to the giant holiday billboards and white lights. Seeing such merriness cheered her slightly. "Everything looks prettier at Christmas," she said.

"Wait until they light the tree later this week," Max said as they were passing Rockefeller Center. "That's when the decorations really kick into high gear."

The famous tree stood like a towering shadow amid the brightness. "I'm looking forward to it. I've seen photographs, but never the real thing. The one we have at home isn't quite as tall."

"Not too many trees are, unless you live in a mansion."

Or a palace. Arianna bit her lip. "Do you decorate

the Fox Club?" Considering how much attention he'd paid to period details, she was curious as to what the place would look like for Christmas.

"Are you kidding? The staff would have my head if we didn't. Day after they light the big one, we light our own tree. Make a party out of it."

"Sounds nice."

He shrugged. "Personally, I'd prefer a professional decorator, but they have fun."

"I always loved decorating the Christmas tree." When she was little, her parents would have a separate tree in their suite to celebrate the family's private Christmas. The four of them always decorated it themselves, even Father, who insisted he was the only one who could properly align the star on top. This year, her father and Armando would decorate it without her.

And what of Christmas in the future? Would her child's Christmas be filled with love and excitement? Would they be sharing traditions with a man who did not love them, or would they be decorating alone?

"Hey, everything all right?" Max asked.

Arianna blinked back the moisture from her eyes. Goodness, but she was a seesaw of emotions today. Max placed his hand, solid and sure, on her arm. She suddenly wanted to curl even closer, with his arm wrapped tight about her shoulders. What was it about him that his simple presence improved her spirits? "I was feeling nostalgic again, that's all."

"You've been doing that a lot tonight."

"The decorations bring back a lot of memories. Doesn't that ever happen to you during the holidays?"

"Thankfully, no. I'm much too busy focusing on the present to worry about those days."

*Thankfully?* This was supposed to be a happier subject. Did he not want to remember? Stealing a look at his profile, Arianna tried to picture him as a child, imagining him as a smaller, younger version of the man she saw now.

"Christmas was always a special time for my family," she told him. "When I was a very little girl, my brother, Armando, and I would stay up late on Christmas Eve, hoping to catch Babbo Natale."

"Babbo Natale?"

"Our version of Santa Claus." One of the many traditions Corinthia shared with its Italian neighbor. "Armando and I would watch out for him every Christmas Eve. I was determined to catch him in the act." The two of them would tuck themselves under blankets near the fireplace, flashlights in hand for when he made his appearance.

"Did you? Ever catch him, that is?" Max asked.

"Never," she said with a smile. "No matter how late we managed to stay awake, we always fell asleep before he arrived."

"Sneaky guy."

"What about you?" she asked, curious. She hadn't forgotten his *thankfully* comment from a moment earlier. "Did you ever wait up for Santa?"

"Santa was kind of hit-or-miss in our house. Is that your hotel?"

He pointed ahead to where a pair of police cars were parked, their blue lights flashing, and any follow-up questions Arianna might have had regarding his comment took a backseat. "Why are the police here?"

"Good question. Wait here and I'll find out."

She was too curious to wait. When Max opened the door, she climbed out after him. "I am the one staying here," she said when he shot her a look.

A policeman stood guard at the front door, his heavy blue coat seeming to swallow him whole. When he saw them approaching, he stepped into their path. "Sorry," he said, his breath heavy with the smells of coffee and cigarettes, "but you can't go in."

"But I'm staying here," Arianna replied. "Can't I go up to my room?"

The officer looked them both up and down. "You are?" She wasn't sure what was more incredulous, his voice or his expression. "You might want to find a different hotel."

"Why? What happened?" Max asked.

"One of the guests was attacked in their room."

Immediately Max shot her a look. Arianna ignored him. She didn't need to see his eyes to hear the silent "I told you so" hanging between them.

"How?" she asked. Surely when he said "attacked" he meant by a fellow guest. Someone staying in the room.

"From the looks of things, they kicked in the door."

Kicked in the door… He was exaggerating, right? "What about security? Why did they not stop them?"

"What security? We're not talking five stars here. She just left in an ambulance," he said to Max. "You'll be able to go in as soon as they're done processing the scene. Although, honestly, I would consider someplace else if I were you." Arianna didn't miss the way the policeman's gaze slid to her as he said the last part.

"Don't have to tell us twice," Max replied. "Come along, Arianna."

Trailing behind him was becoming a habit as, once again, Max took hold of her hand and led her away. At least this time, she matched his long stride immediately. "What are you doing?"

"You don't think I'm letting you stay at that place now, do you?"

She didn't know he'd been given the authority to *let* her do anything. "I can't afford to stay anywhere else."

"You let me worry about that."

Except it wasn't his job to worry, was it? Or his decision.

Yanking her hand free, she stopped in her tracks, arms folded across her chest. "I appreciate the concern, Mr. Brown, but don't you think that where I sleep is my business?"

"Are you…?"

Whatever he intended to say, he bit the words back and took a deep breath. "Did you miss the part where the cop said *she* left in an ambulance?"

"Of course not. I heard him." It scared her half to death, too, the idea of being alone in her room while there was an attacker on the loose. If she hadn't been able to sleep soundly before, there was no way she would sleep at all now.

"Then why are you being stubborn?"

Because she had been tossed around by circumstance enough these past few days and needed to keep some tiny bit of control over her life, that was why. "Surely, whoever did this isn't coming back. I mean, the police are standing guard…"

"Sweetheart, you don't think that cop is going to stay, do you?" He flashed her an indulgent look that, under different circumstances, would have infuriated her. Unfortunately, she was too unnerved by his comment to be angry. "They might do that where you come from, but here, the police are way too busy to stick around longer than necessary."

Where she came from, there wouldn't be an attacker. He would be stopped by security before he even entered the building.

But this was New York, and here she lived in a cheap hotel where men kicked in doors. Looking around, she saw a small gap between cars, and wedged herself onto the curb.

"Hey, buddy," she heard the taxi driver say, "are you coming or going?"

"Give us a minute, will ya?" Max replied.

A second later, she felt his warm body wedging itself into the space next to her. They sat so close that Arianna thought he might wrap an arm around her shoulders. Looking over, though, she saw he had both arms tucked awkwardly between his long legs. Like a perfect gentleman. Although it shouldn't have, the thought left her feeling even more tired.

"You think I am being a stubborn brat, don't you?" she said.

"What I think is that you're tired and not thinking straight. Plus..." He straightened his legs with a groan. "I'm guessing circumstances make trusting strangers difficult."

"I trust you," she replied. Strange as it sounded.

"If that's the case, then let me take you to stay

somewhere else. At least, for tonight. I'll sleep a lot better knowing you're somewhere safe."

Arianna looked down at her lap. She *was* being a child. It wasn't only about her anymore. She had another life to think of.

And she was tired. So very, very tired. "I would like a good night's sleep," she said, shoulders sagging.

"Same here. So, what do you say?" The narrow space must have gotten to be too much, because he stood up and offered his hands. "How about we tuck you in someplace safe, so we can both sleep soundly."

Why not? She was too tired to argue. Without his body pressed against hers, she felt cold and empty.

Letting out a sigh, she took his hands. "Just not someplace too expensive," she said, struggling to her feet. "I'm staying here for a reason."

"Oh, don't worry." He was already guiding her toward the taxi. "This place won't cost you a penny."

Arianna stiffened. What did he mean, it wouldn't cost her anything? "Why is that? Where are we going?"

Good thing he was holding her hands, because otherwise she would have slapped the smile off his matinee-idol face. "My apartment."

# CHAPTER FOUR

"SEE? ISN'T THIS better than a hotel?" Having punched in the security code on the keypad, Max turned to see Arianna's reaction.

It'd taken some effort to convince her his intentions were honorable. Thankfully he'd been holding her hands when he'd announced his plan, because based on the way Arianna's eyes flashed, she'd wanted to clock him. Even after he explained that it was too late at night to look for a suitable hotel, her eyes had remained suspicious.

He could understand why.

Thing was, he hadn't told her the entire truth. Of course they could find a suitable room, but he wasn't comfortable with her spending tonight in a hotel, period. When that cop said someone had been attacked, his brain ran through every concern he'd had since she'd told him during her interview where she was staying. Instantly, he'd pictured her being carried to that ambulance, her delicate face covered with bruises. With that kind of image in his head, how was he supposed to then take her to another hotel? He didn't care if it was the St. Regis itself; she'd still be checking in alone in the middle of the night.

He wanted her with him. Where he could keep an eye on her. And okay, maybe take things a little further, if Arianna wanted the same. After all, it had been a long cab ride, with her body sliding up against his every time they turned a corner. He had barely recovered from sitting next to her on the curb.

So, while some vein of compassion might have suggested the arrangement, the male part of him longed to take advantage.

Arianna was surveying her surroundings. While he'd been punching the keypad, she'd walked from the foyer into the living room, stopping at the sectional sofa. Yesterday's suit jacket lay draped over the back from when he shucked it off, along with his shoes, which lay on the floor nearby. This morning's coffee and newspaper sat on the coffee table. "Sorry. I wasn't…"

Why was he apologizing? His penthouse was one of the most impressive ones in the city. What were a few pieces of clutter? "The spare bedroom is behind the kitchen. You should find spare toothbrushes and things in the bathroom."

"Do you host a lot of overnight guests?" The suspicion had moved from her eyes to her voice as she stepped around the sofa to look through the windows lining his back wall.

"Not in that bedroom." He couldn't help but flash a grin when she glanced over her shoulder. They both knew exactly what he meant. "Anyway, I've only had the place about nineteen months." A birthday gift to himself. The culmination of years of blood, sweat and tears, not all of which had been his.

"It's lovely. Especially the view." In the distance,

the tower lights on the Empire State Building glowed Christmas red and green.

"That's one of the things that sold me on the place," he said, joining her at the window. "The windows and deck wrap around three walls so you see practically all of Manhattan. There's a lap pool on the terrace as well. It's closed up for the season, but in the summer it feels like you're swimming on top of the world."

"I imagine it does."

The tone of her voice, casual and blasé, made him feel like a bragging idiot. None of this was out of the ordinary for her, was it? Not the million-dollar penthouse or the breathtaking view. With all the business about the Dunphy, he'd forgotten, but seeing her now, he realized how overwhelmingly natural she looked amid the luxury. It startled him, and raised a million questions, not the least of which was why a beautiful woman so obviously from a world of breeding and wealth would want to leave that world? She said she wasn't in trouble? Stupid him for dropping the subject earlier.

He watched as she took in the view, mesmerized by her profile. Despite her pallid skin and the dark hollows beneath her eyes, she remained the most captivating woman he'd ever seen. The way she stood, head high with near-regal bearing, inspired a kind of reverence in him. That had to be why he wasn't peeling her coat from her shoulders.

Instead, he found himself moving toward his kitchen. "Go ahead and make yourself comfortable. I'm going to grab a drink. You want one? Beer? Wine? Herbal tea?"

"You keep herbal tea here?"

"Don't sound so surprised. I'm in the restaurant business. We spend our lives anticipating guests' needs." Actually, the tea was something he'd grabbed at the last minute when he'd cooked dinner for a yoga instructor, thinking a woman into meditation and Zen wasn't the caffeine type.

He found the tin pushed to the back of a kitchen cabinet. A little dusty but unopened. Apparently he and the yoga instructor never got to dessert. "It's something called Moroccan mint," he called out. "Will that do?"

"Wonderfully," she called back. "I love mint."

"See? Anticipating guests' needs." Although, from the way her enthusiasm sent pleasure rippling through him, you'd think he'd delivered on a promise to give her the moon.

"I would have taken any flavor so long as it was not chamomile." Her answer sounded unexpectedly close, causing him to nearly drop the teakettle. Looking behind him, he saw that she'd moved to the island that separated the kitchen from the rest of the living space. She'd shed her coat as well as her shoes, if the height the marble countertop reached on her was any indication. Her uniform looked more like a cocktail dress than ever, the shiny fabric blacker next to the white marble.

Or was the marble whiter because of the black?

Realizing he was staring, he turned back to the stovetop. "Bad memories?" he asked, turning on the flame. She'd been drinking chamomile when she got sick the other day.

"I seem to have developed a dislike of the smell. Mint is far more soothing."

"If you say so. Personally, I'd rather a nice cold beer." To prove his point, he reached under the island to take a bottle from the built-in cooler. "Do you mind?"

"Not at all."

Good, because he needed a drink. Popping the cap, he tilted his head to let the cold liquid run down his throat. Slowly, his insides relaxed.

A part of him felt uncomfortable, enjoying the occasional drink the way he did. With every bottle or glass, he had to remind himself that he wasn't the old man. That a drink did not a drunk make.

Tonight was one of those nights when he had to remind himself twice. All that talk about Shirley and the stupid things people did for love.

It'd been callous of him, pointing out that her parents' marriage ended as unhappily as all the others. He'd spoken the truth, though, hadn't he? Sooner or later "true love" kicked you in the teeth. If you were lucky, the person simply died and left you alone. The unlucky ones got to stick around for twenty, twenty-five years before a heart attack set them free.

So why bother, right?

"I think I see where you got the idea for the Fox Club," Arianna said. While he'd been lost in thought, she'd left the kitchen island and walked to the opposite wall, where his vintage film noir posters were hung. Her swanlike neck curving as she looked closer at his favorite, *Call Her Murder*, a 1940s movie about a murderous femme fatale that showed the killer lounging like a cat in a blue evening gown beneath the title.

"Or did owning the Fox Club inspire buying these?"

"A little bit of both. The movies inspired the club. The club financed buying originals." He took another drink. "You know, a lot of people thought I was crazy when I first opened the club."

Too risky, they'd said. Opening a high-end restaurant during a recession. Who would want to eat in a club that looks like it's from the 1940s?

"I owned a stake in a bunch of bars that were considered sure things as far as income. I got a lot of 'a bird in the hand is worth two in the bush' kind of lectures." Presented in a far coarser way, of course. Definitely too coarse for a woman like Arianna.

"Looking around, I would say you proved them wrong."

"That I did." She didn't know the whole story by half. About all the years he worked in dive bars and sleazy surroundings before finally breaking free. Self-reliance. Now *that* was something worth fighting for. He smiled, allowing himself a moment of self-satisfaction.

Meanwhile, Arianna had turned her attention back to the posters, leaving him to study the way her dress drew to a *V* between her shoulder blades. As his eyes traced a path downward, he mentally counted the knobs of her spine like they were pearls on a string. What he wouldn't give to run his finger over each tiny bump.

"What made you pick detective movies?" she asked.

"Not detective movies—*film noir*."

"There's a difference?"

"Absolutely. Film noir is a very specific kind of detective movie. Much darker. More cynical." The door having been opened, his inner film geek stepped out. "And they have a lot more style."

"You studied film."

"I wouldn't exactly call what I did studying."

A high-pitched whistle cut him off. Turning off the burner, he poured the water into the waiting mug and carried it out into foyer.

"There was a library not far from our apartment when I was a kid. They played old movies every Saturday afternoon," he said, handing over the cup. Their fingers tangled as he transferred custody of the handle, and he felt the heat swirl around his stomach again.

"I used to go there to hang out," he explained, trying hard not to focus on the way her lips puckered when she blew at the steam. "Or rather, my mother used to send me there to hang out."

"Why? Was she trying to get you to study more?"

"More like keeping me away." Her futile attempt to shield him from reality. In spite of himself, he let out a sigh. "My father liked a quiet house, so the less things there were to set him off the better."

As if anything his mother could do made a difference. The old man inevitably exploded whether Max was in the apartment or not.

"I'm sorry."

"S'all right. I didn't like being around him, either. No one did."

No one but Mom, that was. He took another drink so he wouldn't have to see the pity in Arianna's eyes. Amazing that he said anything at all. Usually if a guest asked about the movie posters, he said he liked detective movies and moved on. His past—especially anything to do with his rat of a father—was best left there.

And yet twice tonight he'd made reference to what his childhood had been like. What Arianna would think if she knew the whole story? If he told her how when he came home from the movies, his mother would pretend everything was normal, as if her hair wasn't mussed and her eyes weren't rimmed red. Would she look at him the same way if she knew he came from a world that was cheap and violent as the movies he used to escape it?

Pushing down the heat threatening his cheeks, he walked into the living room. "Anyway, I used to sneak into the room where they were screening the movie so I could sleep without some librarian bugging me. One afternoon, I couldn't sleep, so I watched. Some kind of shoot-out, pretty lame as far as gun battles go, but I couldn't stop watching. After that, I started staying awake."

"And a fan was born."

"What can I say? They sucked me in," he replied, flopping back on his sofa. Stretching his legs out on the coffee table, he let his head lie back against the soft leather cushion and remembered how it felt, sitting in the dark, lost in a world of grit and mystery.

"Sometimes, I wonder if it was the movies themselves or just being able to lose myself in someone else's story that hooked me. Who knows, maybe if they'd been showing foreign films, I'd have opened a French restaurant."

"Or a cabaret if they had shown musicals?" Arianna took a seat on the cushion next to him and smiled.

"Exactly," he replied, smiling back. All of a sudden he was feeling quite relaxed. The alcohol was going to his head.

Why else would he be sharing stories he spent most of his time trying to forget?

"I'm glad they weren't. Showing musicals, that is," Arianna said. "I might have ended up applying for a job in the chorus line instead of waiting tables and that would have been a true disaster," she added, before taking a drink.

"Oh, I don't know. I bet you'd have made a great chorus girl," Max replied. He forced himself not to look at her legs as he said so. "We already know you can play the piano. And sing." Granted, she wasn't so great that record producers would be banging down her door, but her throaty voice made you want to hear more.

What he'd like right now was to see more. More leg. More of that gorgeous expanse between her collarbones. Giving in to temptation, he traced the length of her with his eyes, only to discover the dress had too much material to give him the view he craved. The skirt spread across the seat cushion like a black satin tarp, covering her legs down to the ankles. He found himself itching for even the tiniest of peeks.

Making matters worse, she insisted on perching on the edge of the cushion, poised to take flight at any moment.

"You know," he said, slipping a fraction closer "it's all right to sit back and relax. I don't bite, I promise."

"Forgive me if I question the sincerity of a man whose guest bedroom has never been used before."

Gaze shifting to his lap, he scrubbed the warmth from the back of his neck. She had him there. "Well, you have my word I will be on my best behavior." The words *unless you ask otherwise* fell silently at the end of the sentence.

Silent or not, she picked up on the postscript, and narrowed her eyes. "Why do I think you say that to everyone who visits your apartment?"

"In your case, it's true."

"Is it?"

"Yeah, it is," he said, the depth of his sincerity surprising him. "I know you didn't plan on staying here tonight, and that you only came because I twisted your arm."

"Thank you for realizing that."

Those weren't the only reasons, though. The women he usually brought home were all beautiful, desirable and completely interchangeable. One blended into another in an unmemorable, indistinct kind of way. Arianna, on the other hand...

"You're different."

"I beg your pardon?"

"Different," Max repeated. Having said the word out loud, he decided to plunge on with his explanation. Surely he wasn't telling her anything she didn't know already. "You're not like the other women I know. You're..." *A lady*, he almost said. "A cut above."

"A cut above what?" She laughed. A light and airy sound, like bubbles rising up from her chest. It wrapped around his insides, making him regret the promise he'd just made.

"Everything," he replied.

Arianna knew that tone of voice. Gentle yet seductive. Manolo used to use the same voice whenever he was trying to be romantic. Max, however, didn't have to try. The tone came naturally.

Making him all the more seductive, despite his promises.

Setting her tea on the coffee table, she turned to face him only to realize how closely they were sitting when their knees bumped. Quickly, she shifted backward. "Why are you doing all this?" she asked him.

"Doing what?"

Looking innocent didn't come naturally to him. "This. Being nice to me. Opening your home to me." If not to seduce her, then what was his motive? "Why are you doing all this for someone you barely know?"

"I thought we covered this earlier, at the restaurant."

Yes, they had. He'd told her he was a sucker for a sob story. Was that truly the only reason? Was helping her simply another one of his attempts to save the world? It all seemed too good to be true.

She smoothed the wrinkles from her skirt. "How do you know I'm not a murderer like the woman on your poster?"

"Wouldn't that be priceless," he said with a laugh. "Killed by my own obsession. How film noir."

"I'm serious. You don't know."

"No, I don't. But my gut tells me I'm pretty safe."

Much as she hated to admit it, she trusted him,

too. She started to reach for her tea, then changed her mind. Normally mint settled her stomach, but her insides were as squirrelly as ever. "I've never been very good when it comes to intuition," she said.

"Put your faith in the wrong person, did you?"

"More like I didn't trust myself. I let myself be swayed by other people's opinions, when I should have listened to the voice in my head."

"Happens," Max said. "Some people can be very persuasive."

Present company included. "Especially when all you want is to make them happy."

That was all she wanted, only to fail them by falling out of love and running away. The disappointments would continue, too, no matter what future she chose.

The cushions shifted. Max had switched positions again so that his arm was stretched out along the back of the sofa. If she leaned back, Arianna would find herself nestled in the crook of his shoulder. Protected by his warm presence. The notion was scarily appealing; she sat a little straighter.

Out of the corner of her eye, she saw Max's bottle resting on his thigh, balanced in place by his long index finger. "You know," he said, "I always figured Darius would be the first person to use my guest room. In fact, I'm surprised he hasn't, considering how many times he crashed on my sofa before I moved."

She wondered if the bartender would be upset that she had usurped him. "The two of you are very good friends, aren't you?" It wasn't so much a question as a statement of fact. From the start, she'd recognized that theirs wasn't the usual employee-employer relationship. Their banter reminded her of the way she and Armando would egg each other on when they were kids. "I take it you've known each other a long time."

"Since forever," Max replied. "He used to get his mom to let me crash at their place in high school on nights I didn't want to go home. She used to make this dish with pork and coconut milk that was amazing."

No wonder he and the bartender were so comfortable with each other. "He still looks out for you, doesn't he?" she said, thinking of the bartender's glares. "He's protective."

"It goes both ways. We've seen each other at our lowest."

How low would that be? How much lower could a person go when they spent their childhood hiding in a library and avoiding home? It was a life she couldn't begin to imagine, and the man next to her had lived it. Made her problems seem very small in comparison. Small and silly.

"Did you know he got me my first job?" Max asked. "Bar-backing at this bar where he and his crew hung out."

The strange term pulled her from her thoughts. "Bar-backing?" she repeated. "What's that?"

"Like being a busboy, only without the glamor. Paid the rent, though, which was what mattered. Anyway, a few years ago, when I heard Darius was out of...that is, back in the city and looking for work, I paid him back by hiring him."

But, according to him, he didn't have a rescue complex. "That was nice of you."

"Nice had nothing to do with it. I owed him. I wouldn't be here if he hadn't given me my start."

Arianna took a good look at where "here" was. As far as luxury accommodations were concerned, the penthouse was smaller and less opulent than many of the places she'd visited. Certainly when compared to her own home. Nevertheless, the apartment had a unique richness many of the other places lacked. A style. Personality. Max's personality. From the film posters to the Scandinavian furniture, the place reflected its owner's smooth elegance.

That Max lived in style wasn't a surprise. She would have been shocked if he didn't. What did surprise her was learning that he hadn't grown up in such surroundings. The man seemed, to steal one of Manolo's favorite phrases, to the manor born.

"And how did you get here?" she asked.

"You mean, the story of Max Brown's success?"

"Exactly." How did a man go from hiding in the library to living at the top of Manhattan? "Couldn't have been all Darius's doing."

"No, but like I told you, he did get me my start. The rest was a combination of good old-fashioned hard work and a lot of luck," he told her. "Helped that the bar owner took a liking to me. I worked my way up from bar-back to bartender to manager, and eventually saved enough money to buy in to the place. From there, I bought in to another and another."

She hadn't realized. "How many restaurants do you own?"

"Not restaurants. Dives. Places a lady like you wouldn't step foot in."

Considering her current circumstances, his continual labeling of her as a lady amused her. "You mean places like the Dunphy?" she asked, offering a sideways smile.

"Worse. These places made the Dunphy look like the Taj Mahal." Forearms resting on his knees, Max cradled his empty bottle in his hands. "Profitable, though," he said, staring at the label. "Very profitable. And, to answer your question, I owned six. I sold them to finance the Fox Club."

"Your labor of love."

"Yeah," he answered in a soft voice. Arianna waited, curious if there would be more. The faraway expression on his face suggested as much. "I wanted to build something I could be proud of," he said after a moment. "Some place as far away from those dives as possible."

He smiled. "Can't get further away than 1945, can you?"

"No, you can't," Arianna replied. Although he was trying to sound light, she could see the shadows behind his smile. It wasn't only the dives he'd wanted to escape from, it was reminders of his roots.

"It's no wonder you're proud. You've created something really special. The restaurant, that is." Without thinking, she placed her hand on his leg, only realizing what she'd done when she felt the muscles beneath her fingers stiffen, then relax.

"I like to think so," he replied.

The hairs on her arms started to rise as he transferred his attention from the beer label to the back of her hand. She should pull it away, she knew, but for whatever reason, her brain wouldn't send the message. It was too focused on the roughness of his wool slacks, and the strong thigh beneath. Strength that matched the man's character.

She wanted to tell him she understood how he'd felt. While she wasn't running from as significantly terrible a past, she was facing an unwanted future. Surely the two were a little bit similar?

She didn't tell him, though. Saying anything would only open the door to revealing more, and she wasn't ready to trust her secrets with anyone, not even Max Brown.

Slowly, she lifted her hand. "It's getting late."

"You're right. It's been a long night, too. Let me show you the spare bedroom."

"Thank you." The way her insides lagged at his quick agreement she blamed on fatigue. It'd been a long, eventful day. No doubt she'd be asleep the moment her head hit the pillow.

A thought suddenly stopped her. "All my clothes are at the Dunphy," she said. "I have nothing to sleep in." For that matter, she didn't have anything to wear the next day. They hadn't discussed what she was going to do beyond access to a toothbrush.

"Check the bureau drawer. I've got some old T-shirts stored in there. One of them should fit." He pushed the door wide to reveal fawn-colored walls and a satin-covered queen-size bed. "I hope this is okay."

Okay? After two days of dinge and dust, the pristineness of the room nearly made Arianna weak in the knees. Oh, but to slide into what she knew were soft, clean sheets. Her heart bounced at the thought. "It's wonderful. Thank you."

"You're welcome." The tenderness in his voice,

coupled with the gentle softness that had taken up
residence in his gray eyes, knocked her off-kilter,
as though the ground she was standing on had suddenly shifted.

She reached for the doorframe to keep from swaying forward, swearing as she did that Max was swaying, too. His head appeared to dip ever so slightly.
"Arianna…" he whispered.

She should have stepped away. Gone into the bedroom and closed the door. But his slate-colored eyes
hovered so close, gray back-lit with dark blue and
desire, their slumberous gaze rendering her mute.
Before she could think another thought, she rose on
tiptoes, her lips parting in welcome.

His mouth slid over hers, and she sighed. Long
and loud, as though she'd been holding her breath
and only just now remembered how to breathe. He
tasted of beer and spices, a taste so exotic and lovely
she wanted to taste it forever. Max's hands cradled
her face. His fingers tugged at her chignon, pulling
loose the strands. Soft moans punctuated his kisses.
Wrapping her arms around his neck, she pressed herself against his length, their bodies fitting together
so neatly, it made her head spin.

It wasn't until she felt his hand slide down over her
shoulder to rest on her ribs that reality came crashing
back. With a cry, she yanked herself from his arms.

There was guilt along with the confusion in his
eyes. "I'm—I'm sorry, I thought…" He started to back
away. "I'll leave you alone now."

"Max, wait." It wasn't right to let him shoulder
the guilt, not when she was the one who initiated the

kiss. "It's my fault. I should never have kissed you in the first place."

A rueful smile found its way to his face. "Let me guess—you're married?"

"No, not married." Her hand slid across her abdomen. As much as she'd rather keep her secret, he deserved a true explanation. "Pregnant."

# CHAPTER FIVE

PREGNANT? MAX PRESSED his palm to the wall for support. Of all the reasons… He'd thought she might be married, or hiding from a jealous boyfriend, but pregnant?

Suddenly, the pieces started to make sense. The chronic nausea. The herbal teas. *This* was why she was hiding.

She looked as mortified as he felt. "I should have said something before you… I'm sorry."

"No, no, *I'm* the one who should be sorry." What kind of man kisses a pregnant woman like he was on his last breath?

Apparently, *his* kind, since his arms itched to wrap themselves around her again. "I broke my promise. Ten minutes ago I said I wouldn't…"

"Both of us were…"

Yes, they'd both been willing participants, but he was the one who had promised otherwise. It was just that when she looked up at him with those parted red lips, he couldn't help himself. He'd wanted to taste them for days.

Still, she was pregnant? The word refused to leave his brain, as though if he repeated it enough, it would make sense. He looked to her middle, flat and tiny in her dress. "How?" That was a stupid question. "I mean…"

"It's complicated."

"I bet." Ten to one she didn't want to tell him the details, either. Pregnant women didn't run away on a lark. Whatever the reason, he bet it was a doozy. What did she say earlier? About not trusting her instincts?

He was too tired to press for details right now. "It's been a long night," he said. "Get some sleep."

"All right." Her attention focused downward, she stepped into the bedroom, only to step back again. "Max, I—"

He was too tired for the regret in her voice, too. "Good night, Arianna."

Nodding, she disappeared behind the door. Max waited until he heard the latch click before turning around. How quickly circumstances changed. No way he could let her leave the restaurant now, or go back to the Dunphy. Not when there was a child's welfare in the mix.

Memories of her sighs whispered in his ear. Jamming his fingers through his hair, he forced the memories to be silent. No sense tormenting himself over something that wouldn't happen again. Best to just shove aside his thoughts.

He headed into the kitchen, away from Arianna.

Arianna sank onto the bed, no longer enthralled by the clean linen. What kind of woman passionately kisses a man when she is carrying another man's child? She was going to be a mother for goodness' sake—mother to possibly the future king of Corinthia. She had no business kissing anyone, no matter how seductive and strong.

At least she came to her senses before circumstances went too far. Tomorrow morning she would again apologize to Max and explain how she'd been overtired and let pregnancy hormones get the best of her. Then she would focus her energy on whether or not she would marry Manolo, as she was supposed to be doing.

"Don't worry, bambino," she whispered. "I won't let you down anymore."

But as she was slipping out of her dress, her thoughts once again drifted to Max. Her body still trembled from his kiss, a reaction she never had with Manolo. Back then, she'd told herself seeing sparks was nothing more than a myth. If only she had known…

It wasn't more than the sparks that left her longing, though. Being with Max felt so…natural. Beyond feeling like she'd known him forever. When she looked into his eyes tonight, it was as if she were teetering on the edge of something more than mere attraction. Something vast and exciting.

She was playing with fire, that's what she was doing. The last thing she needed was an unwanted attachment to a man who, by his own admission, thought relationships were foolish. She had enough going on without getting her heart involved.

Best that she use her head for once, and keep her distance.

When she stepped from the bedroom the following morning, Max was already sitting at the kitchen island. From the looks of him, he'd been awake a while. Either that, or he woke up looking debonair, which, with him, was a distinct possibility.

He wore a fresh suit, charcoal gray if the pants were any indication, while the sleeves of his white shirt were already rolled to the elbows. Meanwhile, her hair was damp from her shower, and she lacked makeup.

"Sleep all right?" he asked. His eyes remained on his phone screen, last night's warm gaze a thing of the past.

"Very good. You?"

"Fine."

Arianna wondered if he was lying, too. Recalling his shell-shocked expression, she was pretty sure he was.

"There's water in the kettle if you want tea."

"Thank you, but I'd rather… That is, do you mind if I…" She pointed to the stack of buttered toast by his elbow.

He glanced up, then back at his phone. "Help yourself."

"Thank you." They ate in silence, the night before sitting between them like a giant third party. This, she thought, must be what a one-night stand felt like—awkward and stilted. She missed last night's companionship. The ease with which they'd talked. She supposed that was gone for good now. She'd be but another employee.

*Ex*-employee, she corrected, stomach dropping. She'd turned down the only job she was qualified for. And having told him she was pregnant…

She set down her toast. "I'm sorry about last night."

"A mistake in judgment. It won't happen again."

He'd said as much last night. She rubbed her hands up and down her thigh, wondering what to say next. "I feel like I owe you some kind of explanation."

"Not really. You don't owe me anything."

Perhaps, but she knew he had to be curious. The question she had to answer was how much she wanted him to know. Lying awake, she realized the most delicate part was already exposed. What would telling him the rest matter? "Like I told you last night, the situation is complicated. I came to New York to sort everything through."

Max nodded. Arianna knew that if she didn't say another word, the subject would end then and there. For some reason, though, she was the one who couldn't let the matter go. "Mano—the father—he doesn't know."

"I gathered as much," Max replied. "I'm guessing you two aren't together anymore."

"Not for a couple months. I'm afraid when he finds out…"

"He'll take the baby away?"

"What? No, not at all. If anything, he'll insist we get married."

"Ah." The strangest shadow covered his profile. A darkness from within. "And you don't want to get married."

"I don't know what I want to do." Her mind was paralyzed when it came to making a decision.

Appetite gone and unable to sit still, she pushed away from the counter. "Manolo, he was a liar and a cheat. More interested in impressing my father than he ever was in loving me."

"Is that what you meant by not trusting your instincts?"

"I tried to tell myself I was imagining things."

The view from his living room was no less spectacular during the day. A thick carpet of clouds lay in front of her feet, with only the weather lights atop the tallest buildings truly visible. Hugging herself, she watched as the vapor moved slowly past, enveloping Max's building along with all the others. That was how she felt. As though she was being overtaken by forces she couldn't control.

"Do you love him?"

She started at the closeness of Max's voice. Looking over her shoulder, she saw him standing a yard away, hands stuffed deep in his pockets. "I tried to," she replied, "but no."

"Then problem solved. You don't marry him."

If only it was that easy. "You don't understand. The baby—"

"Lots of women raise children on their own."

"I'm not most women," she replied, turning her face back to the window. "For one thing, my father would expect me to marry."

"Your father isn't the one having the baby."

"No, but he is the one with the power."

"I don't understand. Who died and made him king?"

Arianna choked back a laugh. Of all the phrases to use... If he only knew the irony. "My grandfather, for one."

"What are you talking about?"

No sense backing away from the story at this point.

"My father is His Majesty Carlos the Fourth, King of Corinthia."

He blinked. "King who of where?"

"Corinthia. It is a small country near Italy. Most people have never heard of it."

"Ri-ight."

He didn't believe her. He was looking at her like she was Mrs. Riderman. "Here. I'll show you." She walked over to the counter, where he'd left his phone. "This," she said, pulling up an image of the Corinthian royal family and shoving the phone in his hand, "is me with my father and my brother, Armando."

It took an eternity, but eventually, he looked up at her. "You look better as a blonde," he said.

Her shoulders relaxed. "I was trying to make myself look as different as possible."

"Yeah, that's not as effective as you think." With that, he stuffed the phone in his pocket and headed toward the kitchen. "I haven't had enough coffee for this. You have any more surprises? Got a hired killer after you? Stole the crown jewels?"

"If I stole the jewels, I wouldn't have needed the job." When he failed to even smile at her joke, she shook her head. "No. That's everything. But now you understand why I was so hesitant to say anything."

"Sweetheart, I'm not sure I understand anything." Grabbing the coffeepot from the burner, he filled his cup to the brim. "A few days ago, I hired a down-on-her-luck waitress. This morning I find out she's a pregnant princess. You tell me how that's supposed to make sense."

When he said it like that, she didn't suppose it did. Her hunger from before had disappeared, the nausea once again taking up residence, although this time she wasn't sure she could blame morning sickness alone. "Do you mind if I make myself some tea?"

"Be my guest. Or should I be serving you, Your Highness?"

"I can make my own, thank you." Arianna turned on the burner. "I only told you because I thought you deserved a complete explanation. There is no need to treat me any differently than before."

But he already had, backing away when she told him about the baby. How could things not change? She was no longer a down-on-her-luck waitress with whom he could flirt.

That was how it should be, shouldn't it?

Suddenly, she couldn't wait for the water to boil. She needed tea immediately. She looked around for the tea bags. "Where did you put the tea?" she asked.

"I put it back in the cupboard. Hold on." The air behind her warmed as he moved closer. He reached above her, the starched cotton of his shirt making a soft crinkling sound as he stretched. The faint scent of his aftershave drifted toward her, reminding her all too clearly what it felt like to be in his arms. She closed her eyes and inhaled.

"Here you go. Teacup, too." His arm came down, wrapping around her as he set tin and cup on the counter. "Anything else?" He lingered a little longer than necessary, as though to pull her close.

The teakettle whistled. "No," she replied. "I'm fine." Fine, except for the shiver that passed through her when he moved away.

"So who is this Prince Charming? The one your father would want you to marry?"

"His name is Manolo Tutuola. His family's leather goods company is the largest employer in the country. Father adores him." She frowned. "Why do you want to know?"

"Just trying to make sense of everything," he said with a shrug. "Like why you felt the need to dye your hair and hide in a ratty hotel. Seems a little excessive."

"You've never been a princess."

"Last time I looked, no."

From his point of view, her behavior probably did seem extreme. "I wanted to be alone to think. Really alone," she added, before he could say anything. "When you're royalty, that's impossible. Besides the paparazzi, there are guards, assistants, traveling companions. Any trip I took would involve itineraries and schedules. Solitude is not as easy as you would think.

"Then there's my father. If I insisted on being alone, he would want to know why." And coward that she was, she didn't want to have to face him.

In her teacup, the tea seeped from its bag like green smoke. "I've never been able to lie to him," she said, watching as the tendrils dissipated. "And the truth…"

"So to avoid disappointing him, you ran away?"

Childish, she knew, but hadn't that been a theme lately? "I left a note saying I needed a few weeks on my own, and that I would be home soon. This…" She gestured around the kitchen, "Joining the Fox Club. They were never part of the plan."

She told him about the pickpocket in Times Square. "I was planning to call home when Darius mentioned the job opening."

"And now here you are."

"Here I am."

Letting out a loud breath, Max left her by the counter and paced his way back to the living room. Talk about a story. Most men, upon hearing all that, would usher her out the door as fast as they could, before the craziness got any worse. Only, she was telling the truth. There was no mistaking that had been her in the photograph she showed him.

Hadn't he known from the start that she was different from other women?

What kind of idiot was this Manolo guy? A pretty big one from the way she frowned when talking about him. "What did he do? Your boyfriend?" he asked, looking out the windows rather than at her. If he looked at her, he'd be too tempted to stand close. "You said your boyfriend was a liar and a cheat. What did he do?"

"I found a pair of women's panties in his sheets. Another woman's panties."

Definitely an idiot. You don't waste your time playing with rocks when you've got a damned diamond in front of you. Arianna was right to kick him to the curb.

Only she hadn't kicked him completely; she was debating marrying the creep. Turning to look at her, he said, "Surely, your father wouldn't make you marry him. Considering."

He wouldn't be the first father to insist a man step up, a voice in his head argued.

The look she gave him was just as doubtful. "Corinthian tradition is very old and very conservative.

There are rules…and expectations regarding my behavior. Prior to marriage."

Prior to marriage? "You mean…?" Arianna nodded. She was expected to be a virgin. "Isn't that pretty archaic?"

"Perhaps, but it is tradition. Normally people wouldn't care, but for me to have a child out of wedlock would cause an incredible scandal. My father would be crushed, and he's already suffered enough sadness these past few years between Mama getting sick, and then losing my sister-in-law. I promised myself I'd never add to that."

"Instead you'll raise a child in a loveless home." Such a wonderful solution. He didn't bother asking whether Manolo would agree to a wedding. Marrying royalty was a terrific business move; didn't take a liar and a cheat to know that.

"I told you, the decision isn't that easy. It's…"

"Complicated, I know."

"It is," she said, coming around the island to join him. "I have a duty to uphold Corinthian tradition."

Maybe, but part of her clearly didn't want to or else why run away to think?

"I also have a duty to do right by my child," she said, reading his mind. "Whatever I decide affects his future."

"No kidding."

"I mean more than psychologically. If I do not marry Manolo, then this child will forever be the king's *illegitimate* grandchild."

He was missing something. The way she emphasized *illegitimate*?

"Illegitimate children cannot inherit the throne.

What right do I have to make that decision for him? For my country?" She looked at him, blue eyes shiny with moisture. "So you see, I have to decide which choice is the lesser of two evils."

Sounded like she'd already made her choice; she simply hadn't accepted her fate. Max's insides ached for her. If the situation was different—if she wasn't out of his reach—he'd close the distance between them and hold her as tightly as possible.

But he couldn't. She either belonged to another man, or if by some miracle she did decide to go against tradition, she was having a child. That involved way too much commitment for a man like him.

Ignoring the tightness in his chest, he took a long sip of coffee. "Well, one thing's for certain," he said when he finished. "There's no way we can let you go back to the Dunphy. Or any other rat hotel for that matter. Not in your condition." All it would take is one push by a careless drunk.

"Does that mean you're going to help me?"

"No, I'm going to kick you out on the street." Her eyes lit up like Christmas lights when he spoke. "Of course I'm going to help you."

"But the restaurant. I thought you didn't want me..."

"We'll work something out." Seeing how he'd nearly dragged her to bed last night, the phrase *didn't want me* wasn't the best choice of words. "In the meantime, we'll stop by the Dunphy to get your belongings and you can unpack them later tonight."

"Unpack? You want me to stay here?"

"Where else would you stay? By now I'm sure your father has figured out where you've gone, and has people checking every hotel in the city." If Max was her father, that's what he would do. "You're not going to get any thinking done if you're looking over your shoulder."

"I can't."

Her fingers brushed her lips. He wasn't supposed to notice, but he did. The same thought was going through his mind. "Look, if it's about last night, you have my word I'll be on my best behavior. For real," he added, trying to catch her eye.

To his relief, she smiled. "It was nice sleeping in a decent bed," she admitted.

"You have my guarantee there will be no police raids in the middle of the night, either. You'll have all the privacy and solitude you want. What do you say?"

"All right. I'll stay."

"Great." He ignored the way his pulse picked up at the news. After all, she would be there only for a couple of weeks. And then she would leave.

Because that's how things worked.

Darius was on the phone taking a reservation when they arrived at the Fox Club later that morning. The first thing he did was drop his attention to the suitcase Max had in his hand.

"Going somewhere?" he asked, once he'd finished the call.

"There was a problem at the Dunphy," Max replied. "Arianna decided to stay somewhere else."

"What a surprise. About the Dunphy, that is." Grabbing the coffeepot from the burner behind the bar, he poured a cup and slid it across the bar in Max's direction. "If you want hot water, you'll have to get it in the kitchen," he said to Arianna.

"Or, you could go to the kitchen for her," Max replied.

The bartender shot him a look. "Why should I?" he asked, lines forming along his dark brow. "Everyone else helps themselves."

"Because I'm asking you to." Normally, he'd let his friend's attitude roll off his back; Darius treated all new hires with the same disrespect. Knowing Arianna's true identity, however, he no longer felt right. Arianna cut off any reply he might have made.

"No need to argue," she told them. "I don't want any tea right now anyway. When I do, I will gladly get it myself. What I would really like to do is get to work, if you don't mind."

"Work? Who you going to play for? The place is empty."

"Arianna is going to help me with the menus for the upcoming holiday parties," he told Darius. Before they'd left his penthouse, they argued over her wanting to earn her keep. Max thought about insisting that her company was compensation enough, but that sounded as though there was more to their arrangement than him providing shelter. Plus, she would have rejected the comment immediately. This was the only compromise he could think of.

"Menus?" Darius's frown grew more pronounced, and with good reason since it was usually his job.

"I've got to have her do something since she can't wait tables," Max replied.

"I thought she was taking Shirley's old job?"

"She doesn't want to."

"Doesn't want—what does that mean? She sucks at everything else, you finally find something she's good at, and you give her a choice? What's going on?"

"You two do realize the lady is standing right here," Arianna interrupted. "There is no need to talk about me in the third person."

"Fine." Darius turned and looked her in the eye. "Why don't you want to play piano?"

"It's complicated." Her eyes darted to Max, wariness darkening the blue. "I am not in a position to be onstage at the moment."

"Oh." It took less than a second for understanding to make its way to Darius's face, as Max knew it would. After all, the bartender had been around the block enough times to connect the dots. He just forgot himself when he got annoyed. Or, in this case, felt disrespected.

"Oh," Max repeated. He took a drink of coffee. At the rate he was consuming the stuff today, he'd burn a hole in his stomach by dinner. Which, thinking about it, might not be a bad idea. It would give him something to focus on besides the woman next to him.

Who smelled and tasted way too delectable for her own good.

Meanwhile, just because he understood why Arianna wasn't playing the piano didn't mean all was settled with Darius. Max still owed him an apology for yanking the rug out from under him.

"Why don't you go ahead and get settled in my office," he said to Arianna, "and I'll join you in a couple minutes. Darius and I have a few things to go over first."

"Are you sure I shouldn't stay?" She looked back and forth between them. "In case…"

"It won't take long," he assured her. "I just want to talk to him about some supply orders."

"Supply orders," she repeated. She didn't seem sure if she believed him. There was doubt lacing each word.

"Yeah, supply orders. I promise. It won't take long." Hopefully she understood what he was really promising, that her secret would remain safe with him. What he wanted to do was take her hands and really reassure her, but that wouldn't be appropriate seeing how he'd promised to keep his distance. "I'll be there in five minutes."

"So that's how it is now," Darius said, once she was out of earshot. "She's your new right hand?"

"Look, I know you're ticked I gave her part of your job."

"No, hey, I'm cool," he replied, raising his hands in a way that said he clearly wasn't. "I'm the one who told you to get her out of your system. I just need to know if this is going to become a regular habit. 'Cause if you're gonna promote every woman you sleep with, things are going to get awkward real fast."

"It's not like that," Max replied, surprised by the defensiveness in his voice. He wished he could explain to his friend that Arianna was officially off-limits. "Believe it or not, I'm only interested in helping the woman."

"Uh-huh." Leaning over the bar, he nodded at Arianna's suitcase, which sat where Max left it, next to a bar stool. "Out of curiosity, where did your newest employee sleep last night?"

Max's cheeks grew warm.

"I thought so."

"In the spare bedroom." So he could wipe that smug smile off his face. "Nothing happened." Nothing except two whopper revelations and a kiss he couldn't stop thinking about.

Instead of his smile fading, however, Darius let out a laugh. "You are kidding me. Max Brown took a woman home and didn't sleep with her? Let me get the calendar. Someone's got to mark this date down."

Max curled his lip into a sneer. "Very funny. You act like I've never gone out of my way to help someone before. May I remind you you're the one who says I'm always trying to save the world?"

"Save the world, sure. But I've told you from the start, this chick is different. I figured it was because you had the hots for her, but now you tell me she's in the spare bedroom, and she's working in your office planning menus? I don't get it. What's the big deal about this particular woman?"

"She's special." The words came so easily, they scared him. *Special* was another one of those words with implications.

Then again, Arianna was special. She was royalty, for crying out loud. She was carrying the possible king of her country. Of course he would go out of his way to help.

Although that didn't explain why he felt protective of her before he knew her story, or why he was still fighting the urge to hold her in his arms.

"I'm sorry, sir. We don't open for another hour."

At the sound of Darius's voice, Max turned to see who had walked in. The man standing in the doorway was tall and swarthy, with salt-and-pepper hair. He wore a navy blue coat remarkably similar to Arianna's in terms of style and expense. His posture reminded him of Arianna as well. Straight and tall.

Regal.

A chill ran down Max's spine. "He's not here to eat," he told Darius.

"How do you…?"

"May I help you?" He didn't have time for the bartender's questions right now. There was no doubt in his mind this man was looking for Arianna.

The stranger regarded him with an imperious stare. "I am not here to eat," he replied, in a lilting accent similar to Arianna's. "I am Vittorio Mastella, head of security for His Majesty King Carlos of Corinthia."

"King who of where?"

Darius had come around the bar to join him by the door. Max immediately shot him a look.

"How can we help you, Mr. Mastella?" He noticed the man's red tie was dotted with what looked like small black dragons. A similar combination, this time in the shape of the flag, was pinned to his lapel. The Corinthian flag. Max recognized it from the website Arianna showed him.

"I am looking for someone. A young woman. I am wondering if she has been in your establishment recently." Reaching into his breast pocket, the man produced a photograph. It was a cropped version of the one Arianna showed him online, with her hair blond and piled atop her head.

"Have you seen her?" he asked.

For the first time in his life, Max actually thanked

God for his years of working the underbelly. It took all his experience to keep from reacting.

"Sorry," he said. "She doesn't look familiar."

Mastella looked over at Darius. Thankfully, the bartender could be trusted to follow Max's lead and had a better poker face. He shook his head. "Nope. Sorry."

"Are you certain?"

Something about the man's stare made the hair on the back of Max's neck stand straighter. He seemed to be fixated on a point past his shoulders. *Where Max's office was located.*

"Positive," he replied, shifting to his left. "I think we'd remember if a gorgeous blonde walked into our place. Wouldn't we, Darius?"

"Yeah, we don't get too many people wearing crowns. Unless you count Mrs. Riderman, but that's only on special occasions."

"I see." If the stranger was listening, Max couldn't tell. The man seemed intent on whatever it was he saw over his shoulder. "Are you going on a trip?"

Dammit. The suitcase. That's what the guy was looking at. "Yes, I am." Hopefully the man didn't notice the catch in his breath before he spoke. "I'm heading to Connecticut right after work."

"Connecticut?"

"It's the next state over," Darius chimed in.

"I have a meeting with a supplier in Hartford first thing in the morning. Figured I'd get a head start. You know, beat the traffic."

"Of course." He sounded about as interested in Max's travel plans as he would a listing of menu ingredients. Returning the photo to his breast pocket, he pulled out a leather card case. Expensive leather. Probably from Manolo's factory. Max fought a sneer.

"I am staying at the St. Regis," Vittorio was saying. "Should you see Princess Arianna, please let me know. It is imperative that I speak with her as soon as possible."

He bet it was imperative. Max pretended to study the card. "Sure thing. I'm sorry we couldn't be of more help."

Vittorio, who was pulling on a pair of leather gloves, barely spared a glance. "On the contrary, you've both been very helpful. Thank you." Giving a quick nod of his head, he turned on his heel and left.

No sooner did the door shut, than Darius locked on him like a laser. "Princess Arianna?"

"You never heard a thing," Max replied. "Not a single word."

"Including the word *princess*?"

"Especially that word."

"Does that mean you're not going to tell me what's going on?"

Max sighed. He didn't like leaving his friend in the dark, but he'd promised Arianna. "Not my story to tell. Let's just say it's complicated."

"No kidding." The bartender shook his head. "Man, you've gotten involved with some crazy women, but this time… You know what? I take it back. I don't want to know."

"Good." Max headed back toward the office. Arianna had to have heard Vittorio's voice. Hopefully she hadn't tried to bolt through the back door.

* * *

As soon as Arianna heard Vittorio's voice, she'd leaped from the chair she was sitting in and wedged herself in the space behind the office door. Thankfully, Max's office was set at enough of an angle that Vittorio shouldn't notice the movement.

She could not believe the head of Corinthian security himself was going door to door looking for her. Knowing Vittorio's sense of order and propriety, he no doubt found the task completely beneath him. On the other hand, his personal involvement made sense. If Father wanted discretion, Vittorio would be the only man he would trust.

Thinking of Father made her insides twist with guilt. Was he angry or worried about her? Both, she imagined. That was how she would feel if it was her child. More weight piled onto her already guilty conscience.

What was she going to do? Choose duty or disgrace?

*You already know,* a voice whispered.

Did she? All her life, she had come down on the side of duty. Father wanted her to stand in for Mama. Father needed a goodwill ambassador. Father wanted her to date Manolo. Was she destined to choose duty again? If so, then why was she hiding behind a door? Why not step out, show herself to Vittorio and be done with the whole silly scheme?

"You can relax. He's gone now."

The tension seeped from her shoulders. Funny how quickly Max's voice could put her soul at ease. Letting out her breath, she let her head fall back against the wall. "Thank goodness. I cannot believe he walked in while I was sitting in plain view. Do you think she suspects that I am here?"

"Nah." Shaking his head, he planted himself against the edge of the desk, once again demonstrating the natural grace Arianna admired. With his hands stuffed in his pockets and his legs crossed at the ankles, he looked calm and collected. Nothing at all like a man who lied to a Corinthian official. "I'm pretty sure Darius and I chased him off the scent," he said.

"Darius?" Her pulse began to race. "He knows who I am?"

"Don't worry. He won't say anything."

"How can you be so sure?" The bartender had shown only disdain for her. What incentive did he have to keep her secret? Especially in the face of a reward. There would be a reward.

"I told you, we've known each other since we were kids. Darius might be obnoxious at times, but he's loyal to a fault. I told him to keep his mouth shut, and he will."

Arianna wished she could share his confidence. Now two people knew her secret. If Darius chose to tell just one person...

Was all this worrying and subterfuge worth it, simply to have some time to think over a question with an obvious answer? For a couple more weeks of Max's company? The knot that had replaced her heart twisted in her chest at the question.

"This is ridiculous," she said, coming out from her shadows. "I should call Vittorio and let him—"

"No!"

"What?"

Max had straightened to his full height, like a soldier at the ready. "You said you needed a couple weeks."

"That was before…"

Before the voice in her head started gaining strength.

"Before I realized how silly this whole idea was," she said. "I have no business running away from my problems like a child."

"There's nothing childish about wanting to think things through. About making the right choice. What will going back today solve that can't be solved two weeks from now?"

He had a point. Her life would be exactly the same in two weeks or even in a month. It was the intensity of his argument that stirred her thought. Reached inside her and squeezed at the part that wished for a third alternative.

She ran her fingers over the brass gussets that lined the edge of the chair in front of her. "If I didn't know better, I'd say you didn't want me to go." She was only partially teasing.

"It's not about my wanting you to stay or leave," he replied. "It's about you being absolutely sure you know what you're doing. This is your future we're talking about."

Wrong, she thought, hand coming to rest on her belly. Her future was inside her. What was left was to decide what life would be best for the baby. She had a feeling she knew.

"I suppose a few more days wouldn't hurt," she said.

Max's smile was far more animated than she

would have expected. "Exactly. You'll stay, you'll take it easy and you'll decide whether or not marrying Manolo is right."

"I hope you're right."

"Trust me." He raised his arm, and for a second Arianna thought he was going to stroke her face, only to watch as he combed through his hair instead. "You'll be glad you stayed."

Would she, though? She wondered as a tremor of disappointment trailed through her. The voice in her head, the one who had all the answers, was telling her staying would only make things more complicated.

Because it knew why she wasn't ready to leave.

# CHAPTER SIX

*"DID YOU REALLY think you'd get away with it?"*

Max recognized the actor's voice soon as he heard it; the movie was one of his favorites.

He didn't expect to come home to it playing on his television set however. Tossing his overcoat over the chair by the door, he walked into his darkened living room, only to stop short at the threshold.

There was a Christmas tree in his window. Four feet high and lit with tiny white lights. Candles, too. A half dozen of them in jars strategically placed around the space. They turned the apartment into a cornucopia of holiday aromas: cinnamon, pine and sugar cookies.

Sitting in the midst of everything, wrapped in a blanket, sat Arianna, her attention glued to the television screen. She had a cup of tea cradled in her hands, the rim hovering by her mouth as if she couldn't tear herself away to take a sip.

Max's chest tightened. They'd been sharing a space for only a few days, yet finding her tucked in the corner of his couch already felt normal.

Frighteningly so.

"You've been busy," he said, finally finding his voice.

She started, then smiled. Max's chest constricted a little more. It was the oddest of sensations. Not desire so much as a kind of warmth wrapping around his center. "When I sent you home early I thought you would get some rest, not decorate."

"There was a man selling them from the back of his truck. I saw them, and decided your apartment could use a little Christmas spirit. The doorman helped me bring it upstairs."

"And the candles?"

"The man was selling those, too. You don't mind, do you?"

In other words, she'd bought herself a load of questionable Christmas goods. Max smiled as he walked over to the tree. "No, I don't mind. Usually, I don't bother. I figure the one at the club is enough."

"I'm afraid it's not very well decorated. I thought the ornaments would go further than they did. If I had known, I would have purchased more candles."

"It's okay. I like the sparseness." He poked a particularly large red ball and watched as it swung back and forth catching the light. It'd been a long time since he'd had any kind of Christmas decoration in his place. Always seemed a bit silly since he spent most of his time at work. This little guy looked like he belonged though.

Much like the woman behind him on the sofa.

It dawned on him she must have spent her entire paycheck, or much of it. Less than a week's worth of hours wasn't much. "You should have told me you wanted to decorate. I would have bought a tree."

"I know, but I wanted to do this myself. To thank you for everything you are doing."

"You didn't have—"

"I told you, *I wanted to*. Consider it an early Christmas present."

Because more than likely she wouldn't be here on Christmas Day. Max swallowed the lump that had all of a sudden stuck in his throat. He was used to being the one who did people kindnesses, not the other way around. "Thank you."

"You are most welcome." There was the sound of rustling behind him, as she shifted position. "I have been thinking that this situation can't be easy on you."

"What? Harboring a princess?" He turned with a smile. "I do it all the time, don't you know."

"I'm serious. I know how much I've disrupted your life this week. Yours and everyone else's at the club. You've been kinder to me than I could ever imagine."

"It's nothing." What else could he say? Truth was, he didn't understand his excessive kindness himself. Since they first met, he'd been trying to figure out what made her different from the other people he helped, so that he seemed willing to do just about anything. He couldn't explain it any more than he could explain the desperate feeling that gripped him when she mentioned leaving.

"You know most people who do as much as you have expect something in return," she told him.

"How do you know I don't?"

"My gut."

"Ah, so we're listening to that now, are we?"

"Better late than never, right?"

In the darkness, her lilt was more pronounced, giving her voice a husky, come-hither quality that went straight through him. Answering the call, he left the tree and joined her on the sofa. To his delight, she moved a couple inches to give him space, but didn't tuck herself tighter into the corner. He toed off his shoes and stretched his legs across the coffee table. "Interesting choice of movie," he said, pointing to the big screen. "Not that I'm complaining, of course."

"I thought it was going to be a musical. It has the word *Holiday* in the title."

"You could have turned the channel. I'm sure there are more festive programs on, even at this hour of the night." This time of year, every channel had a dancing elf or sappy holiday romance.

"I know, but once I realized what it was, I decided to keep watching. I wanted to see what it was about these movies you found so fascinating."

In other words, she was trying to understand him. Max knew the drill. When a woman started delving into his psyche, it meant she was looking for more than a good time. Usually that was the signal it was time to let her down gently.

So, where were the warning bells? The quickening pulse telling him to pull back?

Maybe it was because he knew Arianna was leaving anyway that her question made him lean back with a smile. "What have you discovered?"

"I don't know yet. This movie is definitely attention-holding."

"I'm sensing a *but* coming."

"It's just that I can't help wondering…" She chewed her lower lip. "Are all of them this…unbelievable?"

"Says the runaway princess sitting on my couch."

The way she wrinkled her nose in response made him chuckle.

"I am serious," she continued. "The heroine keeps going back to the husband no matter how many horrible things he's done, including trying to frame her for murder."

"Doesn't sound so unbelievable to me." Probably the most realistic part of the whole movie if you asked him. "You said yourself people do stupid things when they're in love."

"You mean like your pianist friend, Shirley."

"Yeah. Like Shirley. Sticking with a loser even when they know it'll end bad." His gaze drifted back to the Christmas tree. Or like his mother.

He felt Arianna shift closer. Sensing the thoughts he was holding back. Why not say more? She wasn't staying.

"The Christmas before my mother died, she and my father didn't have a tree," he said. "My father told her it was a waste of money. She wouldn't let me buy one for them, either, because she didn't want to tick him off. Instead, she spent the last month of her life in a joyless house."

"I'm sorry."

Max kept his eyes on the tree. He wasn't ready to turn his head in case there was pity to be seen in Arianna's eyes. Wouldn't matter if she sat in the shadows or not, he'd see it.

"That's how it works. No matter how bad he made her life, she stuck it out. Said love meant taking the good with the bad. 'Course in her case, good meant getting through the day without a backhand."

It was a running theme in his neighborhood. His

mom. Darius's mom. Mrs. Manning on the first floor. Stand by your man until your loyalty dragged you into an early grave.

"They never should have gotten married in the first place really," he said.

"They must have loved each other once."

"Nah. Only reason my dad proposed was because my grandfather made my dad do the right thing."

"Oh." If it was possible for a word to convey a thousand meanings, that one word did.

"Yeah," he replied softly. "Funny, but as far as I can tell, doing the right thing didn't do any of us any favors."

The two of them sat quietly while his words settled between them. On screen, the heroine and her husband fought for control of his gun. It wouldn't end well for one of them.

"It would be different, you know," Arianna said from her corner. "When—if—I marry Manolo. I wouldn't be ruining his life. If anything, this child is the best thing to ever happen to him."

"Lucky Manolo," he drawled.

She was right, though. Her situation was different than his parents' It involved power, money, tradition—everything that had been absent from their lives. He didn't hear any mention of happiness, though. That didn't change.

Why did the thought of her marrying this man bother him so much anyway? It was of no consequence to him what she did. If anything, maybe a political marriage was a good thing. If neither of them loved each other, then there was little chance one of them would spend their days heartbroken and alone.

Who knew? Maybe one day Arianna would learn to love this Manolo guy. She cared enough to try before. And who's to say the cheating jerk wouldn't change his spots over time as well? God knew, if Max was in his shoes and had a woman like Arianna to come home to he would.

His chest constricted yet again.

"Is your stomach still bothering you?" Max noticed she'd taken up her tea again. The nausea was why he'd sent her home early. She'd begun looking pale and tired shortly after lunch.

"A little," she replied, between sips. "I thought I was feeling better, but it started churning again."

"You've been sick a lot." There it was, that overwhelming desire to protect her coming up again. This time, he welcomed the distraction. Rushing in to solve a problem was a lot easier than dealing with the other thoughts clogging his brain. "Is that normal?"

"From what I read, I believe it is."

"Still, maybe you should see a doctor to make sure."

Her hand came down to rest on her stomach. "I'd like to, but I can't figure out how without identification. I thought perhaps a hospital emergency room…"

But that would mean giving her name, which meant being discovered and heading home before planned. "Leave it to me," he said. "I'll get you an appointment with someone who won't ask questions."

"You will?"

"Sure." Because she was special and he was destined to keep bending over backward for her. "Now, what do you say we dump this gangster film and find some dancing elves?"

She smiled. "Sounds lovely."

Yeah, it did. He reached across her to get the remote from the end table. Their eyes met as he pulled back. Her lips glistened, shiny and bright. Would he ever be able to sit on this couch again without thinking of mint tea? He wondered. The scent had already become a staple in his world. Mint and pine and vanilla cookies. Another lump rose in his throat.

"Thank you again for my Christmas tree," he whispered.

"Thank you for everything," she whispered back.

The words rolled through him, settling somewhere near the center of his chest. Squeezing the remote in his fist, Max prayed Manolo Tutuola appreciated the gift he was getting.

"You do not have to come with me," Arianna said a few days later.

"Actually, unless you want a lot of questions from the front desk, I think I should. I'm not sure how much Carol has told her staff."

"How much have you told Carol?" She stopped to adjust her scarf before stepping through the door Max was holding. Winter weather had arrived in earnest. November's rawness was gone, replaced by a crisp cold that turned every New Yorker pink-cheeked.

Greeting them with a hearty good-morning, the doorman raised his arm to signal a taxi, only to have Max wave him off. Arianna had already said she wanted to walk, despite the cold. She'd been inside too much lately, and craved the fresh air.

"As little as possible," Max replied in response

to her question. "I sort of implied you were here illegally."

"I see." They were on their way to a friend of Max's who'd agreed to examine her "on the down low," as Max put it.

"You'll like her," he continued. "She's smart. Very dedicated to her patients."

As well as very fond of Max to do him such a big favor, she mused. The thought sat sourly on her tongue as she voiced more charitable concerns. "Still, she is taking a risk, is she not? Aren't there rules about these sort of things?"

"If there are, she didn't mention them. Though I think she would have done the favor regardless." He flashed one of his knee-buckling grins. "I can be pretty persuasive when I want to be."

She bet. Arianna didn't want to know any more. Thinking about Max charming her obstetrician made her morning sickness worse.

That she should feel possessive at all was ridiculous. Max had a love life before she arrived, and he would continue to have one when she returned home. Nevertheless, whenever she thought of another woman sharing Max's company, sitting on his sofa, drinking tea in his kitchen, she found herself fighting an overwhelming urge to stake her claim.

The reason why was too scary to contemplate. Her life didn't need another complication.

*You mean beyond dragging out your decision so you can spend more time with Max?*

"Are you sure you want to walk?" Max asked. "Carol's office is a good fifteen blocks."

"I do. The fresh air feels good. Besides, shouldn't

you be cold when you are looking at Christmas decorations?"

To illustrate, she pointed to a store window filled with artificial snowflakes. "Perhaps we can buy more ornaments for your tree."

"I like the tree the way it is decorated."

He'd said as much two nights ago. Buying him a Christmas tree had been a spur-of-the-moment idea. When she'd spotted the man unloading them from his truck, she knew an evergreen was exactly what the apartment needed for Christmas cheer. She hadn't forgotten what Max said about Christmas being hit-or-miss as a child.

She had a feeling she'd remember a lot of things about Max. Such as how he smiled at her differently from the way he smiled at others. His eyes lit up more. Or like how he looked right now with his reddened cheeks and his perfect hair blown askew by the wind. One particularly thick shock of hair lay across his forehead like sloppy bangs. It made him look like the boy Arianna imagined he used to be. Before cynicism took over.

Yes, she would definitely remember Max for a long time.

She dabbed her scarf at the moisture gathering in her eyes. "I think the wind is making my eyes tear."

"Definitely stings when it hits your face, that's for sure. Maybe, if you pulled your scarf higher…"

Or maybe if he put his arm around her shoulders, she thought. In the protective circle of his arm, she wouldn't care what the wind did. Since their kiss, he hadn't touched her at all beyond the casual brush of his hand. There was a moment the other night when they were watching television, when she thought he might, but no, he'd remained a perfect gentleman, taking grcat pains to avoid physical contact. Even when his arm had been stretched out behind her and she'd shifted close.

He was keeping his promise.

She was the one with the problem. The one longing to toss aside all common sense, curl against him and rest her head over his heart. To pretend for a few hours she was more than the latest person he was trying to help.

"If you're uncomfortable now," Max said when she sniffed away her thoughts, "wait until it starts to snow."

"Snow?"

"Uh-huh. Weren't you listening to the radio this morning? The city is supposed to get two or three inches."

"Really?" The thought of fluffy white snow banks cheered her immediately. "We rarely get snow in Corinthia, and when we do, it melts almost immediately, except at the top of Mount Cornier. Manhattan is lucky."

He laughed. "You might want to ask a few New Yorkers before saying so. Snow isn't so great when it's mid-January and you haven't seen the sun for two weeks."

"But in this case, it means they'll have a white Christmas. I would love one of those."

"You could always stick around for this one."

"Perhaps I will," she replied.

Neither of them was serious. Max was simply making conversation, and Arianna…she could only hide from her decision for so long, despite visions of a snow-filled Christmas Eve in Max's penthouse.

"Do you miss it?" Max asked. "Corinthia?"

Funny question. Wasn't it only a week ago she was wishing she were home in bed waiting on a servant to bring her tea? "A little," she replied. "I love my country very much. And I miss my family. My father. Other things, however, I don't miss at all."

Max made a strangled sound, something between a cough and a snort. He thought she was referring to Manolo.

"Other things," she told him. "Additional things."

"Like what?"

"For one, I do not miss having to sit through father's diplomatic dinner parties."

"Bad?" Max asked.

"Horrible. Do you have any idea what it is like to spend an entire evening listening to people talk about themselves? I would never tell Father, but there are nights when I'd rather put my eye out than listen to one more self-important windbag."

"Why wouldn't you?"

"Put my eye out?" she replied with a laugh. "That would cause a spectacle."

"No, I mean why wouldn't you tell your father how much you hate them?"

"Because..." Because he was her father. "With my mother gone, he needs me to act as his hostess. Besides, it makes him happy to have me there."

For some reason, her response made him look down at his feet. "It makes *him* happy," he repeated with a frown.

"Yes. Very." For a long time, it was one of the few things that did.

"Sounds like that means a lot to you."

She stiffened a little at his tone. What was wrong with wanting to be a good daughter? "Of course it does. He's my father. Did it not mean a lot to you to make your mother happy?"

"That wasn't possible."

Not as long as she'd stayed with his father. Arianna kicked herself for asking the question. At the same time, she knew he *wanted* to make his mother happy. Especially if...

"A month after Mama died, I went to my father's office unannounced," she told him. "He was sobbing. Not crying—sobbing, in agony." She could see him still, with his head in his hands, crying as though his heart had been torn from his chest. "This man—the most powerful man I knew—was broken and there was nothing I could do except be the best daughter possible."

Max nodded. "So that's what you did."

"Yes. I became the consummate princess. And then, when Armando's wife died and everyone was thrown into mourning again..."

"You stepped up even more and started dating Daddy's favorite industrialist?"

"He was thrilled. The entire country was thrilled." Max still didn't understand, did he? The responsibility that sat on her shoulders. "Corinthia is a small country. It's not like America, where your leader is some person thousands of miles away whom you might never meet. We consider our countrymen to be like our family, and us theirs. When my mother and Christina died, the people mourned as strongly as we did. They needed something positive to focus on as much as my family did."

She looked up at his face, which was frozen in a frown. "Tell me you would not have done the same in my shoes? If there was a chance for you to make your mother smile, even just for a little while, that you would not have taken it?"

"Yes, but..." He shook his head. "Nothing."

"What?" If he had an argument, she wanted to hear it.

"It's just that, despite everything in her life, what would have made my mother the happiest was knowing I was happy. We're here."

He reached around her for the door handle, ending the discussion. Just as well. Arianna wasn't sure how to respond.

It turned out that, in addition to being a kind person and a respected obstetrician, Dr. Carol Miller was also blonde and statuesque. Arianna spent the entire examination vacillating between appreciating her kindness and hating her guts. It was much too easy to imagine this woman sitting in Max's kitchen. Or in Max's bed for that matter.

Speaking of Max, was it necessary to look that pleased when Dr. Miller greeted them in the lobby? Surely he didn't have to hug the woman for as long as he did.

"Everything looks good, although I'd like to see you on prenatal vitamins," the doctor said, when she finished. "Otherwise, development seems to be right on schedule. Looks like you've been taking care of yourself."

"I have to, don't I?" Arianna replied. "It's not only my health anymore."

"I'm glad to hear you say so. You'd be surprised, but every once in a while we get a patient who insists they don't have to change their lifestyle one little bit, including tossing back a few cocktails every Friday night. Trust me, that little baby in there is going to appreciate the fact you didn't."

Arianna tried to smile. "Do you think he or she could pay me back by not making me so sick to my stomach?" Darn morning sickness had been acting up since Dr. Miller walked out to greet them. As soon as the woman put her arms around Max's shoulders, Arianna felt like she was going to lose her breakfast.

"Max mentioned you were sick a lot. I don't see anything to indicate it's abnormal, though. Some women are simply more prone to morning sickness than others. You should be feeling better soon."

"I hope so," Arianna replied. She'd had enough churning for a lifetime. "Personally, I do not know why they call it morning sickness since I've been sick twenty-four hours a day."

"One of the great mysteries of pregnancy life," the doctor replied. Uncrossing her abnormally long legs, she stood and walked across the exam room. "Lifestyle factors can exacerbate the problem, though. Have you been under any stress lately?"

"A little," Arianna said as she scratched at the seam on the exam table. *Stress* was hardly the right word for the thoughts swirling in her head.

"Well, that won't do you any favors, for sure. Try to take it a little easier if possible."

"I'll try."

The doctor took no notice of her reticence, as she was busy opening the exam room door. "Maribel? Would you bring Mr. Brown back now?"

Arianna immediately propped herself on her elbows. "Why are you calling for Max?"

"Oh, I'm sorry. I figured he would want to be part of this," Dr. Miller replied. She had crossed the exam room yet again, to retrieve what looked like electronic equipment sitting on a wheeled cart. "I have to admit, it was funny hearing him be all papa bear on the phone. I forgot how protective he could get."

"Yes," said Arianna. "He certainly goes above and beyond for his employees."

"Employee?" The doctor frowned. "I'm sorry. I thought the two of you were…"

*Together.* Arianna's heart leaped at the thought, only to immediately fall hard. "No," she replied. "We are not together. I'm merely someone he's trying to help."

"Wow, I'm sorry. The way he sounded on the phone, I assumed…"

"Assumed what?" Max appeared in the doorway. He looked at her from over the doctor's shoulder. "Is something wrong?"

The probing concern in his eyes made Arianna feel more exposed than the paper gown.

"My mistake. I thought… Never mind." Dr. Miller waved her hand. "You can go back to the waiting room. I'll send Arianna out as soon as she's heard the heartbeat."

"I can hear the heartbeat?" Any embarrassment she felt vanished with a flutter. She could hear her baby? "I didn't think I was far enough along."

"You're just far enough that we should be able to pick up something with the fetal Doppler."

Arianna's pulse stepped up its pace. Her baby's heartbeat. She couldn't believe it. Except for the morning sickness and her clothes feeling a bit snug, she didn't feel all that pregnant. Yet she was about to hear definitive proof there was a life inside her. She looked to Max, who was still standing in the doorway.

"Would you like to stay?" she asked him.

"Me?" His self-assuredness, which she thought was a permanent fixture, slipped slightly. "I don't think…"

"It's not exactly protocol," Dr. Miller told her.

"Please." Nothing about this appointment fit protocol, so why change now? "I'd like him to hear the heartbeat, too." She couldn't explain why, other than it felt important he share in this moment with her.

"If Max wants to stay," the doctor replied.

"Please?" Arianna repeated, looking him in the eye.

The restaurant owner wore the strangest expression. Fearful, almost. His eyes were wide and distant. "I…"

Cutting off whatever he was about to say, he nodded instead. "Okay, if you want me to."

"Now that that's settled, I'll need you to lie back down," Dr. Miller replied. "Max, you can either stand by the sink or you can step a little closer."

Max opted for the sink, a choice that left Arianna disappointed. While she didn't expect him to hold her hand, she'd hoped he would at least want to stand near her.

At least he was sharing the moment.

Lifting one side of the paper gown, Dr. Miller squirted a dollop of cold gel on her abdomen, before reaching for what looked like a plastic microphone.

"Sometimes it takes a couple minutes to find him or her," she said, pressing the tip into the gel. Arianna held her breath while the doctor moved the device left, then right. Suddenly, she paused the microphone an inch or so above Arianna's pelvic bone. "Hear that?"

A low rapid drumbeat was coming from the machine. "Is that it?" Arianna asked. Dr. Miller nodded.

In a flash everything became a thousand times more real. The baby. Gone was the nebulous concept that she was pregnant. This was a real child, a living breathing being whose heart beat inside her. Tears sprang to her eyes.

"Can you hear?" she asked, looking at Max. It felt incredibly right, sharing this moment with him.

Max's eyes were glassy as well. "Yeah," he croaked. "I can hear. I— Excuse me."

Skin white as a sheet, he rushed from the room.

# CHAPTER SEVEN

GRIPPING THE SIDES of the sink, Max stared into it, the sound of running water drowned out by his breathing.

The look on Arianna's face when she'd heard the heartbeat... Pure joy. When she turned to look at him, her eyes radiating with the love she felt for her child, his heart had stopped dead in his chest. And it hit him: they were listening to the heartbeat of a child who, when born, would be as special as its mother.

He wanted to grab her hand then and there, and share this moment with her. As if they were having this baby, she and him. It was such a ridiculous thought, he'd had to get out of there. Clear his head. There was no *them*. No relationship—even if he wanted one.

Someone knocked on the men's room door. "Max? Are you all right?"

"Fine, Carol," he answered with a sigh. "I'll be right out." Turning off the tap, he dried his face and opened the door.

Carol was leaning against the opposite wall, arms folded across her chest. "Arianna's getting dressed. She'll be out in a moment."

Schooling his features into something close to collected, he smiled. "Great. I'll meet her in the lobby."

As much as he wanted to make his exit, it felt rude not to say something before he left. "Thanks again for seeing her today. I hope I didn't put you in too tight a spot."

"Don't worry about it. I'm glad I could help," she replied. "She's sweet. I can see why you wanted to help her."

"I would help her whether she was sweet or not. It's the least I can do."

"Sure it is." Carol's smile came with a sharp, unreadable expression.

Whatever. Originally, he figured on paying back the favor by suggesting a dinner. If he recalled, Carol had been a fun date. A little too focused on babies for his taste, but good for some smart conversation and laughs. In fact, this would be the perfect time to ask her out, only his plan didn't seem like such a good idea anymore. Every time he looked at her, he would hear the tiny drumbeat of Arianna's baby.

"Well," he said, trying not to sound too abrupt, "I should see if Arianna's made it to the lobby yet..."

Carol's hand stopped him. "Are you sure you're all right? You got pretty pale in there."

"I skipped breakfast, is all. Standing in that stuffy room got to me."

Once again he started to leave, and once again her hand kept him in place. "It's funny," she said. "The entire time we were seeing each other, I can't recall you ever getting as worked up about something as you did just now. Reminded me a lot of the new fathers we get in here."

"I told you, I skipped breakfast." Defensiveness kicked in good and strong, causing him to deny a little more vehemently than necessary. "Trust me, Carol, I'm fine. And I'm not the father of that baby, either."

Although for a moment, he did wonder...what if he was?

It had started snowing by the time their appointment ended. Giant fluffy flakes, straight out of a movie, turned Manhattan into a surreal winter wonderland.

"Isn't it beautiful?" Beside him, Arianna had spread her arms wide and lifted her face to the sky.

"Gorgeous." The flakes dotted her hair and eyelashes. He'd always thought it a cliché when he read how melted snow looked like diamonds, but dammit if it wasn't true. Her eyelashes glittered with them. Like a snow angel.

*A snow princess.*

Flakes blew into his eyes, blurring his vision and bringing him back to reality. "It's really coming down," he said, brushing the snow from his hair. Snow was sticking to everything, including the street and sidewalk, turning both slick. Everywhere pedestrians were waving at the yellow taxis, trying to catch drivers' attention. Raising a hand, he joined them. "Hopefully we'll be able to get a cab." Visions of Arianna losing her balance and falling filled his head.

Her gloved hands grabbed at his wrist and tugged it down. "Are you kidding?" she replied. "Take a taxi and miss my first American snow? Absolutely not."

He knew she would say something like that. "It's a snowstorm, Arianna. No one walks in this weather."

"I do." Grinning, she draped her scarf over her

head, turning it into a gray cashmere veil. "You make it sound as though it is a blizzard. It's beautiful out. The perfect day for walking."

A snowflake melted on his nose. "I wouldn't say perfect."

"Please? This could be my only chance to experience a white Christmas."

Her comment reminded him she would be leaving soon. Back to her real life, and he would be nothing but a fond, distant memory.

That's how life worked, right?

Arianna was still looking at him, her eyes as bright as the lights on a Christmas tree. How could he say no? Besides, if he was going to become a memory he might as well give her a day that was worth remembering. "Sure, but will you at least hold on to my arm in case you slip?"

You would have thought he had given her the Hope Diamond—or replayed the baby's heartbeat—the way she smiled. "If you insist," she said, hooking an arm through his.

Covering her hand with his, Max told himself his insides had not just turned upside down when she touched him.

He took her along Fifth Avenue, where she oohed and aahed over the elaborate window displays, her favorite being an over-the-top animatronic display of the twelve days of Christmas.

"Don't they have Christmas decorations in Corinthia?" he laughed when she forced him to stop at yet another display, this one portraying a Victorian Christmas scene.

"Of course we do, just not on such a grand scale. We are, after all, a small country."

"That's New York for you. When we do things, we do them big."

"In Corinthia, it's more about tradition," she replied.

Sounded like everything in Corinthia was about tradition. After all, wasn't tradition the reason behind her leaving? Keeping his thoughts to himself, he let her continue.

"The castle, of course, is decorated elaborately, as is Corinthia City, but once you move to the outskirts, things look the same as they have for centuries."

"How's that?" he asked.

"Well, for one, there are no outside lights. Instead, the houses decorate their window boxes with boughs of green. Then they place a single candle in the center of each window. The green is supposed to represent life, and the candles the blessings that are to come in the future."

Interesting. He tried to picture the image in his head. Never having been much for fancy Christmases anyway, there was something appealing about simplicity. "Sounds nice."

"Oh, it is. If you drive to the top of Mount Cornier and look out, all you can see are single white lights for miles and miles. It's one of the most beautiful things I've ever seen. No offense to your Manhattan."

"None taken."

She was wrong, though. The most beautiful thing was the look on her face when she described the scene. He loved the way her mouth turned upward when she spoke, in the barest hint of a smile. He wanted to brush her lips with his fingers and let her delight sink into his skin.

What he really wanted to do was to kiss her. To hold her like he had that first night in his apartment and kiss her until he couldn't breathe.

Instead, he pulled her closer, pretending it was to protect her from a pedestrian rushing the opposite way. She leaned close, her cheek pressing against his shoulder. Even with the snow swirling around them, he could smell traces of perfume on her damp scarf. Orange blossom.

"Sounds like I'm going to have to plan a trip to Corinthia," he said as he released her. His body felt the absence immediately, making him wish the sidewalks were more crowded.

But then she turned her smile on him, and he felt better. "Oh, you should! You would love it. The air smells of grapes and ocean, and in the summer the sky is so blue you swear you could swim in it. We call it Corinthian blue."

Like her eyes, he bet. "When I visit, will I get a personal tour from Her Royal Highness?"

"Of course. You'll be a royal guest. You can even bring Darius," she added.

"Darius in a castle? Now, that I'd like to see."

It was a pipe dream. By the time he visited, if ever, she would be married and have a whole new life. He didn't want to think about that right now. Today was about making memories. Good memories.

He took her hand. "Come on," he said. "I've got some even better decorations to show you."

* * *

"Only a block farther," he told her.

"I can't believe you won't even give me a hint as to where we are going," Arianna said. Although at the moment, she didn't really care where they went or whether it was close by. She'd heard her child's heartbeat, the snow was falling like in a fairy tale and Max was holding her hand. If only every day could be this magical.

She glanced at the man next to her only to get a playful smirk in response. "Honestly, I would have thought you'd guess by now without one. Guess you're just going to have to wait and see when we get there."

So it was some place she knew? Looking around Fifth Avenue, she couldn't see anything other than storefronts. Beautifully decorated storefronts, but nothing that seemed special enough to warrant a surprise. Wherever he was taking her, if Max thought she would enjoy herself, then she probably would.

How different it was being with Max. When she was seeing Manolo, there had always been a kernel of doubt in the back of her head. Well-warranted, it turned out. With Max, though, she'd trusted him from the very start. He made her feel safe. More than safe—special. In a way that being royalty or rich never could.

She had better enjoy it while she could. A week from now, her time in New York would be nothing more than a memory. She would leave and Max would find a new person to help—to make feel special—while she was relegated to the past. Just another face in a never-ending line of charity cases. If she needed proof, she need only look at how he left the exam room while they were listening to the baby's heart-beat. She yearned to connect with him; he couldn't leave fast enough.

For now, however, they were sharing the day, and she planned to savor every moment. There would be plenty of time to be melancholy later on.

"And, we're here," Max announced. He pointed.

Here, apparently, was a block-sized opening between stores. "You brought me to an alley?"

"Promenade," he amended.

They turned the corner, and Arianna gasped. The promenade, as he'd called it, was a long narrow garden lined with illuminated angels and toy soldiers. Their white lights guided people along a walkway dotted by Christmas trees and plastic candy canes. At the opposite end, barely visible in the snow, Rock-efeller Center's famous statue of Prometheus held court by the skating rink. And in front of him stood the Rockefeller tree, a tower of white-tipped branches.

"You did say you wanted to see the tree."

Yes, she had talked about it. In the taxi, the first night he brought her home. Or rather, to his apartment. And he remembered. There weren't words to describe what the gesture meant to her.

"This is a much better view than from 30 Rock."

"It's beautiful," she said, looking up at one of the angels. The decoration's white frame disappeared in the snow, making it look like a collection of daytime stars. "I had no idea."

"In the summer time, the center aisle is a series of reflecting pools," Max said, pointing to the strip of red carpet. "I remember my mom took me here once when I was little and I fell in trying to grab the change from the bottom. I had to ride the train home soaking wet. And worse, she wouldn't let me keep the money."

"Poor baby."

"You have no idea. I had at least twenty-five cents."

Arianna laughed, imagining a childhood Max sitting on a subway car in wet clothes, pouting over his lost quarter. "Striving to be successful even then."

"Hey, don't mock. A quarter is a lot of money to a five-year-old. I could have bought a half a candy bar."

More likely, he would have put it in his piggy bank. A man didn't make himself a millionaire from nothing without a well-ingrained respect for money. She respected that about him. Most of the men in her circle had been born into wealth. To have ample money was a fact they—and she—took for granted. Max, on the other hand, not only understood what it was like to have nothing, but now that he had money he also made a point of helping others.

It made him all the more a man in her book. She wondered if any woman would be lucky enough to win his heart or if he would remain cynical about love for the rest of his life. Seemed wrong. That a man as good as he be without a partner.

Not nearly as wrong, though, as it was to be jealous of a woman who didn't yet exist.

To save herself from her thoughts, Arianna pointed to the pavilion where a lot of activity was taking place around the tree. There were people running back and forth, and what looked like scaffolding being erected. "What is going on there? Do you think something is wrong with the tree?"

"Doubt it," Max replied. "More likely they're getting ready for tonight."

"Tonight?"

"The lighting ceremony. Looks like they're setting up the stage and cameras for the television broadcast. Probably doing a light check, too. Would be pretty embarrassing if the thing didn't light up."

"That happened to my father at the annual palace open house. Someone forgot to connect a switch so only half the tree lit. He laughed it off with a joke about elves, but afterward he was not pleased."

"Imagine if that happened in front of thirty million people."

"I'd rather not," she replied, turning her attention back to the stage. "I hadn't realized the ceremony would be such a spectacle. Can we stay to watch?"

"Afraid I should go to the restaurant. You can go, though. In fact, I could probably make a few calls and get you a spot near the dais so you wouldn't have to stand out in the cold waiting for the show to begin."

"That's all right," she said. "It wouldn't be the same alone." *Without you.* That was what she wanted to say. Everything about today was enhanced by his presence. "I'm sure I'll see it another time, and if I don't... It's only a tree, right?"

"Right." His answer didn't sound as firm as she would have expected, perhaps because he was distracted by something on the platform.

"Wait right here," he said suddenly. "I'll be right back."

"All right. Where are you...?" There was no sense finishing her question; he'd already jogged away.

Cold without his presence beside her, she wrapped her arms around her midsection and watched as his figure disappeared behind the ice-skating rink. What was he up to? A silhouette that looked like it could be him appeared on the stage, but between the snow and the distance, she couldn't be sure.

Ten minutes later, he returned and announced, "Mission accomplished."

"What mission?"

His eyes had an awfully mischievous sparkle. "Stand right here, just like this…" Moving behind her, he put his hands on her shoulders and turned her toward the stage. "And you'll see in…five, four, three…"

The Christmas tree came to life. Thousands of dancing colored lights sparkling in the snow.

"Merry Christmas, Princess," he whispered warmly in her ear.

Arianna fingers flew to her lips. This was why he had disappeared? She looked over her shoulder to find him smiling down at her. "You asked them to light the Christmas tree?"

"I might have persuaded them to test the lights a little early."

For her. "I can't believe…" The words stuck in her throat, blocked by a floodgate of emotions filling her heart. "Thank you."

"It was nothing. You gave me a tree, now I'm giving you one. Sort of."

Arianna shook her head. "Not nothing." She touched his cheek. The stubble of his five o'clock shadow scratched against her glove, making her wish the weather were warmer so she could feel skin against skin. But she was touching him, and they were standing toe-to-toe in the snow, and that would have to be enough. "It is the perfect ending to the perfect day."

His smile sobered, the playfulness growing tender. "I'm glad," he said, knuckles brushing her cheek in return. Lifting her hand from his face, he pressed a kiss in her palm. "Now you'll have something to remember New York City by."

Remembering New York City wasn't the problem, Arianna thought as she looked back at the tree. It was getting her heart to forget.

# CHAPTER EIGHT

THE NEXT NIGHT, the Fox Club celebrated its own tree lighting. Max sat at the bar and watched as his staff sang and drank their way through decorating the restaurant. Usually he joined in the merriment, but this year he had too much on his mind.

What had he been thinking? Romantic walks in the snow, paying guys to light the tree early? All so he could enjoy watching a woman's eyes shine like Christmas lights?

That wasn't like him. As far as he was concerned, romantic gestures led to mistaken impressions. Implying a commitment he wasn't willing to make. Yet with Arianna, the gestures came naturally. He wanted to make her happy. He wanted…

And there was the problem. *He wanted.* He'd wanted yesterday to never end. He wanted circumstances to be different. He wanted Arianna… About the only thing he didn't want was for her to leave. Which was the only thing with any basis in reality.

When had this happened? When did he go from wanting to help a woman out…to wanting the woman herself?

On the other side of the room, Arianna laughed as

Darlene chased Javier around the tables with a can of scented aerosol. The sound went straight to his insides, leaving his chest with a funny kind of fullness.

It was the same feeling he'd had hearing her baby's heartbeat.

"Oh, come all ye faithful, with a bough of holly…" Darius suddenly joined him at the bar, his off-key voice drowning out whatever song was playing on the sound system. The bartender wore a scarf of silver garland, and had a red paper ribbon stuck to his curls. Easing himself onto the stool next to Max, he flashed a grin. "Yo! How do you like Santa's Little Helper?"

Max blinked. "Who?"

"The drink, Max. How do you like it?"

"Oh, right." He looked at the red martini concoction sitting on the bar, untouched since Darius poured it. "Sorry, I've had other things on my mind."

"No kidding." Reaching over, the bartender picked up the drink and downed it in one swallow. "These are going to be a big hit this month," he said. "Put some sugar on the rim and the ladies will eat 'em up."

"Don't you mean drink?" Max muttered.

Darius's raucous laugh was the opposite of Arianna's. "Good one! Glad to know you've still got your sense of humor."

"And you're drunk."

"Possibly. But isn't that what Christmas parties are for?" He followed Max's line of sight, before turning back and setting the glass on the bar. "You know, you can take your eyes off her. She won't disappear."

Max felt his entire face heat. "That obvious, huh?" He supposed it was.

"Like a neon sign," his friend replied. "Look, we

totally threw that security guard off the scent. He ain't coming back."

"I hope so."

At least Darius blamed Corinthian security for his obsessiveness and not the fact that Max simply couldn't get Arianna out of his head. Knowing his friend, Darius blamed both, but at least he was being kind in only mentioning the security.

"I know so. By the way, you never did tell me her story."

"Told you, it's not my story to tell." Darlene had twirled a strand of garland on Arianna's head like a crown, causing another ripple of laughter to filter through the room. "Besides, you wouldn't believe it if I did."

"If you say so." In other words, he wouldn't push. That trust was one of the things Max liked about the man. He might talk big, but when push came to shove, he respected Max's privacy. "It's got to be good, though, if she's got you this whipped."

Max whipped his head around. "I'm not—"

"Speak of the devil," Darius said, gesturing with his head. "Nice crown."

Wearing a trio of paper bows stuck to her hair, Arianna gave them both a regal wave as she approached. Seeing how brilliant her smile was, Max's stomach did a backflip. "Darlene and the others have decided to go someplace called Xenon," she announced. "They want to know if you two are interested in going."

Darius was off the bar stool in a flash. "I am primed and ready. How 'bout you, boss? You up for some dancing?"

Max looked to Arianna, who shook her head. "Maybe next time, Dar."

He should have realized the bartender caught the exchange. Darius looked back and forth between them. "Did you two get married and not tell anyone?"

"Very funny. Someone has to stay back and clean up after you people."

Sliding off his stool, he used retrieving the empty martini glass as an excuse to hide the way his insides reacted to the comment. For the first time, the word didn't generate a wave of cynicism. Instead, his stomach backflipped again.

"Unless you all want to do it tomorrow morning while you're hung over?"

"No way. I will happily give you that pleasure," Darius answered. He started toward the coatroom. "Oh, and just so you know, we're all going to be a little late tomorrow," he called over his shoulder. "So you might have to do the opening yourself."

"Like I don't every year," Max called back.

"They certainly know how to have a good time," Arianna said as the crew filed out a few moments later, Darlene leading them in a conga line.

"Yes, they do," Max replied. "Did you?"

"Very. I think they are starting to forgive my ineptitude. Everyone was very friendly."

"Of course they were. You're easy to like." He adored the way her cheekbones pinked whenever he complimented her. "And they are good people," he added.

"It's obvious they like working here. I think they were disappointed you didn't go with them. You didn't have to stay behind on my account."

"Soon as they get on the dance floor, they'll forget all about me. Besides, I was serious about someone having to clean up." Plus, there was nowhere he'd rather be than with her.

Man, he had it bad.

There was also something he needed to do. His own personal holiday tradition that none of the staff, not even Darius, knew about. He moved around to the back of the bar, taking the glass with him.

Wedging herself into the space beside him, Arianna leaned back, elbows against the bar rail. "The tree looks wonderful, don't you think? It makes the entire club smell like pine."

"I think that might be Darlene's air freshener."

"What about you? Did you have a good time?"

"I always have a good time," he said, setting the glass in the dish bin.

"Every time I looked over, you looked so serious. Is something wrong?"

"Not at all." Only a bunch of emotions he couldn't describe and the knowledge that time was slipping through his fingers every time he looked at her.

The cardboard box was still where he'd stashed it last year, tucked behind the spare napkin caddies. "Ah, found it," he muttered.

"Found what?" He could feel her looking down on the back of his neck, trying to see.

"My lucky tree," he answered. His one sentimental nod to Christmas, or to anything for that matter.

"What do you mean? I thought the tree onstage was your tree."

"Oh, it is. This is to hang *on* the tree." Rising, he set the box on the bar. The red corners had started to tatter, and the white cover had grayed a long time ago. "I'm afraid the box is a little worse for wear these days." He'd snatched it out of a recycling bin a few years ago in an attempt at preservation. What was even more sad was that as bad as the box looked, it was in better shape than the contents.

His palms were sweating a little as he lifted off the cover. When it came down to it, his tree ornament was as ugly as sin. Chunky and dull, with several branch tips missing, it looked more like a green acrylic blob on a string. Anyone in their right mind would laugh themselves silly.

He held it up by the string and held his breath. "Presenting my lucky tree."

Arianna didn't laugh. She simply tilted her head to get a better look. "What makes it lucky?" she asked.

"Well, for starters, it came from the very first bar I ever worked at."

"The place where you bar-backed."

"You remembered the term. Nicely done."

Arianna lifted the ornament from his grasp. "I never would have guessed you to be the sentimental type."

"Normally, I'm not." At least he never thought himself to be, but the last few days had revealed his hidden emotional side. "This ornament is special, though. It saved my life."

"It did? How? It's a two-inch plastic tree!"

"Remember how I told you the bar was a dive?" She nodded. "That was putting it mildly. It was the kind of place where your feet stuck to the floor. I'd mop up, but I'm pretty sure all I was doing was putting dirty water on top of dirt. And you know how we've got frosted windows? The windows there were frosted, too, but with dirt."

"Eww!"

"Yeah." A woman like her didn't belong within a hundred miles of such a place. "Anyway, my first year, one of the waitresses decided to decorate for Christmas. We didn't have a tree so she hung this thing on one of the window hooks. I think it came attached to a bunch of bubble bath she had or something." He remembered the sound it made clicking against the dirty pane. The bright green had been out of place amid all the dirt. "Wasn't much, but it was something."

"How was it lucky, though?"

"One night while I was cleaning up, I knocked it off the hook. When I kneeled down to pick it up, someone shot out the window."

Arianna gasped. "Shot? With a gun?"

"Uh-huh. If I hadn't been under the table looking for this sucker, who knows what would have happened." Touching his finger to one of the few undamaged branches, he gave the tree a small tap. "It's been my good-luck charm ever since."

"As well it should be." Her hand shook slightly as she lifted the ornament into the light.

It was nothing but a tacky piece of garbage, and yet she was holding it as though it was made of Baccarat crystal.

"Amazing how the small things turn out to be some of the most important," she said. "I'm glad you knocked it over that night. I'd hate to think of a world without a Max Brown in it."

"Oh, I doubt it'd be that much different," he replied, pretending to study the box the ornament came from. A lump had jumped to his throat that he couldn't swallow away, causing his voice to turn gravelly.

"You sell yourself short."

"Not really. I'm just one guy."

"I'm not so sure about that," she said. "I know my life is better."

She smiled, and just like that, the emotions he'd been battling found a name. A big, scary four-letter name that jammed its way into his heart.

He curled his fingers around the hand holding the ornament. "In that case, let's hang it together."

Arianna's pulse skipped. Was he really asking her to share in his personal ritual? She looked down at the tree dangling between their joined hands. "Are you sure?"

"I wouldn't ask if I wasn't."

He was just being kind—that was all. Including her because she was there. He had no idea how the gesture squeezed at her heart.

"Why?" Glutton for punishment that she was, she had to ask.

He shrugged. "Maybe I thought we could both use the luck this year."

"We certainly could." Although something told her all the luck in the world wouldn't be enough to solve her troubles. Not unless it could change reality.

His hand hovered by the small of her back as they crossed the room, a fitting reminder of the distance between them. While they were together tonight, she could never truly be with him. Would it be so horrible, she wondered, if she pretended for one more day that she wasn't leaving? To freeze time for just a little while longer?

"Where should I hang it?" she asked when they reached the tree.

"I usually hang it in the back, near the top where no one can see. Can you reach?"

"I think so. If I stand on my tiptoes." They were, it appeared, the magic words, because suddenly his hands were on her hips, steadying her. Keeping her safe, as he always did. She looped the ornament over a branch just below the peak. Safe in its new home, the green blob swung back and forth, the plastic catching the overhead light and looking almost decorative.

"What do you think?" she asked.

"Beautiful."

His voice was rough and low, sliding down her spine until it pooled at the base, where it set her insides aching. Turning slowly, she found herself face-to-face with eyes dark with desire. Heavy-lidded, they searched her face, looking for what, she wasn't sure. Permission? She shivered. He needn't look very hard.

"Beautiful," he repeated. Suddenly, his fingers were tracing her jaw. Slow and soft, their path stoked memories of their first kiss. The ache inside her grew stronger. She could feel the vibrations of his breath against her breasts. Shallow and ragged.

His hand moved to the back of her neck. Arianna's eyes fluttered shut. She let her head fall back, baring her neck in silent acquiescence. She felt his breath on her lips and then, the rest of the world vanished as his lips covered hers, his unique, indescribable flavor traveling over her tongue and into her soul. Wrapping her arms around his neck, she returned the kiss as deeply as she could.

Time and reality could wait.

"Arianna!"

Her heart froze. *Father?*

# CHAPTER NINE

ARIANNA SPRANG FROM Max's arms, practically shoving him in an effort to be free before Father saw her. She couldn't believe he was here. How did he know where to find her? A quick look at Max said he was as shocked as she.

Was it possible she heard wrong? Maybe it was someone else with an accent that sounded like Father.

"Is anyone here? I demand you show yourselves immediately!"

It was definitely Father. Smoothing her hair, and praying it wasn't too obvious what she and Max had been up to, Arianna stepped out from behind the tree.

There, in the middle of the dining room, surrounded by discarded garlands and plastic cups, stood His Majesty King Carlos IV, wearing a scowl to beat all scowls.

"I thought you said she was here," he hissed to Vittorio. "Aria—"

She took a deep breath. "Hello, Father."

"Arianna!" The scowl vanished in favor of relief as he rushed to the stage, his arms around her before she could say another word. "Oh, my precious little girl! I'm so glad to see you." He crushed her to him, enveloping her in a ferocious cocoon of wool and fatherly affection.

Arianna closed her eyes. While she'd had bouts of homesickness, she hadn't until this moment realized how much she missed her family. She clung to him just as ferociously, feeling his body tremble with emotion. His coat smelled of nicotine, the aroma sending guilt stabbing through her. He only smoked when he was extremely distraught. "I'm sorry, Father," she murmured against his shoulder. "I didn't mean to make you worry."

She pulled back to see unshed tears glistening in his eyes. "Worry?" he said. "You frightened me half to death."

"Didn't you get my note?"

"You mean that slip of paper telling me you needed a couple weeks alone to 'think'?" He tossed up his hands and made a scoffing sound. "How was *that* supposed to keep me from worrying? When I didn't know where you were or what had happened? I was afraid I'd…"

His words might have drifted off, but Arianna heard them anyway. He was afraid he'd lost her, too. Like her mother and sister-in-law.

Now that she looked closer, she saw how badly the uncertainty had taken a toll. He looked older. Weary. Normally pale, his face looked even gaunter than usual, the bags under his eyes looking more like bruises than circles. It was the same face he'd worn for weeks following Mama's and Christina's deaths. Realizing she was responsible for its return made her sick to her stomach.

"But you found me now," she said, touching his cheek. "I'm all right."

"Thank goodness. And thank goodness Vittorio tracked you down to New York, or I would still be… What did you do to your hair?"

"My…?" Her fingers brushed the ends. Right. Her hair. She'd grown so used to the new color, she'd forgotten.

"I suspect she changed colors so she would be harder to spot in a crowd," Vittorio replied, with, to her surprise, a hint of admiration.

"But why? Why run away in the first place? Did something happen? You look pale. Are you sick?" He cupped her face, like he used to do when she was little and came to him crying, a tender gesture that only made her feel guiltier.

"No, Father, I'm not sick."

"Then I don't understand? If you needed time to think, why not go to the apartment in Milan or have Sergio take you on the yacht? Why hide yourself in some…" He shook a piece of tinsel from his shoe. "Some common nightclub."

"I beg your pardon. The Fox Club is hardly common."

Max. Distracted as she'd been with her father's appearance, she'd forgotten he was standing behind her. She watched him as he stepped off the stage, the familiar tingle running through her from his presence.

From the way his eyes widened, Father hadn't noticed Max, either. "Who are you?" he asked, in his best dismissive tone.

"Max Brown. I own this establishment."

She heard Vittorio suck in his breath as Max extended a hand. Royal protocol dictated that commoners wait until the king offered his hand. Doing otherwise was considered not only presumptuous, but a huge breach of decorum.

Her father shook it. Arianna and Vittorio exchanged a look. The last time someone broke protocol, Father stared him down. Either he was too tired to protest, or he actually saw Max as someone worthy of respect. Considering Max's natural air of authority, she liked to think it was the latter.

Especially since Max acted as if shaking hands with royalty was something he did every day. "It's a pleasure to meet you, Your Majesty," he said. "And, nice to see you, too, Mr. Mastella. I wasn't expecting to see you again."

"So I gathered," Vittorio replied. "How was your trip to Connecticut, by the way? The one you planned to take with Princess Arianna's luggage?"

He closed his eyes at the security chief's question, the way someone did when they realized they'd been fooled. "You recognized the suitcase."

"All members of the royal family carry luggage with very specific markings for security purposes. Although I'll admit, you and your friend put on a very entertaining show," he added with a superior smile.

There was regret in Max's eyes as he turned to her. "I'm sorry. I didn't know."

"It's not your fault," she replied. Neither of them could have predicted Vittorio recognizing her suitcase. Nor had she known about the security markings. It was simply a case of bad luck. "Max has been helping me," she told her father.

"By lying to Vittorio." Having been assured of her

safety, her father had reverted to his imperial self. He jutted his chin, giving the impression of looking down even though Max was several inches taller. "Forgive me if I do not thank you, Mr. Brown."

"But you should," Arianna said. Heaven knew what Vittorio told him, but it was important that Father knew the kind of man Max was. That he wasn't the bad guy in all this. "You have no idea how much he helped me. Without him, I would have... He went out of his way to make me feel safe," she said, smiling in his direction. "I'm not sure what I would have done without him."

"It was my pleasure."

He smiled back, and it was as though they were back behind the tree, sharing a moment meant for only the two of them.

"If that is true..." Her father's voice interrupted the moment. "Then you have my gratitude, Mr. Brown."

"Like I said, it was my pleasure. Your daughter is a special lady."

"May I remind you to whom you are speaking?" Vittorio looked about to have an aneurysm from the lack of protocol. He took a step forward only to be waved off.

"It's not necessary, Vittorio. I'm sure Mr. Brown means no offense. As for you..." He turned to Arianna. "I trust you are ready to come home?"

The question made her heart ache. She would never be truly ready to leave. Not when her heart wanted to stay in New York. With Max, who was ten times the man Manolo would ever be. But, as she was learning, the heart couldn't always have what it wanted. It was time for her to stop running away and face reality. She pressed a hand to her stomach. Face her responsibilities. And that meant letting Manolo know he was going to be a father, and letting her child grow up with every advantage possible.

It was the decision she knew she'd make all along. She just hadn't wanted to face it.

Shoulders heavy, she nodded. "I have to pick up my belongings." It would give her a chance to see Max's apartment one last night.

"Wait. You're going?" Grabbing her arm, Max turned her around to face him with a force that would have had him pinned to the floor if she hadn't stopped Vittorio with her hand.

Even so, his face looked like it had been slapped, all wild-eyed with disbelief. "Just like that?" he asked. "You're going to go back?"

Surely, he wasn't that surprised. They'd both known her returning to Corinthia was inevitable. "I have to. You know that."

"But what about…?" He looked down to her stomach and back up again. The answer must have shone in her eyes, because his suddenly darkened with remorse. "No."

"It's the right thing to do," Arianna whispered. There was so much more she wanted to say, but with Father standing behind her, she couldn't. Then again, she wondered if her words would have made a difference. From the look on Max's face, she didn't think so, but she tried anyway. "It won't be the same," Arianna added.

"Not the same," he repeated in a rough voice. His jaw was tensed, a tiny muscle twitch revealing precisely how tightly he was clenching his teeth. She waited for him to release her arm. Instead, his grip tightened. "Come with me," he said.

"I don't think…" Without waiting for an answer, Max pulled Arianna across the dining room, and before her father or Vittorio were able to respond, pushed her into the room and closed the door behind them.

As a deterrent, it wasn't the best. If they didn't come back out, Father would only instruct Vittorio to kick the door in. "You do know—" she began.

"Marry me."

Arianna froze where she stood. He did not just ask her to…

"Marry me," Max repeated, this time taking her hands in his. "Tell him I'm the baby's father and marry me."

Marry Max. They were the two most incredible words. In her mind, she could see it all. The three of them. A happy, loving family.

Only, Max didn't say anything about love, did he?

She looked down at their joined hands. Max's grip was solid and warm, like the support he offered. "You want to take Manolo's place?"

"Why not? You said yourself you don't love Manolo. This way you'll be in control. You can please your father and not have to spend your life stuck in a bad marriage."

Of course she wouldn't, because when the time came, Max would no doubt devise a way for them to part amicably. What he was offering was a business partnership complete with an exit strategy. It was an incredibly generous and selfless offer.

"The lesser of two evils," she said flatly.

No need to ask him why. He was stepping up, the way he always did. Trying to save the world, or at least trying to save her from falling into the same hopeless morass as his mother.

*Too late*, she wanted to tell him. She'd fallen the moment he'd had the tree lit in Rockefeller Center for her. Maybe even before.

"It's the perfect solution," he said, his certainty painful to listen to.

On the contrary, it was no solution at all. Spending a month, a year, married to Max, knowing he'd only agreed out of some overblown sense of nobility? The fantasy of what she wished could be would haunt her forever.

Nor could she do it to him. Tie him to a woman and child that weren't his. She cared for him far too much.

If anyone was going to make a sacrifice in this room, it would be her.

The pounding started on the door. "Your Highness, is everything all right? Do you need help?"

"I'm fine, Vittorio," she called back. "I will be out in a moment." Reluctantly, she pulled her hands free. "We'd best open the door or they will knock it down."

"They better not. That's solid oak." He strode across the room and turned the latch. The tumbler clicked loudly. Vittorio, standing on the other side, had to have heard.

Max pressed a hand against the wood. One hand wouldn't be enough to stop Vittorio entering, but it didn't matter. They only needed a moment; they would be leaving soon enough. "How do you want to tell them?" he asked her.

Her stomach twisted into a knot. "I'm not."

"What?" Door forgotten, Max's hand dropped to his side. "What do you mean?"

"I'm not telling them you're the father," she replied. She couldn't.

A storm flashed behind Max's eyes as they widened in disbelief. What had been cool and gray had become mottled steel and navy. "Why the hell not?" he asked. "I just told you, it's the perfect solution."

Except there was no love. If he would offer but one tiny word to make her believe he cared... Anything at all. It didn't even have to be the word *love*. One word and she would stay with him forever.

But all he had to offer was a business partnership and an exit strategy. It hurt to look him in the eye. She had to turn to his desk. "I cannot keep the truth from Manolo. He has a right to know he is going to be a father."

"Even if he doesn't deserve to be? The child deserves a happy home."

"He will have one. His mother will love him. His grandfather, his uncle. He will be surrounded by love. Besides, people can change. Who is to say fatherhood isn't exactly what Manolo needs? People do grow up." She had. Just now.

"Besides," she added, her fingers tapping out a nervous rhythm on the desktop, "being honest with him is the right thing to do."

"The right thing..." There was a thud, and she realized Max had punched the door. "So that's it? You're just going to walk out of here and marry a man you don't love—who doesn't love you—because it's the right thing."

Better than marrying a man she *did* love who didn't love her. "Yes, I am."

"Unbelievable," he muttered.

Arianna wanted to punch a door herself. She was tired of having this discussion. Max could remind her about Manolo until he was blue in the face, but it wouldn't change anything. She would still be pregnant, and neither man would love her.

"I told you," she said, whirling around. It was the first time she'd looked him in the eye since he'd offered marriage. "The rules are different for people like me. There are traditions, expectations I'm expected to live up to. My father—"

"Your father would want you to be happy," he growled. "How does sacrificing yourself accomplish that? Tell me."

"It doesn't…"

*Matter*, she was going to say, but Vittorio chose that moment to open the door. Max attempted to push it shut, but the security chief wedged his foot in the space, blocking him.

"Your father is wondering if you're ready to leave. We have a rather long flight ahead of us."

There was certainly nothing more to be said here. At least nothing she could say aloud. Slipping back behind her regal facade, she offered Vittorio a cool and efficient nod. "Of course. I was just leaving."

When she reached the office door, she paused long enough to steal one last memory of Max's movie-star face. The storm still raged in his eyes. "Arianna," he said, trying one last time.

"Goodbye, Max," she replied. "Thank you for everything."

*Do not turn around,* she told herself as she joined her father. *Do not cast a final glance at the club that you will never forget. Do not think about how soon there will be another desperate soul who needs help, making you a dim memory. Above all, do not let anyone know that leaving the Fox Club is killing you on the inside.*

Head held high, she followed her father out the door.

Max stood shell-shocked, his feet frozen in place. That was it? She was just going to leave? Less than an hour ago the two of them were kissing behind the Christmas tree. The most mind-blowing kiss of his life. And now she was walking out without so much as a look back?

The door closed. The sound of the click reverberating in the empty club did what the sight of her leaving couldn't and that was prod him to move. Rushing to the entrance, he yanked open the door and stepped outside, making it to the sidewalk in time to see the limousine's taillights pulling into the traffic. He stood there in the cold, and his gaze followed the red lights until they became one with a sea of taillights and disappeared into the night.

She was gone.

He could try and intercept her at his apartment, but what good would it do? The woman had made up her mind. Chosen to throw her life away and subject her child to a loveless marriage.

At least he could say that he'd tried. Offered her a chance to please her father and control her destiny.

Why on earth did she reject him?

He didn't want to think about the panic that had spurred him to ask in the first place. The same icy fear that was squeezing his chest right now. The one that felt like the earth was crumbling beneath his feet, leaving him without purchase.

Slowly, he made his way back into the restaurant. Someone had decided to create a display atop the reservation desk. Boughs of evergreen and holly surrounded one of the hurricane candles he'd bought for the dining room. He twisted a branch between his thumb and forefinger.

Green for life; candles for the blessings to come in the future. The tradition of Corinthia.

He'd have Javier remove the greenery tomorrow.

Right now, he needed to clean away the remains of the day. Maybe by the time he had done that, this hollow, off-balance sensation would have faded.

Honestly, he didn't know why he was disturbed in the first place. Arianna's leaving was hardly a surprise; he'd known all along her stay was temporary.

After all, wasn't that how life worked?

The feeling didn't go away. If anything, the sensation worsened until by the following night it had grown to a heavy ache that weighed him down. He couldn't seem to do anything. Paperwork sat on his desk untouched while he stared into space for hours at a time. After a couple of luckless attempts, staff members started going to Darius with questions. And as for going home… He didn't. He thought about it, but then he recalled the image of his Christmas tree in the window, and the inertia would grip him stronger than before.

Shortly after midnight, a knock sounded on his office door and Darius's head appeared. "We're down to just a few tables. I'm going to go ahead and announce last call."

"Sure." His voice sounded as distant as his thoughts. "What about that paralegal party? They still here?"

"That's tomorrow, boss."

"Sorry. I lost track of the day."

"You've been losing track of a lot today. I'd blame last night's party, but you didn't drink." The bartender stepped inside and closed the door. "Everything all right?"

"Everything's fine," Max replied. "I'm just a little out of it, is all."

"No kidding. I noticed your new roommate isn't around tonight, either. You two have a fight?"

"You could say that." If by fight he meant Arianna walking out. "She's gone."

Darius's jaw dropped. He sat down, wearing a look of confusion. "What do you mean gone? Where'd she go?"

"Home. Back to Corinthia."

"You mean, where that guy the other day was from?"

Max nodded. He thought about sighing, but exhaling seemed like too much work. "That's the place."

"But I thought she didn't want to go back. What happened?"

Max told him about King Carlos. When he finished, Darius sat back, his jaw lower than before. "An actual king here in the restaurant. So that dude wasn't kidding about Arianna being a princess."

"Nope."

The swear word he muttered under his breath was the same one Max had been mentally repeating since last night.

"Apparently His Majesty decided to retrieve his errant daughter in person."

"Wow." The bartender shook his head. "That sure don't happen every day, not to guys from our neighborhood. You think you might want to tell me the whole story now?"

"Not much more to tell," Max replied. "I didn't know she was a princess until the night she played piano. Before that, I thought she was just another hard-luck case. Turns out she simply wanted a few weeks of anonymity." Some things, like Arianna's pregnancy, still weren't for him to announce. Funny, how he felt honor-bound to keep her secrets, even after she was gone.

He did tell Darius about her being robbed, though, and how she impulsively applied for the job when the bartender mentioned it.

"So, I'm the reason we ended up with her," he remarked. "This explains why she sucked as a server. And why she was staying at a pit like the Dunphy, too."

"Yep." Attempting to project an indifference he didn't feel, Max leaned back and perched his legs on the edge of his desk. "And why I had her move into my spare room. Once I figured out she was royalty, I couldn't very well let her go back to that dive." Not when he could come home to her sitting on his sofa. His apartment was going to feel very different now that he was back to living alone.

"So, that's it, huh? She's gone for good?"

"She never planned to stay long to begin with."

"Too bad. She was just beginning to grow on me. You going to be okay?"

"Me? Sure, I'll be fine," he said, waving off the question. Wasn't as though Arianna was the first person to pass through his life. She was just another woman. Another lost puppy. A new one would replace her soon enough.

"You sure?" Darius asked.

"Of course. Why wouldn't I be?"

"I don't know, maybe because you're wearing your emergency suit, which tells me you didn't go home last night."

"I was busy cleaning."

"For twenty-four hours?"

His friend got up and walked around to Max's side of the desk. "Look," he said, "why don't you just admit you had a thing for the lady. Last time I looked, it wasn't a crime."

"Maybe not, but it never did anyone any favors, either. Or have you forgotten what it was like in our neighborhood?"

"That's because the people we grew up with were losers. Or hooked on losers."

"Present company excluded," Max replied automatically.

"Half of it anyway," Darius replied. "You're not like the people in our neighborhood, and Arianna definitely isn't. In fact, she's about as far from our neighborhood as you can get. Like, 'out of this world' far."

"What's your point?" His head was beginning to

hurt; the last thing he needed was to be reminded of Arianna's uniqueness.

"My point is… I don't know. I just don't think the world will end if you like her, is all."

Tell that to the hole in his chest. "Well, it doesn't matter now, does it? She's gone."

"What? They don't have phones where she's from? Or email?"

"It's not that simple," Max said. "There are complications."

"These complications have anything to do with the lady being nauseous all the time, and scarfing down saltines from the salad bar?

"I heard the waitresses gossiping," he said when Max failed to hide his surprise. "I wasn't sure if they were being catty or what. Is it true?"

He plucked at the seam on his pants. So much for keeping his end of the bargain. "She didn't want anyone to know."

"Now I get why you backed off. I mean, pregnant with another man's kid? That's some serious baggage. I know I couldn't—"

"I asked her to marry me."

"Say what?" Darius looked at him bug-eyed.

"I told her to tell her father I was the one who got her pregnant and that we would get married."

"What the…? Why would you do that?"

"To give her a choice," Max explained. "So she wouldn't have to go back to Corinthia and marry a man she didn't love." So the light in those beautiful blue eyes wouldn't fade under the weight of disregard.

"Yeah, but to step up when the kid's not even

yours?" For the second time in the conversation, Darius swore. "That's brave even for you."

"Doesn't matter. The lady said no." Max could still hear the door clicking as she walked away.

"Of course she did. Getting out of marrying a guy she doesn't love by marrying another guy she doesn't love? Talk about a crazy idea."

"Her father was getting ready to take her away. I had to come up with something to keep her from leaving."

"So you proposed? What would you have done if she actually said yes?"

"What do you mean, what would I have done? I would have married her."

"And spent the rest of your life raising some other dude's kid."

To his surprise, the thought didn't make his pulse race. If anything, his heart grew heavier.

"It wouldn't have been so bad." Max could have given the child everything his father never gave him. Attention, affection. "The three of us could have made a pretty decent family."

But she didn't want it. She'd rather lock herself to a serial adulterer for the rest of her life.

Why? Why wasn't his proposal good enough? He'd been asking himself that question since she walked away. It was the one piece of the puzzle he couldn't figure out, and he was tired of trying to find it. Tired of everything.

He needed a drink. And not a beer, either. He needed something hard enough to silence the thoughts spinning through his head. Like tequila or whiskey.

His dad liked Kentucky bourbon. Maybe he should go with that? Take a page from a professional.

"Man, I knew I should have set up a pool." Darius followed him from out of the office and behind the bar. Taking two tumblers off the top shelf, he set them on the counter, then took the bottle from Max's hand. "I called this thing from day one."

"Called what thing?" He pushed the nozzle back toward the glass to keep Darius from pouring.

"You falling for Arianna. Soon as I saw your face, I knew you were a goner."

"I was not." It was a feeble protest, at best. Darius was right. He had fallen when he saw Arianna. Who wouldn't? She was beautiful, sweet, kind...

*Special.*

The hole inside his chest ripped open, and all the emotions he'd been pretending didn't exist came pouring out. Years of telling himself love was a waste of time and what happened? He fell anyway. Hard.

Thing was, in the end, he was right anyway. The only thing falling in love did for him was make Arianna's departure ten times worse.

Groaning, he banged his head against the shelves. "I'm an idiot."

"I take it that's your way of saying you got feelings for this woman."

Feelings? They were talking way more than just feelings. "I love her." As soon as he said the words, he knew he meant them. He loved Arianna. "What am I going to do?"

After he got good and drunk, that was. How would he ever feel complete again?

Darius handed him a drink. "Does she know how you feel?"

"I asked the woman to marry me."

"Yeah, but did you tell her *why* you wanted to marry her?"

"No." So far as Arianna knew, he was offering another solution to her problems, like staying in his apartment or working at the restaurant.

"Well, I'm no expert," Darius said, "but I spend enough time behind here listening to drunk people complain to know that if a lady gets a marriage proposal, she wants to know it's because the man loves her. Especially if she's already got one potential fiancé who doesn't."

In other words, Max had messed up badly. He should have told Arianna how he felt before she walked out. "I'm going to need more than one bottle," he said. It was going to take a good long drink before he stopped kicking himself. If he ever did.

Darius's hand grabbed the bottle before he could. "It's not too late, you know. You could still tell her."

"How am I supposed to do that?" Max asked, tossing back the one drink he did have. "She's halfway across the world."

The bartender arched his brow. "They've got airports, right?"

"Of course they do, but…"

"But what?"

What if going to Corinthia didn't change anything? He'd already had his heart ripped open. Was it worth getting his hopes up only to have it ripped open anew? "Who's to say she cares?"

"Who's to say she doesn't?" his friend immediately replied. "You won't know unless you ask."

Max reached for the bourbon.

"Of course, it's up to you," Darius said, grabbing the bottle before Max could and pouring out the smallest of swallows into Max's glass. "I gotta say this, though—if you'd been this cautious when we worked at Mac's, we'd still be bar-backing."

He turned and shelved the bottle with the rest of the inventory. "I better let the waitstaff know I'm closing the bar."

With that, he left Max alone to stare into his glass. Darius was right. At age eighteen, he didn't think twice about risks; he leaped at any opportunity to raise himself up. Then again, that was about making money. Failing didn't leave him feeling shattered.

Did he dare fly to Arianna and bare his soul? Was it possible she felt the same?

There was only one way to know for certain, and that was to ask her. Otherwise, he would be spending the rest of his life wondering. And if she said no...? What was the worst that could happen?

His heart didn't really have that much left to break anyway.

# CHAPTER TEN

"ARE YOU SURE you're all right, sweetheart? You haven't been yourself since we left New York."

That was because she'd left part of herself behind. Noting the worry in her father's eyes, Arianna replaced the thought with a smile. "I'm fine, Father. Just a bit jet-lagged from the time change, that's all."

Her acting skills needed work because her father did not look convinced. "I wish you would tell me what is going on. You know Armando and I would do whatever we can to help."

"I know." Sadly, there was not much they could do.

After they had left Max, she'd told her father to head straight to the airport rather than stop to retrieve her luggage. The few pieces of clothing she left behind weren't worth the hardship of visiting Max's apartment. There was no way she would be able to maintain her composure while being assaulted by memories. While it had only been a few days, in her mind it felt like a lifetime. There'd been such an overwhelming sense of rightness to sharing breakfast with him, or sitting next to him on the sofa.

If her father had suspected the yearning behind her suggestion, he said nothing.

She hadn't told him about the baby yet, either. Almost did, on the plane, but she changed her mind at the last minute. In spite of everything, she felt as though Manolo deserved to hear the news first.

Hugging her midsection, she wandered from her seat on Father's sofa to the large bay window. Corinthia was readying for the holidays. The grounds crew was hanging garlands of evergreen along the palace walls. The interior had already been decorated. The tree had been erected in the archway and candles had been placed in the windows. Next door, in her mother's music room, a large spray of green sat atop the grand piano.

As they did every year, the designers had outdone themselves. The palace was a Christmas wonderland of red, gold and purple.

It all paled in comparison to cheap store-bought garlands and a misshapen piece of plastic.

And tomorrow, when Father lit the palace tree and announced to Corinthia that the holidays had begun, it, too, would be lacking because it wasn't a snowy afternoon in Rockefeller Center, and Max wouldn't be standing behind her.

Oh, Max. She pressed her forehead against the glass. *Marry me.* His words refused to leave her alone. Every time she thought about the baby or Manolo, there they were, clear and strong. *Marry me.*

Why did he have to say anything? Why couldn't he have remained silent and simply let her go, instead of teasing her with an unachievable fantasy?

The soft knock on the door made her stomach drop. Fate had arrived. Taking a deep breath, she recovered her composure in time to see her brother's secretary, Rosa, step inside. "I'm sorry to bother you, Your Highness, but Signor Tutuola is here to see Princess Arianna."

"Manolo?" Her father's face brightened at the announcement, making her anxiety worse. "That is a surprise. How did he find out you had returned?"

"I called and asked him to come," she told him.

Her father smiled. "I would be lying if I said I wasn't pleased to hear it. I always thought the two of you made an attractive couple."

"I know." Even now, there was a smile on Father's face, eclipsing the concern that had been there the past thirty-six hours. She could but imagine how happy he would be about her and Manolo marrying.

Her father happy and her child's life scandal-free. That's why she was doing this.

"You can send him in, Rosa," she said.

When Father said they made an attractive couple, it wasn't parental bias. Manolo Tutuola was a handsome man, more runway model than industrialist. His sandy brown hair was perfectly styled, as was his closely cropped beard. When they first met, Arianna had been impressed by his sense of fashion. In a room full of men in dark suits, his flashier, continental style stood out.

That was before she'd learned what the right man could do with a simple dark suit.

Manolo flowed into the salon, and immediately bowed to her father. No extended hand for him. His protocol was flawless.

"It's good to see you again," her father said, nodding in return. "Arianna just told me she asked you to pay us a visit."

"And I was thrilled that she did. I've missed you," he said, bowing in her direction. She could see him struggling not to frown as he took in her dark hair. "You look lovely, as always."

Arianna nodded in return. She had bags under her eyes and was not wearing an ounce of makeup, not to mention that she had a foreign hair color, all of which left his sincerity open to question. "Father, would you mind if Manolo and I had a few moments alone?"

"Not at all, sweetheart. I need to speak with Armando before our meeting with the minister of finance anyway. Manolo, it is good to see you again. Perhaps we'll have the opportunity to talk afterward."

"I'd enjoy that, Your Majesty. Would you please give Signor Baldecci my best as well? I found the interview he gave the Italian press to be quite insightful."

"I will be sure to let him know. I will see you later as well, sweetheart."

As her father leaned in to kiss her cheek, Arianna couldn't help but think it a seal of approval. "Have a good meeting, Father," she said with a smile. Manolo bowed his goodbye.

Once the door shut, he turned to look at her again, his dark eyes shining triumphantly. "I'm glad you called, Arianna. I was afraid you were going to let our misunderstanding drive a wedge between us."

"Would that be the misunderstanding where you slept with another woman?" she admonished. Crossing her arms, she marched back to her place at the window.

"I told you, Maria is just a friend who needed a

place to stay. I was helping her out of a difficult situation."

"And I suppose her panties happened to appear in your bed completely by accident.

"Our laundry…"

"That's enough, Manolo." Did he really expect her to believe he was playing the Good Samaritan? A real Samaritan did not limit his good deeds to models and aspiring actresses.

He might as well learn right now that she would not be patronized. "I spoke to Maria, and I know all about your extracurricular activities. Frankly, I find your behavior, and your lies, adolescent at best."

One could call the added comment adolescent on her part as well. Considering how the man had humiliated her, however, she was owed at least one insult. The sight of his face darkening with embarrassment left a warm feeling.

It was a short-lived victory at best. Before she had a chance to say another word, he'd crossed the room to join her. "Not so childish that you didn't call and request that I visit," he replied. "Is that because you missed our…closeness as much as I did?"

She shivered as he ran an index finger along her arm. Not a good shiver, like the ones that traveled through her whenever Max came near had been, but rather a cold tremor that left a sour taste behind.

"I have missed you, Arianna," he whispered. "More than you can imagine. Just the other night I was thinking of you… How lucky I was to have you in my bed. A poor, humble servant." Lifting her hand, he brushed his lips across her knuckles.

Throughout, Arianna kept her eyes on his face and

noticed that his eyes never once changed expression. There was no sign of sincerity. There wasn't even a flicker of desire. At least not on an emotional level.

No wonder instinct told her something was off about him. The man was a total phony.

"I didn't call because I missed your bed," she said, snatching her hand back. "I called because you and I needed to talk."

"All right." Taking the rejection in his stride, he leaned against the window molding. The shoulder pads of his jacket shifted, giving him a cockeyed posture. "What did you want to talk about?"

Time to bite the bullet. Arianna breathed in deeply. "I'm pregnant."

For several seconds, Manolo said nothing. "Does your father know?" he asked finally.

"Not yet. I thought…" The words tasted stale on her tongue, forcing her to swallow and start again. "I thought we could tell him together."

"Yes. That makes sense. Good thinking." He paced away, toward the center of the room. "He'll be displeased that we took so long to tell him, of course, but I can say you were afraid something was wrong, and didn't want to get his hopes up until you knew everything was going to be all right."

He glanced over his shoulder. "How far along are you anyway?"

"Nine and a half weeks."

"Great." Resuming his pacing, he began working something out in his head. "It'll be tight, but we should be able to fit in a wedding. You will definitely need to watch your diet. Plump up too much and it will show in the photographs. Although, the right designer gown should be able to camouflage any protrusion."

Camouflage? Gown? "Surely, you're not talking about having a state wedding." Considering the circumstances, would it not be better to have a small, family-only ceremony?

"Of course we're having a state wedding. We are Corinthia's most prominent couple. We can't marry with anything less than pomp and circumstance. What would people think?"

"That you wanted to keep things intimate?"

He waved her answer away with a scoff. "Are you serious? Intimate is for commoners. A royal wedding is supposed to make a statement."

Wasn't he making a statement already? Arianna's insides deflated. She perched on the windowsill, and wondered how long it would take for her to shrivel up and die. Not once had Manolo expressed any interest in the baby itself. He didn't even ask about her changed appearance. In fact, so focused was he on the logistics of their prospective union that she could have left the room without him noticing.

She didn't expect him to greet the news with hearts and flowers, but surely he could show some curiosity about his child.

"I heard the baby's heartbeat."

Manolo barely looked up at her announcement. "Good for you."

"You don't care how it went?"

He stopped his pacing to look at her. "I am sure if there was a problem, you would have told me. By the way, if we are smart, we will have the palace press office drop a few hints to the papers about an engagement. It is important that we avoid looking as though I *had* to marry you."

"Even though you did," Arianna muttered.

"Yes, but the world does not need to know that. I do business with a number of conservative countries. I do not want to give them the wrong impression."

By all means, let them protect his reputation.

Look at him, she thought, ratting off tactics like a man planning an acquisition. Wasn't he, though? Had he not won the lifetime rights to the royal family? The prize he worked so hard to attain with his charm and ingratiating behavior?

She was wrong about there being no emotion in his eyes. They gleamed with triumph.

*Marry me.*

She closed her eyes as Max's final plea mocked her. This was what she wanted, she reminded herself. A marriage that wouldn't haunt her with if-onlys. There would never be any doubt as to Manolo's feelings toward her. Or lack thereof. It was a cold and lonely future, but what did it matter? Without Max, her future would be cold and lonely anyway.

Suddenly, she saw herself ten years down the road, angry and alone with a child desperate for its father's attention. That was the future she was creating for her child. A life full of misery for both of them. Two unhappy people living for duty. No love. No warmth besides what they gave each other.

She thought of a woman living a joyless Christmas and a son longing to buy a tree.

Her child deserved better.

"I can't do this," she said, jumping to her feet. "I can't."

Manolo stopped his pacing and stared at her. If she didn't know better, she'd say he'd forgotten she was in the room. "What are you talking about?" he asked. "What is it that you cannot do?"

"Marry you."

"Don't be silly. You and I are having a child. We have to marry. Your father would expect no less."

"My father will have to understand." At least she prayed that he would. Either way, the die was cast. Having spoken the words, there was no way she would take them back. No way she wanted to. Free of responsibility's mantle, she felt lighter. Truer to herself. "Because there is no way I am marrying you. Not now, not ever."

"But..." When she looked back, she would probably chuckle over the stunned expression on Manolo's face. He looked as though he had been struck. This was a man who was used to succeeding. "But the baby."

"I would never keep the baby from its father. You may have as big a role in its life as you wish. Always. Just not as my husband."

"Hardly see the point otherwise."

The words were barely a whisper as he ran a hand over his face, but they were loud enough for Arianna. Her child definitely deserved better than this man. Filled with the rightness of her decision, she drew herself to full height and gave Manolo the most imperial glare she could muster. "You may go now. My secretary will keep you informed of the baby's progress."

Leaving him in the living room, she turned and disappeared into the music room.

* * *

She decided to play Chopin's *Nocturne in C minor*. The desolate-sounding concerto seemed an appropriate choice for a woman who had dismissed the father of her unborn child, was about to shame her family and was in love with a man who didn't love her back.

Mostly she played because of Max. Playing piano no longer reminded her only of her mother. Memories of playing in New York joined the mix. When her hands drifted over the keys, it was his smile of approval that she pictured. That smile was the moment when everything had begun to change. When the nerves that had been plaguing her started to shift into something more.

As for sending Manolo away, the moment she heard him mutter those words, she knew she'd done the right thing. Just as she refused Max's proposal because she didn't want to spend her days wishing he loved her, she could not marry Manolo and subject their child to the same fate. Better to live in disgrace than let her child be raised by a man who didn't love it.

Finally, she knew the answer to her no-win situation. Too bad she had to break her heart to figure it out.

Which brought her thoughts full circle back to Max. Closing her eyes, she ran through every detail of their week together. The way his voice rumbled in his chest when he stood close. How the snow dotted his hair with tiny drops of water. The warm, safe feeling she got whenever he wrapped his arms around her.

Then, after she'd remembered everything, she folded the memories up into a tiny square and forced them into the back of her mind. From here on in, she would use what was left of her heart to be the best mother possible.

"It is good to hear music in these rooms again." At the sound of her father's voice, she opened her eyes. He stood in the doorway.

"It has been a long time since you played," he said. "Such a sad song, though, for this time of year."

Arianna switched to a carol, one of his favorites. "Better?"

"Much," he said, coming to stand behind her. She felt him press a kiss on top of her head. "It's good to have you home."

"It's good to be home," she replied, smiling. On the inside, however, she was far from cheerful, knowing this was nothing more than a brief moment of tranquility. She'd postponed the inevitable long enough.

Meanwhile, her father sat down on the settee a few feet away. It was the same piece of furniture she had sometimes napped on while her mother practiced. Out of the corner of her eye, she saw her father unbutton his jacket and settle back against the cushion.

"How was your meeting with the financial minister?" She didn't really care; it was a way of avoiding the subjects she should be discussing.

"Very well. Armando has developed a real knowledge of fiscal policy. He's going to make a very good king when I decide to step down."

"Was there ever any doubt?" Her brother took his position as heir apparent as seriously as she took her own as princess. More, actually. He would never have run off from his responsibilities. Even during the darkest days of his grief, he managed to fulfill his duties.

Had he been in her shoes, Armando no doubt would have married Manolo, too.

Her father made himself more comfortable. "I am surprised to find you alone. I assumed Manolo would be with you when I returned. Did something happen?"

Arianna's fingers slipped, and she hit a wrong note. Fortunately, Father didn't notice. "It was good to see him," he continued. "For a while, I thought the two of you might be having problems.

"Or are you still?" he asked after a pause.

It was time to stop running. Taking a deep breath, she rubbed her hands on her skirt and turned to face the one man whose opinion had always meant the world to her. "Manolo and I are no longer seeing each other," she said.

"Oh." The corners of his mouth turned downward in disappointment.

Arianna bowed her head. "I'm sorry, Father. I know you liked him."

"Very much," he replied. "I had hoped… That is, Manolo had hinted the two of you…"

"Manolo might have hoped," she said, shaking her head. "But no."

"Really? Here I thought you were fond of him."

"I tried to be." Lord knew she tried.

It was clearly not the answer her father expected, because the lines on his forehead grew more pronounced. "What do you mean 'you tried'?"

"I knew how much our being a couple meant to you. I wanted things to work out between us so that you would be happy, but in the end…"

Rising from the bench, she walked to the left-hand side of the room, where there hung a series of seventeenth-century panels by an artist whose name she never could remember. "Manolo isn't the man we thought he was." She told him about Maria and the other women. "He was more interested in currying your favor than he ever was in courting me."

"That—" Behind her, she could hear the settee cushions crinkle as her father's posture stiffened. "I treated him like a member of this family, and this is how he pays me back? By mistreating you? If I had known…"

There was another pause, and a few moments later, he was on her side of the room, drawing her into a hug. It felt disingenuous accepting the embrace, but Arianna relaxed into it anyway.

"This is why you went to New York, isn't it?" he asked. "Because of Manolo?"

"Yes…" She broke free of his arms. "And no." There was only one way to deliver the news, and that was as quickly as possible. With her hand on her stomach for strength, she looked him in the eye and said, "I'm pregnant."

You could hear a pin drop. Arianna watched as her father's expression changed from disbelief to the anger and disappointment she'd been dreading. Seeing it stabbed as deeply as she knew it would, and she ached to take it away.

"Pregnant," he finally repeated.

"I'm sorry, Father." It was the best she could do. Tears threatened to burn her eyes, but she blinked them away. Regardless of how badly his disappointment hurt, she needed to stay strong.

Somewhere in the back of her mind, a voice said Max would be proud of her for doing so.

Letting out what sounded like a low growl, he started pacing. "Manolo. He knows?"

"Yes, he does. And before you say anything, I have already told him that I would not marry him. I can't. Not knowing the kind of person he is."

She held up her hand before her father could interject. "I'm sorry. I know I've let you down, and I know it breaks with every tradition Corinthia has ever had, but please understand. I can't let my child grow up with a father who only loves himself. If I can't have a marriage like yours and Mama's, then I don't want any marriage at all. I would rather leave Corinthia than—"

"Leave Corinthia? What are you talking about?"

"To avoid a scandal. I know tradition expects me to—"

Her father stared at her in disbelief. "And you think I would ask you to leave Corinthia because of that?" he asked. "Never."

"But, the baby would be..."

"My grandchild. And you would still be my daughter. I will admit, this is not the path I expected your life to take, but I would never want you to spend your life married to a man you didn't love." Drawing close, he cradled her face in his hands. "Your happiness is far more important to me than any tradition or scandal that might erupt. Surely you know that."

*Your father would want you to be happy.* That was what Max had said.

She closed her eyes before the tears could break free. "I've been so stupid," she whispered.

"No, my darling daughter, I am the one who was stupid for letting you think even for a second that you had to sacrifice your happiness," her father said, gathering her in his arms.

With his arms tight around her shoulders, Arianna finally let loose the tears she'd been fighting. Outside in the courtyard, the workers were hollering about the decorations; she could hear them through the window. At the moment, though, all that mattered was that she had been afraid for nothing. She cried a little harder, this time for her foolishness.

"It's all right," her father said. He rubbed small circles on her back. "The three of us, you, me and Armando, we will deal with Manolo and any scandal he might cause. Because you are right. You should not settle for anything less than what your mother and I had."

At that, Arianna had to sniff back a fresh batch of tears. Beautiful as his words were, they made her feel more foolish. "I'm afraid it's too late for that," she said, breaking out of his embrace once more.

"Why is that?"

Suddenly, the commotion she'd heard outside grew closer. No, this was a different commotion, coming from the corridor outside the salon. "Is someone arguing with Armando?" she asked. The two of them headed into the salon, just in time to see the door fly open.

"Call the damn national guard if you want. I'm going in there," the intruder barked.

Arianna gasped.

There, in the doorway, his coat half off his shoulders, stood a wild-eyed Max Brown. "You and I need to talk," he said.

# CHAPTER ELEVEN

HE'D MADE IT.

It wasn't until he'd landed in Corinthia and saw the large royal portrait hanging in the airport that Max discovered a major flaw in his plan. This wasn't New York, where all he had to do was unlock his penthouse door to see Arianna. Visiting her here was going to be like trying to see the President of the United States. A person couldn't walk into the palace and ask for Arianna Santoro. You needed a royal invitation or special permission, which could take days—or weeks—to wrangle.

He didn't have days to spare. Not with Arianna planning to marry Manolo and leave his life forever.

Fortunately for him, he still had Vittorio Mastella's business card in his pocket. Either the head of security had a romantic streak, or he appreciated Max's skills as a fast talker, because he agreed to let Max pass through security without credentials.

"You are on your own after that," he'd said. "If Her Highness refuses to see you, I will throw you out personally."

Max had no intention of that happening. Not even

when Arianna's brother tried to bar him access, and he had to push his way through.

Now, he was face-to-face with Arianna at last.

She looked horrible, eyes puffy and red-rimmed, her skin the color of chalk. "You and I need to talk," he said. With all the adrenaline of the last few minutes, the words came out far harsher than he meant, so he added in a gentler voice, "Please."

He'd just finished shrugging his jacket into place when a hand clamped down on his upper arm. "I'm sorry, Father. He pushed his way through," its owner said. "Security is on the way."

"It's all right, Armando. I know him." Arianna's eyes were two large pools of blue, shimmering with surprise and...were those tears?

His stomach clenched. The pallor, the crying... Wrenching himself free, he rushed closer only to stop short of taking her in his arms. He wanted to—God knew, holding her again was all he thought about since leaving New York—but the despair in her eyes held him back. "Are you okay?" he asked. "Is the baby...?"

"The baby is fine," she replied. Max let out his breath. He hadn't realized how scared he'd been to hear her answer until she alleviated his concerns. If there had been any doubt in his mind about raising another man's child, it died then and there. Who cared who fathered the child? The baby was part of Arianna; therefore he loved it with all of his heart.

*Loved it with all of his heart.* Who would have guessed those words would ever enter his thoughts? He, who avoided love like the plague.

"What are you doing here?" Arianna asked.

"I told you. I needed to talk to you."

She hadn't moved since he burst into the room. Now, she walked toward one of the room's large windows, her hands twisting back and forth in front of her.

"What could we possibly have to talk about that we did not say in New York?" she asked.

A lot. Their entire lives. "Just give me five minutes. After that, if you want me to go, I'll leave and never bother you again."

Blood pounded in his ears thanks to his racing heart. *Please let her say yes.*

She didn't answer.

"I think you should leave now, Signor Brown." It was King Carlos. Focused on Arianna as he was, he'd forgotten the king was in the room. "My daughter obviously does not wish to see you."

Turning slowly, he looked at the man Arianna served so devotedly. "If you don't mind, I'd rather hear that from her directly."

"Who do you think you are? Do you have any idea who you are talking to?"

Arianna's brother—at least he assumed it was Arianna's brother—reached for his arm again, only this time Max was ready and sidestepped the attempt. He backed toward the window as well, meeting the gazes of the king and his son glare for glare. They could try and intimidate him all they wanted. He wasn't leaving unless Arianna threw him out herself.

From the corner of his eye, he saw Arianna hang her head. "Let him stay," she said in a soft voice. "I'll listen to what he has to say."

"Alone," he added. Again, King Carlos and his son glared at him. Again, he returned the glares.

"It's okay," Arianna added. "I'm not in any danger."

Far from it, Max wanted to say. If anyone was in danger it was him. One well-placed rejection, and his heart would shatter.

"That might be the first time anyone has ever ordered them to do anything," she said once the others left the room.

"Thank you for backing me up."

"The only reason I did was to avoid a scene." Finally she turned away from the window to look at him. "Why are you here?"

Max opened, and then shut his mouth. He'd had an entire speech planned, but seeing her up close, the late-day light behind her forming a gray silhouette, all his impressive words failed him. The only thing he could come up with was "You left your suitcase."

"I decided I didn't need it. Is that why you flew halfway around the world? To return my luggage?"

"No."

"I didn't think so." She looked down as if just noticing her twitching hands and quickly clasped them tight. "So what did you want?"

Was there a note of expectation in her question? His quickening pulse said yes, but he refused to get his hopes up. "Are you still planning to marry Manolo?"

She answered with a haughty sniff before walking away. "I don't think that's any of your business."

None of his business, but she hadn't said yes.

He followed her into the next room, which turned

out to be a lavishly decorated space containing a very large piano. Arianna was making a production out of straightening a pile of sheet music, a portrait of anger and sadness. He wondered what she would do if he rested his hands on her shoulders and cradled her close. "Why did you turn my proposal down?" he asked instead. "Why did you walk away?"

"Because…"

"'Because' isn't an answer." Why was he dragging this out? The words *I love you* were right on his tongue. All he needed to do was say them.

But he was still afraid. He needed to know this wasn't one-sided. "Was it because you didn't think I meant it?"

"No. I know you meant it."

"Then…?"

"Because I didn't want to be another one of your charity cases, that's why!" Music scattered to the carpet as she whipped around. "I didn't want to be someone you had to rescue. I wanted…"

"Wanted what?" Max asked, heart pounding.

She looked away again. "Nothing."

There was no need for her to answer; he knew. He heard it in the way her voice cracked when she spoke. And with that confession, the last of fear's grip on his heart disappeared.

Slowly, he reached out to brush the hair from her cheek. "You were never a charity case," he told her. "Not for a second."

"Of course I was. I was no different than Darius or Shirley or any of the others who crossed your path," she said. But she leaned into his touch nonetheless, giving him the confidence to carry on.

"Do you remember the first time we shared a taxi? You said people do crazy things when they're in love. Remember?"

"I remember."

Her breath hitched. Closing his eyes, Max pressed a kiss to her temple. Being close to her again was like coming home after a long absence. "Does flying halfway around the world to stop a wedding count as crazy?" he whispered in her hair.

Arianna's heart stopped. Was he saying what she thought he was saying? She was afraid to look him in the face, in case this was all a sick, terrible joke.

But here he was, holding her. His fingers tracing her jaw. Lifting her chin until she had no choice but to look into his eyes.

Which stared down at her with slate-blue sincerity. "I'm not rescuing you," he whispered, his words hoarse with emotion. "You're the one rescuing me. I need you in my life."

Was he saying...?

"I love you, Arianna."

They were the most beautiful four words she'd ever heard. Words she had hoped and wished for, but never thought she'd hear pass his lips. "I love you, too," she whispered, and she kissed him with all the love she had in her heart. A deep, soul-searing kiss meant to say everything she couldn't put into words.

It ended much too soon. She could have stayed that way forever, wrapped in his arms, but suddenly Max backed away, his eyes bright and unreadable.

"I'm not finished," he said with a smile.

With that, he dropped to his knee. "Marry me, Arianna. Tell Manolo and your father and everyone else to go to blazes and marry me. I promise I will spend the rest of our lives making you and the baby happy."

He already had. She was happier at this moment than she could ever remember. So happy, she couldn't hold back the tears. "Yes," she said, dropping to her knees and throwing her arms around his neck. "Yes, yes, yes."

They clung to each other, laughing and crying at the same time. "I love you," Max repeated over and over. "I love you."

When they'd recovered, he brushed back the hair from her face. "I never thought to bring a ring."

Arianna laughed. Later, she would tell him about dismissing Manolo and her talk with her father. What mattered now was that they were going to spend the rest of their life together. "It doesn't matter," she whispered against his lips. "I have you."

# EPILOGUE

MAX LIFTED TWO glasses of sparkling cider from the tray on the table, and handed one to his bride. "So what time does Babbo Natale show up?"

"I don't know. I told you, Armando and I always fell asleep before his arrival."

"In other words, this whole thing is an excuse to stay up all night."

"Would you rather we fall asleep early?"

"Absolutely not. I can't think of a better way to spend Christmas Eve than under a tree with you." He clinked the rim of his glass against hers. "Merry Christmas, Your Highness."

"That's Mrs. Brown to you," Arianna replied. She giggled as the carbonation danced over her tongue.

Officially, they were now to be referred to as Conte di Corinthia, Prince Maxwell, and Her Royal Highness Princess Arianna, but she liked plain old Mr. and Mrs. Max Brown. The names had a simple, sincere ring to them.

The two of them were sequestered in their new private quarters at the palace, having been married exactly twelve hours. Tomorrow, Christmas Day, they would be officially presented to Corinthia as husband

and wife. Tonight, however, was about them. Knowing the pomp and circumstance that awaited them, Arianna wanted their wedding night to last as long as possible. Apparently Max agreed because when she came up with the idea of staying awake for Babbo Natale, he enthusiastically agreed.

She curled closer to her husband, draping the sheer robe of her peignoir across their laps like a blanket. Nearby, next to the fireplace, a tree laden with white lights twinkled merrily. "I might be biased," she said, "but as beautiful as that tree is, it is nothing compared to the one at the Fox Club. That might be the most beautiful tree I've ever seen."

"Better than the one in Rockefeller Center?"

"Absolutely. You didn't kiss me behind the one at Rockefeller Center."

"Ah, good point, Mrs. Brown." He bent his head over hers. "I can, however, kiss you under this one."

"Mmm, as much as you want," she replied. There would be a lifetime of kisses under Christmas trees. Not to mention children laughing and begging for their own late night Christmas Eves. This was but the first night of forever.

As she'd suspected, Manolo was far more interested in making royal connections than he was in being a father. Therefore, it wasn't a surprise when he agreed to let Max adopt the child as his own. It also wasn't a surprise that Max refused to let Father make Manolo sign away his parental rights. "Someday he might realize what an idiot he is," he'd said.

Perhaps, but Arianna suspected that would never happen. She and Max would raise the child—their child—in a home filled with family and love.

With a happy sigh, she thought of the smile on her father's face as they said their vows. Who would have guessed that in risking his disappointment, she'd made him happier than ever? "Thank you for agreeing to have the wedding in Corinthia."

"I've already told you, I didn't care where we got married, so long as we did. Besides," he said, nuzzling her neck, "watching Darius having to bow to your father and brother was totally worth it."

"That was your favorite part of the ceremony?"

"Second favorite," he said. "Hearing you say 'I do' was the best part."

Arianna had to admit, that was her favorite part, too.

Her eyes were getting heavy. Apparently when it came to dragging out her wedding night, the spirit was willing, but the pregnant body was not. She nuzzled closer to Max, letting his scent lull her to sleep.

Suddenly, a rippling sensation traveled across her abdomen. Like bubbles. Instantly, she awoke and grabbed Max's hand.

"What—?"

"Shh…" she said, placing his hand on her stomach. "Feel that?"

The ripple repeated.

His jaw dropped. "Is that…?"

"I think the baby is trying to wish us a merry Christmas."

Nothing in the world would ever match the smile that split Max's face. She wanted to weep with happiness at the joy that shone in his eyes. "Not *the* baby," he said. "*Our* baby."

Leaning over, he placed a kiss right above her belly

button before returning to kiss her. "Merry Christmas, Princess."

As far as she was concerned, it already was.

\* \* \* \*

*For more Corinthian Christmas magic,*
*don't miss Prince Armando's story in*
*WINTER WEDDING FOR THE PRINCE.*
*To learn more about*
*WINTER WEDDING FOR THE PRINCE*
*as well as Barbara Wallace's other titles,*
*visit www.barbarawallace.com.*

# "You went to an awful lot of trouble for me today. I guess I have to wonder why."

"I didn't want you dropping from exhaustion at the day care center," Hudson said wryly, skirting the question.

Still, she kept her gaze on him. "So you'd do this for any of your employees?" She motioned to the meal and the house and he knew what she meant.

"No, I wouldn't. You're special, Bella."

Her pretty brows arched. "Usually when a man does something like this, he wants something in return."

He put down the wing he was about to eat. "Maybe I do. That kiss just didn't happen out of the blue. There's been something simmering since we met. Don't you agree?"

She looked flustered. "I don't know what you mean. I—"

"Bella, tell me the truth. If you can honestly say you don't feel any sparks between us, I'll drop the whole thing, take you home, not approach you again with anything in my mind other than a boss-and-employee relationship."

"That's what we should have," she reminded him. "Maybe. Are you going to answer my question?"

\* \* \*

**Montana Mavericks:**
The Baby Bonanza—
Meet Rust Creek Falls' newest bundles of joy!

# THE MAVERICK'S
# HOLIDAY SURPRISE

## KAREN ROSE SMITH

First Published in Great Britain 2016
By Mills & Boon, an imprint of HarperCollins*Publishers*
1 London Bridge Street, London, SE1 9GF

© 2016 Harlequin Books S.A.

Special thanks and acknowledgement are given to Karen Rose Smith for her contribution to the Montana Mavericks: The Baby Bonanza continuity.

ISBN: 978-0-263-92031-4

23-1116

Our policy is to use papers that are natural, renewable and recyclable products and made from wood grown in sustainable forests. The logging and manufacturing processes conform to the legal environmental regulations of the country of origin.

Printed and bound in Spain
by CPI, Barcelona

To my dad,
who would have been 100 years old this year.
With his 35 mm camera, he gave me my love
of capturing memories with photography.
I miss you, Daddy.

# *Chapter One*

Hudson Jones was used to getting his own way. But as he stood in the doorway of his office at the Just Us Kids Day Care Center, he had a feeling he wouldn't get his way this time. Bella Stockton had him stymied.

The day care manager was beautiful—tall and willowy with wispy short blond hair. He'd tried to flirt with her over the past month that he'd been here to see to the day-to-day running of the center. After all, a cowboy could get lonely underneath the big Montana sky. But unlike the other pretty women he'd flirted with over his thirty years, Bella didn't respond to him.

He studied her as she talked with a mother, one who'd apparently been involved in the parent-teacher conferences scheduled at Just Us Kids after normal business hours. Hudson recognized the expression on the parent's face. Over the last couple of months, he'd dealt with his share of upset parents. An outbreak of RSV—respiratory syncytial virus—had hit Just Us Kids, sending one of the children to the hospital, which had prompted her parents to file a lawsuit. The day care had been cleared, but the damage to its reputation had been done.

He moved a little closer to the main desk in the reception area where Bella sat.

Marla Tillotson was pointing her finger at Bella. "If I even see another child here with sniffles, I'm pulling Jimmy out and enrolling him in Country Kids." She turned on the heels of her red boots, gave Hudson a glare and headed for the door.

Although Hudson usually didn't commit too much time to any one place, he had taken this job more seriously than most. After all, it was an investment he didn't want to fail. He owned the property the day care sat on; his brother Walker owned the franchise. He'd let his brother talk him into staying for a while in Rust Creek Falls to oversee the staff and handle the PR that would put Just Us Kids back in the public's good graces. But, to be honest, mostly he stayed in town because he wanted to get to know Bella better.

As soon as he saw Bella's face, he didn't hesitate to step up to her desk. "It wasn't your fault," he said adamantly.

As day care manager, Bella ran a tight ship. She enforced policies about not signing in sick kids, incorporated stringent guidelines for disinfecting surfaces and educated the staff. But it seemed she couldn't put the whole awful experience of the lawsuit behind her.

Bella brushed her bangs aside and ducked her head for a moment. Then she raised burdened brown eyes to his. "I just can't help thinking that maybe I slipped up somehow. What if I wasn't vigilant enough before the outbreak? What—"

Hudson cut her off. "I'm going to say it again, and I'll say it a thousand times more if you need to hear it. You didn't do anything wrong," he assured her. "I read numerous blogs about day care and RSV when Walker asked me to take over here. RSV looks like a cold when it starts. Kids are contagious before they show symptoms. That's why it spreads like wildfire even with the best precautions. It's going to be *our* job—" he pointed to himself, and then he pointed to her "—to make sure an outbreak doesn't happen again."

Bella met his eyes intently. Suddenly the day care center seemed very quiet. Maybe it was just because he was so aware of her gaze on him. Was she aware of him? They could hear low voices in one of the classrooms beyond where tables were set up for the parent-teacher conferences. But other than that, the facility suddenly had a hushed atmosphere.

Hudson noted that Bella seemed to be gazing intently at him. That was okay because he was studying her pretty oval face. He missed seeing the dimples that appeared whenever she was with the kids. That's when she seemed the happiest. Her hair looked so soft and silky that he itched to run his fingers through it. But he knew he couldn't. This was the first time she'd even stopped and looked at him like this. Had she thought he was the enemy, that he'd pick apart everything she did? That wasn't his style.

He found himself leaning a little farther over the desk. He thought she was leaning a little closer to him, too.

All at once there was a *rap-rap-rap* on the door.

Sorry that they'd been interrupted, he nevertheless

excused himself and went to the door. When he opened it, the brisk November air entered, along with Bart Dunner, a teenager who was a runner for the Ace in the Hole. Hudson had ordered a mess of ribs from the bar for anyone who was still around when dinnertime came. He paid Bart, gave him a tip and thanked him. On the way to the break room, he glanced over at Bella. *Nothing ventured, nothing gained*, he told himself.

"Have you eaten?" he asked her.

"No, I haven't. I've been making out schedules and ordering supplies for the new year."

He motioned to the bag. "Come join me."

At first he thought she was going to refuse, but then to his surprise she said, "I skipped lunch. Supper might be a good idea."

As they washed their hands at the sink, Bella kept a few inches between them, even when she had to reach around him for a paper towel. Was she skittish around all men...or just him? Maybe she was just shy, he told himself. Maybe she was a virgin. After all, she was only twenty-three.

At the table, they each took one of the Styrofoam containers with ribs, crispy fries and green beans. "These ribs smell delicious," she said, and he didn't think she was just making conversation. But it was hard to tell.

As they ate, he tried to get her to talk. "You know, we've been working together for over a month, but I don't know much about you, except that you live with your brother and help with his triplets. I also know lots of people in town signed up to create a baby chain to care for the kids." Jamie Stockton had lost his wife, leaving him with the newborns to care for and a ranch to run. "That says something about Rust Creek Falls, don't you think?" If he could just get Bella talking, maybe she'd realize he was interested in her.

"That's the way Rust Creek Falls works," she responded. "Neighbors helping neighbors. And what you know about me is probably enough."

"Come on," he coaxed. "Tell me a little more. Did you grow up here?"

"Yes, I did. I was born here."

"Have you and your brother always been close?" he prompted.

"We have. I love my nephews and niece dearly." She took a forkful of green beans, then asked, "What about you? I know Walker is your brother."

"I have four brothers. But we aren't that close. Maybe because we've always had our own interests, or maybe because—" He stopped.

Bella studied him curiously. "What were you going to say?"

Hudson hesitated and decided he had to give to get. "Maybe because my parents never fostered closeness."

She gave him an odd look at that. "Our parents died in a car accident when I was twelve and Jamie was fifteen. We always had to rely on each other."

No wonder she didn't talk about her childhood. Losing parents had to be traumatic. "I'll bet you did rely on each other. Who took you in?"

"Our maternal grandparents took us in—the Stockton grandparents had both died. But Agnes and Matthew Baldwin didn't really want that responsibility."

"How can you know that, Bella? What starts that

way sometimes can turn into something else—a real family."

Looking troubled now, Bella shook her head. "When our grandmother died of a heart attack, I was fifteen. Jamie was eighteen. Our grandfather blamed us."

"You can't be serious." Hudson was outraged for her. How could her grandfather have even given that impression? But then he thought about his own parents and how cold his mother seemed.

"You don't know the situation," Bella said gently. "Jamie and I weren't the easiest kids to raise, and our grandfather was probably right."

Hudson was horrified that Bella actually believed that. She was one of the sweetest women he'd ever met. "You can't blame yourself for what fate hands out." But he could see she did.

Bella had torn apart her ribs at that point, and instead of trying to eat them with a fork as some women might, she nibbled the meat off the bone. Her fingers were sticky, and so were her lips. Hudson couldn't stop looking at her lips. She was in midchew when she realized he was staring. She stared back.

All eating stopped as they gazed at each other, and it was quite possible there was even a hum in the air. He wondered if she was just a little bit attracted to him.

But he never got to ask because one of the teachers popped her head into the break room.

"Got enough for me?" she asked.

That broke Hudson out of his trance. "Sure do, Sarah. Come on in and join us."

As the boss, he knew that was the right thing to do. But as a man, what he really wanted was to be alone with Bella. To find out more about her. To get to know her.

To kiss her.

Hudson let himself into the ranch house on the Lazy B, thinking that living in Rust Creek Falls for a while wasn't a chore. He tremendously liked where he was staying. He'd met Brooks Smith, the town's veterinarian, on one of his first trips to Rust Creek Falls. He knew the town vet could always recommend the best place to ride or rent out a horse. Brooks had done better than that. He'd suggested Hudson rent Clive Bickler's ranch.

Clive, an eccentric wealthy man who'd bought the property after the big flood several years ago, traveled a lot. Besides the main ranch house there was a smaller log home on the acreage where an older couple lived. They'd lost their ranch in the flood, and they lived on the Lazy B now and ran the place. Clive rented his home to high-end clients who appreciated his art collection and other niceties. Hudson, basically a trust fund cowboy, filled the bill. Living here was not only convenient but downright pleasant.

As he tapped in the code for the security alarm, he heard noise in the kitchen. That didn't bother him because he knew who was there—Greta Marsden. She wasn't only the wife of the foreman, but she also made sure Hudson had meals and treats to eat. Now she was loading a casserole into the refrigerator. The kitchen was all shiny stainless steel and high-end appliances. Not that Hudson cared because he didn't do much cooking.

Greta was in her fifties with silver hair that fluffed around her face. She had a wide smile and a kind disposition. She might have been a few pounds overweight, but she was fit in jeans and a plaid shirt. Her wool jacket hung over a nearby chair.

She glanced over her shoulder at him as she made room in the refrigerator for the casserole dish and smiled. "Do you need supper?"

"No, I had ribs. Not that they could stand up to anything you make."

She closed the refrigerator door, blushing a little. "You sure do know how to charm a woman, but save that for the ladies your age. I'm beyond it."

Hudson laughed. "You're not."

She waved his comment away. "When kids are grown, companionship and affection mean more than anything else. I'm relieved I don't need to look hot for anyone."

So that was what marriage developed into—companionship and affection. He wasn't sure his parents had that.

On the drive here, he'd thought about everything Bella had told him about her family. In fact he hadn't been able to get her story out of his head. He was still distracted by it now.

Greta bustled around the kitchen and pointed to a plastic container on the counter. "Oatmeal raisin cookies. These cold nights they'll go good with hot chocolate before you turn in."

"So you think I'm still a growing boy."

She laughed. "No, just a hardworking man with a big appetite."

Hudson wasn't sure about the hardworking part. He'd never really had to work too hard because his family was wealthy, so he was wealthy. He tended to take on jobs as he liked and then move on. His last project in Cody, Wyoming, had been about helping a friend start up a ranch—buying horses, choosing computer programs to manage the place efficiently. Over the years he'd managed ranches, wrangled cows and trained horses. This gig with Just Us Kids Day Care Center was something entirely new to him.

Greta looked around the kitchen and shook her head. "Edmond needed me to do bookwork today, so I didn't clean up here," she explained. "I'll be back to do that in the morning."

Hudson wasn't concerned about collecting a few dust bunnies. "No problem."

As he remembered Bella saying *Our grandfather blamed us when Grandma died,* he considered Greta's comments about marriage.

"Do you mind if I ask you something personal?"

Greta shrugged. "I suppose not."

"How would you feel if you suddenly had teenage grandchildren to raise? What if it happened overnight? What would you do?"

Greta didn't even hesitate. "Edmond and I would try our best to love them to bits. The people who come in and out of our lives are gifts."

When Hudson thought about Bella, he realized how she usually seemed sad unless she was around the kids. Had that been because of the way she'd been raised?

Apparently her grandparents hadn't considered her

and her brother as gifts. That had to color the way she looked at herself and the rest of her life.

Hudson nodded, suddenly a bit pleased with the evening. Though she hadn't revealed too much over their quick dinner, he had learned quite a bit about Ms. Bella Stockton.

When Hudson entered Just Us Kids the following morning, Bella was already there.

As he walked into the reception area, he tipped his Stetson and gave her a cheery good morning. Yet she simply murmured hello and hardly lifted her head. What was *that* about?

He wondered that same thing again when she wouldn't meet his gaze at a brief staff meeting before the children began arriving. He was sure something was wrong midmorning when Bella dropped time sheets on his desk without even looking at him.

She didn't act like a beautiful young woman of the millennia. It wasn't that she lacked self-confidence, because she didn't. With the staff, with the kids, with every aspect of organization, she was confident in her abilities. But not around him.

He had to get to the bottom of it.

Hudson had found he enjoyed being with the kids. It was odd, really. As an adult, he'd never been around children much. Several times a day he'd wander through the sections of children in different age groups. He knew many of the children by name, and they knew his name. He often stopped to help with an art project or just to converse with a curious four-year-old. They came up with the darnedest questions.

He pretty much stayed away from the babies, watching over them from afar. The teachers didn't seem to mind him wandering through. They often gave him a thumbs-up, and he praised them for the way they handled the kids. It wasn't an easy job, and he knew it. He'd handled two-year-old horses, and *that* task had seemed easier.

Throughout the day he often glanced at Bella and wondered why he was so interested in her. Her beauty, for sure, that pretty face, that pixie hairdo, that slender figure. There was something else, too, though—something that both unsettled and intrigued him.

He'd never been seriously involved with a woman. He'd never wanted to settle down because he'd seen the coldness in his parents' marriage. When he had dated, he'd seen that women wanted to tie him to one place. Moving from place to place gave his life the excitement romance couldn't. No woman had ever meant as much to him as not being tied down.

However, something about Bella Stockton made him want to get to know her a little better. He wanted to know why she'd gone all shy on him.

Late in the day, when only a few stragglers remained to be picked up, he had his chance.

He went to Bella's desk and asked, "Can I see you in my office?"

She looked up at him with startled eyes. But then she asked, "Do I need my tablet to take notes?"

He shook his head. "Not about this."

That brought a frown to her pretty face. But she followed him into his office, and this time he closed the door. He didn't claim to be a human resources expert.

Yes, he could spin a good story. However, this moment called for some honesty.

"I suspect you're not happy that I'm here to oversee Just Us Kids. But I want to reassure you I know you do a good job. My being here is just necessary in the wake of everything that happened."

"I know that," she murmured.

"Do you?" He looked at her directly, making eye contact, not letting her look away.

"It's not just *you*," she said. "It's *me*. I don't want to make a mistake. I don't want anything to jeopardize Just Us Kids."

"I understand that. Up until yesterday, I thought we got along just fine. At least we could have a simple conversation."

She didn't say anything to that.

He went on. "And yesterday, I thought we were finally getting to know each other a little better. I'm glad you told me a bit about your childhood."

"I shouldn't have," she quickly said.

"Why not?"

"Because Jamie and I don't like to talk about it. We don't like to think about it. Those were hard times for both of us, and we don't want anyone to feel sorry for us."

"And you think I feel sorry for you?"

"Possibly."

Hudson shook his head. "I'm sorry you and your brother went through that. I'm sorry your grandparents didn't treat you as the gifts you must have been." He found Greta's conclusion absolutely fit the situation.

At his words, Bella looked surprised.

They were standing near his desk, she at one corner and he at the other. But now he took a few steps closer to her. He could smell the light flowery perfume she wore. He could see the tiny line across her nose because it wrinkled there whenever she laughed or smiled. She didn't wear much makeup, but what she did wear was perfect—just a bit of lipstick and a little mascara from what he could tell. Simply looking at her caused heat to build inside him. He tried to throw a dash of cold water on it with logic, but it was hard to douse the kind of attraction he hadn't felt for a very long time.

However, he kept his voice even when he said, "It's a good thing when people who work together share bits of their personal life. They have a better understanding of what the other person has gone through. Do you know what I mean?"

She considered that. "I guess the way I grew up taught me that children should all be treated with respect and kindness and love."

"I can see that."

"And why do you treat them as if you're one of them?" she asked as if she really wanted to know.

"Because I never grew up." He was half joking and half serious.

Bella finally broke a smile. She looked him up and down, from his wavy brown hair, to the razor stubble on his jaw, to the open collar of his snap-button shirt, to his wide leather belt, jeans and boots. Then she said, "That's easy to believe when I see you with the kids. But it's hard to believe when I look at you as the supervisor of this place. You wear the role very well."

"It *is* a role, Bella, believe me. I'm only here until we're sure Just Us Kids has its reputation back, then I'll be off again somewhere else. That's what I do. That's what I mean about never growing up."

She shook her head as if she didn't understand. "But what's your purpose?"

"My purpose?"

"Before this job, what made you want to get up every morning and face a new day?"

"A new adventure. I went looking for it, whether it was gathering wild mustangs in Wyoming or managing the books of a friend's ranch during start-up. I have skills, and I have purpose, but that purpose isn't always the same. I find a purpose in the places I travel."

"With no commitment or responsibilities?"

"No commitment and no personal responsibilities. It's an easy, uncomplicated way to live."

"My life is full of complications," she responded with a little shrug. "I guess I wouldn't know what to do without them. But my commitment to Jamie and the triplets, and eventually finding my own future, gives me purpose each morning. It's a continuing purpose. Do you know what I mean? It's going to take me into the years to come. Yours seems like it could fall apart easily and leave you adrift."

Oh, he'd been adrift. He'd been adrift in between jobs, and he'd been adrift when he'd just enjoyed the scenery. But Bella seemed to think adrift was a bad thing. He didn't.

They gazed at each other for what seemed like minutes, even though it was only seconds. He found himself wanting to slide his fingers through her hair. He found himself wanting to step even closer. There was a sparkle in her eyes when she looked at him that made him believe that maybe she was attracted to him, too. But he was sort of her boss, and she already thought he was judging everything she did. How stupid would it be to get involved with her? Yet *he* set the rules here, didn't he? If he and Bella ever did really connect...

He suddenly cleared his throat. "I'd better open the door before anyone gets second thoughts about what's going on in here. I wouldn't want there to be any gossip about your reputation."

A shadow passed over her face, a definite shadow. Maybe he'd learned a little personal information about her, but not nearly enough. Just what was that shadow from?

But she wasn't going to confide in him any more than she already had. He could see that. She was already stepping away from his desk toward the door.

"Bella?"

She stopped.

"Are we okay?"

"We're fine," she said, raising up her chin a bit.

*Fine*. That was a wishy-washy word that didn't nearly begin to describe what he felt when he was in the same room with Bella Stockton. But he just nodded because he could see that's what she wanted him to do. He wasn't going to push anything...not yet.

## Chapter Two

On Saturday afternoon, Bella was thankful for the baby chain that was helping her brother at Short Hills Ranch. This afternoon, Lindsay Dalton, one of the volunteers in Jamie's baby chain, had stopped by. She was taking over care of baby Jared while Jamie and Bella handled the others. By the stone fireplace in the family room, Bella was holding Henry and sitting in an old pine rocker she'd found at a flea market. His little eyes were almost shutting. Jamie had taken Katie upstairs to the nursery to try to calm her down. She was teething and couldn't be easily consoled today.

Lindsay sat on the sofa cooing softly to Jared. "If Henry starts crying again, he will, too," she whispered.

Lindsay was a pretty brunette and Bella could easily see why Walker, Hudson's brother, had fallen for her. Her own friendship with Lindsay had been strained by the lawsuit against Just Us Kids since Lindsay had been the lawyer suing Walker. But now Lindsay and Walker were engaged, and Walker was going to work mostly from Rust Creek Falls and travel when necessary. Lindsay and Bella were finding common ground again by helping Jamie.

"How goes everything at Just Us Kids?" Lindsay asked her, truly interested.

Bella continued to rock back and forth, watching Henry's fists curl. Holding a baby absolutely melted her heart, yet it made it hurt at the same time.

"Everything's going well," she told Lindsay. "At least it seems to be. We had a mother tell us that if she saw one baby with the sniffles, she'd pull her child and enroll him at Country Kids." Country Kids was their rival for clients.

"Sniffles and kids just go together," Lindsay said with a shake of her head. "Especially this time of year."

"One sniffle now and Hudson asks the parent to keep their child home. That's the way it has to be. I know that's a hardship on the parents, but we can't have another outbreak."

"I'm glad we can talk about this," Lindsay said. "I hated being on opposite sides of the fence."

Bella nodded. She'd missed Lindsay's friendship, too. "How are you and Walker?" she asked.

Lindsay's face broke into a wide smile. "We're wonderful. *He's* wonderful."

Then Lindsay asked, "How are you and Hudson getting along?"

"Fine," Bella responded airily. There must have been something in her voice, because Lindsay asked, "How fine?"

Bella felt her cheeks flush.

Lindsay said gently, "You know, don't you, that

Hudson has a reputation for being a love-'em-and-leave-'em cowboy."

"His reputation doesn't matter," Bella said. "He's my boss. That's it."

Still she remembered the way they'd sat together eating those sticky ribs, the way they'd stood close and she'd felt heat from Hudson and her own heat in return.

"You don't resent him overseeing you anymore?"

"I'm still not sure how I feel about that," Bella admitted. "But I'm not as resentful as I was at the beginning. I understand that both Hudson and Walker have to safeguard the business. I just didn't want someone judging every move I make."

"Is Hudson doing that?"

"Actually, no, he isn't. His managerial style is hands-off, unless he has to step in."

She thought about how Hudson had stepped in after a parent had dressed her down. She also thought about Walker's brief visits to the day care center and his sometimes condescending attitude to Hudson because he was the older brother.

"I wish Walker would tell Hudson he's doing a good job. After all, Hudson handled the PR for the whole problem and managed to keep most of our staff and our clients. But I get the idea that Walker doesn't understand what a huge achievement that is."

Lindsay rubbed her finger along Jared's chin, studying his baby face as if maybe she was contemplating having a child of her own someday.

"I hear what you're saying," Lindsay assured Bella. "But you know, brothers will be brothers. I get the feeling that Walker and Hudson's relationship is complicated, so I think it's better if I stay out of it."

Bella admired Lindsay's honesty. "You're probably right. I wouldn't want anyone interfering in my relationship with Jamie."

After the babies fell asleep, Bella and Lindsay took them upstairs to their cribs in the nursery. Since Katie was still fussing, Jamie carried her to his bedroom so her restlessness and cries wouldn't wake the other two.

Downstairs once more, Bella and Lindsay cleaned up the living room and den. There were always baby things scattered everywhere, from bottles to diapers to receiving blankets to toys. After Lindsay left, Bella went to find Jamie, still in the recliner in his bedroom, rocking Katie. In a pink onesie with a teddy bear embroidered on the front, she looked like a little angel. He was looking down at her as if she *were* one.

"She's almost asleep," he told Bella. "But she's still restless. I want to make sure she's really into a deep nap before I put her down with the others."

"I can take her," Bella offered. "Why don't you go riding? You need a break." He'd been up half the night with Katie.

"I want to make sure this is merely teething and not something else. She doesn't feel hot, but I want to be certain she's not running a temperature."

Bella could hear the fatigue in Jamie's voice, and he looked exhausted. He hadn't shaved today, and beard stubble lined his chin. His blond hair fell over his brow as if he'd run his hand through it many times. But as he looked down at his daughter, his blue eyes were filled with love.

Jamie was often overwhelmed; she could see it on his face and hear it in his voice. Yet he never gave up on the ranch, and he never stopped putting the babies first. He always gave them every ounce of love and caring in his heart, even if that meant he didn't have much of a life anymore.

She'd never regret quitting college and moving back in here with him. She loved helping him take care of the triplets. She loved being around the babies. But it was also painful. She so wanted to be a mother, but she knew she might never be able to have kids. Just how fair or right was that?

"What are you thinking about?" Jamie asked her. As a close sibling, he always could read her moods.

Her past played through her mind like a mocking newsreel. She could never forget about it, even though she tried. So she answered him truthfully.

"I'm thinking about how wild I was as a teenager."

"You were dealing with our parents' deaths."

"So were you, but you didn't jump off the deep end."

"Our grandparents didn't want us. I pretended I didn't care. I put my energy into sports. But you—" He shook his head. "You were younger. You needed Grandma's arms around you. You needed them to want you. They didn't. That's why we were separated from the others."

Bella sighed. Their sisters Dana and Liza had been younger, more adoptable, and had been sent to a group home for that purpose. Their brothers Luke, Daniel and Bailey had been over eighteen and had been turned out on their own.

"Don't you ever wonder where they all are?" Bella asked.

"Sure I do. But the fact remains that you and I haven't left Rust Creek Falls. Our siblings could find us if they wanted to. They obviously don't want to. Case closed."

Bella understood Jamie's attitude. After all, they'd been rejected by their grandparents. They didn't need sibling rejection on top of that.

"Sometimes I don't understand how you help me like you do," Jamie said, looking troubled.

"I'm your sister."

"Yes, but…"

She knew what he was getting at. They rarely talked about it, but today seemed like a day for stepping back into the past.

"I think she's finally asleep," he said, rising from the recliner and carrying Katie into the nursery. There he settled her into the crib and looked down on her with so much love Bella wanted to cry.

Then he turned back to her. "When you got pregnant, I didn't know what to do to help you. After you lost your baby and possibly the chance ever to have another one, I didn't know what to do then either. I don't know how Grandma and Gramps kept everything that happened to you a secret, but they did. Grandma died so soon after you lost your baby, and Gramps blamed you. And me. But keeping the secret about your miscarriage wasn't good for any of us…especially you.

You couldn't talk about what happened. You couldn't express your grief."

"Jamie," she warned weakly, not wanting to delve into any of those feelings.

"I feel like you're still grieving sometimes when you look at the triplets," he explained.

"You're wrong about that. I love being around Katie and Henry and Jared. They fill my life with happy times."

"I know sharing the triplets with you isn't the same as your having your own kids, but I want you to know I appreciate everything you do to help me and to take care of them. And even if you love being around them because they're your niece and nephews, don't you mind being around the babies and kids at the day care center? Isn't it just downright hard?"

"Actually, it's not," she assured him. "I think the day care center has been my saving grace. Your triplets and the kids there…they fill me with joy. I don't have time to be sad."

Jamie suddenly gave her a huge hug, and she leaned into him, grateful to have her brother. In that moment, she thought about having more, too—about having a man to love, a relationship, a life outside the day care center and Jamie's triplets. She thought about Hudson. She'd been attracted to him from the first moment she'd seen him. But she'd also realized what kind of man he was. He had a reputation, and she knew he wouldn't stay no matter what kind of electricity was flowing between them now. She shouldn't get involved…*couldn't* get involved. Besides, she had nothing to give somebody like Hudson. He had experienced the world.

And she was just a small-town girl who couldn't have kids.

Late Monday morning Hudson sat in his office much too aware of Bella at her desk in the reception area beyond. She really was an expert at handling the children. This morning he'd noticed the way she put her hand on a child's shoulder, or gave him a hug. Her smile when she was with the kids was absolutely radiant. Yes, it was safe to say there was a lot about the woman that intrigued him.

As if his thoughts had beckoned her, she stood and approached his office. He invited her inside.

"I set up a meeting for you with the holiday pageant director, Eileen Bennet, next Wednesday afternoon," she told him.

Every year the local elementary school put on a Christmas pageant, and this year they wanted the day care babies to get involved. "The pageant isn't that far off. I hope she doesn't have anything too complicated in mind."

"If she knows babies, she won't," Bella said with a smile. She filled him in on what she knew, then turned to go. She'd almost reached the door of his office when he asked, "What did you do before you managed the day care center?"

He'd heard the gossip that she'd quit college to help her brother, but he didn't know that for a fact.

"I was in college—my second year."

He must have looked puzzled because she added,

"I worked after I graduated from high school to save money for college."

"What did you do?"

"Mostly I waitressed. Lots of long shifts so I could sock the tips away. Four years of that, and I applied for and received a grant from a women's foundation. I enrolled at Montana State University."

"What was your major?"

"Business administration. I eventually wanted to focus on public affairs and learn strategies for helping small towns survive. Maybe that's a pipe dream, but if someone doesn't inject life into a place like Rust Creek Falls, it could become a ghost town. That was especially true after the flood."

"So your college courses gave you managerial skills that come into play here."

"I guess you could say that. I don't know when I'll be able to complete my degree. Working here will help me save the money to do it. But I plan to stick around Rust Creek Falls as long as Jamie needs me."

Bella's eyes sparkled with her dedication to her brother, as well as with the dreams that she still envisioned. More than anything, Hudson wanted to stand up and go over to her. He longed to brush her bangs across her forehead. Even more than that, he ached to tip her chin up, to bend his head, to put his lips on hers.

And that's why he stayed sitting. Yeah, he longed to kiss her, but they were in their workplace. Besides that, he wasn't looking for a long-term commitment, and Bella was the type of woman who deserved one.

This time when she moved to leave his office, he let her.

For the rest of the morning, Hudson felt unsettled. Finally he pushed away from his computer, stood and stretched. Truth be told, he wasn't used to sitting at a desk for most of the day. If he had to choose a job he liked best, it would be one training horses, cutting calves or walking through a field or pasture checking fence. He liked being a cowboy. Even now he rode whenever he could at the Lazy B, but it wasn't the same thing as being on a horse most of the day.

Leaving his office, he spotted Bella. Instead of at her desk, she was on a ladder at the bulletin board in the reception area. Instinctively, he crossed to her, fearful she was going to fall off.

As he stood a few feet from her, he could see that she was putting up photos of the babies who came to Just Us Kids. There had been an explosion of pregnancies after a wedding reception that most of the town had taken part in two summers ago. Rumor had it that old man Homer Gilmore had put something potent in the punch. The result: nine months later, nurseries had been full of babies. Many of those babies were enrolled at Just Us Kids.

He moved a little closer to study the photos, and Bella took notice of him.

"These pictures are good. Who took them?"

"I did," Bella said proudly.

She was still on the ladder, and he stood close to her, his shoulder at her waist. "You just didn't snap quick photos. These are well thought out, artistic even. Look at the eyes on this little guy. They absolutely sparkle." He pointed to another one. "And this expression is priceless. You have a real artist's eye and good timing.

Kids move and change minute to minute, and you've caught some of their best expressions."

She glanced down at him, and their gazes met. "Thank you," she murmured.

Clearing his throat, he said offhandedly, "You'd probably enjoy looking at the paintings at my ranch house."

Bella seemed to almost lose her balance. She toddled, and he put his arm around her to support her. They stood frozen, staring at each other, her face above his but not so far away. Why had she lost her balance? Had she thought he wanted her to come back to his ranch house for other reasons?

Maybe he did.

"You have to careful," he mumbled.

She nodded slowly. "Yes, I do." Then she pushed away from him and made her way down the ladder.

Once she was on the ground, he asked, "Do you have other photos you've taken? Not of babies?"

"I do. I carry my camera with me almost everywhere I go."

"Get it," he said impulsively. "I'd like to see them."

"Now?"

"You're due for a lunch break and so am I, right?"

Bella didn't know what to think of Hudson's suggestion. Did he really want to see her photos? Why? And just what had he meant by that comment about going to his ranch? Did he really want her to see the paintings? Or did he have something else in mind?

Did *she*?

She felt her cheeks beginning to flush. She didn't know what was wrong with her. For years now she hadn't dated. She'd kept to herself. She'd been determined not to get into any more trouble, not to do something foolish or reckless. But in a way, her heart had been frozen during those years. She'd rebelled as a teenager, and that had gotten her into so much trouble. No, she hadn't loved the father of her baby. Yes, she'd been looking for love, and somehow she'd mistakenly thought that sex could give her love. But she knew better than that now. She knew better about a lot of things.

But having Hudson's arm around her when she'd almost fallen, catching the scent of his aftershave, looking into his blue eyes, foolish and reckless and impulsive had all seemed like good ideas.

*No, no, no*, she told herself firmly. *Hudson Jones is nothing but trouble for you.*

Knowing all that, she still said, "My camera's in my bag. I'll get it."

Going around her desk, she opened the bottom drawer. Inside her hobo bag she found her point-and-shoot camera. It wasn't anything special, but it worked for her.

Taking the small white camera to Hudson, she turned it on. Then she hit the button that brought up the display and the photo review. "My SD card is almost full," she admitted, handing him the camera so he could look for himself. She pointed to an arrow button. "Just press that to go backward or forward."

He was silent for a long time as he seemed to spend forever on each photo. When she glanced over his arm, she saw he was studying the sequence she'd taken on Short Hills Ranch. She'd shot the fall foliage with horses in the background. She'd captured Jamie astride a horse as well as a bay with a star on its forehead looking straight at the camera. There was a shot inside the stable, too, where a yellow light cast a horse in a golden glow.

As Hudson shuffled through one photo after another, she watched his expression. He had an expressive face, not stoic like her grandfather's. She saw his eyes widen with surprise when he glimpsed at a photo he especially liked. She spied his mouth turn up at the corners as he went through a sequence of the triplets more than once. There was Katie with cereal all over her face... Henry with his thumb in his mouth... Jared crawling toward a favorite toy. She'd also caught Jamie standing in a window at dusk, his profile in shadow.

Hudson suddenly lowered the camera. "Do you know how good these are?"

She analyzed every crease on his face, the openness in his eyes. Was he feeding her a line?

But his next words told her he wasn't. "I can see you don't know how good you are. Did you ever think about hiring out your services?"

"It's just a hobby."

"It's a hobby that could take you someplace. What if I tell you I know someone who might like to hire you to take photos?"

"Of what?" she asked suspiciously. After all, she'd learned to be suspicious of men and their motives.

"Do you know Brooks Smith?"

The name sounded familiar, and all at once she placed it. "He's a veterinarian. I've never met him. His dad usually comes out to Short Hills when we need a vet."

"Brooks and his dad have separate practices but cover for each other. His dad is cutting back his hours. Anyway, Brooks and his wife, Jazzy, run a horse rescue ranch out at the edge of town. The ranch is a passion with them, and they're going to have pamphlets printed about the facility. Jazzy mentioned she just hasn't had time to put it all together. Do you think you'd be interested in taking photos of the horses on the ranch?"

She was so busy now that she didn't know what to say. Between work and the triplets, she sometimes didn't have time to breathe. But the idea of taking photographs and making extra money was downright inviting.

"When would I have to do this?"

"Pretty soon, I guess. They mentioned handing out the pamphlets at their holiday open house."

"I don't have much spare time," she admitted.

"I know you don't, but this would probably only take a few hours."

"You don't know if Brooks and his wife would really want me."

"I can set up a meeting."

"Let me think about it. If Jamie has enough help, it would be a possibility."

Hudson motioned to the photos of the babies on the bulletin board. Then he pointed to her camera. "You have a gift, Bella. You see with your camera what most folks can't see with their eyes. You really should share that."

She thought about that, then asked, "Why? I mean, everyone sees what they want to see for the most part."

"But what if you can broaden someone's outlook? What if you could give them a positive spin instead of a negative one? What if you can make a difference?"

"We're talking about shooting a few photos." She couldn't keep the amusement from her voice because she thought maybe he was joking.

"No, not just a few shots. Each of your photos is a study of your subject that you've captured for eternity. That's not something to treat lightly."

She never expected something so deep to come out of Hudson. That just proved she didn't know him very well. And he certainly didn't know her.

"I'll check with Brooks and Jazzy," he said. "You think about it. I'm going to take a walk and get some lunch. Would you like some fresh air, too? You're welcome to join me."

She could hear the sound of children's laughter coming from one of the rooms. When she looked up at Hudson, she saw interest in his eyes. The children were safety. Hudson was danger.

As she had for the past few years, she chose safety. "I'd better stay here in case anybody needs me."

"You like to feel needed, don't you?"

"I do. It gives my life purpose."

He shrugged. "I've never had that kind of purpose. I'm not exactly sure what it feels like."

"Walker needed you here. Isn't that why you took over supervising Just Us Kids?"

"I never looked at it that way," he conceded. "I guess you're right." He motioned to the bulletin board. "It looks good. It will capture people's attention. Soon we'll have to decorate for the holidays."

"It's not even Thanksgiving yet."

"Not so far off," he reminded her as he moved toward the door. He opened it and looked back over his shoulder at her. "I won't be long. If anything comes up, you have my cell number."

She nodded. She did have his cell number. But she doubted she'd ever use it.

## *Chapter Three*

As she approached Jamie's front porch, Bella couldn't stop thinking about Hudson and the way he'd studied her photos. He'd really seemed interested. She'd never thought of taking pictures for actual payment. That would be a breeze if it panned out because she loved photos and she loved horses, so she knew they'd be good. She hoped Hudson would really follow through with his offer.

As she opened the door to the ranch house, Bella heard commotion in the kitchen. Taking off her coat, she hung it in the closet and headed for the voices and the squeals.

She smiled when she saw the scene in front of her. Fallon O'Reilly was helping Jamie with the triplets by trying to feed Katie while he fed Henry and Jared. Bella felt warmth spread around her heart at the generosity of Fallon and others who were giving of their time so easily. However, the way Fallon looked at Jamie, Bella suspected there was more there than a friend helping a friend.

Fallon was a year older than Bella and came from

the kind of family that Jamie and she wished they'd had. She was a product of parents who had been married for decades and who loved their kids dearly. In turn, Fallon was great with kids. She should be; she worked at Country Kids Day Care.

When Fallon spotted her, she smiled. "As you can see, applesauce is on the menu. Katie is wearing it exceptionally well, don't you think?"

The baby had obviously waved her hands around with applesauce-covered fingers. There was even some on the little pink ribbon in her fine hair. She smiled when she thought how Jamie always dressed her in pink and tried to keep the ribbon in her hair so everybody would know she was a girl. He was such a good dad.

On the other side of the table, Henry and Jared had smeared it all over their mouths, on the high chair trays and even on Jared's nose.

"This looks like fun," Bella said with a laugh. "Can I join in?"

Jamie motioned to a chair on the other side of Henry. "Pull it up and have a go at this."

As Bella settled in, she said to Fallon, "How's everything at Country Kids?"

She brushed back her curly red hair. "Busy as usual. I had a four-year-old today who hit another child, so I had to call his parents to come pick him up. He was having a tantrum."

"How did the parents react?"

"Not well. But I explained that he couldn't disrupt the whole class just because he couldn't get his way. The mom admitted she and her husband are having some problems at home and that's why he's acting out. Her husband lost his job in Kalispell, and he's taken two part-time positions to try to make up for it. But they're having financial difficulties and arguing. All of that affects kids."

Bella exchanged a look with Jamie. Everything regarding home life affected kids. That's why she and Jamie were trying to give the triplets all the love and attention they could muster. With others joining in, the triplets should have a good start on life, even though they'd been born prematurely and had had to catch up. Even though they'd lost their mom.

"Fallon, I don't know if we say it often enough, but we're so grateful for your help," Bella said.

"I love helping." She turned her blue eyes on Jamie and then the triplets. "When these little ones follow me with their eyes, as they grab hold of my finger, or they eat their food instead of wear it, I feel like I've accomplished something important."

"I know what you mean," Bella agreed. "That's why I love working at the day care center, too. Babies are so easy to love." She thought about her background and Jamie's and added, "Unlike teenagers, who are angry and ungrateful sometimes."

"Our grandparents did their best," Jamie murmured.

Bella supposed that was true. People could do only what they knew how to do. But it seemed love should be easier to give than to withhold, and she'd always felt their grandparents had withheld their affection. She always surmised that they'd taken in her and Jamie out of guilt. Years before, they'd disowned their only daughter, Bella's mother Lauren, when she'd gotten pregnant out of wedlock, and Bella suspected they regretted that decision. When Bella had gotten pregnant, it had brought back for her grandparents all those unwanted memories and stress—stress that no doubt contributed to her grandma's death. At the end of the day, she had blamed herself for all of it. She'd ended up believing that she was a burden who should have never landed on her grandparents' doorstep.

Jamie's thoughts must have been following the same course because he said with regret, "I wish things were different with Gramps, but that's too much water under the bridge, isn't it?"

"I wish things were different around the holidays especially," Bella agreed.

Gramps still lived in the same house in town, and they never heard from him or saw him. She wished he could be part of their lives, but he'd disowned her after she'd gotten pregnant, even though she'd had a miscarriage. That hadn't made any difference to him. He'd been cold and mostly unspeaking until she moved out when she was eighteen. There was so much resentment there—resentment for his wife dying, resentment for the financial burden they'd caused, resentment that Bella had acted out when she was looking for love. No, there was no going back there. She just had to look forward.

"Family is complicated," Fallon agreed.

"Yours doesn't seem to be," Bella offered. "You're close to your brothers and sisters, and your parents would do anything for all of you."

"That's true, and my parents are great role models

for the marriage I'd like to have someday." Again her gaze fell on Jamie, but he was oblivious.

Bella knew her brother had always thought of Fallon as a kid sister. Would that change now that she was helping him with the triplets? Could that change when he was still grieving over Paula? Thank goodness for the babies and the others who were helping. Although Jamie didn't want to be beholden to anyone, the baby chain's presence in his life kept him from brooding, from being too solitary.

And then there were the babies. As she watched her brother wipe applesauce from Henry's little mouth, she knew the triplets had saved Jamie from grief that could have swallowed him up.

"As soon as we're done feeding them, we'll start supper," she said to Fallon. "Would you like to stay? I just plan to make tacos."

"I can chop tomatoes, lettuce and whatever else you want to put on them," she offered after she accepted the invitation. "That is if we get these rapscallions settled so we can have supper."

"We can take turns watching them and cooking, even if we have to eat in shifts. We'll manage it," Jamie insisted.

Her brother's gaze met hers. Yes, they were managing. But life was about more than managing, wasn't it?

She thought again about Hudson. All too easily she could picture his face and his mesmerizing blue eyes.

Bella stopped in the break room the following morning for a bottle of water to take to her desk. She was surprised to see Hudson there, opening a carton he'd set on a side table. Every time she looked at him, a little tremor started inside her and she wished she could will it away. It wasn't like she ogled calendars with pictures of buff firemen or handsomely suited *GQ* models for a little female thrill. But whenever she looked at Hudson, she felt a quiver of excitement.

She wasn't sure if it was caused by his long, jeans-clad legs—those jeans fit him oh so well—or the Western-cut shirt with its open collar where a few chest hairs peeked out. He was long-waisted and lean, and she could imagine exactly how he'd look seated on a horse. His brown leather boots made him seem even taller. Even without his tan Stetson, there was a rugged-Montana-guy feel to him that had to do with the lines of his face, the jut of his jaw, his dark brows. His thick hair waved a bit as it crossed his brow, and she found her fingers itched to ruffle it.

Crazy.

He smiled at her now as he flipped open the carton and took out...a blue teddy bear. Then he dipped his hand inside again and produced a green one and then a brown one.

She couldn't help but smile, too. "What are those?"

"Christmas presents for the young'uns. The day before Christmas they can each take one home."

"Did you do this?"

"Do you mean did I pick them out and order them? Yes, I did. It seemed like a great idea. There are three more boxes of them out in my truck. I'll stow them in the storeroom until Christmas Eve."

She approached him, telling herself she just had to pass by him to get to the refrigerator. When she did walk past him, she caught scent of his aftershave, something woodsy that made her think of pine forests.

She took a closer look at the bears. "They look child safe with their embroidered eyes and noses."

"That's what the online description said," he assured her. "I know how careful the teachers and parents are about those things. I learned that the first week I was here."

"You had a crash course in child rearing from the teachers."

"I did, along with the most tactful way to speak with parents. But it's darn tiring being politically correct all the time. It's much easier just to say what you think."

"You usually say what you think?"

"I try to. Less misunderstanding that way. I've had a few sharp lessons in life, teaching me to get to the bottom of people's motives really quick. Straight speaking does that."

She nodded, opened the small refrigerator and pulled a bottle of water from the shelf.

Now he moved a few steps closer to her. She wrapped her hand around the cold bottle of water, suddenly feeling hot. He unsettled her so, and she didn't know what to do about it.

"You were busy all morning, and I didn't want to interrupt you. I spoke with Jazzy Smith, and she'd like to see your photos."

Bella had considered the project but had doubts about becoming involved in it. "I don't know, Hudson. I don't even have a professional camera, and I don't know when I'd have the time."

Hudson gave her a long studying look. She had a

feeling he was debating whether to say something. But then he said it. "You're around babies and kids all day at the center, and you're around your brother and the triplets the rest of the time. Don't you think you deserve something of your own?"

She didn't know why his comments felt like criticism of her life. She'd had a whole ton of criticism from her grandmother and her grandfather. She didn't need any more from outside sources, making her second-guess what she was doing. Even her friends had been judgmental when she'd quit college to help Jamie. So before she thought better of it, she decided to say what *she* thought.

"You've no right to tell me how to live my life."

He didn't look shocked or even surprised, but rather he just gave her that same steady stare. "No, I don't have any right to tell you how to live your life. But maybe, just maybe, it wouldn't hurt for you to talk about it with someone." After closing the flap, he hefted the box of teddy bears into his arms and left the break room, heading for the storage closet.

*See?* she thought, mentally chastising herself. *Say what you think and it causes tension.* Yet on the other hand, her retort wasn't quite fair, not when he'd just seemed to be looking out for her. She sighed and went after him.

He was shuffling things around in the closet, apparently making room for the teddy bears.

Teddy bears. How many men would have thought of that? Let alone gone ahead and taken care of it.

He didn't look her way as she entered the closet, so she went right over to him and stood in his path.

"Hudson, I'm sorry. I shouldn't have responded like that. I guess you just hit a sore spot. That was my rebellious teenage side making an appearance."

He didn't seem angry. In fact, the look in his eyes made her breath hitch a little when he remarked, "I can't see you as a rebellious teenager." His lips twitched up a little in amusement.

If only she hadn't been, her life might be so much different now.

"You have no idea," she told him. As soon as she said that, she was afraid he'd ask questions. To forestall those, she said simply, "I'd like to meet Jazzy Smith. Did she have a particular time in mind?"

"Matter of fact, she said this evening would be good. If you're free."

Bella thought about it. "I'll have to call Jamie and make sure he has help for dinner."

"No problem. Just let me know. I can pick you up at your brother's. No reason for us to take two vehicles."

She considered riding in Hudson's truck, maybe finding a common interest that didn't include diapers and rattles.

"I'll call him now," she assured him and took her phone from her pocket, heading back to her desk. She could think better and breathe easier when she wasn't in Hudson's presence.

When Hudson picked up Bella a few hours later, Jamie was upstairs giving Henry a bath while Fallon finished feeding Katie and Jared downstairs. She called upstairs to her brother that she was leaving.

Bella explained to Hudson, "Giving a baby a bath can be tricky. Henry has his full attention."

"I'll meet him another time," Hudson assured her.

But Bella wasn't all that sure she wanted Jamie and Hudson to meet. Jamie was too intuitive, and her brother would sense her attraction to the man and zero in on it. She didn't want that happening. It was difficult enough to deal with her reaction to Hudson, let alone Jamie's reaction, too.

Hudson easily made conversation with Fallon. "I suppose you're getting ready for the holidays at Country Kids, too."

"We are. Artwork turkeys everywhere."

Hudson laughed.

"Fallon's such a good help with the triplets because she knows exactly what to do most of the time," Bella explained.

"Experience definitely helps when you cope with kids," Fallon agreed.

"I'm surprised you stop in here after work," Hudson noted. "Kids can be draining. I admire the way Bella works and then comes home and helps with the triplets."

"It's easy for me just to stop in on my way home," Fallon said. "And, like Bella, I love kids."

Katie banged her spoon on her high chair tray while Jared pushed round cereal pieces into his mouth.

"Are you sure you're okay for me to leave?" Bella asked.

"I'm fine. After Jamie's done with Henry, I'll take Katie up and give her a bath."

After goodbyes, Hudson walked Bella outside to

his truck. He went around to the passenger side and opened the door for her. "Need a leg up?"

Oh, no, he wasn't putting his hands around her waist and giving her a boost into the high truck. She could just imagine those long fingers and those big hands and the warmth she'd feel through her jacket...

Quickly she assured him, "I'm used to boosting myself up onto a horse. No problem with a truck."

Fortunately she was telling the truth. Clutching her purse and the photo album she was going to show Jazzy and Brooks, she hopped onto the running board and slid inside. Hudson closed the door for her, and she wondered if he was this chivalrous with every woman. Rumor had it he wasn't seeing anyone in town, but he could have a long-distance relationship with someone.

Once he was inside the truck and they were on their way, she felt she had to make conversation. Dusk had already fallen, and the inside of the cab seemed a little too intimate.

"Is the rescue ranch far?"

"Just about a mile from here."

"You said you're staying on a ranch."

"The Lazy B."

"That's a big spread," she said. "Any horses?"

"Oh, yes, some fine ones. Clive, the owner of the spread, has a good eye. He has two quarter horses, an Arabian, a Tennessee walker, a horse who pulls the buckboard and a Thoroughbred that was supposed to be racing but wasn't real successful at it. She's a beauty, though."

"Do you have a favorite?"

"I do. The Arabian, I have to admit it. I'm used to

quarter horses for cutting cattle and rodeo training. But that Arabian has eyes that can see into your soul. She seems to intuitively know what I want to do next, with a flick of the rein, with a slight pressure of a boot. Amazing, really."

"What's her name?"

"It's Breeze. Clive found her at the rescue ranch. Someone had abandoned her. After Jazzy worked her magic and got her back into shape, the mare actually trusts humans again. Clive named her Breeze because she runs like the wind. She knows her name now. At least, I think she does. She comes when I call her."

After a moment, he asked, "What's your horse's name?"

"How do you know I have a horse?"

"You said you liked to ride. So my guess is, Jamie has one just for you."

"Her name's Butterscotch. I ride her in the mornings when I can."

"I can almost picture her. Flying blond mane?"

"You got it."

Horses were an easy conversational gambit for them. Horse lovers were like any animal lovers. Talking about the beautiful creatures created a bond.

After a bit of silence, Bella decided to be a little bolder. "So what life did *you* leave when you dropped in here to take care of Just Us Kids?"

He glanced over at her, maybe to gauge how much she wanted to know. She could see his profile by the light of the dashboard glow. She imagined he could see her face only in shadow.

"I was helping a friend in Wyoming who'd bought a ranch. He needed help with the start-up."

"I imagine traveling place to place, you meet a lot of people."

"I do."

"Do you make friends easily?" From what she'd seen, he did. But she wanted to know what he'd say.

"I find something to like in most people. That allows for friendship, especially if I go back to a place more than once. It's really hard to keep up a friendship once you leave. I know the tech age is supposed to make it easier, but friendship still requires commitment."

He was right about that.

"Have you ever been committed to a woman?" she asked. She supposed that was one of the better ways to phrase it.

"No. Never anything serious," he answered with a shrug. "How about you?"

That was the problem with asking questions. The questionee thought he should return the favor. "Not lately," she said nonchalantly.

"Did you leave someone behind at college?"

"No. I really had my mind on my studies, so I didn't date."

He seemed to mull that over, and she wondered if he'd ask more about her past.

To her relief, he flipped on his turn signal and they veered down a lane to the ranch. "Brooks could move his practice out here, but he prefers to keep it in town."

Since darkness had fallen, Bella couldn't see much except for the floodlights on top of the barn that glowed over their surroundings. There were at least three barns and a house that looked like a typical ranch house but was much newer. It appeared big for two people, but maybe Brooks and Jazzy were planning on having a large family. Bella felt that stab of pain again that was never going to go away. It was one regret that haunted her.

Apparently divining her thoughts, Hudson explained, "Brooks and Jazzy plan to fill this house with kids. But they also have a first-floor suite set up for Brooks's dad when he's ready to move in with them one day."

"Then they must have a wonderful sense of family," Bella said, thinking about her absent brothers and sisters and whether she and Jamie would ever see them again.

When Jazzy opened her door to them, Bella admired her natural beauty right away. She was slim in skinny jeans and a tunic sweater. But her smile was wide as she welcomed them. She didn't hesitate to give Hudson a hug.

"It's good to see you again." She held out her hand to Bella. "It's nice to meet you."

"And you, too."

Bella handed the photo album to Jazzy. "I thought you might want to look at these. I don't have a professional portfolio, but I keep an album of the best ones."

"I can't wait to see them," Jazzy said. "Come into the living room. I fixed a few snacks. Brooks is out in the barn. He'll be in shortly."

Bella quickly glanced at the cheese tray, the biscuits that looked warm from the oven, jam and butter for those, and a fruit platter, too.

"You didn't have to go to all this trouble."

"It's no trouble. Brooks and I often don't eat till much later. I have something simmering in the slow cooker. I grab a snack with him when he gets home, and then we go out to the barns for a couple of hours. Rescue horses need a lot of kindness, soft talk and gentle touches. That takes time."

"Do you have help?" Bella asked.

"Some part-time help. There are also a group of kids from the high school who mount up service hours for working here. They learn from the horses, and the horses learn from them." She motioned to the food again. "Help yourself. I can't wait to take a look at these." She positioned the album on her lap and began turning pages. After a few pages, Jazzy glanced at Hudson. "You were right. She has a good eye—for scenery, for animals and for kids. That's a winning combination."

Just then Brooks emerged from the kitchen. "I came in the back way," he said, "so I could wash up. Hey there, Hudson."

Hudson introduced him to Bella.

"Look at these," Jazzy said.

"Before I even look, I can hear it in your voice. You like them," her husband guessed.

She just smiled at him and handed him the album. Bella lifted her camera, pressed a button and showed Jazzy photos she hadn't yet had printed. They were the same ones Hudson had seen of the triplets and of Jamie's ranch.

"Those are unedited," Bella told her. "I play with them a bit when I have time—cropping, adding a little light, studying them with black-and-white effects."

"I can see that with these," Brooks said, motioning to the album. "I think we should hire you."

Jazzy nodded and named a sum Bella could easily accept.

"I'd like a day with perfect weather," Bella said, and they all laughed. "Well, near perfect," she amended. "Do you mind if we do a last-minute shoot? I'll keep checking the weather day to day and, when I can get free, I'll text you to see if it suits you. Is that okay?"

"That's fine."

Now that business was taken care of, they snacked and talked, and Bella felt she really liked the couple. It was easy to see that they were deeply in love, as well as passionate about their work.

After she and Hudson left and they were in the truck, she said as much to him.

"You'd never believe they married for convenience's sake, would you?" Hudson asked.

"You're kidding."

"No. It had to do with Brooks's dad and him letting his son into the business. Then his father had health problems, and Brooks felt marriage was the only way to convince his dad to slow down."

"But they have more than a marriage of convenience."

"Oh, yes, they do. Jazzy and Brooks will be the first ones to tell you that they thought they were marrying for convenience, but they were really marrying for love."

Bella and Hudson didn't talk after that, and she wondered if they were both thinking about what he'd said. She couldn't remember much about her own parents' marriage, but she believed they'd been in love. She remembered them holding hands. She remembered them kissing when they thought their children weren't looking. But she'd never know that kind of love. Men wanted children, and she couldn't have them.

Back at the ranch, she'd thought she'd just hop out of Hudson's truck and that would be it. But no, he was being chivalrous again. He came around to her side and opened the door for her. He even took her hand to help her out. That was the first they'd touched all evening. His fingers seemed to burn hers. And when she was on the ground, she looked up at him, confused by all of it. They walked side by side to the front door, then just stood there gazing at each other.

"It *was* nice," he finally said, "sitting there with Jazzy and Brooks, talking like we're friends."

"Yes. Most of my friends are single women."

"They really liked your photos. This could be just the first of many assignments. Word gets around, you know."

"It would be fun to take photos to pay bills. I can also save some money for college."

"No splurging?"

She could hardly think straight looking into Hudson's eyes. "No splurging," she said softly.

He took a step closer to her, and Bella knew she should back away. But she didn't.

Hudson reached out and touched her cheek. Her face was cold from the winter night air, and his hand was large and warm. She could feel calluses on his fingers, and that was exciting. Everything about Hudson was exciting. When his hand went to the nape of her neck and he slid his fingers into her hair, she should have protested. She didn't. And when he bent his head, she knew exactly what he was going to do.

## Chapter Four

If he'd thought this kiss was going to be something easy or quiet, Hudson had been dead wrong. Bella had a sweetness about her that revved up his male instincts and all his male needs. The hunger that welled inside him wasn't going to be satisfied with just a quick tasting.

Some essence of her made him want to get closer and know her in an intimate way. He wrapped his arm around her, maybe to steady them both.

He'd kissed a lot of women, and he'd wanted to demonstrate finesse with this kiss. But finesse floated out the window when his tongue breached Bella's lips. He swept her mouth with an intensity that disconcerted him. No, one brief kiss wasn't going to be enough. He felt intoxicated by their passion and confident in her response. She was tasting him, too, giving back passion as well as receiving it.

But then suddenly she wasn't. It was as if a switch had been flicked off. He felt her stiffen, and he knew exactly what was going to come between them. Rational thought. It had invaded her head before it had found its way to his.

Suddenly she was breaking away, her arms stiff at her sides. She was shaking her head, and he knew whatever she said wasn't going to be good.

Still, he was old enough and experienced enough and respectful of females enough, not to take what a woman didn't want to give. He tried to shut down the heavy beating of his pulse. With a deep breath, he willed his body to calm down, letting her escape his arms. He kept his hands by his sides even though he wanted to still touch her, even though he wanted to wrap her in another embrace.

"What's wrong?" he asked, surprised his voice had come out as even as it had. After all, that kiss had practically knocked his boots off.

"I can't do this," she said, shaking her head again. "I need my job. I can't get involved with you."

As if a bolt of lightning had made him see more clearly, Hudson suddenly realized that everything about Bella's life was so much more precarious than his. Although his parents had been distant emotionally, he'd had four brothers. Someone was always there. And besides his family, his father's wealth had been a life raft. His own trust fund had given him opportunities and saved him from embarrassing situations. When something didn't work out, he moved on to the next endeavor because he didn't have to count on a paycheck. Bella didn't have that luxury. She worried about her brother and her niece and nephews and about Jamie's financial situation. She worried about her own.

She was trying to save enough money to finish college, and Hudson knew how expensive that was these days.

The porch lamp softly glowed across her face. He saw her expression that said she already might have done something that would put her job in jeopardy. That was because she didn't know him. She didn't know what kind of man he was, and that he'd never punish a woman for backing away from him.

"Bella, it's all right. I understand."

"You're not mad because I wouldn't—" She stopped, seemingly embarrassed to go on.

"Nothing's going to interfere with your job, whether we kiss or whether we don't."

"It's too dangerous for me to even think about getting involved with you," she responded. "I can't risk one of the few jobs in Rust Creek Falls that pays decently. It isn't just you. It's Walker, too. He owns Just Us Kids. If anything happened between you and me, he could blame me."

This time Hudson took hold of her shoulders. He couldn't help touching her. "Stop, Bella. I do understand. No repercussions. I read the signals wrong."

At that she blinked, and then she sighed. "I can't let you think that. You didn't read the signals wrong. But I remembered my responsibilities. I remembered who I am and who you are. We come from different worlds, Hudson."

"It was just a kiss, Bella."

After she studied him for a few seconds, she nodded. "Okay, it was just a kiss. I have to go inside. I'm sure Jamie heard the truck, and he'll wonder why I'm still out here."

Hudson dropped his hands away from her because he knew she was going to run. He couldn't blame her, for all the reasons she'd mentioned. Yet when she turned the knob on the door, when she glanced at him over her shoulder, he got the feeling she didn't want to go inside at all.

She said good-night, and so did he. But as he went to his truck, he remembered everything about their kiss, and he wondered if she was doing the same.

Hudson understood Bella's avoidance of him—he really did. That didn't mean he was less attracted to her. Nor did that change the electricity that zapped between them whenever they had to deal with each other. First, when he stole glances at her and saw the dark circles under her eyes, he wondered if the tension between them was causing it. But as the week passed, he didn't think that was it at all. Bella worked all day, and he'd heard her tell one of the teachers that two of the triplets had kept her and Jamie up for the past few nights teething. He might not understand what that was all about, but he did understand sleep deprivation. She wasn't smiling at everyone the way she usually did. The next day at lunchtime, he walked into the break room and found her arms crossed on the table with her head down on them. She was asleep.

She didn't stir as he approached her and stood at the table looking down at her. Her eyes were closed, the lashes fanning her cheeks. Her hair wisped along her face, looking as silky and soft as always. He couldn't let her try to function like this.

Placing his hand on her shoulder, he said gently, "Bella?"

Her eyes fluttered open immediately. She turned her head, spotted him and sat up straight. "Sorry," she murmured. "I was just—"

"You were catching forty winks."

"It's my lunch break," she said, almost defensively, as if he'd caught her doing something terribly wrong.

"I understand that, and if we had a cot in here where you could take a nap like the kids do, you'd be fine. But you're not getting enough sleep, are you?"

"Katie and Henry have new teeth coming in. They're miserable. At first Jamie and I took turns, but it's hard to handle two at once. So we've both been up rocking and walking them."

"You have to get some sleep. Take the afternoon off, go home and go to bed."

"I can't do that."

He suddenly realized she meant *can't* in a couple of different ways. "You mean because you're needed here?"

"Yes, I am."

"I can take over for the afternoon. It's Friday. Things have slowed down for the week."

But Bella wasn't convinced, and then he realized what the other problem might be. "You won't be able to rest if you go back to Jamie's, will you? I should have realized that. Let me take you to my house so you can get a few hours of sleep without disruption."

Bella's eyes went wide, and he knew exactly what she was thinking. "I'll let you in, turn off the alarm and then I'll come back here. You can sleep on the sofa or a bed or wherever you want. The place will be yours for a few hours."

"Hudson, it's your home. I can't just barge in and take over."

"Sure you can. Tell me, how much time have you had absolutely alone since you moved in with Jamie?"

The question obviously didn't need much thinking about. She answered immediately. "I'm alone in my drives to and from work, and if I manage to go for a ride to exercise the horses."

"And how often do you do that?"

"I haven't for a couple of weeks," she admitted.

"Exactly. You have noise and kids around you almost twenty-four hours a day. Give yourself a break, Bella. Just take a few hours for yourself. Come on, get your coat. I'll let Sarah know I'll be gone for about twenty minutes."

"I can just drive myself," Bella said.

"In your condition, you might fall asleep at the wheel. This is no big deal. Grab your coat and let's go."

As if she didn't have the energy to resist, she nodded, went to the closet and pulled out her coat.

Bella opened her eyes when Hudson switched off the ignition of his truck. They were in the driveway of the ranch-style house. She must have dozed a little on the way here even though it hadn't been that long a drive. She was really that exhausted. It was the only reason she'd taken Hudson's offer seriously.

Was he really going to just drop her here and leave? That's exactly what she wanted, right?

"We're here," he said cheerily. "And a good thing,

too. I don't think that seat belt could have held you upright any longer."

"You're exaggerating."

"Not by much. Let's get you inside."

The stone-and-timber home was one story and sprawling, and it sat before her like a quiet haven. Hudson came around and opened her door. He offered his hand, and she took it to step down from the high running board. The cold air felt damp, as if snow was on its way. 'Twas the season.

As she walked beside Hudson, she felt…small. His height and broad shoulders made him tower above her. He was a substantial man, especially in his boots and suede coat with its Sherpa lining and trim. At the door, he dug into his pocket and pulled out a key. There was an overhang above the door, and as she stepped up beside Hudson, she felt as if the two of them were the only people in the world. She figured it was sleep deprivation muddling her thoughts.

He turned the key in the lock, opened another dead bolt, then pushed open the door. As soon as they stepped inside, he was pressing buttons on the security system on a panel on the wall.

The floor of the foyer was some kind of black stone. With just one look, she could tell this house was built with quality materials.

To the right, Bella caught sight of a dining room with a hand-carved oak table and chairs, and a beautiful hutch that showcased stoneware plates. Looking ahead into the center of the house, she saw an open-concept family room and kitchen.

Hudson motioned through the family room. "There are two bedrooms over that way." .

Then he motioned to the left. "I've set up an office over there, and there's a master suite behind that. Where would you like to settle?"

The lone couch in the family room was upholstered in blue and rust in a chevron design and looked cushy with its back pillows for support and comfort. She didn't pay much attention to the accompanying leather recliner and wing chair with side tables and lamps. That sofa was exactly what she needed.

"That'll be fine." As soon as she reached the sofa, she took off her coat and laid it over the back. She sank down onto the couch, and it was like sitting on a cloud.

Hudson laid the key on the immense rough-hewn coffee table. "I'm going to leave you that key. I have a spare. Do you want me to set the alarm or not?"

"I don't want to set something off by mistake."

Hudson pointed to the hangings on the walls. "Clive owns some expensive art. That's why there's a security system."

"Not to mention this beautiful furniture and that huge flat-screen TV," she said, motioning to it.

Hudson chuckled. "Yeah, not to mention that." He took out a card and a pen and jotted down the alarm code. He slid it under the key ring. "I'll set the alarm. There's the code in case you need to turn it off."

"I'm not going to move," she assured him, settling back against the cushions.

A Pendleton blanket was folded over one of the side chairs. Hudson picked it up and brought it to her, spreading it out on the lower end of the couch. "Just in case you get a chill. This will warm you up."

Just looking at Hudson Jones warmed her up, but she wasn't exhausted enough to say that. She did have a few faculties about her.

"I'll come back here after the last kid's gone from the day care center and drive you back there to get your car. You have my cell number, just in case you need me for some reason."

When her gaze caught Hudson's, their kiss became a vivid memory once more. She had the feeling he was remembering it, too.

His eyes darkened. He took a step closer but then said, "The refrigerator's stocked if you get hungry. Greta takes care of that for me."

"Greta?"

"Her husband, Edmond, is the foreman on the ranch. They live in the log cabin just around the bend from the house."

After a last look at her, he turned and headed toward the door. She had the feeling if he stayed longer he could sit on that sofa beside her, and then who knew what could happen?

"See you in a few hours," he said.

She heard the beep of the alarm as he set it and the click of the door when it closed. She heard his truck revving up in the driveway and backing out. Taking one of the throw pillows from a corner of the sofa, she positioned it, curled up with her head on it and pulled up the blanket.

She saw Hudson's face in her mind's eye, right before she succumbed to her fatigue.

* * *

When Hudson returned to the Lazy B that evening, he let himself in and switched off the alarm. He'd stopped at Wings to Go, hungry himself and sure Bella was, too. Greta had left salads in the refrigerator, and they'd go great with the wings. He knew Bella would want to get home, but sleep and food and quiet had seemed to be a necessity for her today.

When he switched on the small side light in the family room, she didn't stir. He watched her from a few feet away. She was curled on her side facing the sofa, the blanket pulled up to her shoulders. He wanted nothing more than to go over to that sofa and finger her hair, touch her cheek, kiss her. Even sleeping, she awakened his appetite for more than barbecued wings.

Still, he let her sleep while he went to the kitchen and set the table for dinner. By the time he put out the salads and the wings, he heard the rustle of movement from the sofa.

"Hey, sleepyhead," he said with a smile. "Are you hungry?"

Pushing off the blanket, she sat up and tried to wipe the sleep from her eyes. "I didn't hear you come in."

"You got a good nap."

She yawned. "I did. I feel like I got more sleep than I have all week." She checked her watch. "Oh my gosh. I've got to get home. Jamie will wonder what happened to me."

"Text him. You can take another fifteen or twenty minutes to eat supper. You've got to take care of yourself, Bella. You won't be much help to him if you get run-down or sick."

She looked torn, but then she nodded. "I know you're right." She'd left her purse on the coffee table, and now she took her phone from it and quickly texted. Afterward she said, "Something smells great."

"I picked up wings. The rest of the meal was in the fridge. I'm a lucky guy."

He saw her look around as if she hadn't really done it before. He spent a lot of time in the family room. A flannel jacket lay over the top of one chair. His laptop sat on the coffee table beside an unfinished cup of coffee. Another pair of boots sat near the gas fireplace.

Standing, she started toward him. "It looks as if you've settled in."

"For now," he said, meaning it. After all, he didn't know how long his wandering spirit would keep him here. He motioned to one of the ladder-back chairs at the table. "Have a seat."

She washed up at the sink and then sat across from him, studying him rather than the food.

"What?" he asked.

"You went to an awful lot of trouble for me today. I guess I have to wonder why."

"I didn't want you dropping from exhaustion at the day care center," he said wryly, skirting the question.

Still, she kept her gaze on him. "So you'd do this for any of your employees?" She motioned to the meal and the house, and he knew what she meant.

"No, I wouldn't. You're special, Bella."

Her pretty brows arched. "Usually when a man does something like this, he wants something in return."

He put down the wing he was about to eat. "Maybe I do. That kiss just didn't happen out of the blue. There's been something simmering since we met. Don't you agree?"

She looked flustered. "I don't know what you mean. I—"

"Bella, tell me the truth. If you can honestly say you don't feel any sparks between us, I'll drop the whole thing, take you home, not approach you again with anything in my mind other than a boss-and-employee relationship."

"That's what we should have," she reminded him.

"Maybe. Are you going to answer my question?"

Stalling for time, she spooned potato salad onto her plate. Then she looked up at him with guileless brown eyes. "Yes, I feel the sparks, but I've been doing my best to ignore them."

He pushed the broccoli salad dish toward her. "That's only going to work for so long."

She sighed and took a sip of her sparkling water. Then she said, "Can we table this discussion for now?"

"Am I making you uncomfortable?"

"No. It's just I have my mind on getting home because I know Jamie's going to need my help."

"And you're afraid if we get embroiled in this type of discussion, you won't get home soon enough."

She picked up a wing. "Yes."

He nodded. "Okay, let's eat."

They were quiet as they ate but still aware of each other. Their gazes met often. Their fingers brushed when they reached for another wing at the same time. He noticed the pulse at the hollow of Bella's neck. He caught her studying the scar under his eye.

"I fell out of a tree house when I was a kid," he said, "and got scraped up pretty good."

She blushed a little. "Stitches?" she asked.

"Yep, twelve of them. How about you? Were you adventurous when you were a kid?"

She was silent for a few moments, then she said, "Not in the tree-climbing kind of way." She hesitated. "But after Jamie and I went to live with our grandparents, I was difficult—acting out, truancy, that kind of thing."

She looked as if there was a lot more to that story, but he didn't press. He just responded, "You don't look like the type. Now you seem to want to go by the book and obey every rule."

"Maybe because I stepped over the line one too many times." With that conclusion, she stood and carried her plate to the sink. Then she asked, "Can you point me to the powder room?"

He waved down the hall. "It's right across from the office."

She nodded and went that way.

He cleaned up in the kitchen, still wondering about her "acting out" escapades. When he heard her in the hall off the foyer, he met her there and pointed to the office. "Did you peek in there?"

"No."

"Not the nosy type?" he asked with a grin.

"Not usually," she answered agreeably.

"I'd like to show you the paintings in there. Come on. It will only take a minute."

He led her into the office, and when she joined him,

she gave a little gasp of pleasure. "Oh my. Are they originals?"

"They are. Clive considers Barclay the best Western painter in America."

He gave his attention to the landscape of a Montana ranch near Billings, then another near Missoula— mountains with a stream running through.

"I noticed the wall hangings in the family room right away when I walked in. They're beautiful, too. Mr. Bickler has wonderful taste and deep pockets."

"Deep pockets can't buy taste," Hudson assured her. "But, yes, Clive has both. I'm fortunate this place was available when I was looking around to find somewhere to live. I thought you might appreciate these."

"I do."

He pointed to a vase sitting on a wide windowsill. "Most of his pottery is signed, too."

She came closer to the window to examine the vase. The darkness outside and the quietness of the house wrapped them in a type of intimacy. He was very aware of the master suite right down the hall.

When Bella looked up at him, he wanted to kiss her so badly that he could remember her taste. But he didn't want to scare her away. He was afraid another kiss right now might just do that. Timing, he knew, was everything.

His voice was husky when he said, "I'll take you back to the day care center, then I'm going to follow you home to make sure you get there safely." He put his forefinger to her lips. "And don't say I don't have to do that. I know I don't. I want to."

Her lips under his finger were warm, pliable, sexy,

and he knew exactly how sweet. When he removed his finger, she was still looking at him. He suspected there was a depth to Bella that not many people probed. She kept up a wall of reserve, and that held them at bay. But he was going to break through that reserve.

One day.

A short time later, Hudson and Bella stood next to his truck at Jamie's ranch. Bella didn't know how to thank Hudson for what he'd done for her this afternoon. He confused her. She hadn't expected the kindness that seemed an innate part of his nature. She felt she had to return that kindness and maybe even take a figurative step toward him, toward admitting those sparks they both knew they felt.

"Can you come in for a few minutes?" she asked. "I'd like you to meet my brother." If Jamie saw the attraction between her and Hudson, he could help her sort it out.

There was a bright moon in the sky, and even though his face was shadowed, she caught the surprise on it. "I'd like that," he said.

And just like that, Hudson took her hand and they walked toward the door. He let go as she opened it. Inside the house, the TV was blaring. Paige Dalton Traub was on the sofa playing with Katie. Jamie was on the floor with Henry and Jared building a structure with colored blocks. He looked up when Bella came in.

"I'm glad you got some dinner," he said. "It was hit-and-miss here."

She'd texted him about the wings and eating with Hudson. She and Jamie had no secrets from each other.

Jared crawled quickly toward Bella. Bella dropped her purse, shrugged out of her coat and laid it over a chair. Then she scooped up the baby, hugging him close.

"Hi there, big boy. I hope you're not giving your dad too much trouble."

"He and Katie aren't as fussy today," Jamie said, getting to his feet and hauling Henry into his arms. "I'm hoping the teething crisis is over."

Bella introduced the two men.

They shook hands, and Bella noticed they seemed to be sizing each other up. They were about the same height and supremely fit from their outdoor work, though Hudson was a bit huskier. Then Jamie introduced Paige—Sutter Traub's wife, elementary school teacher and mom—to Hudson.

Paige said, "If you'll excuse me, I'll get this little girl started on her bath."

Jared suddenly leaned toward Hudson, holding his arms out. Not sure how Hudson would react, Bella said, "You don't have to—"

But Hudson didn't hesitate. He lifted the little boy from Bella and held him high in the air. "Hi there, big guy. I hear you've been stealing sleep from your dad and your aunt. I hope those teeth have settled down."

"Until the next one pops up," Jamie said wryly.

Hudson transferred Jared to the crook of his arm, and the little boy seemed satisfied to stay there for the moment. "I can't imagine caring for three of them," he said to Jamie with a shake of his head. "This is like having your own day care."

"I hope Bella's told you we have nothing against

Just Us Kids. But since the triplets were preemies, I don't want to take the chance of putting them in day care yet. You understand, don't you?"

"Of course I do. And they're in good hands from what I hear."

"Our helpers are the best," Jamie said. "And so is Bella," he tacked on.

It was easy to see the bond between brother and sister and the way they communicated with their eyes, with a gesture, with no words at all. Jamie deposited Henry in his play saucer and then held out his arms for Jared.

Placing him in another saucer, he said, "Come on, fella, you're going to be next for a bath."

"I'd better be going," Hudson said. "It was good to meet you."

"Likewise," Jamie agreed with a nod. And then he maneuvered the two saucers into the kitchen.

Bella walked Hudson to the door. "It's always chaos here."

"Just like the day care center," Hudson said with a smile.

They were standing very close, and neither of them seemed to want to move away. Bella wasn't sure how to say goodbye to Hudson. She wasn't sure where they were headed. They were in between a working relationship and a personal one, and she wasn't even sure she should step into the personal one. But when she looked into Hudson's eyes, she wanted to.

"Thank you for this afternoon," she said sincerely. "I needed the sleep and the quiet, and those great wings."

Hudson chuckled. "Here I thought you were going to say you needed supper with me."

"All of it was really kind of you."

Hudson reached out and touched her cheek. "It was more than kindness, Bella. Sometime we'll continue the discussion we started over dinner."

Then he was stepping away from her, opening the door and leaving. She stood in the doorway, watching him until he drove away.

She found herself disappointed he hadn't kissed her. Confusion? Thy name was Bella.

# Chapter Five

On Saturday morning Hudson rose before sunrise. After downing a protein shake along with one of Greta's cinnamon rolls, he went for a ride on Breeze, contemplating his day. He considered what Bella had said about purpose and realized except for handling the day care's PR problems, he didn't have one. He thought about last evening, meeting Jamie and watching him handle the triplets, as well as his ranch. The guy needed more than a baby chain. Since he'd noticed fencing on Jamie's ranch that needed to be repaired, Hudson decided what he was going to do with his day before bad weather moved in. Throughout his adult life, he'd never had to consult anyone when he wanted to go somewhere or do something. So he didn't now.

He drove his truck to the lumberyard, bought the supplies he needed and headed out to the Stockton ranch, down a rutted road on the side field. The ground was frozen, so he couldn't repost fence. But he could replace slats and make repairs that would keep cattle in and horses safe.

Before 9 a.m. he was working on the fence line, the

physical labor feeling good. He'd missed it. After an hour, he sat inside his truck, warmed up with another cinnamon roll, then went back at it. It was noon when he spotted Jamie rushing out the back of the house and across the field. Hudson didn't at all expect the reaction he got when Jamie was within earshot of him.

The rancher asked, "What are you doing out here?"

"I thought you needed help with the fence line. You don't want your cattle or horses getting out, do you?"

Hudson could see the angry expression on Jamie Stockton's face now that he was closer. "Of course I don't want them getting out. But I don't want *you* doing my work."

"I was trying to help out, just like the baby chain helps you with the triplets."

Jamie's words puffed white in the almost frigid air. "That's different. I have to accept help so Katie, Henry and Jared stay healthy and happy and content. But as far as the ranch goes, I can handle it on my own. Did Bella tell you I needed help out here?"

"No," Hudson said honestly and quickly. "I saw it when we drove by. Your fence slats are falling off. Your posts are leaning. I would have helped with those, but I can't with the ground frozen. If the snow rots them and takes them down, you might have to put up something temporary."

"That's *my* worry, not yours."

To top things off, Hudson caught sight of Bella running toward them. He could see she hadn't even taken time to zip her parka. She jogged toward them and came to an abrupt stop. When she did, he saw how troubled she looked. He hadn't meant to make things harder for her or for her brother.

He addressed Jamie again. "I understand if you want me to stop. But I already bought the supplies. What if I unload them in your barn?"

"I don't need charity," Jamie insisted stubbornly. "You can take your planks and nails and leave."

Bella went to her brother and put her hand on his arm. "Jamie."

"I mean it, Jones," Jamie said tersely. "You took over the day care center under Bella's nose when she'd done nothing wrong. Maybe you had to because you were invested in it. But you have no investment here. Just let me and mine take care of ourselves."

Hudson knew about pride. Walker had been the big brother who bailed Hudson out of scrapes and then tried to tell him what to do. Hudson had always balked and his pride got in the way of a good relationship with Walker.

Jamie had lost his wife. He had to juggle more than a man should have to. At the end of the day, his pride was a valuable asset.

So Hudson didn't argue with him. He just tipped his Stetson to Bella, nodded to Jamie and said, "I understand. I'm out of here."

He gathered up the few supplies he had lying about and stowed them in the back of the truck. When he stole a glance at Bella, he saw she was caught in the middle. He wouldn't want to be in her position. She had to support her brother, and if that meant watching him turn down help, then that's what she had to do.

Hudson climbed in his truck, and as he drove away,

he peered into the rearview mirror. Bella looked appalled that he was leaving like this. But he'd had no choice. He'd miscalculated badly. What was that old saying? *No good deed goes unpunished.*

He'd found that out today. Wandering, rambling, not being connected to anyone seemed to be the easier road to take. Yet he realized now it might be a road that no longer satisfied him, a road that had kept him from forming real connections and friendships.

The Monday morning influx of babies and children under the age of five was the ultimate mayhem. But somehow Bella managed it and kept everybody, from parents to kids to teachers, smiling when she did it.

Hudson hadn't had a chance to talk to her, and he wasn't sure she'd want to talk to him. Now when he looked back on what he'd done, he saw how it could be misconstrued. His actions could be considered high-handed, arrogant, maybe even condescending. She might want to stay far away from him. So he was surprised when, after the last child was logged in for the morning, Bella came to his office and rapped on the open door.

He stood and came around his desk, not wanting a barrier between them. It seemed as if they had enough of those, though he wasn't even sure what some of them were.

"I wanted to talk to you," she said, looking as if she had something serious on her mind.

"I wanted to talk to *you*," he returned.

They were about two feet apart, and Bella looked lovely today in a pale blue sweater and navy slacks.

She'd worn boots, too, no doubt in anticipation of the snow that was predicted for later. It seemed Bella was the type who liked to be prepared.

They both said "I'm sorry" at the same time. He stopped and waved at her to go first. "Go ahead," he said. "But you have nothing to be sorry for."

"I'm sorry for Jamie's behavior," she apologized.

"His behavior was my fault," Hudson assured her.

Shaking her head vigorously, she responded, "No, it wasn't. One thing I've learned is that we have to own our actions. Jamie simply overreacted. It was a wonderful thing you tried to do."

Hudson stuffed his hands in his pockets so he didn't think as much about reaching out and touching her. "*Wonderful* didn't turn out so well."

"It's nothing against you, Hudson. Jamie's already accepting so much help with the triplets, he's touchy about it. He feels as if his life is running him instead of him running his life. Do you know what I mean?"

Thinking about what she'd said, he nodded. "Yes, I do. I can see the responsibilities he has sitting on his shoulders. They're wearing him down. I think they're wearing you down a bit, too."

"I'm fine," she assured him. "But I am worried about Jamie. I had a break on Friday, thanks to you. I really needed that afternoon nap. *And* that dinner. But Jamie won't take a break."

"Maybe he feels if he does, everything will fall apart. I should have discussed fixing that fence with him before I did it. I never meant to cause such a ruckus."

"You did fix the worst part, and whether he realizes it or not, he's going to be grateful when he thinks about it." She took a step closer to Hudson, and he felt his heart beating faster.

Before he realized what she was going to do, she stood on tiptoe and kissed him on the cheek. That kiss was as light as the touch of a butterfly's wings, but he felt it in every fiber of his being.

When she stepped away, she said simply, "Thank you," and then she was gone from his office.

Hudson brushed his fingers over the place on his cheek where her lips had touched his skin.

He did that often over the next hour, aware that he'd been touched by that gesture as he hadn't by anything in a long time.

Throughout the morning, he found himself staring out the window more than at his computer. Around noon he watched the first snowflakes begin to fall. They didn't start lightly but multiplied quickly, coating the grass and the pavement in no time.

The phone began ringing, and he knew why. Parents would want to pick up their kids early. To his surprise, every single one of them did. Usually there were stragglers but not today. And that gave Hudson an idea.

After the teachers had left, Bella was reaching for her parka in the break room when he found her there and asked, "How would you like to go riding in the snow?"

She zipped up her parka. "Are you serious?"

"I am. If you're game, I'll follow you to your brother's, where I can apologize to him for my high-handedness, then we can go for a short ride and chase the snowflakes. What do you think?"

"At your place?"

"Yeah, at my place. There's a horse who will be perfect for you, a little chestnut named Boots. She's got four white ones."

Bella laughed. "Okay, I'm game. Let's go."

A short time later, they pulled up at Jamie's ranch. He parked behind Bella and walked up to the door with her. She opened it, went inside and called "Jamie? Somebody's with me who'd like to talk to you."

Jamie came from the kitchen, his finger over his lips. "Not too loud. All three of them are napping. I think it's a first. Country Kids let out early, and Fallon's upstairs sorting the triplets' clothes. Some of them are already too small."

As Jamie spotted Hudson, he went silent. But Hudson didn't hesitate to walk right up to the man.

"I'm sorry," he said. "I never meant to overstep. You want to run your ranch and your life your way. I get that. I should have talked to you before I brought in supplies and did anything."

Jamie was silent as he studied Hudson, maybe trying to figure out if he was being sincere. Then he extended his hand. "No hard feelings. You did a good job and saved me a lot of work. But I want the bill for those supplies and the time you put in."

"How about if we split it down the middle? I'll give you the bill for the supplies, but my time was free."

Bella's brother considered Hudson's words, then he nodded. "All right. But I owe you one. If you need a favor for something, you come to me."

"Deal," Hudson said with a grin. "For right now,

though, I'd like to take your sister riding in the snow at my place. Is that all right with you?"

Cocking his head, Jamie seemed to weigh what Bella might want.

She said, "I'd like to go if you don't need me. Is Fallon going to stick around?"

"She is. She said she can stay the night if need be."

"I'm just going to change into warmer clothes. I'll be quick—five minutes."

As Bella hurried up the steps, Jamie murmured, "Riding in the snow. We did that when we were kids."

"Before your grandparents took you in?" Hudson asked, still curious about Bella's upbringing.

"Oh, yeah, before they took us in. After that, we didn't have a whole lot of fun."

"Bella told me they didn't want you. I can't believe that."

"Oh, believe it, because it was true. I'm surprised she talked to you about it. She never talks about our childhood. Did she tell you anything else?"

"Just that she believed her grandfather blamed the two of you for your grandmother's death."

"True, too, and he might have been right."

The way Jamie was looking at him, Hudson wondered if he expected him to go on, to say more that Bella might have told him. But there wasn't anything else. Now Hudson was even more curious.

He forgot about Bella's past, though, when she came rushing down the stairs in jeans, riding boots and a pretty pink-and-white turtleneck sweater. He had a sudden urge to cuddle her in his arms. To be honest, he actually wanted to do more than that. But the cuddling sure would be nice, too.

She grabbed her parka and made sure she had her gloves and hat.

"Let's go," he said. "I'll call Edmond on the way, and he can get the horses saddled up."

As Bella rode beside Hudson in his truck, she wasn't sure what had made her agree to this crazy proposal. Maybe it was Hudson's enjoyment of the idea. Maybe it was his enthusiasm. Maybe she just needed a little fun in her life.

Hudson didn't pull into the driveway at the house but rather drove farther down the lane and pulled over at a big red barn. She spotted a log cabin not far away.

"Is that where the foreman lives?"

"Yes. It's a homey place. Greta's into crafts as well as cooking. I think you'd like it. Maybe we can stop there afterward."

At the door to the barn, snowflakes swirled lazily around them as Bella said, "I feel guilty for leaving Jamie back there with the triplets."

"They're his kids, Bella, not yours."

For a moment, she was almost angry at the remark, and Hudson must have seen that. "I'm sorry. I shouldn't have been so blunt. But it's true. At some point he's going to have to be able to handle his own life. He said Fallon was there, so you don't have to worry about him, at least not for the next few hours."

"You can look at the situation pragmatically. I can't."

He took a step closer to her and held her by the

shoulders. "Someone has to. Maybe I can help you find a balance."

"And what can I do for you?"

The way Hudson was looking at her, she knew exactly what she could do for him, and it involved a kiss. She kept perfectly still, but he didn't bend his head. He didn't squeeze her tighter.

Rather he said, "Not everything's a negotiation, Bella. I meant it with Jamie when I said I don't want anything in return, and I mean it with you, too. I just enjoy being with you. Maybe that will work to both our advantages."

"How's that?"

"You think I need purpose in my life. Maybe I'll get a better sense of that by being around you."

"Sometimes, Hudson, I can't tell if you're making fun of me or if you're serious."

"I will never make fun of you, Bella. You're a beautiful, intelligent woman who deserves to be listened to. Why would I want to make fun of that?"

A snowflake landed on her nose, but she didn't care, didn't move. Suddenly it had become more important that Hudson understand her and where she'd been, at least part of it. So she explained.

"My parents were great, at least what I can remember. I have some pictures of them in an album. Thank goodness, our grandparents let us keep those. In those photos, Mom and Dad were laughing and playing ball with us, and even jumping under the hose on a hot summer day. We felt listened to…important…loved. But after my parents were gone, my grandparents talked only to each other. They made decisions with each other. They never consulted us. They sent—"

She stopped. She wasn't going to tell him about the brothers and sisters they never saw. She didn't want him to feel sorry for her. She just wanted him to know the way it had been and why she reacted sometimes now the way she did. "My grandparents just didn't listen, and after Grandma died, my grandfather shut off. It was as if he wasn't even there. He put food on the table. He barked orders at us. But he was never kind the way a parent should be kind. He was never there to listen to what happened at school or after school. He was cold and hard, and I couldn't wait to leave."

Now Hudson did put his arms around her. The brim of his Stetson kept snow from falling on her face. He admitted, "I know about cold parents. My mother's that way. But she calls it reserved. It comes down to the same thing."

"I think Gramps was born that way. Then when he was in a situation he didn't want to be in, burdened with us, he withdrew more into himself. Why do you think your mom was cold?"

"I'm not sure. My guess is she wasn't happy in the marriage. When you're not happy, when the other person doesn't try to make you happy, what's left but resentment and maybe even contempt? That's always what I felt vibrating between them."

"But you had your brothers."

"Yes, I did. We established our own rules, kept each other safe, fought, yelled, but told each other our secrets."

"Like brothers should. Is that why you helped Walker when he needed you?"

"That's one of the reasons."

He brushed snowflakes from her hair, and the stroke of his hands almost made her purr. "Let's get you inside before you become a snow woman."

She laughed, and he opened the barn door for her.

"Edmond, how goes it?" Hudson called when he saw his foreman in one of the stalls.

"Just getting Boots ready. Your Breeze is champing at the bit. She can't wait to get out there."

"They might not be so happy once that snow's falling all around them. But we won't keep them out long."

"Greta wants to know if you'd like to come to supper when you get back. She has a huge pot of chili on the stove, and she says it's just what you'll need after a ride in the snow."

Hudson looked at Bella. "Do you think Jamie can do without you?"

She considered everything Hudson had said about having her own life, about Jamie needing a life of his own, too. Yet she knew right now their lives had converged. Still, Fallon was helping him, and she said she'd even stay the night. Bella had the feeling that Fallon wanted to spend as much time as she could with Jamie. Maybe it was a good thing if she stayed away for a little while.

"Let me give him a call and make sure before we saddle up."

The call took only a few minutes, and she was ready to mount Boots. Hudson stood next to the pretty horse holding its reins. "What did he say?"

"He said I should have supper here with you. Everything is under control back there."

"Good. I lowered the stirrup a bit so you could mount easier. Once you're up, I'll fix it for you."

He could have just given her a leg up, but she was glad he'd done it this way instead. Hudson's touch made her skittish, and maybe he knew that. What she'd heard about Hudson, about him being a love-'em-and-leave-'em cowboy, just didn't mesh with who he really was. She'd found him to be a gentleman, and she liked that. She liked it a lot.

She'd been right about the way Hudson sat on a horse. His back was straight and his shoulders square. Yet his body had enough flexibility that he seemed one with the horse. He looked as if he'd been made for riding. And he looked incredibly handsome, especially against the snow that frosted the landscape.

She followed Hudson since he knew the terrain better than she did. Besides that, she trusted him to lead. Odd that she thought of that now. She hadn't trusted him when he'd first come to Just Us Kids, but she'd learned better. Her experience with men—other than her brother—had been anything but positive. Trusting seemed as far away as dreaming or loving someone who would love you back forever.

The atmosphere out here was positively church-like. The tall pines, the hushed silence, the pure whiteness of fresh snow. Bella felt herself relaxing into the moment, simply enjoying being alive.

Hudson suddenly changed direction and gestured for her to follow him due south. They rode along a copse of pine and aspen and rounded a corner. She felt a gasp come from her soul when she saw a pond before her with white softness edging its borders. The water reflected the gray sky, but there were places where it picked up sparkle from somewhere.

Hudson waited for her to ride up beside him, then he asked, "Are you game to dismount for a while? Those trees will protect us from the snow." He motioned to a canopy that looked like a little haven.

"Sure," she said, giving him a smile. "It's beautiful out here."

He gave a nod and then dismounted first so he could give her a hand. She would have just jumped off her horse, but Hudson was right there, his hands on her waist, helping her to the ground. He lifted her down, and she felt like air in his arms. There was strength there and a sure grip that assured her she wouldn't fall.

He took hold of their horse's leads. They walked about twenty feet into the copse of trees, and she saw immediately why he'd wanted to bring her here. It was a more in-depth view of the lake, the snow on the reeds, the white birch on the far shore, the pine canopy that kept snow from falling on them.

"Sometimes we don't realize how much noise surrounds us all day until we're in a quiet place like this."

"Do you come here often?" she asked, almost in a whisper because that seemed fitting here.

"I do. I have that luxury because I don't have to take care of triplets when I go home."

Facing him, she asked, "Are you trying to make a point?"

He gazed down at her with sincerity in his eyes.

"Nope. Just attempting to show you the other side of having a purpose."

She felt mesmerized by him...so drawn to him. "I think you have a purpose when you come out here."

"What would that be?"

"To connect with something outside yourself, something bigger than yourself. My guess is you find here what many people find in meditation or in church."

"Wide-open space has always meant freedom to me. I don't like fences or boundaries that predict where I have to stay."

That statement prompted her to probe deeper. "Do you think you were *born* to be a risk taker or an adventurer? Or did you learn it?"

"I only take calculated risks. And as far as being born an adventurer, I'd say I learned it, in order to escape my siblings and my parents."

"I wish I had gone that route," she admitted with a sigh, and then was appalled she'd said it. What she didn't want to do was get into her background. What she didn't want to do was explain what had happened when she was a teenager rebelling against her grandparents who didn't love her, against fate that had taken her parents from her, along with her other siblings, too.

Apparently Hudson's thoughts ran in another direction from her teenage years because he turned to face her, adjusted the chin strap on her hat and said, "You can still be an adventurer. It's never too late to start."

The darkening of his eyes, the heat she suddenly felt between them, the vibrations that were all about male and female awareness made her ask jokingly, "You mean I should catch a plane to Paris?"

"No," he said honestly. "I was thinking that you should kiss me again."

When Hudson wrapped his arms around her, she didn't hesitate to let him pull her close. He dragged his thumb down her cheek and kissed the trail his finger had taken. His sensual touch sent tremors through her, and in spite of herself, she envisioned them naked in his bed. She should have stopped the thought right there. If she had, when his lips sealed to hers, maybe then she wouldn't have felt like melting into his body. The cold seemed to swell around them, but they were warm, getting hot, even hotter. His lips seemed to burn hers, and when his tongue breached her lips, forged into her mouth, took the kiss deeper and wetter, she wrapped her arms around his neck and held on for dear life.

Hudson stopped the kiss suddenly...didn't end it... just stopped it.

She knew he wanted another one because he kissed along her lower lip, then the corner of her mouth. After a deep breath, he said, "You make me feel too much."

"You make me shake," she admitted.

His soft chuckle said he liked that idea, and he came back for another kiss, and then another until time didn't matter. The swish of pine boughs didn't matter. Snow mounting around their boots didn't matter. Only Hudson's desire, his hands at the nape of her neck and his body heat mattered.

He broke away again, then he looked down at her, breathing hard. He assured her, "If we were someplace else, someplace warmer and more comfortable, we'd be doing more than kissing."

*But we shouldn't be,* a voice inside her yelled. *Why not?* echoed back. She ignored both and said to Hudson, "I'm not sure we *know* what we're doing."

"That's the fun of it—the adventure of it," he reminded her. "Let's just see where this goes, Bella." Just in case her response wasn't what he wanted to hear, he brushed her lips with his again and wrapped his arm around her. "I think that chili at Greta and Edmond's is good and done. Let's go get a bowl and warm up."

She didn't need chili to warm up. She'd been plenty warm when Hudson had been kissing her. She had a feeling she'd be plenty warm every time she thought about it, too. Could she be an adventurer and take it further?

Thank goodness, she didn't have to answer that question now.

# Chapter Six

As soon as Bella walked into Greta and Edmond's house, she felt as if she were surrounded by warmth, and not just warmth coming from the woodstove. Whereas Clive Bickler's house was decorated with expensive paintings, fine-quality wall hangings and artist-signed pottery, Greta and Edmond's little house was simple and cozy. It was a log home, and Greta had kept the country look about it.

Everything was spick-and-span, shiny and authentic. The wide-plank flooring was worn. The living room's magnificently colored, large Southwestern rug needed repair in one corner and wore a straggling fringe in the other. The appliances weren't state-of-the-art, but Bella could tell they were used and used well. The colors migrating through the cabin—whether the fabric was striped, flowered or solid—were burgundy, green and yellow.

"I love your house," Bella told Greta. "It's charming."

Greta motioned to the curtains and the valances. "I made those myself. I still have an old treadle machine that works just fine. We managed to save it from the flood."

Edmond motioned to the table where a crock full of chili sat in the center. "Take a seat and we can talk while we eat."

"Our ranch was almost wiped out," Greta told Bella. "We saved what livestock we could first, then a few other things like my sewing machine, photo albums, framed pictures, a set of dishes my grandma handed down. But that was it. Everything else was wiped out when the house filled with water up to the second floor."

Edmond sat next to his wife and covered her hand with his. It was obvious that thinking about the flood was still an emotional experience for the couple.

Bella stole a glance at Hudson. He was watching Greta and Edmond, obviously trying to understand.

Greta's husband went on to explain, "We were living in the boardinghouse, not knowing what we were going to do next. No job, not much in the way of possessions. We basically had each other. We could have gone to live with our kids, but we didn't want to do that. They have their own lives. I was using my phone every day to search for jobs and not coming up with anything because lots of folks in town were in the same boat."

"But then fate stepped in, I guess," Greta said. "The owner of the Lazy B wanted to leave Rust Creek Falls, didn't think it would ever come to life again, and Clive Bickler saw the good deal that it was. Edmond and I had helped organize one of the old barns that wasn't underwater where we could give out supplies to people who needed it—bottled water, blankets, some clothes.

Clive heard about that somehow, and the fact that Edmond knew horses and cows. So he asked us if we'd manage his place, room and board free. It was a deal we couldn't refuse. We just hope he never sells the place."

During the next hour, Greta and Edmond were full of lively stories about times on their own ranch when they'd had it, as well as this one. Eventually, Edmond and Hudson got to talking about horses while Bella and Greta spoke of good meals to make on the go. Bella was thoroughly enjoying herself and could see why Hudson liked spending time with these people. As a couple they were cute together, bumping each other's shoulders, touching each other often, and Bella could tell from the sparkle in their eyes that they were still deeply in love.

They were eating dessert, a delicious gingerbread with whipped cream, when Greta and Edmond exchanged a look. Edmond nodded, and Greta addressed Hudson.

"We have some really great news."

Hudson gave a chuckle. "What would that be? You can't make me any more food than you already do. It won't fit in the refrigerator or on the counter."

Greta waved his comment away. "This has to do with our children."

Edmond added, "One specifically. Our daughter Gracie is pregnant. She and Cole are overjoyed, and so are we."

Greta cut in, "Edmond can't wait to teach a little one how to ride a horse."

Hudson said to Bella, "Their daughter lives in Kalispell, so they'll be able to see their grandchild often."

"A little girl," Greta said with glee. "Can you imagine? Bows and pigtails and shiny shoes."

Edmond shook his head. "Not if she's a tomboy like Gracie was."

Bella saw Greta's and Edmond's radiant faces, and Hudson's happiness for them. She felt happy for them, too. "A baby is something glorious to look forward to," she said, and she meant it.

But inside she felt as if the evening had suddenly wilted because reality had struck again. These good people had reminded her what family was all about—meeting someone you loved, getting married, having kids. A sudden sadness washed over her, especially when she thought about her kiss with Hudson and what it could mean...what it *did* mean. They were so attracted to each other, and if she let that kiss go further, the next time—

There shouldn't be a next time. If they started a relationship, it couldn't go anywhere. No man wanted her because she couldn't have kids. She could not carry a baby to term. When would she finally let that reality take hold?

Maybe she could find love later in life, she told herself. When she was fifty? When having kids didn't matter to a man? Was that ever the case? She knew what Hudson was like with kids. She'd seen it over and over again. He enjoyed them. He could get down on their level. He could even *be* one at times. He would want children.

Somehow she managed to be part of Edmond and Greta's conversation, talking about kids, toys and even the day care center. She managed to smile and share in their excitement. But deep down, she hurt. That hurt would never go away.

Hudson was confused as he drove Bella home. They'd had a marvelous afternoon. Their ride had been romantic and fun—the snow falling around them, riding together, the grove in the trees that had sheltered them while they'd kissed. He knew he hadn't been mistaken about Bella being as involved in it as he was.

Dinner with Edmond and Greta had seemed to be enjoyable, too. But then suddenly, he could tell there'd been a change in Bella. She'd grown quieter, though not a lot quieter. He'd only noticed her gaze hadn't met his as often. There had been a tension there when he'd spoken to her, even about something as mundane as a child's toy. And he wanted to get to the bottom of it.

He felt as if he'd done something terribly wrong. Maybe once that wouldn't have bothered him so much, but this was Bella, and it did bother him.

When he arrived at the Stockton ranch and parked in the drive, he hadn't even turned off the ignition when Bella said, "You don't have to walk me to the door. I'll be fine."

That almost made him angry. He switched off the motor and said, "That sidewalk looks slippery. I'll walk you to the door." He knew his firmness brooked no argument.

Bella seemed to accept his decision, but she didn't

look happy about it. She didn't wait for him to come around to her door. She opened it herself and hopped down.

When he rounded the truck, she was already on her way to the door. His legs were a lot longer than hers, and he caught up easily. He clasped her elbow and made sure she wasn't going to slip on the walk. At the porch she turned to him, and it seemed that she steeled herself to meet his gaze.

She smiled and said, "Thank you for today. I had a lovely time."

She'd said the words, but there was some kind of underlying message in them that he didn't like and he didn't accept. It was as if this was the last time they were going to have a lovely time.

"Bella, what's wrong?"

"Nothing's wrong," she said with a little too much vehemence.

"I don't believe that. Everything was fine, and then suddenly it wasn't. I want to know what's going on in that head of yours."

She gave him an almost defiant look that said maybe he didn't have the right to know what was going on in her head. She was correct about that, so he tried a different tack.

"If I did something wrong, I'd like to know what it was."

Now the defiance was gone, and she looked genuinely concerned. "Hudson, you didn't do anything wrong. I enjoyed the ride, I really did. And Greta and Edmond are a wonderful couple. I can see why you like spending time with them."

"But?" he prompted.

She shook her head. "No *buts*. It's just that our situation hasn't changed. You're my boss. I think we should keep our relationship colleague to colleague."

Settling his thumb under her chin, he tipped her face up and studied her. That might have been one of her concerns, but it wasn't the only one. Still he couldn't force her to confide in him. All he could do was try to gently persuade her with actions rather than words.

"We're more than colleagues, Bella. Deep down you know that."

Reluctantly he took his thumb away from her soft skin. Reluctantly he took a step back. "But I respect what you're saying. I respect you."

He turned to go. "I'll see you at Just Us Kids." Then suddenly he stopped and looked over his shoulder at her. "If you ever want to change our colleague status, just say so. I'm flexible." He left her standing on the porch contemplating his words.

As he climbed into his truck, he saw her step inside. He just hoped that someday soon she would confide in him what was bothering her.

Because if she didn't, they would just remain colleagues...until he left Rust Creek Falls.

On Tuesday afternoon, Bella stopped in Hudson's office. They hadn't had contact all day, and he was glad to see her now. She motioned to the classrooms.

"All the children are gone early for a change. We had a light day with the snow keeping some of the kids home. So I'm going to scoot. I called Jazzy, and I'm going out to the ranch to shoot photos. I have about an hour and half of daylight. With the snow and the sun on the horizon, I should be able to get some good shots."

"After I close up, do you want company?" he asked.

"I might be finished by the time you get there," she said. Then she paused and gave him a small smile. "You can help convince Jazzy that if she doesn't like the photos, she doesn't have to take any. So sure, come on out."

Because of Bella's attitude toward a relationship, he didn't want to push. But he wasn't beyond coaxing a little. Just being around her would help convince them both exactly what they should or shouldn't do. Besides, he still wanted to find out what had happened at dinner last night, and why she'd turned suddenly...*sad*. That was the only word he could find to describe her mood.

After Bella left, he finished up some work, chatted with the teachers, then when they left, he made sure the facility was locked up tight. As he drove to Brooks and Jazzy's ranch, he felt energized at the idea of seeing Bella again. Had other women ever done that to him? Sure, he'd looked forward to dates, to finding satisfaction in the most physical way. But the idea of seeing Bella again just...lightened him. That was the only way he could put it, and he felt almost happy.

He didn't think about happiness often. He just lived his life. It was one of those things that if you searched for it you couldn't find it. But he'd figured out happiness had nothing to do with what he owned. It had something to do with where he went. Maybe that's why he traveled. This lightness he felt around Bella, however, was something different altogether.

At the ranch he parked beside Bella's car. Climbing

out, he adjusted his Stetson and headed for a purple-coated figure standing at the corral fence.

Jazzy was staring into the pasture where Bella was shuffling through the snow, crouching down to get a shot, then standing to take a long view of another horse. He and Jazzy watched her as their breaths puffed white every time they breathed out. Bella wouldn't want to be out here too long in this cold, but she was dressed for it with practical boots and a parka, a scarf and knit cap. He couldn't see her expression from this distance, but her stance said she was intent on what she was doing.

"She's good with the horses," Jazzy said.

As he watched her approach one of the animals and hold out her hand, maybe with a treat, the horse nuzzled her palm. She stroked his neck and put her face close to his.

"As good as she is with kids," Hudson noted. He could feel Jazzy's gaze on him as he watched Bella.

"You like her," Jazzy said, as if it were a foregone conclusion.

"You mean it shows?"

"If someone's looking," Jazzy answered. "It's in the way you look at her. The thing is, I've heard rumors that you don't stick around very long. Are you planning to settle in Rust Creek Falls?"

"No." The word popped out of his mouth before he thought better of it. "I'm going to be moving on soon. Walker can easily find someone else to oversee the day care center."

"That might not be as easy as you think. Rust Creek Falls isn't teeming with cowboys like you with managerial experience. I hear you've done a magnificent job of getting the business back on track since the lawsuit."

"I hope that's the case. It's hard to wipe out the impression of something gone wrong. But we're steadily signing up new clients, and the old ones are staying. That's what's important."

"Do you find what you're doing fulfilling?"

He thought about it. Then he said with a shrug, "Kids or horses. That's a tough decision to make. I sure do miss being outdoors, though, working with horses most of the day."

"So you like Clive's ranch?"

"Oh, I do."

"Do you really want to move on?"

"It's my nature," he said quickly, as if he had to convince himself of that, too.

Instead of focusing on Bella, Jazzy turned to him and looked him deep in the eye. "Maybe it's only your nature until something or someone convinces you to stay."

Jazzy's words were still echoing in his mind a half hour later as Bella waved to them that she was finished and came over to the fence, her camera swinging around her neck on its strap. She climbed the crossbars and swung her leg over the top.

Jazzy said, "I'll start inside and make us hot chocolate. Maybe we can thaw out our fingers and toes."

Hudson held out his hands to Bella. She hesitated only a moment, and then she took them and let him help her down. They glanced at each other now and then on the walk to the house but didn't speak. Hudson wanted to ask her how she thought the shoot went, but he knew she wouldn't answer, not until she got a look at those photos on more than her camera screen. And he had an idea.

"Did you bring along the cord to hook your camera up to the TV?"

"Brooks and Jazzy have a smart TV?"

"Oh, I'm sure they do. We'll check when we get inside. That way you can see what the pictures look like."

"I brought my laptop," Bella said.

"Wouldn't you rather see them spread across fifty-two inches?"

She laughed. "It's a guy thing, isn't it? Having a huge TV."

Hudson stopped and studied her. "Is that a sexist remark?"

"No, it's the truth," she said.

"You don't want to watch a chick flick on fifty-two inches?"

"When I watch a chick flick, it's for the content. I don't care how big the screen is."

He just shook his head. "Venus and Mars."

"You think men and women are from two different planets?"

"I think they have two entirely different perspectives on the world."

"You might be right."

They were no sooner inside than Jazzy brought hot chocolate and sandwiches into the living room and set the tray on the coffee table.

Brooks grinned. "Perfect."

He wasn't looking at the food, though. He was staring at his wife. Her cheeks were rosy, her hair mussed. She was wearing slim jeans, boots and a heavy sweater.

"You were out there a long while," he said. "I'll switch on the gas fireplace. Extra heat won't hurt."

After Hudson and Bella had taken off their coats, scarves and hats, they came to sit down, too. Bella rubbed her hands in front of the fire. "That feels nice. I like the idea of not having to carry in the wood."

"It has an automatic pilot, too," Jazzy said, "so if the electricity goes out, we still have its heat. I imagine Clive has something like this," she said to Hudson.

"Yes, he does. It's come in handy the past few nights. No reason to put the heat up in the whole house when I'm just in one room."

Bella gave him a glance that said she was surprised he was economical about it. He had the feeling she underestimated him on a lot of things—his reputation, maybe his brother's sentiments about him, that he was a drifter and didn't settle down long in one place. Yet Walker was probably right.

Not wanting to think about that, he asked Brooks, "Can we hook Bella's camera up to your TV? Then we can all view the pictures on there."

"Without me previewing them first?" Bella asked, sounding nervous about it.

"Up to you," he said.

She chewed on her lower lip for a minute and then said, "I think I got a couple of pretty good shots. Let's do it."

After Brooks and Hudson accomplished the hookup, they all viewed the photos, one by one.

Hudson heard Jazzy's intake of breath at a photo of

a light-colored bay against the sun setting on the horizon and glinting off the snow. He hoped that meant she liked it. There were so many others to like, too. Jazzy took a few steps back so she could get a better perspective and silently watched as one photo after another appeared on the big screen. She oohed over the one of the chestnut near the pine grove when the light was still full. She aahed over a blue sky as a backdrop against pristine snow and a gray equine beauty. Bella hadn't captured only the horses, but the ranch, too. He'd seen her run from one end of the corral to the other, snapping an action shot of three horses together, but then also taking her time, sitting on a fence, snapping barns and trees and Montana's big sky.

After they viewed the photos twice, Brooks said, "Bella, these are fabulous, absolutely fabulous. I don't know how we're going to decide which ones to use."

"You don't have to decide now. I'd like to edit them a bit and do some cropping. I can send you the files."

"I have a photo printer at Clive's place," Hudson said. "Why don't we go back there and print them out. Then you can look at the printed photo as well as the digital file and decide which ones you want on the pamphlet. That might give you a better idea."

Brooks and Jazzy exchanged a look. "That sounds good to us," he said. "Now, let's have another round of hot chocolate."

Bella called Jamie to make sure everything was all right there. He said he had it under control and Fallon was keeping him company. Bella told him about the photo shoot and how Jazzy and Brooks seemed to like her photos. He was excited for her, and she saw that both of them needed something in their lives other than babies and diapers and laundry. She was glad Fallon was there with him.

An hour later they finally left for the Lazy B.

As they stepped inside, she asked, "Why do you have a photo printer?"

"I like gizmos and tech stuff, not just saddles and boots," he told her. "And I've been here long enough to have a collection. I have a camera, too. I sightsee now and then. I've gone out to the falls near Falls Mountain and taken a few shots, but mostly I use it for the day care center. My phone camera is fine, but I get better light with a point-and-shoot. If I see something that can be improved on at Just Us Kids, I take a picture so that I have a reminder of it. It's my way of working."

She followed him into the great room and took off her parka. "I'll pay you for the cost of printing the photos."

"Nonsense. I got you this commission, so to speak. It's my contribution."

As she walked with him to the study, she said, "You're a generous man, Hudson. Have you found people take advantage of that?"

"The ones who need the generosity don't. If somebody does, I chalk it up to experience learned. Giving usually isn't wasted. You give, too. You're generous with your time and your spirit, Bella. I'm sure your brother would attest to that."

When Hudson gave her compliments, Bella wasn't sure what to say. So she said nothing. As they sat next to each other at the desktop computer, their arms brushed. She didn't pull away. Being with Hudson was both unsettling and exciting. The exciting part coaxed her to let it continue. She knew she was headed for deep water and it was quite possible that she'd drown. But the attraction to Hudson was heady, like nothing she'd ever felt before. And she liked dwelling in it for just a little while.

The computer monitor was large enough to do the photos justice. When Hudson downloaded them, all the recent photos on the camera went into the program. He took a long time studying several of them that were taken at area barns and ranches.

"You're really good, Bella, even better than you know. I can frame any one of these for a wall grouping and it would stand out as artistic and meaningful."

"You're too kind," she said.

He turned toward her and pushed a strand of her hair behind her ear. "No, I'm not kind, not about this, not about you. I don't have kindness on my mind when I look at you."

"Hudson," she said on a slightly warning note.

He dropped his hand from her hair, leaned back and sighed. "You don't have to say anything else. I know how you feel about…everything. I can't say you're wrong…unless you want to enjoy the moment. Unless living for today means as much as living for tomorrow."

"Have you used that line before?" she asked, staring directly into his eyes. She knew Hudson was experienced. She knew he'd been around the block, so to speak. She knew he knew what he was doing.

For a moment she thought he was going to get angry, but then he rolled his chair away from hers. "It's not a line. It's just the way I think. It's the way I live. I'm not sure what you think my history is with women, Bella, but I don't need lines."

"No ego there," she murmured.

His serious face turned light, and he chuckled. "I never said I was a humble man. Come on, let's get these printed out. Then I'm going to follow you home to make sure you get there safely."

"No, Hudson. There's no need for that. I don't need a protector."

There must have been something in her voice that convinced him of that, but he was still a negotiator.

"All right. I won't follow you home if you promise to call me when you get there."

"I'll text you," she bargained.

He rolled his eyes but responded, "Deal."

Yet somehow, even though Bella had felt like she'd gotten her way, she knew that Hudson Jones would have the last word.

## Chapter Seven

Bella found herself humming a Christmas carol the following morning as she sat at her computer at the day care center. The holiday was still weeks away, but timing didn't dampen her mood. Nor did the statistics she was examining and organizing for a year-end report.

The photo shoot yesterday had gone extremely well. She loved the work she'd done. She'd been up late editing the photos, emailing files to Jazzy. Already this morning they'd gone back and forth in emails, and Jazzy had chosen seven of the photos she liked the best to use for her pamphlet. She was going to use others on her website. She'd told Bella when she had it updated, she'd let her know.

When Hudson had asked Bella if she minded if he dropped by to watch the shoot, she'd worried that he'd be a distraction. But he hadn't been. She'd liked having him there, sharing in the experience. His ideas were often good ones—like viewing the photos on the big-screen TV. The admiration in his eyes when he'd looked at her had almost made her tear up. She hadn't felt that kind of admiration in a very long time...if ever.

What if Hudson knew about her past? What if he knew she'd mistaken a hungry look in a teenage boy's eyes as love? What if he knew she'd gotten pregnant?

What if he knew she couldn't have children?

The statistics on her computer monitor seemed to blur for a moment. Hudson didn't need to know any of that, did he? After all, he'd said himself that he'd be leaving Rust Creek Falls. But a little voice inside her heart asked, *And what if you do get involved with him?*

The idea had been growing in momentum. It had even taken over many of her dreams. Every time she thought about the two of them together, really together, she had to struggle to push the thoughts and images away. But at night, her subconscious went wild. She woke up wanting his arms around her, needing his arms around her. But then like dreams do, they faded into reality. Her common sense prevailed, and she warned herself to keep her distance, or at least not let anything progress beyond a kiss.

However, Hudson's kisses were unforgettable.

As if she'd conjured him up by thinking about her dreams, he appeared at her desk. "I've been thinking," he said.

She gave him a smile, not knowing what was coming. "I thought I saw smoke coming from your office," she said with a straight face.

He gave her a mock scowl. "That smoke you saw was my coffeepot biting the dust. It's time I buy a single-serve brewer for in there. Any flavor you like best? I'd be willing to share."

The twinkle in his eyes told her he'd like to share

more than coffee. She shook her head. "Break room coffee is fine with me."

"Until I give you Death by Chocolate to taste," he teased. "Just you wait."

She couldn't look away from his eyes, and she didn't want to. It would be so easy to get lost in Hudson and the sparks they generated...in a fire that could consume her. She took a deep breath and slowly let it out.

"So what have you been thinking about?" she asked, getting the conversation back on track.

"I've been thinking about using your photography skills as a moneymaker for the day care center."

She tilted her head, interested.

He could obviously see that because he went on. "How would you like to take photos of moms and their babies? It would be quite a keepsake for them, plus a good promotional tool for the day care center. We can put together a child care book where we lay out the photos with parent tips. I'm sure the mothers would have plenty of those. You've seen those community cookbooks? This would be something like that. Your photos would give it that aaah factor."

"It sounds ambitious, but I'd love to participate in it."

Hudson looked thoughtful. "We could do the photos after hours, or we could commandeer the corner of one of the classrooms. Moms can stop in whenever they like, and you could make it a priority to take the photos."

"Mothers love to be photographed with their kids. I think it would be easy to convince them."

"I'd like to have it all put together by Valentine's Day," he suggested.

"That's quick."

"I know. The owner of one of the ranches I worked at self-published a history of the ranch. I helped him with it. There's a formatter I can contact. I would trust your eye on the basic layout. If we shoot the photos between Thanksgiving and New Year's, it's possible."

"I should send out an email to the parents to explain the project and encourage them to get on board. I can write something up right now and have it to you after lunch for approval."

Hudson was again pensive for a few moments. She studied his expression, the character lines on his face, the way his hair waved across his brow. Standing at her desk, he towered over her and seemed larger than life. His chest was broad, his forearms muscular beneath the rolled-up sleeves of his snap-button shirt. There was strength in those forearms, and she became distracted by the curling brown hair that covered them. Just looking at him, any part of him, sent her pulse racing.

She didn't know how long he'd been talking when his words finally broke through her thoughts. "I don't want you to go to extra work if this isn't going to fly. I'll give Walker a call or text him. After I run it by him, I'll let you know if it's a go."

"It's a wonderful idea, Hudson. It really is. You *deserve* a new coffeepot."

At that he laughed, gave her a little wave and went back to his office. Her heart was still pitter-pattering when she turned back to her computer.

Hudson was eating leftovers from a casserole Greta had prepared when Walker breezed into the day care center and his office later that day.

"That smells good," Walker said, motioning to the chicken-and-broccoli casserole that Hudson had warmed up in the microwave in the break room. "I don't imagine you made it."

"Greta made it. She doesn't let me starve."

"You settled into a good deal there. Not only horses but home cooking."

"In a way, it feels like home, more than our home ever did."

Walker gave him a surprised look. "In what way?"

"I like going there after a day here at work, or after a ride. I look forward to it."

Walker glanced around the office and the rest of the day care center. Hudson knew his brother had gone into the business because he wanted kids to have a safe, caring place to stay while their parents worked. Their own childhood with nannies who were overseeing them only because of a great salary was probably one of the reasons.

The lawsuit Walker had been involved in had also given him a new perspective. He was setting up a foundation, The Just Us Kids Pediatric Pulmonary Center, for children who need specialized medical care.

Walker returned his attention to Hudson. "So you wanted to talk to me about a scheme to make money?"

"It's not a scheme, it's a project." Hudson kept the defensiveness out of his voice. He was prepared with Bella's photos. He spread them across the desk, faced Walker and explained exactly what he had in mind.

"It would help if we could get some kind of child care expert to give quotes, too," Hudson suggested.

Walker seemed to think about all of it. "I'm surprised you came up with this."

Walker's comment irked Hudson. Yes, Walker was the CEO type, the business-oriented brother, but Hudson knew he had good ideas, too, just in a different vein.

After Walker took another look at the photos, and at the schedule Hudson had devised along with the cost estimate, his brother nodded. Then he stared at Hudson as if he were seeing him in a different way.

"I have one question," Walker said. "Will you be staying until the project is finished?"

Hudson considered his brother's question. He also considered Bella and spending more time with her. "Sure, I can stay until it's finished."

That seemed to settle everything in Walker's mind. "Go ahead," he said. "Get it started. It will be good for the day care center. It's something the other franchises could pick up and do. We could even sell it on the biggest ebook seller there is. Child care tips can be relevant to moms across the country. Quite a moneymaker you've thought up here." He extended his hand to Hudson. "Good job."

Hudson shook his brother's hand, feeling a connection with him he hadn't felt in a long time.

After Walker left, Hudson told Bella the good news. "He feels it will be a good moneymaking project and that the idea will catch on with the other franchises. He thinks we might even be able to sell it through a nationwide channel."

Bella's face was all smiles. She threw her arms around Hudson's neck and gave him a huge hug.

The impulsive gesture made him catch his breath, which only made it worse for him as he took in the scent of her perfume or shampoo or whatever smelled like flowers and Bella. He couldn't help but tighten his arms around her, and for just a few moments, she tightened her arms around him. He could feel she was breathing fast, and so was he. He wanted to bury his nose in her hair, kiss her temple and more. But she leaned away, moved her hands to his chest and looked up at him. He had to give her time. He had to give her the opportunity to come to the realization on her own that they'd be good together. One thing he was sure of—he couldn't push Bella, or she'd run. He didn't know why. He wished he did.

As if she were suddenly embarrassed, she pulled out of his arms. "I'm so happy about this. I know it's not the same as professional credits, but if I wanted to do more of this photography work, I'd have a strong recommendation."

"You might want to change what you study at college when you go back," he offered.

She looked pensive. "You might be right. On the other hand, maybe I could have a major in business administration and take photography classes, too. The best of both worlds."

Wasn't that what everybody wanted, the best of the worlds they chose? He felt as if he had one foot in an old world and one foot in a new one. He knew the old world brought him satisfaction, and he was comfortable in it. A new world? That was always a risk. But was it a risk he wanted to take?

Bella gave him a look that said she didn't know if

she should say what she was thinking, but then she seemed to make up her mind. "I couldn't help but notice you and Walker shaking hands as if you meant it."

"That's a novelty?" he joked.

"You have to get along for business's sake, I suppose. But you've never seemed...close."

"He really doesn't know what I've done on past jobs when I've worked at ranches. I guess he thinks I only wrangle calves."

"You don't talk about it?"

"Don't you know cowboys are men of few words?" Again he was teasing, but she seemed to take him seriously.

"Few words, maybe. But if they're the right words, they count."

"You and Jamie are different from me and my brothers. Maybe as kids we commiserated and told each other secrets but not as adults."

"That's a shame. But miles do make a difference. When I was at college, Jamie and I didn't talk as much or often."

"Distance can be a wedge," he agreed.

She said brightly, "But you and Walker are here now. Maybe you'll have a new start."

"Maybe," he agreed, wondering if that could be true. After all, the holidays were coming up. Weren't they the time for a new start, or a deepening of what was already there?

Bella glanced at the clock on the wall. "I told Sarah I'd help her with an art project with her class. Her aide is out this morning."

Hudson nodded. "And I have that meeting with the

pageant director, Eileen Bennet, over at the school this afternoon."

"Let me know how it goes," she said as she stepped out into the hall, giving him one of those smiles that seemed to make his heart turn sideways. He stared at her until she stepped into Sarah's classroom.

Then he looked back down at the photographs he'd printed out that were still spread across his desk. Walker had really studied them and admitted they were as great as Hudson thought they were. If Bella needed credentials to get more photography work, maybe he could help her out. He took out his cell phone and checked his contacts list. Yep, there it was. Miles Stanwick. He was the owner of a few galleries, including one in Kalispell. His headquarters, however, were in Billings. That was the great thing about cell phones. No matter where Miles was, Hudson could reach him. After two rings, Miles answered.

"Hi there, Hudson. Are you in Billings?"

"No, I'm in Rust Creek Falls. I've been taking care of business for Walker here."

"Your dad has always been one of my best clients. What can I do for you?"

"You scout out new talent, don't you?"

"I do, but I have a lot of fresh painters right now. What do you have?"

"How about photographers?"

Miles seemed to think about it. "With point-and-shoot digitals, everybody's a photographer these days. But I'm always on the lookout for something special."

"I think these photos are special, but I don't have

a gallery owner's eye. Would you consider taking a look at them?"

"I'm getting into my busy season. But sure, I can spend fifteen minutes looking over photos. Do you have my email address?"

"I do. I can send you the digital files, but I also printed them out. I think you'll see they really come to life in the glossies. I can overnight them." After Miles gave him the Billings address, he asked, "If you feel the photos have merit, do you think you'll be able to place a few?"

"If they have merit, I can always make a place for them." He paused a second, then asked, "If you're working on business for Walker, then you're not traveling much, I take it?"

"Not right now."

"Well, if you're still in Rust Creek Falls when I come over to Kalispell for the holidays, I'll give you a call. Maybe we can have dinner."

"Sounds good. And thanks, Miles. I really appreciate this."

After he ended the call, Hudson gathered up the photos. He'd email Miles the digital photos, then he'd package up the glossies and mail them on his way to the school for his meeting.

He really did think the photos were something special. He hoped Miles did, too.

He decided to keep the whole gallery query a surprise. After all, he didn't want Bella to be disappointed if nothing came of it. For now she would be happy photographing moms and babies.

An hour later, before he left for his meeting with

the pageant director, he went looking for Bella. He wanted to make sure she didn't need anything before he left. He found her in Sarah Palmer's classroom, where she was still helping with the art project, and what a project it was.

The four-year-olds were having a stupendous time with the art supplies. They were gluing and coloring without knowing they were practicing hand-eye coordination and fine motor skills. Sarah concentrated on that with every art project as well as burgeoning young talent. There were turkey heads and feathers cut out of construction paper, and feet, too, made of some fuzzy cord. Bella and Sarah were helping the children paste them all down on a plate that served as the turkey's body. The kids talked and laughed as they wielded crayons as if they were true artists, drawing faces on the plates.

Tommy, one of Hudson's favorites, pushed back his chair and came running over to him. "Mr. Hudson, Mr. Hudson, look at what I'm doing."

His turkey had black eyes and a mouth, and Tommy was coloring his body purple.

Hudson crouched down to Tommy's eye level. "So you've seen purple turkeys?"

Tommy looked at his turkey and the pictures of turkeys that Sarah had attached to the bulletin board.

"I didn't *see* a purple turkey," Tommy admitted. "But there could *be* purple turkeys."

At that Hudson laughed out loud. Anything was a possibility in a child's mind.

Hearing his laughter, Bella looked up. Their gazes met and Hudson could swear he felt the room shake.

But no feathers scattered, mock or otherwise, so he knew it was his imagination. Purple turkeys could give a man delusions.

The curly-headed blonde four-year-old next to Bella tapped on her arm. Hudson remembered her name was May.

"Miss Bella, I made a mistake. My line went crooked."

Hudson walked over to where Bella was seated, and he could tell the little girl's picture was supposed to resemble a house. A purple turkey. A house in a turkey's tummy. What was the difference? he supposed.

Bella rested her arm around May's shoulders. "A crooked line doesn't have to be a mistake. Let's look at what you're trying to do." She gave the plate a quarter turn. "What if we made your crooked line part of the fence that goes around the house? Sometimes they're straight and sometimes they're crooked. Your line will fit right in."

"But it can't be red. Red is for the bricks on the house," May insisted.

Bella picked up a brown crayon. "Here, give this a try on top of the red. It will make it look just like wood."

May did as Bella suggested and then looked up at her. "It does."

"You'll have a fine fence there," Hudson encouraged her. "I see you have a house with a second floor. Does it have windows on the second floor?"

No windows were showing now.

May put her finger to her lips, and then her eyes sparkled. "My house has windows. I can put in windows."

Bella said to May, "You work on that for a little while. I'll be right back." She pushed her chair away from the table and stood.

Even so, Hudson was still a head taller. For some reason, Bella made him feel ten feet tall. He wasn't sure why. Maybe it was just this "thing" between them. He felt their breathing almost synchronized as they stared at each other. He wasn't sure why that happened when he thought about kissing her, but it did.

How could he think about kissing her when they were in the middle of a room with four-year-olds?

He waved at the table and the projects spread out everywhere. "Do you think you'll ever get this cleaned up?"

"Maybe with the custodian's help," she joked. "But it's amazing how little ones like to help when you ask them. They'll pick up their scraps."

"Their feathers, you mean?" Hudson said with a straight face.

"So you got sucked into a world of purple turkeys and green feathers?"

He laughed. "It's hard to resist. Maybe that's why I like being around the kids so much. It makes the real world go away."

"Or they take you back to when you were four."

"I don't even *remember* when I was four."

"I bet if you and your brothers got together you would. No clubhouse, jungle gym, forts made out of a blanket on the sofa?"

"Are you kidding? A blanket on the sofa? Our mother would have called the maid."

Bella blinked. "I forgot."

"Forgot what?"

"You grew up very differently than I did."

What Bella meant was, he'd grown up with money. Yes, his family had been wealthy. There had been maids and housekeepers and nannies.

"Maybe I did," he said. On the other hand, though, maybe their worlds hadn't been so different after all. "But that fort you speak of...my brothers and I escaped to the woodpile now and then and rearranged it. It was a grand fort. What my mother didn't know didn't hurt her."

Bella studied him. And maybe in the atmosphere with four-year-olds around, and Sarah not too far away, she felt brave to delve into his life a bit because she asked, "How else did you escape?"

"Riding did it the most, or just wandering the pasture with the horses. How about you? How did *you* escape?"

"Books. Books took me anywhere I wanted to go, with anyone I wanted to be with. They still do. When I get the chance to settle down with one."

One of the kids dumped a canister of crayons onto the table. The scattering noise took Bella's attention for a moment. Then she asked, "Are you leaving now?"

"I am. I just wanted to remind you to call me if you need anything."

"Will do. And if I may, I'd like to remind you of something. With the pageant being held the Sunday after Thanksgiving, we don't have a lot of time to get costumes together. I'm definitely not a seamstress, and I don't know if any of the teachers are. So if we have to do any type of costumes, we need to keep it simple."

Hudson nodded. "I'll talk to Eileen about that. You should definitely sit in on the next meeting. Or maybe you should be going instead of me."

"I can go to the next one if you'd like me to. We'll have to get permission slips from parents, work up the PR for the kids being in the pageant and get that out in emails and on the website so the parents know exactly what we're doing, too."

"All good points."

Tommy waved his turkey at Hudson. Hudson went over to the four-year-old and pointed to the turkey's neck. It was still white. "Are you going to color that?"

"Maybe I'll make his neck red."

"You'll have a colorful turkey," Hudson proclaimed with a straight face.

"Maybe Miss Sarah will hang mine up high so everybody can see it."

Bella came to stand beside Hudson. "She's going to hang everyone's turkeys so when your parents come to pick you up, they'll see what a good job you did."

"And we can take them home for Thanksgiving?"

"Yes, you can."

Thanksgiving. Hudson still had no idea what he was doing for the holiday next week. He supposed Bella was planning to spend it with Jamie. Maybe in their next conversation he'd ask her. He'd spent many holidays alone, and he'd told himself he liked it that way. Memories of long-ago holidays were faded and ghostly. He almost had a hard time imagining what a real holiday would be like surrounded by family and friends he actually cared about, and who cared about him.

He should be more grateful about what he'd had growing up. After all, look at everything Bella had lost.

"Is something the matter?" she asked him.

He was going to say no, but decided to tell the truth. "I was just thinking about holidays and families and expectations that aren't usually fulfilled. Look at these kids' faces when they study their turkeys. They're totally in the present. Maybe somehow that's what we have to do to appreciate Thanksgiving and Christmas."

"When you learn how to do that, you let me know," she responded, then added, "Maybe this year the triplets will teach me their secret."

"I'm always open to hearing secrets," he said.

Bella looked startled for a moment, and then she backed away from him. "I'll see you later," she told him. "I have to get back to pasting on those feathers."

The word *secret* seemed to have spooked Bella. He supposed no one got to adulthood without a few of them.

Just what was Bella Stockton's secret?

## Chapter Eight

Bella sat at her desk that afternoon, composing letters to send to parents explaining about the photos she wanted to take and the child care tips they might want to contribute. Usually moms were eager to share everything they knew about kids. She'd certainly gotten experience helping Jamie with the triplets.

Despite the work, she found herself missing Hudson. The place just wasn't the same when he wasn't there. Yes, she'd resented him when he'd first moved in, so to speak, to check up on her. But now they worked in tandem. Not only that, she missed his physical presence, the sparkle in his eyes, the energy he projected. Cowboy or businessman, he was one difficult man to ignore.

When the phone rang, she picked it up. "Just Us Kids Day Care Center, Bella Stockton speaking. How can I help you?"

"Is Hudson Jones there?" a gruff male voice asked her.

"He's not available at the moment. Can I help you?"

There was a pause. "No, I need to speak to Jones. If I leave a message, will you make sure he gets it?"

"Of course I will. Or I could put you through to his voice mail."

"I don't trust that stuff. I'd rather you hand deliver it."

She smiled and wondered how old this man was. She pulled a pink message pad and a pen from her desk. "As soon as he comes in, I'll hand it to him."

"Tell him this is Guy Boswick from Pine Bluff Ranch. He can reach me at…" And he rattled off a number. "I have a problem for him to handle."

"Can I tell him what this is in regards to?"

"No. I need to talk to him. Don't worry. He'll know who I am when you give him my name."

That was a cryptic message if she'd ever heard one.

"All right, Mr. Boswick. I will do that."

"If I don't hear from him today, I'll call back tomorrow," he assured her.

"That's fine. I understand."

She hardly had the words out when Mr. Boswick said "Goodbye" and hung up.

A half hour later, Hudson blew through the door along with the wind and a few snowflakes. He had a smile on his face.

Bella couldn't help but smile back. Hudson Jones was infectious. She just hadn't figured out if that was a good thing or a bad thing.

As he took off his jacket and hung it in his office, she followed him inside, the message in her hand. "You look as if you had a good meeting."

"I did. We figured out how to keep things easy for the babies."

"I'm not sure anything is easy with babies," she warned him.

He chuckled. "Probably not. But how's this for an idea? Reindeer antler headbands for the babies, and we put them all in carriages. That way, volunteers at the school can decorate the carriages and we don't have to worry about costumes."

"I think that's brilliant," she agreed. "Did you come up with that or did Eileen?"

"A little bit of both. Eileen knows kids and what will work and what won't. I'm sure some parents must have carriages. If they don't, I'll buy a few and we'll use those."

"Is that in the budget?"

He arched his brows. "If I have to make a purchase outside the budget, we just won't tell anyone, right?"

"I don't know. Walker could mark me down for being a coconspirator."

"Not if we pull off the pageant with a big kick."

When their gazes met, Bella experienced that shaken-up feeling all over again.

Hudson hung his Stetson on the hat rack. With his flannel shirt open at the collar, dress jeans and brown boots, he was as tempting a man as she'd ever seen. But that's all he was at this point—a temptation.

She broke eye contact first, remembered the message in her hand and held it out to him. "You had an odd phone call, a Mr. Guy Boswick. He wanted me to hand deliver this to you."

Hudson took the message and studied it. "He has a problem?"

"He wouldn't tell me what it was. He just said you

knew him and you should call him back. He warned me that if you don't call him back today, he'll call again tomorrow."

"And keep calling until he gets me. That's Guy, all right."

"So you *do* know him."

"Yes, I do. I worked on his dude ranch a couple of years back. He became a father figure to me for a while. He's a tough old cowboy, but he has a good heart. I can't imagine what he wants now, though. I'd better give him a call." He looked back up at her, and she thought she could be wrong, but it seemed his eyes twinkled when he thanked her.

"Anytime," she said, meaning it.

As she went back to her desk, she realized she hadn't closed Hudson's door, nor had he. Apparently he didn't expect the conversation to be private. She liked Hudson's transparency. He said what he felt, and he meant what he said.

Bella couldn't help but overhear the beginning niceties of the conversation. After all, her desk wasn't that far away from Hudson's open door. She wasn't trying to listen, not at first. But then she heard, "You want me to accept a position in Big Timber with you at Pine Bluff? Why would I want to do that?"

He was being offered a job? Now Bella was all ears.

"I understand you have a problem you want me to solve," Hudson said. "But public perception can't be swayed easily. I have a commitment right now. Any PR firm can help you."

Bella supposed Guy Boswick was raging a powerful argument to sway Hudson to Big Timber, away from Rust Creek Falls. Maybe an emotional argument if he'd been a father figure. After all, Hudson didn't really *need* a job. He was wealthy.

"All right, I'll agree to that." Hudson listened, then asked, "How soon do you need an answer?"

Boswick must have told him and said a few more things because Hudson ended with, "It was good talking with you again, too, Guy. Take care," and he set down the cordless phone.

Hudson looked Bella's way, and she couldn't pretend she hadn't heard. Rising from her desk, she went into his office. "Maybe I'm sorry I gave you that message. I couldn't help but overhear. Did he offer you a job?"

"Yes, he did. But I don't know all the details yet. Someone from the ranch is going to be contacting me. Then I'll know more."

"When would it start?" she asked hesitantly.

"Bella, there's really nothing to talk about. Everything's supposition at this point."

"But when we talked about putting together the child care book, I was under the impression you were going to stay until Valentine's Day, right?"

"I don't want to talk about this now, Bella. I have a lot to think about and information to get. I *will* tell you I'll be out for a couple of hours tomorrow. Actually, maybe I'll just take the whole day. I need to clear my head, go riding, maybe work some colts. That will probably be the best thing for everyone. If you need me, you can reach me on my cell."

Bella decided not to mope. She'd known what kind of man Hudson was when he'd arrived. He'd told her point-blank he was a traveling man and not one to remain in one place. So she certainly hadn't been weaving dreams about him staying, had she? Valentine's Day or sooner, he was going to be leaving again, and she'd better get used to the idea.

She raised her chin when she replied, "I won't need you, Hudson. I managed Just Us Kids just fine before you got here. I can certainly handle it tomorrow."

As she turned to leave his office, he called her back. "Bella?"

She stopped but kept her shoulders squared and her back rigid, her head held high.

"Life is about choices, and they happen every day. This is just another one of those choices."

"Commitments happen every day, too," she returned, then went to her desk and ignored Hudson for the rest of the day.

The atmosphere between Bella and Hudson remained excruciatingly strained after his phone call to Guy Boswick. This was one time when she had no idea what he was thinking. Could he seriously be considering taking a job in Big Timber? Riding the range again? Training horses? He was a man of many talents, that was for sure.

As she worked at her desk all day on Thursday, she couldn't stop herself from wondering where he was and what he was doing. Couldn't stop herself from missing him. It was odd when you got used to a person's presence. When the individual was gone, a piece of your heart was, too. No, not her heart, she told herself. She couldn't care that much about Hudson. Could she?

She thought about the days and weeks and months

after she and Jamie had been split up from their other siblings. Each minute at first, and then each hour, and finally each day, she'd wondered where they were and what they were doing. She and Jamie had been too young and hadn't had the means to keep track of them. Their grandparents had made it clear their sisters and brothers were no longer their concern. Were Liza, Dana, Bailey, Daniel and Luke bitter and resentful? Was that why they never called or returned...because Rust Creek Falls had nothing but bad memories of the split-up after their parents' deaths? And sadness. All good reasons not to return, she supposed.

The day rolled along even though Bella didn't put much gusto into it. At least not until she visited the classrooms to talk and play with the kids. But when she returned to her desk, she fell into the same thoughts, missing Hudson and wondering if he was actually considering the job offer. Knowing she could only make herself crazy, she forced herself to stop. Her life certainly didn't revolve around his, and his would never revolve around hers. At least not with any permanence.

Could an affair assuage some of what she felt for Hudson? Or was it already too late for that? He could even be gone before Christmas.

In an effort to get her mind off him, she returned to her year-end report. She didn't pick her head up until one of the moms, the one who had threatened to take her son to another day care center if she saw evidence of a sniffle, entered Just Us Kids to pick up Jimmy. Marla Tillotson never seemed to be happy. Bella had glimpsed a smile on her face once in a while when she was with her son, but not often. Bella had also noticed that Marla stirred up gossip with the other moms. She managed a new laundromat that had opened up recently, so she was in contact with many town residents. When she heard news, she spread it around.

As Marla approached the desk, Bella pulled out the clipboard with the sign-out sheets. She handed it to her with a smile and asked politely, "Is it getting any colder out there?"

"Cold enough to trade leather boots for fur-lined ones," Marla said. Her gaze went to Hudson's office. "So Mr. Jones took the whole day off?" she asked. "I noticed he wasn't here this morning either."

Bella wouldn't gossip, but she would be honest. "Mr. Jones took a personal day today."

Marla gave her a wicked smile. "I'll say it was personal."

Bella couldn't keep her eyebrows from arching up. "Excuse me?" she asked, knowing she shouldn't pursue it, yet interested in most anything about Hudson.

"I stopped in at the Ace in the Hole for takeout for lunch. He was there with a very beautiful redhead. They seemed to know each other well, at least from the way he was patting her hand. They didn't seem in any hurry to eat and were enjoying glasses of wine."

Bella felt as if she'd been stabbed. Hudson had taken off today for a date? A long lunch with afternoon delight afterward?

Should she be surprised?

With Hudson's charming nature, he'd been in Rust Creek Falls long enough to make friendships, to meet lots of women. She turned back to Marla. "Mr. Jones's business is his alone," she said, her voice devoid of inflection. "Go ahead back to Jimmy's classroom. I'm sure he'll be ready to leave."

Marla gave Bella an odd look, then a little shrug. She went down the hall to her son's classroom.

Bella was not going to give another thought to Hudson Jones.

Not one more thought.

When Hudson came to work the next morning, he looked somber as he gave Bella a nod then went to his office. He didn't say good-morning. He didn't ask how the day had gone yesterday. In essence, he was quieter than she'd ever seen him, and he stayed that way.

Was it because of the kisses they'd shared that she now felt piqued that he was ignoring her? Was it because of their argument? The possibility he'd be leaving?

As the day progressed, and he stayed in his office on his computer, she imagined exactly what he'd been doing yesterday. Maybe he was so quiet because he'd had a marvelous afternoon and evening in bed with the redhead. Maybe the redhead had turned his head. Maybe...

Maybe too many things. She was tired of her mind running in circles or supposition playing havoc with her thoughts. Maybe they should just get everything out on the table and then worry about digesting it.

The afternoon seemed tediously slow as she thought about what she could say, what she could ask. Eventually she signed out the last parent and child, and she watched all the teachers leave.

That left her and Hudson. Now was the time.

He was still at his computer, studying the screen as if it held the answers to the universe, when she marched into his office.

He swiveled away from the monitor and gave his attention to her. "Are you leaving?"

"In a minute. First I have something to ask you."

"Go ahead."

"Why did you ignore me all day? Because I'd like to know whether you're keeping your commitment to Just Us Kids or not."

"I didn't ignore you today."

"I don't know what you'd call it. You hardly said two words."

"I have a lot on my mind. My mood had nothing to do with you."

For some reason that conclusion annoyed her more than anything else. It seemed she was becoming of no importance to him. Or was it that he had become too important to her?

Because she wasn't used to caring for a man, because she had too many thoughts spinning around in her head, she blurted out, "Oh, I understand it had nothing to do with me. That's probably because you must have had a spectacular time yesterday with the redhead."

After his brows arched and he leaned back in his desk chair, she realized Hudson looked totally surprised at her outburst. Meeting her gaze directly, he said, "Lunch with that redhead was all about business. Period."

Bella felt a red flush begin at her neck and start to creep up into her cheeks. She felt like an absolute fool, and she couldn't stand here and face Hudson another second. In one continuous motion she left his office, grabbed her coat that she'd laid over her desk chair, as well as her purse from the bottom drawer, and made for the door.

By that time, Hudson was standing in the doorway to his office. "Bella—"

But she couldn't look at him right now. She couldn't talk to him reasonably, not after she'd acted like a foolish teenager, the foolish teenager she'd once been. She rushed out of the day care center and into her car, then pulled away in a burst of speed.

Hudson had two reactions to Bella's sudden departure. The first—he was worried about her. But the second... Was that jealousy he'd detected? If she was jealous, did that mean she cared about him a bit?

He could go after her, but he expected she needed time to calm down, time to realize they were going to have to talk about this eventually. As he walked through the rooms, closing up the place, he realized he'd been wrong when he'd said his mood today had had nothing to do with her. It had actually had a lot to do with her. Yes, their argument. But more than that, everything else that was on his mind, too.

The woman Guy had sent to meet with him was basically his ranch manager; she took care of the books, scheduling, vet appointments, and kept all running smoothly. She had been a looker, that was true. And in the past, Hudson had wanted to look.

This time he didn't.

He hadn't cared at all what she looked like. But he'd

listened to what she'd said, and that had caused him more turmoil. He tried to decide whether he should stay or leave Rust Creek Falls. Point one, did Just Us Kids still need him? The day care center was back on track now, the client base saved, rumors put to rest, the scare of another epidemic almost resolved. Was there a need for him to stay?

He'd told Walker he'd stay until the book project was completed. No, it hadn't been a hard-and-fast promise, but he did always keep his word. Besides, he'd found he actually liked living in Rust Creek Falls, especially at Clive's ranch. But there was one more reason compelling him to stay. And her name was Bella.

Bella drove home, her face still flushed from her encounter with Hudson and her own stupidity. She usually filtered what came out of her mouth. What had happened?

At the ranch house, she jumped out of her car and practically ran inside. This ranch had become a safe haven. But as she stepped over the threshold, she realized it might be safe, but it was noisy, too.

The babies were squalling for their dinner, and Jamie just shook his head. "Paige couldn't come tonight, so I said I could handle them on my own."

She could see that he was trying to, but more than anything, she could see how exhausted her brother was. Slipping out of her coat, she hurried to help him feed the triplets. With two of them catching spills, wiping sticky hands and playing airplane games, they soon had the babies fed. Bathing, however, took a little longer.

By the time they'd settled all three in their cribs and returned downstairs, Jamie looked at Bella with a weak smile. "You didn't get anything to eat."

"I'm not hungry," she said honestly, still remembering what had happened with Hudson. How was she going to live that down?

Her brother's shoulders slumped a bit as he picked up dirty dishes from the table and took them to the sink. She could tell he was practically dead on his feet, and she knew he needed more than a good night's sleep. He needed a break.

She pulled out a kitchen chair and pointed to it. "Sit."

"I have to clean up the kitchen," he reminded her.

"No, you don't. I'll do it. I want to talk to you."

"That sounds ominous," he said as he sat in the chair, obviously too fatigued to argue with her.

"You have to take a break from everything or you're going to collapse." When he started to protest, she held up her hand. "I'm going to ask for Monday off. I want you to call a motel in Kalispell and leave tomorrow morning for a few days. I want you to get some rest while I take charge of the babies and the schedule and the ranch chores."

"You can't do it on your own."

"You're going to have to trust me, Jamie. The baby chain will help with the triplets, and if I need help with the chores I can call our neighbor's son." When he began to protest again, she cut him off. "You're not going to be any good to the triplets or the ranch if you fall over from exhaustion or get sick. You probably haven't had a solid night's sleep since they were born."

"Since they came home," he admitted. "I think I hear them, and I wake up to check, or I worry that I'm not going to hear them."

"Or one of them cries," Bella added. "Believe me, I understand. That's why you have to do this. You have to depend on me as I've always depended on you."

"What about you?" he asked.

"I've actually *had* breaks—like that afternoon I went riding." Like the afternoon she'd slept on Hudson's couch. "I even get a break at work," she added.

"Around all those kids?"

"I don't have direct responsibility for them—the teachers do. I can take my lunch break without worrying or take a walk."

*Or stop in Hudson's office to talk to him*, she thought. But that wasn't going to happen again.

Jamie got quiet. He actually seemed to be considering her offer. Finally he looked at her and said, "I'll only do this if the neighbor boy can come over and help you with the chores."

"Call him and the motel. Any motel you want."

"Just something with a bed would be good," he admitted.

"I'll call Hudson and ask him about Monday." She hoped she'd just get his voice mail.

But that, of course, didn't happen. He answered his cell on the second ring. But before he could say anything, she launched into an explanation.

After a moment's hesitation, Hudson assured her, "No problem. Take the day off. I can cover for you."

"Great," she said, ready to hang up.

"Bella, about this afternoon…"

"I really have to go, Hudson. I think I hear one of the triplets. I'll see you Tuesday."

And before he could say more, she ended the call.

Was it the cowardly way out? Possibly, but she was also buying time. Maybe in a couple of days he'd forget about her outburst. Simply put, it might not have been that important to him. If it wasn't, she was off the hook.

If it was…she'd deal with Hudson on Tuesday.

## Chapter Nine

Hudson knew the longer a misunderstanding went unattended, the more mucked up life could get. That's why he decided to visit Bella on Sunday. He knew a phone call wouldn't do it. If she was taking care of the triplets with Jamie gone, she'd be too busy to focus on a call. Besides, this explanation required face-to-face time. He had a feeling she didn't believe him about his lunch with the redhead being purely business.

Considering the fact she thought he was the love-'em-and-leave-'em type, it was very possible. Love them and leave them. Yep, that's what he'd done in the past. It was easier than getting involved and getting hurt. He'd always made that clear at the outset with whomever he dated. But Bella?

She seemed to turn his world and his perceptions of it upside down.

When he arrived at Jamie's house and stood on the porch outside the door, he still wasn't sure what he was going to say. He did realize, however, that there wasn't another vehicle in the driveway. That was odd since the baby chain always helped on weekends as well as during the week. Hudson was aware of the sound of squalling babies from inside. Two of them, if he could make out the sounds. He rang the doorbell and heard Bella's voice.

"Oh my gosh, Paige, I'm so glad you could make it after all."

Then she opened the door and saw Hudson.

The baby in Bella's arms was squirming and squiggling and obviously wanted to be let down. He was squalling as loud as his little lungs would allow.

"Which one is this?" Hudson yelled above the din.

Though obviously surprised at his presence, Bella answered reflexively, "Henry."

More crying came from inside the living room. Looking past Bella, Hudson could see a baby dressed all in pink, so he supposed it was Katie, wailing with the best of them. She was seated in a play saucer, but that definitely wasn't occupying her.

He reached out and said, "Give me Henry. You go take care of Katie."

Bella didn't seem sure she wanted to give up the little boy, so Hudson took matters into his own hands. He reached for Henry with a big smile. "Come on, fella. You and I have to talk."

The baby reached his arms out to Hudson, and Hudson took him, raising the baby's face to his own. "You'll get ahead in life better if you don't scream so much. Come on, let's figure out what's wrong."

Hudson walked Henry into the living room and saw the third triplet, Jared, sitting in a playpen playing with blocks. The only cooperative one in the bunch.

Henry had obviously been surprised by Hudson lifting him and talking to him. His cries subsided into hiccups until Hudson settled him into the crook of his arm. Then Henry started all over again.

Puzzled, Hudson jiggled him a bit. "What? Wet diaper? Hungry? Bored? You'll have to tell me."

Henry stopped crying as if he was considering it, and Hudson stuck his finger into the boy's diaper. "He's wet," he called to Bella. "Where are the diapers?"

Bella motioned to a changing table on the other side of the room, and Hudson went that way. He'd learned a thing or two working at the day care center. There, one had to be a man of all trades, so to speak. He not only learned how to change diapers, but also how to give belly rubs and tickle toes. Anything to get a baby to do what you wanted him to do.

Grabbing hold of a rubber ducky on the changing table, he laid Henry down and handed it to him. "You play with this while we take care of business."

By this time Bella had taken Katie out of the play saucer. The little girl had stopped crying as soon as Bella lifted her into her arms.

Now that Henry was concentrating on the rubber ducky, and Katie was quiet, Bella asked Hudson, "What are you doing here?"

"We need to talk." He unsnapped Henry's jeans and took off the wet diaper. "But more important, why don't you have any help today?"

"Fallon caught a flu bug she didn't want to give to the babies. Paige and the others couldn't cover because of church functions or holiday gatherings. Paige said she'd get here as soon as she could."

Hudson fumbled a bit with the dry diaper. He wasn't as adept at it as Bella or the teachers and aides at the day care center. The sticky tab caught on his thumb, bent over and stuck to itself. But somehow he managed to diaper Henry, even if it was a little lopsided.

"I was going to give them a snack," Bella said. "Maybe we can talk if we can get them all eating a cookie at the same time."

"Sounds good," Hudson agreed, snapping Henry's jeans and pulling down his little shirt. When he hefted Henry into his arms, the little boy gave him what Hudson thought was a smile. Hudson felt as if he'd accomplished something big.

After he carried Henry into the kitchen and settled him into a high chair, Bella did the same with Katie. Then she hurried back into the living room to gather up Jared. Soon the triplets were gnawing on cookies.

Bella turned to him. "Would you like something to drink? Soda, milk, juice?"

"Milk would be fine. I'm still a growing boy."

Bella shook her head and gave him a small smile as she went to the refrigerator, poured two glasses of milk and set them on the table.

Hudson was thinking about the best way to start when she plunged in first. "I'm sorry I reacted as I did on Friday. I had no right."

Hudson decided to ignore her remark about her rights. Instead, he said, "Tell me why you reacted as you did."

"Because of what Marla Tillotson said."

After she finished explaining, Hudson pressed,

"And why did that bother you so much? That I might have been having lunch with a redhead."

Bella suddenly gave all her attention to Katie, wiping a few crumbs from her cheek. "Hudson…"

"All right, I'll let that go for now. But let me explain the whole situation to you. Guy sent his ranch manager—who just happens to be a pretty redhead—to convince me he needs me in Big Timber. Apparently he thought she could do a better job at it than he could."

"Because you like pretty redheads?" Bella asked seriously.

Hudson knew a little honesty might go a long way with Bella. "In the past, I've been known to have my head turned by a pretty woman. Guy witnessed that."

"Why does he think you're the right person for this job? Exactly what is it?" Bella asked, moving away from the topic.

"Last season, one of the ranch's patrons had an accident. Guy took an economic hit over it. He had clients cancel their reservations. They're trying to get past it. They've seen how I turned around the reputation of Just Us Kids, and they want me to do that for them."

"Are you going to take the job?"

Hudson couldn't tell from Bella's voice or her expression whether she cared personally or professionally.

He said honestly, "I don't know. Just Us Kids really doesn't need me any longer. Guy is a friend. But any PR firm could help him."

Before she could respond, Bella's phone emitted a lively ringtone. Hesitating only a second, she took it from her shirt pocket and studied the screen. "It's Jamie. I need to take this. Excuse me."

He gave her a wink. "I'll watch this tribe while you talk."

She answered the call. "Hi, Jamie... Everything's fine... I told you, you don't need to check every few hours."

Even though Jamie was taking a break, Hudson realized he still had the triplets and Bella on his mind. Of course he'd be checking in often.

"We're good. Order room service. Eat a lot. Sleep, and watch mindless TV. That's an order."

Her brother said something that made her laugh. "Yes, that is a change, isn't it? Really, we're good. And I don't want to hear from you again until you come home tomorrow night. Fine. I'll text you after they're all settled in for the night. And I'll give them extra kisses from you. See you tomorrow."

Ending the call, she pocketed the phone once more.

"I admire your loyalty to your brother," he said sincerely.

Bella went to the refrigerator and pulled out a casserole dish. She showed it to Hudson. "Cherry cobbler. Our volunteers bring casseroles and desserts when they come. Would you like some?"

"Sure," Hudson agreed. "That will go great with milk."

Efficiently Bella microwaved two dishes of cobbler and brought them to the table. She sat across from him, the babies between them.

Despite everything, Hudson felt a connection to Bella, a connection that was growing stronger. Just now, when she'd offered him this snack, it was as if she'd made a decision of sorts, and he wondered what was coming.

She stirred her cobbler a bit, forgot about her spoon and looked him straight in the eyes. "Jamie and I have been a team for years."

"Anyone can see that," Hudson commented, lost in her face, the point of her chin, the tilt of her cheek bones, the brown of her eyes.

"We became a team for a reason."

"Your parents died. That brought you closer together," Hudson said. She'd already told him that.

"That wasn't the only reason we became a team. We have five other siblings—Luke, Daniel, Dana, Bailey and Liza."

Hudson was stunned. He didn't know what to say. But then he remarked, "No one in town mentioned it."

"Anyone who knows us respects what we've been through. They know we've had a lot of heartache, and some of that is due to not having any contact with our other siblings."

"Why not?"

"After our parents' accident, we were split apart. Dana and Liza were sent away and adopted because they were younger. Our grandparents considered me and Jamie too young to be involved, and they didn't tell us much about it. Luke, Daniel and Bailey were over eighteen and considered adults. Our grandparents said they couldn't handle more mouths to feed, so the three boys left town. They were just as traumatized by our parents' deaths even though they were older. On top of that, I think they were bitter and resentful that my grandparents essentially kicked them out on their own."

"Have you tried contacting them?"

"I've tried. Not directly, of course, because I don't know where any of them are. But I've used search engines. I haven't had any luck."

"And none of them have ever contacted you?"

Hudson could see the anguish on Bella's face as she shook her head. "It hurts," she said. "Jamie has never left Rust Creek Falls, and I've been here except for college. It would be easy to find us. But apparently they don't want to. That's why Jamie and I have been as close as we are."

Finally Hudson thought he understood the depth of Bella's loneliness. As much as he and his brothers squabbled, they stayed connected. Reaching out, he covered her hand with his. "I'm sorry for all you've lost."

"I don't need anyone's pity," she said quietly. "That's why Jamie and I don't talk about it."

"Thank you for confiding in me. That means you trust me."

Bella looked as if she might say more, but then she pushed her chair back and stood. "Maybe we can settle this crew down for a nap. Getting them all quiet and sleeping at the same time could be an impossible feat, but we can try. That is, if you can stay. If you can't, I understand."

Hudson wasn't going anywhere, not until he was sure Bella could handle what she'd taken on.

Although they worked together at the day care center, Bella was surprised to find they also seemed to work well around the babies in the kitchen. She couldn't help sneaking peeks at Hudson as he wiped Henry's mouth or as he plucked a piece of cookie from Katie's hair. He was big and tall, but he was gentle and caring. He was almost as good around the babies as Jamie was.

When he'd thanked her for trusting him, she'd almost told him about her pregnancy and the baby she'd miscarried. She almost told him that she loved taking care of Jamie's babies because she might never have any of her own. Watching Hudson with Katie and Jared and Henry, she could easily see he'd want kids of his own someday.

She thought again about the job offer he'd received. Another good reason not to confide in him. There was no point. Whether she trusted him or not, whether he was attracted to her or not, he was most likely going to be leaving again. Rust Creek Falls was just a stopover in his nomadic lifestyle.

To her surprise, Henry was the baby who quieted first. After they laid him in his crib, he stuck his thumb in his mouth, and his eyes soon closed. It took longer for Katie and Jared. She and Hudson walked them and rocked them until finally they both dozed off. After settling them in their cribs, Bella gave Hudson a smile as they left the room and went downstairs.

In the living room, she made sure the monitor was turned on. "They could wake up in five minutes," she told Hudson.

"Or they could give you a break for at least a half hour or maybe longer."

"Do you always see the world in positive terms?" she asked.

"I try to. But then most of my life has been pretty positive. My family might not be all I want it to be, but I have one. I've never had to think about money. I can pretty much go where I want to go and do what I want. I'm grateful for all that. Every day at the day care center I see single moms struggling and dads working two jobs. I look at folks who were hit by the flood here and what they've lost. I can't help but be grateful for what I have."

"I like your outlook," Bella said.

He stepped closer to her. "Is that all you like?"

She tried to keep the moment light. "I could make a list," she teased.

"And I could make a list of everything I like about you. It would be a long one."

He was right there now, close to her. He loomed over her, but she didn't feel intimidated. In fact, everything about Hudson being near her excited her. Feelings surged through her that almost made her reach for him. When she thought about that redhead, she hated the idea of Hudson kissing another woman, holding another woman, making love to another woman. Bella wanted to *be* that woman.

He must have seen the hunger in her eyes because he took her into his arms and kissed her. His lips were unerringly masculine, supremely masterful, absolutely intoxicating. His arms held her a little tighter, and she pressed closer. His scent, man and aftershave, was intoxicating. He was so ultimately sexy. As they kissed, her hand came up to his cheek, and her fingers trailed over beard stubble. When he groaned, she felt as if she'd accomplished a monumental feat.

As if he wanted to accomplish that same feat, he laced his fingers in her hair. He swept his tongue through her mouth until she had no breath left for anything but Hudson. They kept tasting each other as if they could never get enough and gave in to desire that they'd denied for weeks. He backed her up, and she knew what was behind them—the sofa. She didn't protest or even think about refusing. Her head might know better, but her heart wanted Hudson...wanted him in a primal way.

They'd almost reached their destination...

Then the doorbell rang.

It took a few moments for Bella to realize someone was at the door. She tore away from Hudson, her head spinning, her mouth throbbing from his kiss, her senses filled with him.

"I have to get that," she murmured. "It could be... anyone."

No, she definitely couldn't think straight. That was for sure.

Hudson's eyes held a glazed look, too, and she wondered if he'd been as into that kiss as she had been. Was that even possible? Had she lost her mind? She'd just listed all the reasons she shouldn't confide in him and couldn't get involved with him.

Then what had she done?

She'd kissed him.

To her dismay, that hadn't been an ordinary kiss. That had been a lead-to-something-else kiss.

The doorbell rang again, and she practically ran to

the foyer and pulled open the door. She was so glad to see Paige's face.

But Paige took one look at Bella and asked, "Is something wrong?"

"Oh, no. No," Bella assured her, pulling her inside. "I thought you couldn't get here this soon."

"Our meeting ended earlier than I thought it would. How are you coping?"

"Oh, I'm coping just fine. In fact, Hudson's here. He helped me put the triplets to bed. Believe it or not, they're actually all napping."

Paige was giving her an are-you-sure-I'm-not-interrupting-something look.

But Bella kept shaking her head. "Come on in. I can use your help. Jamie called, and I convinced him I had everything under control." She prattled on, filling the air with chitchat, which was so unlike her.

Paige knew that, and Hudson did, too. But she had to do something to cover up that kiss, to process it, to absorb the way she felt when Hudson kissed her.

By the time she and Paige were inside the living room, Hudson had seemed to compose himself, too. He'd taken his Stetson off the table where he'd laid it when he'd come in and plopped it onto his head.

To Bella he said, "It looks as if you have reinforcements, so I'll be on my way. Nice to see you, Paige."

"Good to see you, too, Hudson."

There was an awkward silence until Bella offered, "I'll walk you out. Paige, I'll be right back. The monitor's on."

It would have been easier and less awkward if Bella had just let Hudson leave. But she'd just have to face him when she returned to work if she didn't deal with their kiss now.

He stepped out onto the porch and then turned to look at her. They were eye level. "It seemed right," he simply said, and she knew what he meant. Everything about that kiss had seemed right.

"Maybe, but I'm glad Paige interrupted. We both need time to think."

He shook his head. "Maybe we should stop thinking and just feel."

"Hudson, there's still a lot you don't know about me."

"So tell me."

If she did that, she'd be plunging into the unknown. If she did that, she'd be asking for rejection. Impulsively, she leaned forward and gave Hudson a light kiss on the lips.

"I'll see you at work on Tuesday morning," she said.

He looked as if he wanted to take her into his arms again, but she backed up, and he seemed to understand. He nodded. "See you Tuesday morning."

When Bella closed the door, she couldn't help but imagine exactly what would have happened if Paige hadn't arrived.

Hudson was out of sorts. When he arrived back at the Lazy B, he went straight to the barn. After a stop at the tack room, he saddled up Breeze, mounted and took a path through the fields where the snow had melted. He needed a horse under him, the wind in his face, the cold against his skin.

As he rode, he realized he just hadn't been able to

go into the empty ranch house. The reason? He wanted Bella there with him. He wasn't sure yet what all that entailed, but he knew he wanted to make a few of his dreams come true—the ones that included Bella in his bed. If they hadn't been interrupted this afternoon, they would have had sex on that couch. The thing was, if Paige hadn't interrupted them, one of the babies might have. That would have been even more awkward.

When he made love to Bella, he wanted no interruptions and no one interfering. He wanted their attention to be focused on just the two of them. He also wanted Bella to be sure…to want him as much as he wanted her. To his surprise, that wasn't just about lust. It wasn't just about the fun they could have in the sheets, the satisfaction of two bodies coming together. No, these feelings went deeper. He felt protective toward Bella. He didn't want her to be confused or unsure. Most of all, he didn't want to hurt her. If they shared a bed, they'd both have to do it freely. Consequences and the future be damned.

The problem was, he'd never felt protective like this about a woman before. He'd never cared about her dreams, her insecurities, her past. He cared about all of that with Bella. She'd lost her parents, her brothers and sisters. He could understand why she wouldn't want to willingly lose any more.

He didn't want to lose anything either…especially not his freedom. He felt vulnerable and didn't like that at all. He didn't like the idea that a woman could cause upset or joy or create a hunger he just had to satisfy.

Bella confused him. That was a first, and he'd like it to be a last.

He had no idea what he was going to do about any of it.

## *Chapter Ten*

Hudson could fry himself a burger. He could even flip an omelet. What he couldn't usually do was bake. But he'd missed Bella at Just Us Kids, as did everyone else, and he wanted to bake something to welcome her back on Tuesday. She did so much for the teachers, the parents and especially the children, making them feel comforted and loved. In essence, she was the poster girl for Just Us Kids. More than that, she was the heart.

At first he hadn't known what to do that would be special yet not over-the-top. He'd nixed flowers right away. Spending tons of money on every rare flower there was and filling her desk with them was too showy and too impersonal. Besides, he wanted to show her another side of him—one that could be caring in ways that counted rather than only spending money.

After consulting a clerk at the grocery store, he found a box of what she said were never-fail cupcakes. He had to do cupcakes, of course, so they could pass them out and share them with the kids. She showed him the muffin pans to buy and colorful little cups. After one look at him, and hearing his woe that he'd never made icing in his life, let alone a cake, she showed him canned icing. That would have to do.

Before he took all his supplies to the checkout, she asked, "Why don't you just buy cupcakes or a cake from the bakery? We'd decorate it really nice and even put her name on it."

But Hudson just shook his head. "That's not the same thing at all. I don't want to buy the cupcakes. I want to make them for her."

The woman gave him a wink and a nod as if she understood, and Hudson left with his purchases, full of hope.

Actually the baking went fairly well, except for a few spills when he poured the batter. The icing, however, was something different. When he realized he'd bought only white and pink, he decided to swirl it and get a little fancy with it. White with a pink swirl, pink with a white swirl. At the end of his project, he had to admit he would never be a cake decorator. But the cupcakes looked presentable, and that's what mattered.

He left early for the day care center, in plenty of time to hang the pink-and-white crepe paper the store clerk had told him would be a good decoration. He wanted everything ready before anyone else arrived.

And he was ready. As the teachers filed in, he was glad Bella wasn't among them. He wanted as many teachers and kids here as possible before she came through that door.

All of the teachers were there and some of the children, too, when she came in, saw the decorations and the big sign that said Welcome Back, Bella. Her mouth dropped open.

KAREN ROSE SMITH 155

Her gaze went to Sarah, but Sarah just shrugged. "Not our doing." She pointed to Hudson.

One of the other teachers, Joyce Croswell, pointed to the cupcakes. "And just look at those. He made them, too." Her gaze went from Bella to Hudson, as if everyone should realize something more was going on than boss and day care center manager.

Bella looked absolutely paralyzed for a moment, but then she recovered and smiled. "I don't know what to say." She went over to Hudson, threw her arms around him and gave him a huge hug. "No one's ever done anything like this for me before. And I was only gone one day."

"Bella Stockton," he said seriously, loud enough for everyone to hear, "you make this place go round. We all felt the length of the day you were gone because you weren't here to experience it with us. We missed your smile and your energy and your caring, and we just wanted to let you know."

Bella looked close to tears now, and he hadn't wanted that. "Come on," he said. "Taste one of the cupcakes, then everyone else can have one, too. I made enough to go around." He took one of the paper plates they used for snacks with the kids and placed one of the pink cupcakes on it. Then he handed it to her. She studied the cupcake with its little white swirl on the top.

They were standing quite close together now, and she murmured again, "I can't believe you went to all this trouble."

"No trouble, Bella, not for you. Not to show you that I think about you and I care about you." He didn't think anyone else had heard what he'd just said, but he could see in Bella's eyes that she had.

"Aw, Hudson."

The door flew open, and two moms and their babies came in. Their special moment was gone.

"I'd better wait to eat this until I can really enjoy it," Bella told him.

"Lunchtime?" he asked.

"Sure, if no crisis erupts. But at least I can taste the icing." Taking her finger, she swiped at the white point on top of the cupcake. He watched her as she slowly placed it on her lip. Her tongue came out, licking the confection, and she closed her eyes and smiled. "It's sweet, Hudson, just like icing should be."

"It came from a can," he said, now wishing he had tried to make it himself.

"It's the thought that counts. It's pretty and it tastes good, and it's perfect on the cupcakes. I'll have a lot more than that little taste at lunchtime. I promise."

Rattled by the sheer sensuality of watching her lick that icing with her tongue, he almost broke into a sweat. Composing himself, he took trays of cupcakes to each classroom and passed them out to the children who were old enough to have them. The others he took to the break room, protecting them with a plastic covering. Then he waited for lunchtime.

Bella had seen that look in Hudson's eyes—the one that excited her. She was never so happy it was finally lunchtime. When she went to the break room, he was already there. Apparently Greta had made him some kind of casserole he could warm up in the microwave.

He had the flowered dish in front of him, and he was forking pasta with ground beef into his mouth.

He stopped when she brought her bagged lunch and a paper plate to the table. "If you'd like something hot, I'll share. There's plenty here."

"I'm fine with this." She nodded at her turkey sandwich. But as she ate it, the smell of the casserole made her mouth water. He must have seen her eyeing it because he took her paper plate and forked some of the casserole onto it. Then he gave her another fork that had been sitting beside his dish.

"Did you expect company?" she asked.

"Sure did. I want to make sure you enjoy your cupcake." And before the electricity zipping between them got a little too hot, he asked, "How's Jamie?"

"He looks better, and he seems rested. I think the time away did him good."

"And you survived," he said with respect in his voice.

"I did...with help. Including yours."

His visit to the ranch house brought to mind that kiss. That kiss she'd never forget.

After that, they made small talk about the day care center while they ate. When they'd both finished, Hudson rose, chose two cupcakes from the tray and brought one over to Bella.

"Coffee with that?" he asked.

"Sure." She'd never had a man serve her cupcakes and coffee before. This was truly a first.

He took milk from the refrigerator and poured just the amount she liked into her mug, then set it on the table. He poured a black coffee for himself.

Trying to be ladylike, she took the paper from the cupcake and then used her fork to take one bite, and then another. "These are really good. Maybe you can give Greta a run for her money in the baking department."

He ate his cupcake in three bites, then responded, "I doubt that. This was just a lucky first try. Or maybe I just had good motivation."

Her fork stopped halfway to her mouth. They gazed at each other, and Bella's heart beat so fast she could hardly swallow.

He leaned forward and with his forefinger touched the top of her lip. "You have some icing there," he said. His touch held fire, and she couldn't help wishing it was his lips that were meeting hers.

"I'd kiss you again," he said, as if reading her thoughts, "but that wouldn't be proper at the workplace."

With Hudson looking at her with those bedroom eyes of his, proper didn't seem to have a place in her world. Should she be fighting this attraction? What if she just gave in to it and enjoyed it? Enjoyed herself with a man? Maybe for the first time ever.

"I should get back to my desk," she murmured, to put that very temptation out of her mind.

But before she could rise to her feet, Hudson covered her hand with his. "Look, I don't know what you've heard about me or my reputation, but I don't just go around kissing random women."

She didn't know what to say to that, so she waited for Hudson to go on.

He cleared his throat, as if putting his feelings into

words was hard for him. "You're such a pretty woman. I'm sure lots of men want to kiss you."

Considering her history and her situation, nothing could be further from the truth. Most of the men in town now considered her standoffish. That was ironic considering her wild teenage years when she was anything but. She couldn't help but laugh wryly at his comment.

But when she did, Hudson leaned away, took his hand from hers and seemed to be insulted. She knew he was when he asked, "Do you consider my kissing you amusing, or our kisses just a joke?"

Anything but. He actually looked a bit vulnerable, and she wondered if she'd hurt him. Could he really care about her?

"I'm just botching this and making a fool of myself," he said, standing.

But before he could stride out of the room, she hopped to her feet and caught his arm. "I didn't mean to laugh, but you don't know—"

"I know how much I'm attracted to you. Are you attracted to me?"

She gave a small nod, and suddenly she was in his arms and he was kissing her again. It was a short kiss, though a deep, wet one.

He set her away from him. "I know you're worried about your job. Considering what happened with my brother and Lindsay, I understand your concern. Believe me. But there are no repercussions with what's going on with us here. You can walk away, and your job will still be safe. I've wanted you for weeks, but I understand that you're young, and I'll back off if that's what you want."

She was deeply touched by everything he'd said because she could see he meant it all. She could also see something else. Because she was young, he could possibly believe she was a virgin, that she was inexperienced. She had to be honest with him and set him straight.

"Hudson, this isn't my first rodeo."

He looked a bit surprised at her comment, so she went on. "You've been on my mind for weeks, too. I have so many decisions to make in my life. Helping Jamie is one of them, and I don't know how long he'll need me. And you're right about my needing this job here. I do. But I also want to go back to school soon. Everything is in flux, so I was trying not to add something else to complicate my life."

"You think I'd complicate your life?" Hudson asked with a crooked smile.

"I don't think it. I'm sure of it. But the more I get to know you, the more I want the complication...the more I want *you*."

His eyes darkened with that unsettling hunger again. He seemed to take in a deep breath, as if he was reminding himself not to hurry anything. "After work, do you want to come back to my place?"

If she answered him affirmatively, she knew exactly what she was agreeing to. Her hand on his arm, she looked up at him with the wanting in her eyes.

She said simply, "Yes."

Hours later as Bella parked in back of Hudson's vehicle and they walked together to the ranch house door, he realized how surprised he'd been at her remark that this wasn't her first rodeo. He'd really thought she might be a virgin, not only because of her age, but because of her demeanor. But apparently he'd been wrong. Had she been hurt terribly by someone and that's why she held back?

After they entered the foyer, they were a bit awkward with each other. He wasn't going to just jump her bones, or rip her clothes off, or carry her to his bed, even though he wanted to do all three. More than anything, he wanted to do this right. Though he wasn't sure why that was so important.

He motioned to the great room. "Would you like something to drink?" he asked. "It might break the ice so we don't feel so rattled."

She smiled at that. "Something to drink would be nice."

"Hot chocolate, coffee, tea?" He wasn't going to suggest wine because he didn't want their senses dulled. He wanted to be aware of absolutely every moment tonight.

"Hot chocolate would be great." Looking nervous, she glanced around the room. Her eyes lit on the photo albums under the coffee table. "I saw these when I was here the last time. Do they belong to Mr. Bickler?"

"No, they don't. They're mine. Believe it or not, I take them wherever I go. Sometimes in a bunkhouse I might not have much else than my boots and my jeans and my sheepskin, and my Stetson. But keeping these with me when I travel helps me stay grounded. I remember I have a family, and I had a home where I grew up. It's just a way of remembering my roots."

"Do you mind if I page through them?"

He thought about that. "No, I don't mind. You'll have a good laugh at some of the pictures in there. They're candid shots, nothing like the photos you take."

"Candid shots are sometimes the best ones." She unzipped her parka, shrugged out of it and laid it over one of the chairs. Hudson felt himself relax. This evening was going to be everything he wanted it to be.

Hudson had learned hot chocolate was almost as important as hot coffee on a cold winter night. He'd become somewhat of a connoisseur and used a mix he special-ordered. Minutes later he carried in two mugs topped by a mound of whipped cream and sat on the sofa beside Bella, putting the mugs onto coasters.

She looked at the hot drink and smiled. "How did you know I liked whipped cream?"

"Just a good guess, I imagine."

She had a photograph album open on her lap. There were photos of him and his brothers as kids. His parents were in a few of them, but it was mostly just them.

"You and your brothers are *all* handsome," she murmured. She pointed to one of the pictures. "Who is who?"

He pointed to each in succession. "That's Autry, Gideon, Jensen and, of course, Walker."

Then she pointed to another picture. "Your mom and dad?"

"Yes."

Hudson's mother looked guarded in that particular photo. His father looked as imposing as ever with a shock of white hair and cold blue eyes. Yet Hudson knew he definitely bore a resemblance to them.

"You look like him—the same jaw, the same high forehead," she noted, mirroring his thoughts.

"I might look like him, but I hope we're different in lots of ways. He and Walker are more alike, all about business and money, maybe even power. Maybe that's why I took a left turn when they took a right."

"Do you respect them?"

"I respect Walker for what he's accomplished. And now he seems a bit different with Lindsay, as if he knows what matters. But my dad, maybe he's just been with the wrong woman all his life and they don't make each other happy. Or maybe they just don't want to work at it."

"I think about my parents often," Bella admitted. "If they had lived, I wonder if the Stocktons would be a close family. Would they have kept us all connected?" She looked up at Hudson. "The way it sounds, you and Walker might be different, but you *are* connected. That's why you're here helping him."

"That's why *you're* helping Jamie."

She nodded her agreement as she sipped the hot chocolate. He saw the whipped cream that gathered on her upper lip and suppressed the urge to lick it off. *Don't rush this. Let her get comfortable. You'll know when she wants you just as much as you want her.*

At least he hoped he would.

Bella placed her mug down as she swiped at her lips. "I have some good memories from before my parents died."

"Tell me," he encouraged her.

"There was this lake where Mom and Dad took us to go swimming. It had a grassy, stony shore, and the older kids would help the younger kids wade in. We had the best times there in the summers, swimming and picnicking. Jamie and I don't talk about those days much because it hurts to think about them. I guess because we miss our siblings. Yet I know remembering would be good for us, too."

Hudson pointed to a photo in the album. "I remember Walker and me being rivals at a lot of things. Roping a calf was one of them. Neither of us was very good at it at first, but our rivalry made us better."

Bella pointed to another photo of him inside a grand room. The Christmas tree he stood before had to be at least ten feet tall. "That's a beautiful tree."

"Mother always had a decorator come in and do the trees, along with other Christmas decorations. That's far different from a tree I'd like to bring in here for the holiday."

"What do you have in mind?"

"I want to go cut it myself and put it right over there." He pointed to a spot by the window. "When I told Greta I wanted to do that, she said she has a box of hand-crocheted white ornaments that she'd made one year for their tree. She has others that she uses now and she said I could have the crocheted ones if I'd like. I *would* like to use them, with lots of tiny lights."

"I'm sure the kids at Just Us Kids would make you ornaments if you asked them."

"I'm sure they would."

Suddenly it seemed that both of them had run out of conversation. Hudson couldn't take his eyes from Bella's, and it seemed Bella couldn't take hers from his. He slowly circled her with his arm and moved closer.

He could smell her floral perfume, like flowers in the middle of winter. Everything about Bella was sweet and pure. Sweeter and purer than he deserved.

"You can still change your mind," he whispered. And he meant it. He wanted nothing about tonight to be uncertain.

"I don't want to change my mind," she said with a small smile that made him ache even more with desire for her.

When he bent his head to her, when his lips captured hers, he felt possessive. He knew his mouth was claiming, and that's the way he wanted it. He wanted Bella to be his. He'd never been so in the moment with a woman before. He was excruciatingly aware of the softness of her skin as he stroked her cheek, the taste of chocolate on her tongue, the small moan that escaped her as they kissed. He gathered her into his arms and wondered how in the heck he was ever going to make it to the bedroom.

"I should have turned on the fireplace," he said when he broke for air.

"Or we could just keep warm under the covers," she suggested softly.

That did it. He rose to his feet and gathered her up into his arms. When he carried her to the bedroom, he felt like a caveman. Somehow Bella made him feel as if he could accomplish anything.

In his bedroom, he settled her on his bed. He found he didn't want to let her go even for a second. So he sat beside her, kissed her again and decided their clothes had to go.

"Light or dark?" he asked her before he started, curious as to what she'd say. The room was in shadows now, and they could hardly see each other's faces even with the hall light glowing.

"Let's turn on the light," she said. "I want to see your face."

Her response pleased him. Loving her in the light meant she felt free about what they were going to do. She felt right about being with him. There was no reason for darkness or shadows or hiding what they were feeling.

After he switched on the bedside lamp and fumbled with a condom packet from the drawer, he reached for her. Not long after, their clothes were on the floor and he'd turned back the covers and rolled on the condom. They were naked on the steel-gray sheets, and he soaked in the beauty of Bella's body.

"Are you cold?" he asked.

"No. Every time you touch me I feel like I'm on fire."

"Same here."

He palmed her breast, wanting her to be ready for him in every way. She moaned, and he kissed her again, this time covering her body with his. He ran his hand up her thigh and then teased her until she wrapped her legs around him.

"I can't wait," he said.

"I'm ready," she whispered.

And just like that, he was inside Bella and he felt as if he'd come home.

She held on to him tightly, but when he kissed her again, he was aware of tears on her cheeks.

"Bella?"

"It's wonderful. *You're* wonderful."

Her words drove him to prolong each stroke, to kiss her more passionately, to touch her everywhere he could. He held off his own pleasure until he felt her body tense, until he heard her cry his name, until she clung to him as if she'd never let him go.

Then he gave in and knew pleasure as he'd never known it before. With Bella in his arms, he felt as if he'd conquered the world.

## *Chapter Eleven*

Bella awoke slowly, realizing where she was and whom she was with. Hudson's arms surrounded her as she lay on her side with him spooned against her. She held no illusions about what had happened last night. She had no expectations. Disappointed before, she didn't want to hope. Yet she couldn't help but remember each kiss, each touch, each word they'd exchanged.

She ran her hand lightly over the hair on his forearm, knowing in her soul that Hudson's strength was more than skin-deep. She admired the man. No, she more than admired him. She'd tumbled over a cliff and fallen in love with him.

Love. How long had it been since she'd known love from anyone other than her brother?

However, she suspected Hudson's feelings didn't run as deep. She'd learned the hard way that men's sexual desire often dictated their actions. Certainly Hudson was no exception. Wanting her and loving her were two entirely different things.

She thought Hudson was still asleep, but a light nip on her shoulder told her that he wasn't.

Could she face him and the fact that one night might have been enough for him? After last night, how would they react to each other at Just Us Kids? She'd followed her heart and now felt foolish.

She started to inch toward the edge of the king-size bed. Better to leave than to face the awkward conversation that told her it was over before it had begun.

But she didn't get very far. Hudson's arm tugged her back to him. He moved over a bit so she could turn to her back, and now she had no choice but to face him.

"Where do you think you're going?" he asked.

"I have to get dressed and go back to the ranch."

"It's not even sunrise," Hudson reminded her.

"When babies are hungry, they don't care if the sun's up or not. I told Jamie I'd be home this morning to help him."

Hudson studied her, then removed his arm from around her. "Do you want to go?"

Just what was Hudson asking her? To be vulnerable and lay her feelings out on the bed? She didn't know if she could do that. "I thought you'd want me to leave."

He stroked a wisp of hair behind her ear. "I don't want you to leave. If it was up to me, we'd stay here all day. I know we can't. We need to talk about how we're going to handle our relationship in public."

She felt heart-tugging joy that he wanted a relationship. Was it possible she could dream again and have that dream come true?

"We should probably keep this—" she motioned to

the bed and everything that had gone on there "—a secret."

"I thought you might say that, but I disagree. We have to think about our situation realistically. I would agree, no public displays of affection at work, even though at times I don't know how I'm going to resist kissing you."

She felt a blush start to creep into her cheeks.

He leaned forward, possessively captured her lips and said good-morning in a way that had her tingling all over.

When he broke the kiss and backed away, he asked, "See what I mean? You smile that certain way and I just want to pull you into my arms. I won't do that at work, but I don't want to be secret about us being together either. If someone sees you here, so be it. We're consenting adults. What we do on our off time is no one's business but ours."

"I don't know how much off time we'll have," she said honestly. "Yes, Jamie has help, and Fallon stayed late last night because he asked her to, but I can't do that often. I can't leave him in the lurch."

"Then I guess we'll just have to steal as much time as we can in between, including lunch hours. My truck is roomy, and the heat we generate should counteract the cold weather, don't you think?"

The idea of a quickie with Hudson was as exciting as spending all day here with him. His crooked grin told her he wasn't just daring her to have sex with him in the truck. He was serious about it.

"And just where would we park your truck?"

"Oh, believe me, I'd find us a secluded spot. And

the falls aren't so far out of town that we couldn't make it there and back in an hour. If we put our minds to being together, we *can* be."

He slid a hand under her and nudged her in his direction.

"You did say we were two consenting adults," she drawled coyly. "And we could practice for that truck rendezvous."

With a low growl, he grabbed a condom packet from the nightstand. After she helped him roll it on, he pulled her on top of him, then ran his hands down her bare back. She could feel him against her, fully aroused and ready whenever she was. Maybe that's why he wanted her on top, so she could set the pace. This morning her pace would be as fast as his. She slid back and forth against him until he groaned.

"Keep that up and this will be the shortest rendezvous on record."

"Practice makes perfect," she teased and rubbed against him again.

"Bella, really, if you don't stop—"

"I'm not going to stop," she warned him. "I'm as ready as you are."

One look into her eyes and he was assured of that fact.

She rose up on her knees and then guided him inside her. She watched pleasure overtake him. Her orgasm came quickly, surprising her.

"We're not done yet," he said as he continued to stroke her. As she kept riding him, she found her body tightening all over again, the tension mounting till she thought she'd go wild. He pulled her down on him, and together they climaxed in a thunderous orgasm.

"Was that quick enough for you?" she asked after she'd collapsed on him.

"*Quick* enough but not *nearly* enough," he responded, and she smiled against his chest.

Hudson felt shaken up, off balance, unsettled and definitely out of his depth. Making love with Bella had blown his mind, and he couldn't seem to sort his thoughts or his feelings. He felt rattled to his core, though he thought he'd hidden it well. He'd tried to be practical about the whole thing. But now at work, catching glimpses of Bella now and then, he just wanted to pull her into his arms and take her to bed again.

Would they be able to work together? He wasn't sure. He had to think about their relationship at work, but he wasn't considering much more than that. The job in Big Timber? Bella's commitment to her brother? His own wanderlust? The questions seemed too big to fit into the mix right then.

Though it was the day before Thanksgiving and many of the kids were home with their families, it was almost noon by the time Bella left her desk. She came into his office, and he braced himself for the feelings that came rushing back when he saw her.

"Are you busy?" she asked.

"No more than usual. What can I do for you?" He hadn't meant the question to have a sexual undertone, but it seemed to.

She blushed a little. "We could talk about that later," she said and gave him a big smile.

He laughed, and that broke the tension—tension that had been caused by mind-blowing sex and possibly the consequences of it. But he didn't want to cut off whatever was happening between them, and apparently she didn't either.

"Jamie has help tonight, so I'm free...free for a few hours. I thought we could spend some time together."

When he didn't answer right away, she hurried to say, "It's okay if you don't want to. I just thought I'd ask." She turned to leave his office.

But he was out of his chair before she could reach the door and blocked her way. "You didn't even give me a chance to think about it."

"I didn't want to put you on the spot. It's okay if you have other things to do."

He was aware of where they were, in his office with glass windows, and teachers and kids not far away. So it wasn't as if he could hold her and reassure her.

"How would you like to put up a Christmas tree with me?" he asked.

"Really?"

He nodded. "Since we're closing early today, we'll have enough light to find one to cut down. Then I'll set it up. I have Greta's crocheted ornaments. We could buy a few more on the way to the Lazy B."

"Sounds good."

"If I didn't have glass windows where everybody can see in, I'd kiss you."

"Later," she said with a wink.

Again, he felt as if his world had rocked on its axis.

Later that afternoon, Hudson could see Bella was excited about the prospect of putting up a Christmas tree at his house. He wondered if she hadn't had many Christmas trees since her parents had died. Would her grandparents have even thought of getting a tree for two kids who needed a little Christmas?

After a stop for ornaments, they'd gone to the Lazy B, then to the stables. Now they were bundled up, riding on a buckboard to a stand of trees he'd seen while on his horse one day last week. "I'm glad we got to the general store early while they still had a collection of balls and garlands. I like your idea of blue and silver mixed with Greta's white ornaments."

"I've always wanted to decorate a Christmas tree with blue and silver," she said.

"Can you tell me why?"

"I remember one like that when my parents were still alive. Mom said it reminded her of heaven and the stars. I've always remembered that."

"Did you have Christmas trees after your parents died?" After all, if they were going to be in some kind of relationship, they should be able to ask the tougher questions.

She was quiet for a little while, but then she told him, "A Christmas tree was too much trouble for my grandparents. I snuck a little one into my room one year, after Grandma died, but Gramps said it would just make a mess and I should get rid of it."

"Did you?"

"No, I didn't," she said defensively. "I put it in my closet. Jamie and I couldn't get each other much. I used my spending money to buy yarn, and I knitted him a scarf. He gave me a card of barrettes for my hair, and we put our presents under the tree in the closet. That probably sounds silly to you."

He transferred the horses' reins to one hand and wrapped his arm around her. "It doesn't sound silly at all. The two of you were trying to make the day special."

After they rode a little bit farther, he asked, "Do you think Jamie will put up a tree this year?"

"I don't know. The triplets are still too young to understand what it would mean, even though they might like looking at all the lights. I'm afraid it would remind Jamie of his Christmases with Paula, so I don't even want to suggest it. If he decides to do it, then I'll certainly help him with it any way I can."

Hudson drew up in front of a stand of pines. He said, "We have to walk a little ways in."

"I wore my boots."

He laughed. He liked the way Bella seemed to take things in stride. He liked the way she was ready for a new adventure even if it was just cutting down a Christmas tree.

"Look around and see if you can find one you like. They might have bare spots from being too close to the other trees, but we can always fill that in with garland or ornaments."

While Hudson took a saw from the back of the buckboard, Bella forged ahead, circling the pines, one after another. He had to smile as she looked at each with a critical eye.

"Imagining those blue and silver balls on them?"

"You bet, and a silver star on the top. We were lucky they had one of those."

Yes, they had been. That silver star could make some of Bella's dreams come true. At least her Christmas tree dreams.

She called from around a pine, "If Jamie doesn't put up a tree, maybe I can bring the triplets over to see yours."

That thought startled him for a moment. The babies in his house. Well, not *his* house, technically. What kind of havoc could they wreak? But once he thought about it, he decided he wouldn't care. Having the babies and their laughter in his house would fill it in a way that it hadn't been filled before.

Bella called from the end of a row. "I think I found one. It will be perfect."

From Hudson's experience, rarely was anything perfect. But he had to admit, Bella had found a pretty nice tree. It was about eight feet tall with no gaping holes. Now all he had to do was cut it down.

As he told Bella to stand back and he scrambled under the tree with the saw, she asked, "Have you ever done this before?"

"Believe it or not, I once worked on a Christmas tree farm."

"Why am I not surprised?"

He looked up at her. She wasn't wearing a hat, and her hair was being mussed by the wind. Her eyes were bright. Her cheeks were pink from the cold air. She'd never looked more beautiful.

"I bet I have a few more surprises up my sleeve. Or maybe not exactly up my sleeve," he said with a wink.

"You're incorrigible."

"You're not the first to tell me that. I think that was my dad's favorite word for me."

"Did you purposely try to live up to that opinion?"

"Sure. It set me apart from the others."

While she was still shaking her head, he took the saw to the base of the pine. It took elbow grease and a bit of work, but a short time later, he called to Bella to step way back, and the tree fell.

"Do you need help carrying it?" she asked.

"No. You run ahead to the buckboard and get out of the snow or you're going to be an icicle."

"No more than you are," she shot back.

"All right, if you want to help, make sure the tarp's laid out across the buckboard. That way when we want to take it in the house, we can just wrap it in the tarp."

Bella made sure the tarp was spread from one side of the wagon to the other. It seemed to cause Hudson no stress at all to pick up the tree by its trunk and load it.

Once he had, she looked at it and said, "It's going to be a beautiful tree."

Beautiful. Just like her. As he looked at her, he felt a wet flake on his nose and realized snow was falling now.

"It's just like in the movies," she said with a laugh of sheer joy. "Cutting down the Christmas tree, putting it in the buckboard and having snow fall." She lifted her hands up to the heavens as if to catch a few flakes.

There were no glass windows around them now, and no one to see them for miles. He captured Bella in his arms and swung her around. "I've never cut down a tree quite like this before."

"What do you mean?"

"Oh, I've cut down trees, but not with someone I cared about. That changes everything."

Still, if he had to list what, he probably couldn't right then. He just knew that this seemed to be the start of something.

He was still holding her when he put her on the ground. "We could have a quickie out here," he whispered into her neck.

"And literally freeze our buns off?"

"Of all times for you to be practical," he grumbled.

"Of all times for us to think about whether we'd want the exciting experience of polar lovemaking, or if we'd rather go back to your place, switch on the fire and think about doing it there."

"Both are tempting," Hudson admitted with a joking air. "Snow, pines, the buckboard and a tarp. Or a glass of wine, a blazing fire, fewer clothes to fumble with."

"I think you're convincing me. But just to make sure, let's experiment a little."

With that he took her cheeks in his hands. They were as cold as his hands were warm. The sensation of touching her like this was a once-in-a-lifetime experience. They didn't kiss at first, but rather rubbed noses. They laughed and teased, snuck cheek kisses and neck kisses before they finally came together in a lip-lock kiss.

Bella had removed the top of her gloves. Although her palms were covered with fabric, her fingers weren't. She could dive her fingers into his hair that way. And when she did, he realized they were taking freedoms with each other, and that was good.

The snow began falling harder as they experimented, him burying his nose at the base of her throat and giving her a kiss there, her reaching her hands inside his coat so she was plenty warm. He could have stood with her all night like that, rocking back and forth, kissing, snuggling.

But the snow was becoming a fuzzy curtain of white now. He whispered close to her ear, "We have to get back."

She nodded as if she knew it were so, but she gave a sigh. What they had done had been fun. They'd just have to do it again sometime.

They both had snowflakes on their hair and their eyelashes by the time they returned to the house. Edmond was at the barn to help Hudson dismantle the buckboard and take care of the horse. Hudson suggested Bella go into the house instead of staying out in the cold. He'd bring the tree inside and set it up, and then they could start decorating.

Bella said, "I'll make hot chocolate to warm us up."

Hudson gave her a look that said they didn't need hot chocolate for that. Edmond no doubt caught the look because as soon as Bella left the barn, he gave Hudson a thumbs-up.

"Something's different between the two of you," he said. "Are you a couple now?"

Hudson shrugged. "We'll see."

Were they a couple now? That was a question to ponder while he set up the tree.

Less than an hour later, Bella watched Hudson string the lights on the tree. They'd chosen tiny white twinkle lights. She thought about their excursion to cut down the pine, and she had to smile. She was so glad Jamie hadn't needed her tonight. She was so glad she could do this with Hudson. She suddenly realized that she wouldn't want to be doing it with anyone else.

The problem was, she didn't know what Hudson expected next. For that matter, she didn't know what *she* expected next. Was this just an affair or a fling? Or could it be more? If it could be more, what would happen if she told Hudson she couldn't have children? Or that at least the likelihood of it happening was very slim?

He was great with kids, even babies, but as he turned to her now and said, "Ready for the ornaments," she pushed questions and doubts out of her mind. It had been years since she'd lived in the moment, and that's what she wanted to do now. Tomorrow, her world could crash down around her. For just today, she wanted to be happy.

Hudson took a break to sip his hot chocolate. "Yours is getting cold."

She went over to the coffee table and picked up her cup. She clinked her mug against his, then she turned toward the tree. "We're doing a fine job. Do we put the star on first or save it till last?"

"Let's save it till last. Are you getting hungry?" he asked. "I put that casserole Greta made into the oven."

"That sounds good," Bella agreed. "I'll start unpacking these ornaments." As she took blue ones from the box and attached little hooks to each one, she heard Hudson moving around in the kitchen. Then she heard the buzz of his cell phone and the rumble of his voice as he spoke with someone. But she couldn't hear the conversation.

Five minutes later he returned to the living room. His expression was thoughtful. "That was Walker on the phone. We were discussing Thanksgiving tomorrow. I know you'll probably want to spend it with Jamie and the triplets. Do you have plans?"

"It snuck up on us so quickly we didn't even buy a turkey. I told Jamie I'd stop at the store on the way home tonight to buy fixings for a dinner."

"I might have a solution for that. Walker and Lindsay want you and Jamie and the triplets to come to dinner at the Dalton ranch."

"All of us?"

"All of you. Lindsay has a huge clan who think the more the merrier. Do you think Jamie will go for it?"

"He might. It would be good for all of us to get out."

"Do you want to give him a call, then I can call Walker back?"

"Sure. I can check in and make sure everything's okay, too."

At first Jamie wasn't sure he wanted to join the Daltons, but then Bella said, "Don't you think it would be good to spend the holiday away and make a new memory?"

After a moment of silence, Jamie responded, "I suppose it would. All right. Tell Hudson to tell his brother he'll have five more at his table."

When Bella did, Hudson laughed. "Apparently it's going to be a big table." He approached Bella and motioned to the ornaments on the coffee table. "We'd better get to tree decorating. What time did you tell Jamie you'd be home?"

"I told him around nine."

Hudson stepped even closer. "When we have limited time together, we have to decide what's most important— decorating the tree, eating or…"

The *or* turned into a kiss that took Bella to a place where happiness was possible, where dreams could come true and where Hudson filled her world.

Hudson was passion and sensuality and all man. Hunger swelled inside her, a hunger like she'd never known. Conscious thought didn't seem possible as Hudson's tongue plundered her mouth, as she chased it back into his, as they kissed each other like they might never do it again. She slid her hands into his thick hair, then needing the touch of skin on skin, she massaged the nape of his neck. When Hudson slid his hand under her sweater, she wanted to give him freer access. She backed away slightly, and he broke the kiss.

"We have too many clothes on," he mumbled, finding the edge of her sweater and bringing it up over her head. After he tossed it onto the sofa, he just looked at her for a few moments.

She was glad she'd worn the bra edged with lace. He unhooked it, then he began unbuttoning his shirt. Not long after, they were on the floor in front of the fire, both naked.

"Decorating the tree seemed important when we were cutting it down, but now this is more important." He whispered his hot breath against her skin as he trailed his lips down to her nipple and suckled it.

Bella thought she was ready to make love with Hudson again. But he apparently had no intention of rushing it. He laid her back on the rug and swept her body with featherlight kisses and butterfly touches, sensual, heady and thrilling. Everywhere they touched, his hands ignited a heat that threatened to sear her skin. As his hands slid down her stomach to her thigh, exquisite sensations bombarded her. This much need, this much want and this much hunger couldn't be right, could it?

She didn't have an answer to that question because she'd never experienced anything like this before. She felt like one of the logs on the fireplace grate that glowed with an inner heat that couldn't be contained.

Although Bella could feel Hudson's hunger in his kisses and his touches, she could also feel tenderness. That's what undid her most of all. Leaning over her on the rug, Hudson kissed her once more while his hand slipped between her thighs. He wanted to see how ready she was. She passed her hand down his back to his backside and heard the growl that came from deep in his throat.

"Do you know what you do to me?" he asked her.

"Probably the same thing you do to me."

"Don't move," he said, sitting up, reaching for his jeans. She knew what he was doing. He was getting a condom from his pocket. She should tell him now. She should reveal that she could become pregnant yet would probably never be able to carry a baby to term. But she didn't say anything. She didn't want to spoil this day by ending it with a conversation that could separate them completely.

A minute later he was poised over her again, looking down into her shadowed eyes, and she wished she could take a picture of him right there and then. Then he entered her, and she held on to him tightly, wishing the moment could last forever. Wishing reality wouldn't poke its head back into her life. Wishing she'd been more responsible as a teenager so that she didn't have a secret to keep now.

She knew she couldn't keep the secret much longer because she wanted honesty between her and Hudson as much as she wanted anything else.

## Chapter Twelve

Jamie's huge SUV maneuvered easily over a light coating of snow on the way to the Dalton ranch—the Circle D. It was located about a half hour out of town.

Bella glanced over her shoulder at the triplets, who were in their car seats behind her. "They seem content for the moment."

"Let's wait and see what happens when we get into a crowd. I'm not sure this was a good idea."

"They have to get out sometime, Jamie. Besides, did you really want to spend the holiday alone?" Sometimes she suspected it was more than protectiveness that kept Jamie from being out and about with his children. Was it grief or was there something else?

"I wouldn't have been alone," he said wryly.

"You know what I mean. Spending the day with the Daltons should be fun."

"We'll see," he responded, obviously not sure of that fact. He glanced at her quickly, then moved his eyes back to the road. "I think this was more about you spending the holiday with Hudson."

He had her there. Still, she said, "It's not like we'll have time alone."

"I'm sure you can steal a few minutes. You're getting more involved with him, aren't you?"

If "more involved" meant sleeping with him, yes, she was. But she wasn't willing to go into that with her brother.

When she was silent, Jamie said, "I worry about you."

"You don't have to."

"You gave up your life to help me. Of course I have to. You *are* going to go back to school, aren't you?"

"Eventually."

"Sooner, rather than later."

"Jamie, I don't know what's going to happen next."

"You mean with Hudson?"

She sighed. "With Hudson. With my job. With the triplets, even. I want to make sure you and the babies are stable before I consider doing anything else."

"We have our routine. We're doing well. If you go back to school, I'll look around for somebody else to help. Even if I have to pay them."

"You can't afford to do that. The ranch expenses are up, not to mention everything you necd for the triplets."

"You're not trapped, Bella. I don't want you to think you are. I would figure something out."

She was sure he would. Still, she felt that he needed her.

"Did you tell Hudson yet about your miscarriage and your...problem?"

"No."

"How serious does it have to get before you do?"

"Everything with Hudson has happened so fast. I have to feel the time is right."

"The longer you wait, the harder it's going to be to tell him."

"I know," she said. But today wasn't going to be the day, not in the middle of a family Thanksgiving celebration. She was sure of that.

Shortly after their conversation ended, Jamie took the turnoff to the Circle D. At the fork in the road, Jamie said, "One of the Dalton brothers lives over there in that white house with the green shutters."

Each Dalton sibling was allotted land within the ranch borders. Although Ben Dalton and his wife, Mary, owned the ranch, Ben was a lawyer and didn't devote much time to it. His son Anderson was in charge and managed it for him. As Jamie drove a ways, Bella wondered what it would be like to belong to a large family and have everyone live close by. That would be nice.

After driving farther, Bella caught a glimpse of the stables. When they reached the main ranch house, she stayed in the car with Katie and Henry, while Jamie took Jared inside. She expected to see Jamie come back out, but instead Hudson did.

He approached the car door and said, "Your brother trusted me to help get the babies inside."

That was saying a lot, she supposed, because Jamie didn't trust just anyone with the triplets. They detached both car carriers from the backseat and carried them into the house.

Already there was a group of adults gathered around Jared, oohing and aahing. When Hudson and Bella brought the other two over, everyone made room. Lindsay and Walker welcomed them, and then the entire Dalton clan descended on them. The parents, Ben and Mary, as well as Anderson and his wife, Marina, with their blended family of eleven-year-old Jake and baby Sydney. There was brother Travis, a bachelor; Lani Dalton with her fiancé, Russ Campbell; and Caleb Dalton and his wife, Mallory, and their ten-year-old daughter, Lily. And, finally, Paige and her husband, Sutter, who cast watchful eyes over their two-year-old son, Carter.

In the center of the crowd, Lindsay smiled. "And this is just the tip of the Dalton iceberg. Uncle Charles is having Thanksgiving with his five kids. My other uncles, Phillip, Neal and Steven, have big families, too, but they live in another part of Montana."

Lindsay's mom, Mary, was particularly welcoming. She picked up Katie from her car carrier and said, "Aren't you pretty? With two brothers to treat you like a princess."

"Or pull her hair," her husband, Ben, said, and everyone laughed.

"We have high chairs so the triplets won't miss any of the celebration." She looked at Bella. "Do you want to come with me to see what else they might need?"

Hudson offered, "I can set up those high chairs."

"Thank you," Mary said. "Come on with me."

"I'll take Katie," Lindsay offered. She whispered to Bella, "It will do Walker good to be around babies."

For the second time in the last few weeks, Bella wondered if Lindsay might be wanting a child soon. Would Walker take to kids as his brother had?

Kids. It always came down to kids.

"What's wrong?" Hudson asked her as they followed Mary to the kitchen.

"Nothing," Bella said lightly. "I'm just hoping we can keep the triplets occupied during dinner so everyone can enjoy it."

"We can always take one out at a time and walk him or her. The Daltons are used to kids. I'm sure everyone will be sitting around the table long enough that a little excursion in and out with a baby won't spoil dinner at all."

In the kitchen, Mary pulled dishes from the cupboard, and Bella chose the ones she thought would be best for the triplets. "I have baby spoons in the diaper bag," she said. "Jamie will warm up their food right before we eat, if that's okay. He likes to maintain a stable diet for them."

"Maybe with a spoonful of mashed potatoes or two?" Mary asked with a twinkle in her eye.

"Maybe," Bella agreed.

A peal of laughter came from the living room, followed by lots of chatter.

"This is a real Thanksgiving," Hudson said.

"Your family doesn't get together for the holidays?" Mary asked him.

"My brothers are scattered all over now, and Mom and Dad are traveling. So, no, we don't. It's rare that even Walker and I are together."

"This *must* be a treat then. One of those holidays to remember. I'm glad you all could join us."

Hudson picked up one of the collapsed high chairs

that were leaning against a wall. "Any place special you want me to set this up?"

"No. Just fit them in wherever you can. I'm sure whoever is next to a baby will see to their needs. This is a child-friendly family."

Hudson carried a high chair into the dining room.

Mary turned to Bella. "What about you, child? I suppose you and your brother spend most of your holidays together."

"Yes, we do."

"I imagine this one is particularly hard for him. I hope being among friends will help. I've heard about the baby chain that takes care of the triplets."

"I don't know what we'd do without them. Not only in the care of the babies, but they've helped Jamie not draw into himself even more. They're kind and considerate, and he almost thinks of them as family now."

"One of the things I like most about this community is that we help others. I'm sorry that Lindsay and the day care center were at odds for a while. You know, don't you, that she was just doing her job?"

"Oh, I know that. I'm just glad everything turned out as well as it did."

"I hear that's your Hudson's doing."

"Oh, he's not *my* Hudson."

Mary laughed. "You can say that, but I see something else."

When Hudson returned to the kitchen for a second high chair, Bella knew her cheeks were flushed. When he left again, Mary said to her, "After dinner, when everyone's settling in to watch TV or chat, you and Hudson ought to take a walk down to the stables.

There's a new horse there you both might enjoy. Her name is Trixie…a fine quarter horse."

As Hudson returned to the kitchen, he heard the last part of that.

"Wouldn't you like to see our new horse?" she asked him.

"I'm always interested in a good horse. I'm sure Bella is, too. She doesn't just ride them, she photographs them. She did some work for the Smith Rescue Ranch."

"Really?" Mary asked.

"Jazzy and Brooks liked some of my shots, and they're using them on their pamphlets and on their website," Bella explained. "The redesigned website should be up by Monday. You should take a look if you get a chance."

"I'm not much into computers, but my husband and all my kids have them. So sure, I'll take a look. Now, come on. We have potatoes to mash, beans to dress and a turkey to carve."

When they were all finally seated around the table for the Thanksgiving meal, it was loud and fun. Many conversations traversed the room, and Bella couldn't keep track of them all. The triplets seemed mesmerized by all the people, let alone the food being passed around. So they were entertained while they ate.

She and Hudson had been seated next to each other. Every once in a while, Hudson would reach over and place his hand on her thigh. That simple contact sent a charge through her body, and she hoped it didn't show on her face. Now and then, however, she saw Lindsay looking at her speculatively. And one time Mary Dalton gave her a wink.

The talk among the men turned to ranching for a while. The women shared recipes, as well as caught up with their careers. Bella felt as if she were somewhere in between. Managing the day care center was not going to be her career. She took care of the triplets with Jamie and could easily discuss that. But she had her foot in two different worlds. Throw in her feelings for Hudson, and it was difficult to come up with a life plan, especially when she didn't know if he'd be staying or going…especially when she didn't know if he could accept not having children of his own.

She joined conversations, but her thoughts were jumbled. The only thing she did know was that she loved being with Hudson. She loved making love with him. She loved *him*.

By dessert time, the triplets were getting restless. Bella, Jamie and Paige took them from the high chairs and set them on their laps, distracting them with rattles and little toys.

Paige said, "The pageant on Sunday is going to be a hoot. Imagine all those babies, kids, costumes and Christmas."

"I'm going to have a look at the carriages tomorrow," Hudson said. "They're at the school and all decorated. I want to make sure there's nothing the babies shouldn't get hold of. I also need to get a few basic instructions to take to my staff. We aren't having a dress rehearsal with the rest of the group." He shrugged. "It's not as if our little ones have a script."

Everybody laughed.

"I'm sure they'll cause a lot of ad-lib moments," Ben said. "You can't have babies around and expect everything to go as planned."

"How about more whipped cream on that pumpkin pie?" Mary asked.

Mary and Ben had blocked off one area of the living room so the babies could crawl around and play with their toys in relative safety. Jamie sat on the floor with them, and Paige did, too. Jamie said to Bella, "If you want to go for a walk or anything, go ahead. We're fine for a while."

Paige waved at her. "We've got this."

Bella looked up at Hudson, who immediately got to his feet.

"I'll go get our coats," he said. "We'll take a look at that new horse."

As they made their way from the house to the barn, Hudson took Bella's arm. "Do you think you can get away for a few hours Saturday evening? I'd like to take you into Kalispell for a surprise."

"I'll have to talk to Jamie and see if he has other help."

"That's fine. I'd just like to take you on a real date. We can get dressed up, go to dinner, and then I'll show you my surprise."

Bella had no idea what Hudson was going to surprise her with, but whatever it was, the idea excited her.

The stables on the Circle D were a classic rectangular shape. Hudson opened the door for Bella and flipped on a switch just inside. The overhead light revealed a long center aisle with stalls on each side and a door at the other end, too. As they walked down the aisle, they saw plaques with the horses' names. They passed one for a giant black horse named Zorro.

"I think they have the heater on in here," Hudson said. "It's not as cold as outside."

Hudson was right, and Bella unzipped her parka as he unbuttoned his. They walked farther in, finally stopping in front of Trixie's stall. She was a cute little chestnut. The horse turned from her trough and gave them an interested look.

Bella held out her hand. "Come here, pretty girl. Let me pet you."

The horse apparently liked the sound of a friendly voice, because she turned and came to Bella, hanging her head over the slats so Bella could touch her nose. "No matter how many times I touch a horse's nose, I'm always amazed at the softness."

"I know what you mean," Hudson said. But there was a huskiness to his voice that made her think he was talking about her rather than the horse.

"You and Mary seemed to hit it off," he said.

"Yes, we did. She's nice."

He laid a hand on Bella's shoulder. "I feel for you that you lost your mother."

"Thank you. Lindsay's lucky. This whole family is lucky that they're still together and have each other."

"I think they realize that. Anderson does a great job managing the place. He wants to do it not just for himself, but for his family."

Bella had noticed more than the family atmosphere today. She'd noticed the couples in love—Lindsay and Walker, Anderson and Marina, Paige and Sutter, Caleb and Mallory. Had she been aware of them because of her own feelings for Hudson? If happily-ever-after was possible for *them*, maybe it was possible for *her*.

Suddenly she was very aware of Hudson beside her. He sidled closer and put his arm around her.

"Every time I'm close to you, I want to kiss you," he murmured in her ear.

She turned into his arms. "I feel like that, too."

Slowly he lowered his mouth to hers. This wasn't one of those quick let's-do-it-before-we-can't kisses. It was one of those I-want-to-take-my-time-with-you kisses. He began it softly but with the firm pressure of his lips. Seconds later, his tongue teased the seam of her mouth.

Her heart was beating so fast she couldn't breathe. But she didn't have to breathe. Not when Hudson was giving her his air, his taste, his desire. Her hand slipped into the collar of his jacket, felt his sweater and then the skin of his neck. Hudson's body was becoming more familiar now. She could feel the tension in it because of the need coursing through him, just like the need coursing through her.

His hand caressed the side of her face, then moved down her sweater to her breasts.

She nipped at his mouth, and he took that for assent of what he was doing. She was assenting all right. She couldn't seem to get enough of him. The stable seemed to spin around her, and she clung to Hudson as if he were the only thing in her world that was stable. He took her tongue deeper into his mouth, and she melted against him. His palm on her breast was replaced with his fingers as he kneaded her and searched for her nipple under the sweater. When he found it, she knew it was hard, and she could imagine him doing things to it with his tongue.

He groaned, dropped his hands to the waistband of the sweater and dived underneath. Skimming her stomach, they came to rest on her bra. Masterfully he flipped open the front catch, and then he was holding her, caressing her breasts, making her want him with a need so strong she could only hope it would soon be satisfied.

He said roughly, "I want you." He brought her hips tight against his so she could feel how hard he was and just how much he wanted her.

All of a sudden, Trixie neighed. The sound penetrated Bella's passionate haze. Then she heard bootfalls and the clearing of a throat.

"I was going to turn around and leave, but you might as well know that I know."

It was Walker's voice.

Hudson backed away slowly, but made sure Bella's coat was closed over her sweater. He wrapped his arm around her and faced his brother. "Don't you say a word," he warned Walker. "Not after what you and Lindsay did."

Bella knew her eyes were wide, and she felt stricken. No matter what Hudson had said, Walker owned the Just Us Kids franchise. Would her job be in jeopardy?

As if Hudson understood what she was thinking, he said to Walker, "This won't affect my working relationship with Bella."

Walker focused on Bella. "Your job is safe. You don't have to worry about that. No one could have handled everything as well as you have, especially with Hudson coming in to oversee you." He motioned to his brother and then to her. "In fact, this attraction between you might have helped that along, encouraged both of you to work for the good of the center."

"Then why does it matter that you *know*? You could have turned around and left and saved us a lot of embarrassment."

"I could have. But I still need to know if you're staying until Valentine's Day, or if you're going to leave before that for the job in Big Timber."

"And you have to ask me *now*?"

"Maybe it's a good thing I am, because Bella has to know, too, doesn't she? Or is she just another diversion until you're on your way?"

Bella's heart sank because Walker knew Hudson's history. And he knew Hudson's nature, too. If she was just a diversion, was she going to let their affair continue?

"I have to give Big Timber my answer on Monday," Hudson said. "I'll give you my answer then, too."

"So you haven't made up your mind?" Walker asked as if he expected nothing less.

"I'm still considering the pros and cons."

Again Walker looked from one of them to the other. And then he nodded and walked away.

They both heard the barn door close. They'd been so engrossed in their kiss, they hadn't heard it open.

Quickly Bella reached under her sweater and fastened her bra. She moved away from Hudson, thinking about everything Walker had said. Then she looked up at the tall cowboy and asked, "So you really don't know yet if you're staying or going?" Though she knew that if he stayed until Valentine's Day, that didn't mean he was going to stay longer.

He took her by the shoulders. "Bella, there's a lot to think about. Believe me, I'll tell you before I tell anyone else what I decide."

She supposed that was something, but it certainly wasn't enough.

"Are we still on for our date Saturday night?" he asked.

She thought of saying no and ending it then, so she could start nursing her heart back to health. But her heart wouldn't let her say it.

"Yes, we're still on for our date." Whether he stayed or whether he left, she loved Hudson Jones. For this weekend, that was going to be all that mattered.

Hudson glanced over at Bella on Saturday evening as she stared out the front windshield, eagerly anticipating where they were going. So far, everything had gone smashingly well. She'd joined him at the dress rehearsal for the pageant, so she'd be able to give teachers direction, too. Although there was tension between them because his decision about Big Timber was still in the offing, they'd seemed to put that aside during the dress rehearsal as well as at dinner tonight.

He'd taken her to the fanciest restaurant in Kalispell. She'd dressed festively in a beautiful long-sleeved red dress. Although the dress seemed modestly cut, its folds accented all her curves in just the right places. When he'd picked her up, she'd looked at him as if he were some kind of *GQ* model, which was crazy since he was wearing a Western-cut suit and bolo tie, a Stetson and boots. She'd given him a smile that had practically twirled his bolo.

Dinner was incredible, but the night wasn't over. He still had one more destination. To make conversation while he drove, he asked, "Do you think we're really ready for the pageant tomorrow? All those babies and kids at one place at one time—"

"We're as ready as we're ever going to be. Sometimes the more you regiment children, the more chaos you provoke. For the most part, all we have to do is make sure the babies are in their carriages and hope that the carriage decorations don't fall off. The one that looked like Santa's sleigh was pretty elaborate."

"The older kids really worked hard on them." Hudson was finding that he liked kids more and more... from babies to high-schoolers. And when he thought of kids, he thought of Bella. He didn't examine that thought too closely because he knew exactly where it might lead—Bella as a mom, him as a dad, a family like the Daltons had someday.

He glanced at Bella again and decided to concentrate on the here and now—on his attraction to her and on her surprise.

There were several cars parked in front of the building already. He pulled up to the curb in front of a bakery storefront.

Bella looked puzzled as he went around his truck and helped her out. She was wearing high-heeled boots, and he didn't want her to slip or fall.

"The bakery's closed," she said in a puzzled voice.

"We're not going to the bakery. I'd have you shut your eyes, but there are some icy spots."

"Why would you want me to shut my eyes?"

"You aren't used to surprises, are you?"

"Not good ones."

Hooking his arm into hers, he guided her along the sidewalk until they came to the Artfully Yours gallery. She looked up, saw the name and blinked. "You want to buy a painting?"

"You never know," he said with a smile.

They went up the steps, and he opened the door to lead her inside. At first, there didn't seem to be a huge selection. The gallery owner was selective on what he hung where, on what sculptures he positioned on pedestals.

The gallery manager came to greet Hudson, and they shook hands. Hudson had spoken with Jim Barringer on the phone several times. Jim gave Hudson a nod, and he led Bella to a side exhibit set in an alcove.

"Aren't you going to let me look at the paintings?" she started to ask, but then her eyes settled on the photographs hanging in the alcove. "Oh my gosh! They're mine. My photos. They're matted and framed."

"As well they should be. This isn't your own show… yet. But it is a showing. Notice the little red dots on two of them? That means they're sold."

Bella's mouth dropped open as she noticed the two sold prints—the landscape she'd shot at sunrise at the Stockton ranch and the close-up of one of the horses. The frames were perfect, rough-hewn like barn wood.

Bella turned to Hudson. "Did you do this?"

Hudson wondered again if he'd been too high-handed by doing it without her permission.

But then she threw her arms around his neck. "I can't believe you did this."

He squeezed her hard. "I didn't do the framing. I left most of that up to Jim, though he did ask my opinion. I just happened to know the gallery owner and asked him to take a look at your photographs. He thought they were well worth showing. You could have more than one career, if you want it, Bella."

Unmindful of where they were and who was around, Bella gave him a smacking kiss on the lips. When she broke away, she said, "Thank you."

"I'd do it again for another kiss like that," he teased.

She looked around the gallery. "I can't believe my photographs are hung here with all these talented artists."

"You're talented, too. You have to know that."

"Maybe I'm starting to."

For the next hour, they went from painting to painting...from sculpture to sculpture...from photograph to photograph until Bella had her fill.

On the drive back to Rust Creek Falls, Hudson thought that Bella might want to call Jamie and tell him her news. But she didn't. She just kept glancing at him, putting her hand on his thigh, looking at him as if he was Christmas all wrapped up in a cowboy package.

"Do you want to stop at my place?" he asked as they neared town.

"More than anything," she answered with such fervor that it took Hudson's self-control to the limit not to press down hard on the accelerator.

When they reached his house, he hurried out of the truck, going around to her side. When he opened her door, he saw longing in her eyes, too. He lifted her down from the truck and held on to her as they walked to the door. He fumbled with the keys as he tried to get the door open. All he could think about was holding her in his arms...naked. Time alone with her was precious, and honestly, he didn't know how much more they'd have.

After he punched in the code for the alarm, he took her into his arms, kissing her the way he'd wanted to kiss her all night. The ride home had seemed endless. He shrugged off his jacket, letting it fall to the floor. She was still unzipping her parka when he helped push it from her shoulders and let that fall, too. Her breath and his heightened and so did every look between them, every brush of their fingers, every touch of their skin. Bella's ability to return his hunger still amazed him. She undid his tie while he found the zipper at the back of her dress and ran it down its track. She unbuttoned his shirt while he pushed her dress down off her shoulders. It weighed on her arms as she was trying to undress him.

He laughed and said, "I can probably do it faster."

By the time he finished undressing himself and her, their clothes lay in a pile in the foyer. They couldn't seem to wait to reach the living room to touch each other. When her hands slid up his chest, he was a goner. He kissed her hard, and she returned his fervor, clutching his shoulders, pressing against him until he thought he'd die from the wanting. Lacing his fingers into her hair, he angled her head for another kiss.

When he broke away this time, she murmured, "I'm ready. We don't have to wait."

"Yes, we do," he said. "I have to grab a condom. Don't move."

She didn't.

"Turn around," he said, and she followed his gentle order, bracing her hands on the wall.

He wanted to give Bella every experience, every pleasure, every peaked orgasm. He just had to hold on a little longer. Stepping close behind her, he ran his hands over her breasts, teased her nipples, then slid his hands down her sides to her hips.

She understood what he wanted to do, and in the next second, he was thrusting inside her, pulling back, then doing it again until she moaned with as much pleasure as he felt. The wall braced them both as he felt her release come first, and then his followed. He rested his chin on her shoulder, and then he just held her.

When he could breathe again almost normally, he said, "Now we can try that in bed and take it a little slower."

She turned into his arms, wrapped hers around his neck and placed a kiss on his lips so tender that he thought he'd fall apart at the seams.

Scooping her up into his arms, he carried her to the bedroom, wanting to make each moment they had together last as long as it could.

## *Chapter Thirteen*

On Sunday afternoon, Hudson felt a bit like a horse in the midst of a cattle stampede. It looked and felt as if everyone in Rust Creek Falls had come to the holiday pageant! That was understandable, he guessed, since the pageant was an important event and there wasn't much else in the way of entertainment in the small town.

Chairs had been set up in rows in the elementary school gymnasium with an aisle down the center. Teachers and volunteers milled about backstage along with a few parents, under the watchful eye of Eileen Bennet.

Classes from the elementary school had already performed. Scenery for the production had been swiveled around for two different segments. The first was an old-time scene where kids in costumes from the 1900s paraded onto the stage. The audience had been invited to sing traditional Christmas carols. The second segment depicted the 1960s with women and girls dressed in maxi-coats, fur rimming their hoods, and men in peacoats. More carols accompanied by the piano had brought a rousing response from the audience.

Now the audience awaited the third and last segment, a modern-day rendition of the holidays. In this segment, children would parade across the stage in Christmas finery. Bella had decked herself out in her red dress. Hudson had complied with the theme by wearing a green sweater and black jeans. Other teachers had dressed in holiday colors, and they would push the decorated carriages onto the stage. They would be followed by a wagon with kids and, of course, Santa Claus, who was actually one of the big, burly, white-bearded dads.

From the sidelines, Hudson heard one of the teachers call, "Quentin spit up! Paper towels, quick."

Another teacher shouted, "Mary's carriage is supposed to be in line before Monica's. Switch them. The parents know the order and will be upset if we don't have it right."

Bella, who was two carriages behind Hudson's, caught his eye. She gave him a thumbs-up and smiled. That smile. He remembered the sleepy expression on her face and the sparkle in her eyes after they'd made love last night.

Suddenly the baby in Bella's carriage lifted up his arms to her. She didn't hesitate to lift him out even though they were almost ready to go on. A baby's needs would certainly take priority over the pageant. She cuddled him and cooed to him, straightened his reindeer antlers and set him back in the carriage, handing him a rattle.

Hudson suddenly felt the need to go to her. Snagging the attention of Sarah Palmer, he asked, "Can you watch this young gentleman for a moment? I need to talk to Bella."

"Sure," Sarah agreed. "We have about five minutes until we push our carriages out onto the stage."

Going to Bella's side, Hudson asked, "How do you think things are going?"

"Great, so far. The audience is really involved. Now, if not too many babies cry once the carriages are on the stage, we'll have succeeded."

He chuckled, then looked over the scene before him with all the carriages lined up and children and teachers milling about. He motioned to the carriages. "I remember all the rumors about how these babies were conceived because of the wedding punch at Jennifer McCallum and Ben Traub's wedding. Supposedly, Homer Gilmore spiked it with a magic potion and there were lots of romantic hookups because of it. When I first came to town, I heard that some couples came here who were hoping to have a baby because they thought the magic might rub off on them."

Bella's face suddenly took on an odd expression. The sadness was back in her eyes, and he didn't understand any of it. But he did understand one very important thing, as if a lightning bolt had hit him. He never wanted her to be sad. He wanted to protect her...forever. He realized that he loved Bella Stockton, and he was going to do something about it.

Someone near the curtain gave a signal, and he gave Bella's arm a squeeze. "I have to get back to my carriage. See you after?"

She nodded and said, "Sure."

A few of the babies did cry as the carriages rolled out in front of Santa and the children on the stage sang "Jingle Bells" with the audience. Hudson, however, wasn't living in the moment right now. All he could do was stare at Bella and wish the pageant was over. He had something to say to her, and he couldn't wait to say it.

He should have seen his love for her before now, but maybe he'd been blinded by the chemistry between them, by the passion that seemed to supersede everything else when he was around her. Bella Stockton was everything he'd ever wanted in a woman without even realizing it. She was smart and challenging and sweet. Most of all, she knew how to care and she knew how to love. That was evident in her loyalty to her brother, her love for the triplets, her care of every child at Just Us Kids.

Hudson realized now that home wasn't so much a place. It could be a person. He wanted to make Bella his home and hoped she felt the same about him. He realized now he could make a life in Rust Creek Falls with her, and he had an idea about that. He was going to get on his cell phone and make sure that dream could come true as soon as he talked to Bella. Maybe he'd always been a rich man, but he hadn't felt rich before. With Bella by his side, he knew he could be a better man than he'd ever been. They'd raise a family together, and they'd hand down values that could last through the years. She'd never said how many kids she might want, but he didn't care about that. Two, four or five. They'd talk about it. They'd kiss about it. They'd make love about it.

Hudson spotted Walker and Lindsay in the audience. Not far away, he spied Jamie with the triplets in their stroller. Fallon was with him. Hudson gave him a big smile and a thumbs-up, and Jamie grinned back. The green headband on Katie's little blond hair tilted sideways. Jamie straightened it with such a loving expression on his face that Hudson knew he couldn't wait to be a dad. Would Bella want to have kids right away, or wait awhile? There was so much to talk about, so much to look forward to, so many dreams to fulfill.

With all the people and babies and kids involved in the pageant, it was almost an hour later until the scenery had been stowed in the wings, until parents had been reunited with their children, until the audience who had come to mingle as well as to watch the show drifted out of the auditorium.

Bella, who had helped stow the babies' reindeer headbands in a plastic bin, snapped on the lid and stacked it with boxes that held other costumes. Hudson was about to burst with what he wanted to say to Bella.

As they walked to the exit, he cloaked his excitement and asked her, "Do you have to get back to the ranch right away?"

She zipped up her parka and hoisted her hobo bag over her shoulder. "I do," she said. "Fallon helped Jamie at the pageant, but she can't stay. I told Jamie I'd be there to help feed and bathe the babies."

Hudson felt a pang of disappointment, but he knew this was Bella's life. They'd have to talk about that along with everything else. But right now, he had to take a few minutes to tell her how he felt. He couldn't hold it in any longer.

"I know we don't have much time..." He took her hands in his. "But I want you to know how much last night meant to me."

"It meant a lot to me, too," she responded. "I can't thank you enough for recommending me to Artfully Yours. But beyond that, Hudson, I've never spent time with a man like you."

"And I've never spent time with a woman like you. And because of that, I have to tell you something, Bella." He drew in a shaky breath and then went for it. "I love you. I want to marry you and make a life with you that includes lots of babies." He gave her a broad smile. "Will you marry me?"

Hudson expected an enthusiastic "yes." He expected Bella to throw her arms around his neck and say that she loved him, too. He expected they'd both be hearing wedding bells instead of silver bells. But none of those things happened. Instead, Bella burst into tears, turned away from him and pushed out the exit door.

It took him a moment to realize what had happened. The door had swung shut, and he pushed out after her.

"Bella, wait," he yelled.

But she was headed to her car.

He took off at a run after her, but when he caught up to her at the driver's side door, she was shaking her head. "I can't give you want you want. Not ever."

Hudson was so shell-shocked he couldn't move, think or talk. In the next few moments, she started the engine, backed up and drove away.

Just what had caused *that* reaction? More important, what was he going to do about it?

* * *

Hudson spent the rest of the evening trying to decide the best thing to do. He could make Bella face him, but he wasn't sure that would do any good. She had to *want* to talk to him. He didn't want to force her.

That evening when his cell phone beeped, he grabbed it up, hoping beyond hope it was Bella. But Jamie Stockton's number showed up.

"Jamie, is Bella all right?" he asked before the rancher could get a word out.

"She asked me to call you. She's taking a sick day tomorrow."

"A sick day? To avoid me?"

He heard Jamie's sigh. Hudson knew Bella might be right there and her brother couldn't talk freely. With insight, he realized talking to her brother might be better than talking to Bella right now.

He asked, "Can you get an hour away at lunch tomorrow?"

Jamie responded cautiously, "I might be able to. Why?"

"Can you meet me at the Ace in the Hole? I need to talk to you about Bella. I only want the best for her. I love her, Jamie."

"All right," Jamie said.

"Around one okay?" Hudson asked.

"If it's not, I'll let you know."

Jamie ended the call without saying more, and Hudson knew Bella was probably listening and Jamie didn't want her to know about their meeting. She might feel her brother was betraying her.

Hudson didn't want to cause a rift between them, but he had to find out what was going on.

The next morning dragged on so slowly Hudson could count each second. He left for the Ace in the Hole fifteen minutes early, found a table there, ordered coffee and drummed his fingers until Jamie Stockton walked in the door.

Jamie saw him and headed toward the table. After he unzipped his jacket, he looked at Hudson's coffee. "I thought you might be drinking something stronger."

"I need a clear head for this conversation," Hudson said. "I need a clear head for this whole situation."

Jamie signaled a waitress and pointed to Hudson's coffee and at his own place. She nodded. Seconds later, he had a mug of black coffee in front of him, too.

"What's on your mind?" he asked Hudson.

"We need to talk, man-to-man, brother to the man who loves your sister."

"I don't know if a talk will do any good," Jamie said.

Hudson felt there was a closed door in front of him, but he wasn't going to let it stay closed. He was going to open it. Heck, he was going to push through it. "Look. I know Bella has a lot of baggage. I want to know the best way to help her deal with it."

Jamie eyed him and asked, "What do you want?"

"I want a future with her. I want a life with her—a family and kids."

A shadow passed over Jamie's face, the same shadow that Hudson had seen on Bella's. Then Jamie seemed to make up his mind. "Yes, Bella has a lot of baggage. She felt abandoned like I did when our parents died. She felt rejected when our grandparents didn't want our siblings and didn't want us either, though they took us in. But her hurts aren't as simple as all that."

"Simple? There's nothing simple about being abandoned. What else is there?"

"I'm only telling you this because I think it's best for Bella. She rebelled against our grandparents' rejection. She became a little...wild. She looked for love in the wrong places. She got pregnant, and she had a miscarriage. Because of that miscarriage, she probably will never be able to have children."

If Hudson had been shocked by Bella's response yesterday, he was even more shocked by what Jamie had told him. He felt numb. She might never be able to have children? It was so much to take in, and he didn't know how he felt about all of it.

He thought about how intimate he and Bella had been, and he couldn't help but mutter, "Why didn't she trust me enough to tell me?"

"I think you can answer that yourself. For a lot of years, I don't think she's trusted anybody but me."

"I feel so sorry for her."

"But?" Jamie asked with a probing look.

"My heart hurts at the idea of not having kids with her."

"That's why I told you this. If you can't deal with the idea of no kids, then you should walk away now. Don't hurt Bella further by rejection later." He nodded to Hudson's coffee cup. "Do you want something stronger than that now?"

Hudson glanced at the bar and all the bottles behind

it. "No, I still need a clear head to think this through. Thanks for your honesty."

Jamie picked up his mug, took a couple of swallows of coffee and set it back down. As Bella's brother rose to his feet and then left, Hudson was hardly aware of it. He was too lost in his thoughts.

The sun was barely up the next morning when Bella stood at Hudson's door and rang the bell. She was shaking. She didn't know if this was the right thing or the wrong thing to do. She didn't know if Hudson would even let her inside after the way she'd left him.

When he didn't answer the door, Bella wondered if he'd gone riding or already left for the day. She could check the garage to see if his truck was there.

Just as she was about to do that, the door opened and Hudson stood there, his expression totally unreadable. She could tell one thing, though. He looked tired, as if she'd gotten him out of bed. His hair was sleep-mussed, there was a heavy stubble on his jaw and his feet were bare under a pair of sweatpants.

"I'm sorry if I woke you," she said.

"No harm," he returned evenly.

She wasn't sure about that. "May I come in?"

He ran his hand through his mussed hair and pulled down his T-shirt. "I haven't even had a cup of coffee yet. Are you sure you want to talk to me now?"

There was an edge of something in his voice, and she supposed she deserved that. She hadn't wanted to talk to him Sunday or yesterday. Coffee or not, she'd take her chances today.

"Yes, I need to talk to you."

His eyebrows arched at the words. He backed up in the foyer so she could enter.

After she did, she closed the door behind her, wishing he'd react more, say something, do something. Like kiss her?

That was wishful thinking.

She had done nothing but think and cry and worry since she'd left him Sunday. She'd helped Jamie with the triplets but told him she didn't want to talk about any of it. She couldn't, not until she figured out what she was going to do. Jamie had pretty much left her alone because he'd known this was her problem to solve and her life to lead. All she could think about all day yesterday and last night was how her heart hurt because she loved Hudson so much. She loved him enough to walk away if that's what he wanted. But she had to be honest with him, and she had to tell him everything first. That was only fair after what they'd shared.

Hudson led her into the living room and sat in the armchair. Maybe he expected her to sit on the sofa, but she didn't want to be that far away. She needed to make eye contact with him, and she needed to be close. So she sat on the large ottoman in front of him.

He looked surprised and maybe a bit uncomfortable.

How could she mess this up any more than she already had? But she wasn't going to scurry away now. "I'd like to tell you...everything."

"Everything?"

"You know most of it, but..." She couldn't lose her courage now. She plunged right into her story. "I felt so lost after my parents died."

She thought she saw a glimmer of compassion in his eyes, but she couldn't be sure. But she hadn't come here for pity, so she hurried on. "Jamie and I missed our five other brothers and sisters. It was like one minute we had a family and the next we didn't. Grandma and Gramps didn't want us, and..." She lifted her hands as if she didn't have to explain any more about that. "I told you I was wild, and you didn't believe me, but I was. I'm not the woman you thought I was, Hudson. When I was a teenager, I wasn't smart or mature. I was fifteen, and I ended up dating and sleeping with an older boy."

"How old?" Hudson asked, and she couldn't tell if there was judgment there or not.

"He was almost eighteen. I got pregnant. I thought he loved me. I thought we'd have a family. But I was so stupid. He didn't want any responsibilities. When I told him I was pregnant, he said it wasn't his."

"You could have proved otherwise."

"I could have. My guess is Gramps would have made me prove it to get child support. But we never had to do that." She heard the quaver in her voice and swallowed hard. When she spoke again, she'd regained her composure. The only way she'd get through this was to blurt it out. "There were complications with the pregnancy. I lost the baby, and the doctor said I might never be able to have another one. I have a weak cervix. I can possibly *get* pregnant, but I'd never carry the baby to term."

Before Hudson could say anything, she pushed on. "My grandparents kept the whole thing secret. I wasn't showing when the miscarriage happened, and I certainly hadn't told anybody but the boy, and he wasn't saying anything to anybody. After Grandma died, Gramps said I caused her heart attack with the stress of my pregnancy and what happened afterward. That's what killed her."

"He was wrong," Hudson said with more expression than she'd heard yet.

"I don't know if he was or not. The only saving grace was that my parents weren't alive to see it."

"If your parents had been alive, the whole situation probably wouldn't have happened," Hudson reminded her.

"I know you probably think less of me now. I know you probably want your own children more than you want me. It wasn't fair that I didn't tell you about all this before we made love."

Suddenly Hudson moved forward in his chair and took her hands into his. "I already know about all of this."

She felt as if the breath had been knocked out of her. Recovering, she asked, "How could you?"

"I had a talk with Jamie yesterday. I don't think he wanted to tell me. He wanted you to confide in me. But he also didn't want you hurt any more than you already were."

"Maybe I should go," she said softly and tried to pull away from him.

But he held on to her and wouldn't let her move. She was as mesmerized by the look in his eyes as she was by the hold of his hands.

"I thought a lot about us in the past two days, Bella, and I know exactly what I want."

She held her breath as panic seesawed in her stomach.

"I love you. I don't want to live without you. I would be fine with adopting kids if that's what you want to do. If you want biological children, there are ways to make that happen. There are advantages to being rich, you know. I can have access to the best doctors in the world, or we can hire a surrogate."

Tears burned her eyes, and she felt a few roll down her cheek.

He went on. "Did I mention that I love you and I can't live without you?"

She was full out crying by then and so in shock she couldn't move or speak until he asked, "Will you marry me, Bella Stockton? Make a family with me? Grow old with me?"

Now the look in his eyes sunk in. It was the look of love. It warmed her, surrounded her and made her free.

"Yes," she said jubilantly. "Yes, I'll marry you!"

Hudson gathered her into his arms and held her on his lap. Then he kissed her with so much promise that she knew she'd remember this day forever.

## *Epilogue*

Hudson and Bella, filled with the Christmas spirit, were decorating Just Us Kids for the holiday. They'd erected an artificial tree in the lobby and were adding ornaments, one by one, their fingers brushing often, their gazes connecting.

They were still working out their plans to get married. Hudson was hoping Jamie would accept some financial help to hire someone to take Bella's place with the triplets. He'd talked to Jamie about it, and Jamie said he'd consider it. Bella's brother was just happy that she was finding happiness.

Hudson had a couple of surprises for her and decided now was as good a time as any to produce one as they put the finishing touches on the tree. Bella had wrapped empty boxes to place underneath it in bright shiny paper and pretty ribbon. It had been only three days since she'd accepted his marriage proposal—three days of giddy happiness, work and, last night, a long night of lovemaking.

Taking a box from his pocket that was wrapped in silver with a gold bow, he handed it to her. "The bow's a little smashed," he said, "But I didn't want you to see it before now. Open it."

"It's early for a Christmas present," she teased.

"We're going to have one long Christmas," he assured her.

She took the bow from the box and set it aside. Then she unwrapped the silver paper and did the same with that. Taking the lid from the black box, she found a velvet-covered one inside.

She looked up at him.

He saw her fingers tremble as she opened the ring box. Inside, on white velvet lay a platinum ring with a large center diamond and tiny diamonds circling it. It reminded Hudson of a snowflake.

He explained, "I hope you like it. I saw this ring at the jewelers, and it reminded me of that day we went riding and the snow started falling. I wanted something unique for you. What do you think?" He took it from the box and slipped it onto her finger.

Bella's face was glowing as she said, "I think it's perfect."

"I hope you'll think something else is perfect," he suggested.

"Uh-oh, another surprise."

"I hope it's a good one. I'm buying Clive Bickler's ranch. We'll have a real home and a place to ride and lots of room to raise a family."

Bella had hung a ball of mistletoe in the doorway of Hudson's office. Taking his hand, she led him to it now. On tiptoe, she wrapped her arms around his neck and gave him a kiss Hudson knew he'd long remember.

His fervor was exploding into downright fiery passion when he heard a noise. Still holding Bella, he broke the kiss slowly, then turned toward the lobby. There were two moms there with strollers with babies. They were grinning from ear to ear.

But Hudson didn't care. He was ready to shout from the mountaintops that he loved Bella Stockton and she was going to be his wife. Bella must have felt the same way because she drew his head down to hers again and kissed him once more.

They were going to have the merriest Christmas of both of their lifetimes.

\* \* \* \* \*

*Don't miss the next installment of the new Cherish continuity*

**MONTANA MAVERICKS: THE BABY BONANZA**

*Everyone has rallied behind Jamie Stockton as he raises his triplets alone—including his lifelong friend Fallon O'Reilly. She's loved him from afar since they were kids. Will Christmas bring the babies a new mummy?*

*Look for*
*THE MORE MAVERICKS, THE MERRIER!*
*by*
*award-winning author Brenda Harlen*

*On sale December 2016,*
*wherever Mills & Boon books and ebooks are sold.*

# MILLS & BOON®

## EXCLUSIVE EXTRACT

Crown Prince Armando enlists Rosa Lamberti to find him a suitable wife—but could a stolen kiss under the mistletoe lead to an unexpected Christmas wedding?

*Read on for a sneak preview of*
### WINTER WEDDING FOR THE PRINCE
by Barbara Wallace

"Have you ever looked at an unfocused telescope only to turn the knob and make everything sharp and clear?" Armando asked.

Rosa nodded.

"That is what it was like for me, a few minutes ago. One moment I had all these sensations I couldn't explain swirling inside me, then the next everything made sense. They were my soul coming back to life."

"I don't know what to think," she said.

"Then don't think," he replied. "Just go with your heart."

He made it sound easy. Just go with your heart. But what if your heart was frightened and confused? For all his talk of coming to life, he was essentially in the same place as before, unable or unwilling to give her a true emotional commitment.

On the other hand, her feelings wanted to override her common sense, so maybe they were even. As she watched him close the gap between them, she felt her heartbeat quicken to match her breath.

"You do know that we're under the mistletoe yet again, don't you?"

The sprig of berries had quite a knack for timing, didn't it? Anticipation ran down her spine ceasing what little hold common sense still had. Armando was going kiss her and she was going to let him. She wanted to lose herself in his arms. Believe for a moment that his heart felt more than simple desire.

This time, when he wrapped his arm around her waist, she slid against him willingly, aligning her hips against his with a smile.

"Appears to be our fate," she whispered. "Mistletoe, that is."

"You'll get no complaints from me." She could hear her heart beating in her ears as his head dipped toward hers. "Merry Christmas, Rosa."

"Mer..." His kiss swallowed the rest of her wish. Rosa didn't care if she spoke another word again. She'd waited her whole life to be kissed like this. Fully and deeply, with a need she felt all the way down to her toes.

They were both breathless when the moment ended. With their foreheads resting against each other, she felt Armando smile against her lips. "Merry Christmas," he whispered again.

*Don't miss*
WINTER WEDDING FOR THE PRINCE
by Barbara Wallace

Available December 2016

www.millsandboon.co.uk

# MILLS & BOON®

## Why shop at millsandboon.co.uk?

Each year, thousands of romance readers find their perfect read at millsandboon.co.uk. That's because we're passionate about bringing you the very best romantic fiction. Here are some of the advantages of shopping at www.millsandboon.co.uk:

* **Get new books first**—you'll be able to buy your favourite books one month before they hit the shops

* **Get exclusive discounts**—you'll also be able to buy our specially created monthly collections, with up to 50% off the RRP

* **Find your favourite authors**—latest news, interviews and new releases for all your favourite authors and series on our website, plus ideas for what to try next

* **Join in**—once you've bought your favourite books, don't forget to register with us to rate, review and join in the discussions

Visit **www.millsandboon.co.uk**
for all this and more today!